Gary Paulsen

McFarland Companions to Young Adult Literature

Gary Paulsen: A Companion to the Young Adult Literature
by Mary Ellen Snodgrass (2018)

Gary Paulsen

A Companion to the Young Adult Literature

MARY ELLEN SNODGRASS

McFarland Companions to Young Adult Literature

McFarland & Company, Inc., Publishers
Jefferson, North Carolina

Also by the author and from McFarland

World Epidemics: A Cultural Chronology of Disease from Prehistory to the Era of Zika, 2d ed. (2017); *Brian Friel: A Literary Companion* (2017); *Settlers of the American West: The Lives of 231 Notable Pioneers* (2015); *Who's Who in the Middle Ages* (2013; paperback 2001); *Isabel Allende: A Literary Companion* (2013); *World Epidemics: A Cultural Chronology of Disease from Prehistory to the Era of SARS* (2011; paperback 2003); *Encyclopedia of World Scriptures* (2011; paperback 2001); *Leslie Marmon Silko: A Literary Companion* (2011); *Peter Carey: A Literary Companion* (2010); *Jamaica Kincaid: A Literary Companion* (2008); *Coins and Currency: An Historical Encyclopedia* (2007; paperback 2003); *Kaye Gibbons: A Literary Companion* (2007); *Walter Dean Myers: A Literary Companion* (2006); *World Shores and Beaches: A Descriptive and Historical Guide to 50 Coastal Treasures* (2005); *Barbara Kingsolver: A Literary Companion* (2004); *August Wilson: A Literary Companion* (2004); *Amy Tan: A Literary Companion* (2004)

ISBN (print) 978-1-4766-7331-8
ISBN (ebook) 978-1-4766-3185-1

Library of Congress cataloguing data are available

British Library cataloguing data are available

Printed in the United States of America

McFarland & Company, Inc., Publishers
Box 611, Jefferson, North Carolina 28640
www.mcfarlandpub.com

For Duncan and Mac, Jasper, the Gussarina,
Cassie, and Arthur Pendragon

There are some who can live without
wild things, and some who cannot.
It was and still is a wonder for me,
what books are.

—Gary Paulsen

Table of Contents

Acknowledgments viii

Preface 1

Introduction 3

Chronology of Gary Paulsen's Life and Work 5

Genealogy 29

Gary Paulsen:
A Companion to the Young Adult Literature 31

Glossary 161

Appendix A: Timeline of Historical References 167

Appendix B: Writing, Art and Research Topics 172

Bibliography 179

Index 187

Acknowledgments

Jill Abahsain, director, Sauk Centre History Museum, Sauk Centre, Minnesota

Ashe County Library, West Jefferson, North Carolina

Charlotte and Mecklenburg County Library, Charlotte, North Carolina

Diane Leukam, editor, *Sauke Herald,* Sauk Centre, Minnesota

Ryan McCormick, reference librarian, Great River Regional Library, Sauk Centre, Minnesota

Special thanks go to expert archivist Lotsee Patterson of Norman, Oklahoma; to reference librarians Beth Bradshaw and Martin Otts of the Patrick Beaver Library in Hickory, North Carolina; and to my publicist and consultant Joan Lail. Bless them all for their forbearance and goodwill.

Preface

Gary Paulsen: A Companion to the Young Adult Literature provides parents, teachers, guidance counselors, librarians, and readers with commentary on 64 topics and a range of literature suited to the situations faced by on-grade and at-risk tweens and teens. By perusing the issues of learning by trial and error in *Canyons* and *Tiltawhirl John* and unsupervised adventuring in *Tracker* and *Brian's Winter,* young readers can apply elements of doubt and hesitance to their own lives and to the iffy choices of their peers, the subject of *How Angel Peterson Got His Name* and *Danger on Midnight River*. Overviews of vulnerability, violence, and fear in *Paintings from the Cave* and *Captive!* spotlight the hardships of growing up in a society obsessed with guns and greed. Entries on adaptation, maturity, literacy, and logic pinpoint episodes that solace and instruct the young on right thinking, the purpose of *Project: A Perfect World* and *Road Trip*. Detailed accounts of parenting, mentors, storytelling, and wisdom answer questions of where and how the next generation of adults can find paths to certainty and self-esteem, the subject of *Guts* and *Puppies, Dogs, and Blue Northers*. Specifics on writing, humor, legend, and kenning explain the methods by which Paulsen crafts his masterful prose, including the art volumes—*Dogteam, Woodsong, Canoe Days, Worksong, The Tortilla Factory, The Island,* and *Clabbered Dirt, Sweet Grass*—co-produced by his wife and partner, artist Ruth Ellen Wright Paulsen.

The glossary pinpoints 211 terms for thorough application to context, as with these six examples:

- *barrio,* a Hispanic enclave in *The Crossing* and *Curse of the Ruins*
- demerits for punishment in the Dunc and Amos books *Crush* and *Molly McGinty Has a Really Good Day*
- Norski, the Norwegian-American women's childhood language in *The Quilt*
- sear, a trigger control in *Tracker*
- deviated septum from a broken nose in *Six Kids and a Stuffed Cat*
- Comancheros, the Southwestern raiders in *Tucket's Gold, Tucket's Home,* and *Tucket's Ride.*

Appendix A: Timeline of Historical References lists events and important figures mentioned in Paulsen's canon, as with Sir William Wallace, the thirteenth-century Scots freedom fighter for whom Abner McDougal names his dogs in *Woods Runner;* the rise of evangelical religion in *The Tent;* and the Emancipation Proclamation of January 1, 1863, an important document in freedmen's future in *Sarny.*

Appendix B poses 44 Writing, Art and Research Topics for study by readers or students in library science, reading, or education courses. Subjects range from comparisons of Paulsen's books with the works of classic young adult authors—Laura Ingalls Wilder, Avi, Cynthia Rylant, Robert Cormier, Esther Forbes, Will Hobbs—to prevalent themes of endurance and survival that dominate *The Boy Who Owned the School* and *A Christmas Sonata*. Questions apply resistance, tradition, curiosity, and heritage to specific titles, as with traits of the disabled in *The Monument,* tolerance toward an outsider in *Harris and Me,* and orienteering in *The River*. A separate listing of primary and secondary sources, both print and electronic, precedes the index, which points readers to fundamental topics and models, particularly dogs, censorship, "Wolfdreams," hunger, music, and libraries. Overall, *Gary Paulsen: A Companion to the Young Adult Literature* scans the tenacity and compassion that fortify a crucial body of works in American literature.

Introduction

The vigor and intuitive accuracy of Gary Paulsen's writing has impacted young adult literature with an honesty and authenticity, the hallmarks of his stellar classic *Hatchet* and of the study of forthright single mothers in *The Glass Café* and *Canyons*. By reliving his exploits in the wild, he has fleshed out memoir and history with eyewitness details as rare as a moose destroying a pickup truck in *Winterdance* and a husky playing tricks on a dog team in *Woodsong*. Quick to outline a story, he strikes at the heart of conflict and confronts protagonists with choices as difficult as keeping a shock victim alive in *The River* and surviving major battles of the American Civil War in *Soldier's Heart*. For characters, he focuses on needy souls:

- fatherless children in *Canyons* and *The Glass Café*
- loners in *The Haymeadow* and *Father Water, Mother Woods*
- neglected and orphaned children in *Call Me Francis Tucket* and *The Cookcamp*
- exploited farm laborers in *The Beet Fields* and *Tiltawhirl John*
- vulnerable delinquents in *Paintings from the Cave* and *The Car*
- refugees of World War II in *Eastern Sun, Winter Moon*.

His cast, which is predominantly male, manages the everyday issues of coming of age while fending off dangers as petrifying as Comanchero and Hessian raiders, terminal cancer, supernatural computer games, a raid by Rawhaz cannibals, and a storm at sea.

Teachers, librarians, and parents gravitate to Paulsen's remarkable list of publications for their freshness and dedication to self-discovery, the dominant topic in *This Side of Wild, The Quilt,* and *The White Fox Chronicles*. From protagonists who accept challenge as opportunity rather than tragedy, readers learn about commitment to the ideals of friendship, loyalty, and daring, the controlling motif of *Grizzly* and "Wolfdreams," and the conservation of nature and historical treasures, concepts integral to *The Grass Eaters* and *Canyons*. His settings favor the purity of creation, especially the snowy wastelands inhabited by the Inuit in *Dogsong* and Apache dwellers in South Dakota's Black Hills in *Tucket's Gold*, but include the perversities and menace of cities the size of New York, Chicago, Manila, Minneapolis, and Cincinnati. By varying plots over a range of topography, he introduces Samuel Lehi Smith to war-torn 18th-century New York City, Nightjohn the literacy teacher to the plantation South, young Gary to Chicago and Okinawa in the 1940s, Mexican survivors in the Dakota beet fields, and mestizo Manny Bustos, an illegal immigrant on his way over the Rio Grande from Juaréz, Mexico, to prosperity in El Paso, Texas, an ongoing political issue of the 21st century. Whether autobiographic or fictional, Paulsen's characters manifest a credible humanity that links their disasters and struggles with the will to succeed, the driving force in interplanetary traveler Mark Harrison in *The Transall Saga* and in the 12-year-old entrepreneur in *Lawn Boy*.

Integral to Paulsen's contribution to satisfying reading lie his tributes to the past and to ordinary settlers and soldiers who bore the brunt of frontier life, rebellion, and nascent democracy during transcontinental travel and virulent wars. The history entry applauds realism in the depictions of the author's signal heroes:

- Samuel Lehi Smith, a fictional survivor of the American Revolution in *Woods Runner*
- a neophyte frontiersman and rescuer of children in *Call Me Francis Tucket*
- a lone deputy U.S. marshal in crime-ridden Indian Territory in *The Legend of Bass Reeves*
- Charley Goddard, a real Union warrior during the Civil War in *Soldier's Heart*

as well as teens growing up in the shadow of the atomic age, the subject of *Sentries*. Background events of the five-part Tucket series disclose tensions between travelers on the Oregon Trail and members of the Apache, Crow, Pueblo, and Pawnee. The Brian Robeson series moves the survey to our own time and to a rethinking of homes and families split by divorce. Twenty-first century conundrums still dividing citizens emerge from *The Rifle* and its perusal of gun ownership and unsuspecting victims of carelessly stored firearms.

The uniqueness of Paulsen's themes draws fans to the search for unconditional love, the yearning for belonging to a family, and dog stories the quality of *Notes from the Dog*. He specializes in the harrowing reflections of broken soldiers, men who return from the front lines bearing the psychological burdens of post-traumatic stress disorder—Sergeant Robert S. Locke in *The Crossing*, Officer Nuts Duda in *Winterkill*, the storykeeper in *Fishbone's Song*, and the stricken Viet survivor in "Stop the Sun." Significant to the pairing of needs from World War I, World War II, and Southeast Asia to 21st-century Middle Eastern clashes, the author finds occasions for veterans to mentor the young by sharing war memories that preserve the hellish wrongs of a series of conflicts, the plot of *The Rock Jockeys*, *The Winter Room*, and *Dancing Carl*. A familiar trope as sturdy as Homer's Trojan War survivors, the value of damaged warriors to civilization enhances simple hearth scenes in which the eyewitness imparts nuggets of wisdom to the untried, the gift of the Foxman and characters in *The Madonna Stories*. By elevating the family circle as a sacred crucible for the forging of character, Paulsen finds relief for his own troubled memories and valorizes his escape to the wild for acquainting him with purpose and self-reliance.

Chronology of Gary Paulsen's Life and Work

A maven of succinct memoirs and candid novellas about humble jobs, wastelands, war, and stark wrestlings with coming of age, Gary Paulsen holds a spot in reader hearts unequaled by other living writers. With some 26 million works in print, many translated into 11 languages, including Kyrgyz, he contributes to American literature a host of compact, eloquent narratives of living to the fullest, despite the obstacles of poverty, broken homes, and world disorder. Overarching his vividly detailed farm and outback adventures, authenticity convinces readers that they are hearing the master teller describing scenarios he knows as well as his own hairline. He distinguishes his process of composition as carving pieces off himself.

May 17, 1939

Born of Scandinavian lineage in Hennepin, Minnesota, to a Norwegian mother, Eunice Hazel Moen Paulsen, Gary James Paulsen resided in an apartment in Thief River Falls 70 miles south of the Canadian border. At the time, his Danish-Swedish father, Oscar Paulsen, was training at a California army base in tank maneuvers.

1941

Paulsen was a toddler when Oscar fought with a tank unit during World War II in Africa and Europe. Gary's paternal grandfather, Hans J. Paulsen, supplemented government checks to dependent wives and children with additional money to Eunice and her son. Filling in for the absent dad was Gary's Norwegian grandmother, Alida Peterson Moen, aided by Uncle George and Aunt Margaret, rural cousins, and Paulette and brother Bill, Oscar's son from a previous marriage. The solution of farming out children from the nuclear family provided the author with serious philosophical musings, the source of *Popcorn Days and Buttermilk Nights* and *The Quilt*. In the introduction to the latter text, he honored Grandmother Alida: "All that I am, I am because of her" (Paulsen, *Quilt*, viii). Kate Larking, a reviewer for the *Calgary Herald,* characterized the story as "unabashedly sentimental … wrenched by events of joy and sadness" (Larking, 2005, ESO5).

July 10, 1943

On the staff of General George Patton, Oscar Paulsen wrote letters about how he participated in the invasion of Sicily, lugging his own body bag. The story "The Cook Camp" implies that Oscar may have taken a French nurse as a love interest. In an apartment alongside the elevated railway in Chicago's South Side, four-year-old Gary lived with his mother, who worked in a laundry and fed her family meager meals of Spam and fried potatoes. At play, according to the story "The Cook Camp," he dressed in a fiber helmet liner and brandished a wood rifle while playing army.

According to *Eastern Sun, Winter Moon: An Autobiographical Odyssey,* a memoir with a cryptic title, Eunice belted twenty millimeter ammunition in a bullet factory from afternoon to midnight while living vicariously on alcohol and adulterous liaisons. At the Cozy Corner bar, she danced and drank without restraint and allowed men to fondle her in front of her pre-schooler. His Grandma Alida sent scorching letters urging Eunice to give up what reviewer Tim Winton called "booze and bitchery" and to behave like a decent wife and mother (Winton, 1993, 1).

Christmas 1943

By train at Christmas, four-year-old Gary traveled from Minneapolis to Winnipah to visit Uncle Ben, Aunt Marilyn, and Cousin Matthew, who was slowly dying of an unspecified illness, the subject of *A Christmas Sonata*. Because Eunice became what reviewer Tim Winton termed a "sexual magnet," Gary shared space at home with his mother's lover, whom he called "Uncle Casey," a character identified in *The Beet Fields* as the boy's poker teacher (Winton, 1993, 1). For her "Punkin," Eunice hired Clara, a foul-smelling babysitter, who listened to soap operas and Charlie McCarthy on the radio, guzzled red wine, and ignored the boy.

1944 summer to fall

Leaving his mother at the Chicago depot, at age five, Gary rode a day and a half alone to spend a summer west of International Falls, Minnesota, with Grandma Alida, a cook for road builders of a Minnesota-to-Canada route. Fictionalizing her as Anita Halverson, he captured her Norwegian culture and gentle mothering in *The Cookcamp,* a critically acclaimed memoir for rugged lessons in coping. The text credits her with six boys and five girls, one of whom died on a Pacific isle while serving in the army artillery. She outlived all eleven. In the short story "The Face of the Tiger," the Gary character survives appendicitis during one of his treks to Minnesota.

The boy eluded a drunken pedophile, whom Eunice kicked to death in an alley with her pointed shoes. "The Face of the Tiger" recalled the pervert as one of the "terrible, sick, depraved, and disgusting men who preyed on children" (Paulsen, *Madonna,* 65). Some 60 years after the episode, Paulsen referred to his louche, but competent mother with the story of Al, a stripper in *The Glass Café.* At local bars, Eunice exhibited Gary, who sang pop tunes for tips. While reading Oscar's letter about a new "friend" in France, she cried over her husband's adultery (Paulsen, *Eastern,* 11). Of unsatisfactory mother-son relationships in a fatherless house, Gary stated in *Canyons*, "The two of them existed in a kind of quiet tolerance" (Paulsen, *Canyons*, 10).

1945

Gary learned to use a box camera, listened to broadcasts of *The Lone Ranger* and *Sergeant Preston of the Yukon,* and saw Gene Autry and Roy Rogers movies at Chicago theaters. From wartime newsreels, he developed hatred for "nips and krauts," a slur he recorded in the story "The Cook Camp" and "The True Face of War" (Paulsen, "True," 25). Two bouts of double pneumonia put him in a Minneapolis hospital under an oxygen tent, which he relived in "The Face of the Tiger" with his mother's attack on a priest to prevent last rites. Gary caught chicken pox on the drive to San Francisco to board a military transport vessel for the Philippines, Oscar's new billet. While recovering, Gary read *Donald Duck* and *Superman* comic books.

At age six, Gary met his father and began formulating a pervasive character study of the alcoholic war veteran, the source of *The Crossing,* "The Madonna," and *The Foxman.* On the journey by naval troop ship from San Francisco via Honolulu to the Philippines, Gary witnessed sharks attacking survivors of a C-54 military transport plane that crashed and broke apart in the Pacific. His mother aided medics in treating savage bites with tourniquets and amputations. When the ship stopped at Okinawa, she distributed candy bars and condensed milk to beggars on the wharf.

Because of Colonel Oscar Paulsen's reassignment from the European war, Gary lived in a stilt house at a Clark Air Base compound in Manila. He spent second and third grade under a private military tutor. With the atmospheric horrors of J.G. Ballard's *Empire of the Sun,* the boy's disaffection for urban life began in the war-torn city, where he and the houseboy Rom combed wreckage they passed on bike rides. Nightly at the island quarters, a Filipino maid named Maria molested Gary. Oscar showed the boy a prison where the Japanese burned prisoners of war to death with flamethrowers. The boy also witnessed stacks of corpses in a cave, where rats chewed on flesh.

In *This Side of Wild,* the author described the ugliness of war as beyond his comprehension "through the hazy viewfinder of alcoholic parents," a perspective he shares with Spokane-Coeur d'Alene writer Sherman Alexie, author of *The Absolutely True Diary of a Part-Time Indian* (Paulsen, *Side,* 63). Tim Winton, a reviewer for the *Los Angeles Times,* surmised: "Even for a war child, his was an extraordinary beginning to life and a terrible story to carry so long untold; it sheds considerable light on the themes of wilderness and survival" (Winton, 1993, 1).

December 31, 1949

Because of Oscar's reassignment to the Pentagon, the Paulsens moved to Washington, D.C., where Gary first entered a public school. Crouched in a coat closet, he remained diffident and made no lasting friends. On his own, he learned how to rummage army surplus stores for such treasures as a canteen with bullet holes in it, flight goggles, and leftover army mittens, an essential detail in *How Angel Peterson Got His Name.* Paulsen was unsuccessful at athletics, but later won acclaim for realistic writing about backpacking, hiking, camping, hunting and fishing, roping, riding, boxing, flying, wrestling, skydiving, and canoeing. His love of risky sports appeared in "Skate-Chuting," a fast-paced article in the December 1969 issue of *Boys' Life.*

1950

Returned to northern Minnesota, at age ten, the author struggled with home turmoil involving his parents' moves to Laporte, Twin Forks, and Thief River Falls and his mother's consumption of beer and gin, bar hopping, and adulteries. He referred to his parents as "the town drunks" (Sides, 2006, B7). In *Harris and* Me, he fictionalized the hassle of yelling and fighting as "pretty much mean whenever they were conscious" (Paulsen, *Harris*, 2). In a parallel situation in *The Foxman,* Carl's tenuous avoidance of a knife-wielding mother recurs when "they started on beer and worked into bourbon" (Paulsen, *Foxman,* 1). His description of the protagonist in *Harris and Me* resounds with personal hurt: "Home became, finally, something of an impossibility for me, and I would go to stay with relatives for extended periods of time" (Paulsen, *Harris,* 2). In *The Beet Fields,* the Gary character summarizes parental derelicts as instigators of "the fights and the screaming and the tears.... It's all bullshit" (Paulsen, *Beet,* 61).

Paulsen's fictional recreations of an inebriated hell became standard motifs for his protagonists. As background for *The Schernoff Discoveries,* he accentuated the problem of compulsive drinking with hyperbole: "If there was a type of alcoholic beverage my parents didn't consume I never saw it" (Paulsen, *Schernoff,* 2). In *The Car,* the author's alter ego Terry Anders, age 14, describes his mom and dad as "two people who just shouldn't have been together" (Paulsen, *Car,* 5). The tone affirms a judgment from the author's anguished memories.

To avoid poverty, instability, and Eunice and Oscar's ongoing whiskey brawls, Gary withdrew to the woods or bedded down in the cellar by a coal-fired boiler. In a warm alcove, he glued together model P-38s, B-17s, Corsairs, and Zeros while subsisting on cartons of milk to top off peanut butter and jelly on Ritz crackers. To fill the family's neglected pantry, he trapped beaver and earned 7¢ a line for setting pins in Ray's bowling alley, a scenario he described in *Winterkill* and *The Beet Fields*. Meager earnings paid for a Hiawatha bicycle and a .410 single-shot Savage shotgun. The beginnings of independence took shape in the bowling alley, where he learned to smoke and inhale. A police officer named J.D. caught him in the act of stealing skis and labored two years at steering him away from crime. Their friendship lasted until 1959, when a punk shot J.D. dead.

In the wilderness, Gary carried bread, a small cookpot, and matches for onsite meals. In adulthood, he honored northern Minnesota in the title of *Father Water, Mother Woods: Essays on Fishing and Hunting in the North Woods,* a veneration of the wild as a source of nurturance and protection. In an interview for the London *Sunday Times,* he accounted for his need for the outback: "I've got to be able to see the horizon, otherwise I get sick" (Scott, 1996, 12).

May

At age eleven, Gary began a pattern of running away from the family chicken farm outside Thief River Falls. His mother sent him to the acreage of Norwegian uncles, who taught him fence repair, horse harnessing, and plowing as well as storytelling. In *Harris and Me,* the Gary character learns to separate cream from milk. Uncle Gordy helped him drag his first buck from the woods. With other boys, Gary rode plodding workhorses and fantasized that the one-ton beasts were Gene Autry's Champion or Roy Rogers's Trigger.

Haphazard placement in homes inspired Paulsen's characterization of Matthew, the child of divorcing parents in *Notes from the Dog,* and Jake in *Paintings from the Cave.* The resulting alienation led to Jake's choice to hide in the cellar and "stay low," a retreat paralleling that of Jacob Freisten's dungeon-like basement in *The Boy Who Owned the School* (Paulsen, *Paintings,* 4). Matthew suffered feelings of being "dropped onto a strange planet," his sci-fi explanation of estrangement (Paulsen, *Notes,* 3). Additional commentary about

Carl's "custodial summer" with his father expressed the writer's empathy for modern kids of failed households (*ibid.*, 12).

1951

At age twelve, Paulsen received a Remington .22 rifle from his uncle and went over the Eighth Street dam in a pickle barrel, a stunt he describes in *How Angel Peterson Got His Name.* With a stray dog named Ike, the pet of a disabled Korean War veteran, he tramped the Minnesota marshes to hunt ducks. Assisting him in retrieving the kill, Ike listened to the boy's troubles. Of their first outing, Gary recalled "with clarity and detail" leaf colors, cold air, and wind on water (Paulsen, *Guts*, 70). To return the woods to quiet, he gave up his .22 and bow-hunted ruffed grouse, ducks, deer, and rabbits, which supplied him with food without disturbing the quiet of the outdoors. At age 50, he altered his thinking by condemning the "unbelievable violence" of hunting and killing (Paulsen, *Woodsong*, 2).

1951 summer

To earn cash for school clothing and supplies, the boy "lived for weekends and holidays and summer," when he hoed beet fields in Jefferson, North Dakota, for $11.00 an acre and grubbed potatoes for 5¢ a bushel (Paulsen, *Alida,* 11). Of his time in the outdoors, in *Father Water, Mother Woods,* he rejoiced in a place where "our lives didn't hurt" (Paulsen, *Father,* xiii).

1952 winter

During the middle grades, Paulsen described the classroom as "a pisshole for me" (Paulsen, *Pilgrimage,* 79). He got passed along because "they did not want him around" (Paulsen, *Alida,* 11). Estranged and desperate on wintry streets, he discovered the Carnegie library on Main Avenue in Thief River Falls and received a borrower's card, a proof of identity and respect for the son of derelicts. Through the reclamation of Jo-Jo the Dog-faced Girl from taunts in *Paintings from the Cave,* the author declares, "Everything about the library was good" (Paulsen, *Paintings,* 86). In the book's third novella, Jamie adds, "It's warm and clean and I like the smell of books" (*ibid.,* 127).

Of Paulsen's introduction to the "voice of the book," he exulted in *Shelf Life: Stories by the Book,* "I consider every good thing that has ever happened to me since then a result of that woman handing me that book.... She showed me places where it didn't hurt all the time" (Paulsen, *Shelf,* 4). He fed a hungry spirit on the warmth and welcome of Sherlock Holmes mysteries, Zane Grey westerns, sci-fi, and classics by Charles Dickens, Jack London, and Edgar Rice Burroughs and Herman Melville's *Moby Dick.* As his reading rate improved, he nestled in a rump-sprung easy chair near the basement coal bin and gobbled the pages like a starved wolf. He eventually read *Moby Dick* 15 times.

Into adulthood, the writer assuaged his yearning for knowledge with a variety of works, including William Manchester's histories, Patrick O'Brien's sea stories, Dylan Thomas's verse, and Robert B. Parker's westerns. The constant feeding on literature kept Paulsen dancing with words. To supplement his love of the outdoors with a bittersweet self-fostering, he read magazines on survival, a niche in his library list that he shares with the fictional Mark Harrison, protagonist of *The Transall Saga* (Paulsen, *Father*, xii).

1953

Because of irregular attendance during moves from school to school, Gary failed grades nine and ten and labeled himself a dweeb and a loser. In *The Schernoff Discoveries,* he chortled that the protagonist, 14-year-old Harold Schernoff, "broke local records for flunking" (Paulsen, *Schernoff,* 3). In summer on the Nelson farm, the author harvested wheat, drove trucks and tractors, and hoed beets for $5.00 a day, a task he reprises in *Tiltawhirl John* and among Hispanic migrant workers in South Dakota in *Sentries.* At home, he sneaked out in the family's Chevy coupe and fantasized about driving a girl to the movies.

Gary's crimes were minor, but potentially self-corrupting. Visits with Grandma Alida "[pulled] him away from the edge and into the center of life" (Paulsen, *Alida,* cover). After five years of retreating to the street, selling newspapers in taverns and hospitals, and cadging spare change from his mother's purse and father's pants pockets, Gary ran away to join a carnival and operate the Tiltawhirl ride. In scruffy surroundings, he polished his poker game. When police investigated a carny knife fight, they declared him underage and forced him to return to his parents.

1955 summer

Gary joined Mexican field laborers in hoeing beet fields. Observation became a lifelong method: "I become very wolflike. Wolves see and listen to every single thing. So I started doing that" (Buchholz, 1995, 53). Self-discipline prepared him for a career in writing.

1956 summer

Paulsen, at age 17, found work on Fourth Street SW in Waseca, southern Minnesota, loading boxes of frozen vegetables for Birdseye. He rode a whizzer motorized bike the 30 miles from his quarters in Mankato. Subsequent jobs involved him in trucking, construction, trapping, demolition with dynamite, teaching, acting, directing, farming and ranching, folk singing, and sailing (Barron, 1993, 27).

1957

A low achiever who hated regimentation, Paulsen admired a teacher named Carlsen and graduated from Lincoln High School in Thief River Falls with a D minus average. In north central Minnesota, he entered the engineering department at Bemidji State Teachers College on funds he earned as a state trapper of destructive quadrupeds. He flourished under the school newspaper adviser, James McMahon, but left after two years because of failing grades, a classroom breakdown he shares with Brennan Cole, the hero of *Canyons.*

Early 1959

By forging Oscar Paulsen's name on army papers, at age 19, Gary initiated a three-year and eight-month hitch, during which he gained discipline from a friendly drill sergeant named Gross. In "The True Face of War," an article for the spring 1999 issue of *Riverbank Review,* he explains, "I was trained for a war that JFK fully intended to fight with Cuba" (Paulsen, 1999, 25). He reported to his maternal grandmother, "I hate it. It was a terrible mistake to enlist" (Paulsen, *Alida,* 3). He suffered nightmares of "a sergeant with a body like Hercules and a head the size of an orange" (Paulsen, *Pilgrimage,* 156). Of the tough discipline, Gary recalled learning, "If you try it again, OK, kawhoomp! Down you go again" (Goodson, 2004, 57).

During basic training at Fort Carson, Colorado, a barracks fistfight cost Paulsen a molar. He exhibited his poker-playing skills, but abandoned hiking, "something I had come to dislike—hate—courtesy of the army" (Paulsen, *This Side*, 2). For $78 per month in White Sands, New Mexico, he tested the Nike Ajax supersonic rocket, the world's first surface-to-air missile. He taught nuclear warhead technology to foreigners at Fort Sill, Oklahoma, and Fort Bliss, Texas, where "once there had been horses tied and where the old gatling gun still sat" (Paulsen, *Madonna,* 81). He later applied the settings to "The Soldier," *The White Fox Chronicles,* a militaristic teen thriller, and *The Tent,* a satire on religious con artists who fleece the poor.

During charity trips to aid children in Juárez, Mexico, the author acquired details for two novels, *Canyons* and *The Crossing,* both winners of ALA citations. In *Pilgrimage on a Steel Ride,* he accounted for his "come-home-on-leave-from-the-army marriage and the siring of his first child, Lance Paulsen (Paulsen, *Pilgrimage,* 12–13). The lengthy road trip impressed on Paulsen a Tennysonian truth: "Not to find, not to end, but to always seek a beginning" (Price, 1997, E3).

1962 May

Because of the Cuban missile crisis from October 16–28, 1962, Paulsen remained in service an extra three months, learning "insane knowledge"—"what practically nobody else could know" about nuclear warheads (Paulsen, *Side,* 66). He left the army with the rank of sergeant and spent a week camping and healing his spirit at the California shore. Some of the buddies he left behind fought and died in the Vietnam War. He found the name of a friend on the Vietnam Wall and "just busted down the middle ... crying on my hands and knees" (Nickelson, 1993). He explained in "The True Face of War" how he stopped beside the "Black Wall where several of them now live, and I sat and thanked them for what they had given" (Paulsen, 1999, 26). In the aftermath of the post–Sputnik frenzy, the author found a job at the China Lake Naval Ordnance Test Station in California at $2,000 a month and took flying lessons in a sporty two-seater Aeronca Champ.

1963

In the wake of a "sudden and unexpected change of heart" in Barstow, California, the author left aerospace technology on satellites for Lockheed and Bendix to proofread a men's magazine in Los Angeles. Lowering his earnings by 80 percent to $400 a month, he obtained the position via a fabricated resume (Lynch, 2009). By day, he composed seven articles on World War I fighter pilot Baron von Richthofen, the notorious Red Baron, and published them in different magazines under the pseudonyms Paul Garrisen, Eldon Tasch, and Carson Dawes.

While living on a sailboat by night in Ventura harbor, the writer mastered composition by completing articles, short fiction, and chapters for two professional authors to critique. The breakneck pace of one assignment per night developed discipline. On return to the Midwest, in town halls throughout Minnesota, he traded recitations of short fiction for home-baked goodies. Of his zeal for writing, his Norwegian grandma affirmed, "That's the Swede in you" (Nickelson, 1993).

Early 1965

Abandoning his wife and children Lance and Lynn, the restless 26-year-old headed to Hollywood in his Volkswagen to be near authors. He worked as a film extra before realizing that, at heart, he was a born writer. For four years, he submitted TV episodes to *Mission Impossible* and dialogue for the 1969 film *The Reivers,* a picaresque Southern comedy by William Faulkner starring Steve McQueen.

1966

With second wife Pam, Paulsen took a break from the Hollywood job of screen writing to retreat to the Poplar, Minnesota, outback to fish, trap, and drink at a cabin in the woods. In "Aunt Caroline," he recalled the union as "the heady-musk-flush of lust" (Paulsen, *Madonna,* 74). At peace in the wild, he lampooned the missile industry for Rand McNally in his first essay collection, *Some Birds Don't Fly,* and joined Raymond Friday Locke in publishing *The Special War.* As described in "The Library," he spent more time reading.

Late 1967

After a three-year marriage, Paulsen left Pam, his second wife, and moved to an artist commune in Taos, New Mexico. He spent six years deep in alcohol and harbored thoughts of shooting himself. As a result of his profligacy, he lost his two children to the husband of his ex-wife.

1968

The completion of *Mr. Tucket,* a boyish escapade set in June 1847 on the Oregon Trail, filled the author with zeal: "God, I'm on the way" (Miller, 1988, 6). Success readied Paulsen for first-person perspectives that enlivened his best works of the 1970s: *The Foxman, Tiltawhirl John,* and *Winterkill,* a fictionalized study of his brush with juvenile delinquency. The latter recapped a two-year relationship with officer Nuts Meyers, a policeman who kept Gary out of trouble in his youth and allowed him to sleep in the patrol car during third shift. The fictional story, which *Kirkus Reviews* called morally ambivalent, took place in 1954 in Twin Forks, Minnesota.

In a downward spiral of boozing and hostility, the adult Paulsen pummeled drunks in bars and let truculence scuttle his marriage. Of his innate restlessness, he admitted, "Like a wildcat in a zoo, I just keep pacing" (Jacobson, 1999, F6). The experience of barhopping and the release of anguish through an alcoholic fog gave him material for Carl Sunstrum in *Winterkill* and for Sergeant Robert S. Locke, the Viet vet and pathetic martyr in *The Crossing.*

May 5, 1971

While following the AA program to quell his drinking, the author married his third wife, illustrator Ruth Ellen Wright. The couple moved to Minnesota from Colorado, birthplace of their son Jim "Gito" Paulsen. Speaking through the character of Isaac, a frontiersman in *Woods Runner,* the author declared, "I don't do particular good with crowds of people" and "wasn't much for conversation" (Paulsen, *Woods,* 14). The author worked in a recycled chicken coop, washed clothes at the town laundromat, and managed on vegetable gardening, poultry keeping and goat herding, cheese making, hunting, and $3,000 cash income per year. Jim recalled a five-hour round trip by bus to elementary school and living without plumbing and electricity until his father struck big time royalties.

1976

Paulsen returned to higher education at the University of Colorado, where he lived in poverty and sobriety. As justification for abandoning drink, he asserted, "Clarity is all we have" (Shadle, 2004, B1). On occasional breaks, he sailed his sloop from Oxnard Harbor, California. He compiled *Careers in an Airport* and collaborated with Dan Theis on black history. The finished work, *Martin Luther King: The Man Who Climbed the Mountain,* featured Gandhi's influence on the assassinated activist and King's role in protesting the Vietnam War.

1977

Emerging from real-life characterization in *Winterkill,* a libel suit pressed by a Minnesota policeman threatened to end the author's burst of fictional éclat. Paulsen won the case, but spent his funds on legal bills. He gave up writing for two years and turned to dogsled running to tend a sixty-mile beaver trap line near Clearwater Lake. The rhythm of Columbia, Obeah, Storm, and Yogi behind a broken sled initiated a oneness with nature that drew him into a week-long trek over northwestern Minnesota.

1978

To finance his hobby, which extended to 30,000 miles of mushing, the author began writing fiction again, viewing characters via "personal inspection at zero altitude" (Paulsen, *Shelf,* 6). He produced a dream tale, *The Night the White Deer Died,* which earned positive feedback from *Kirkus Reviews.* His confidence renewed, Paulsen began selling more stories and articles.

1979

To support his household in Minnesota, Paulsen wrote, tracked satellites, and ran earth-moving equipment on construction sites. As a state bounty hunter, he earned a pittance for the pelts he skinned from beaver and coyote snared on his 20-mile trapline. On frigid nights, he survived by filling his tent with dogs. During moonlit runs, he rejoiced in a view "heart-stoppingly beautiful" (Paulsen, *Woodsong,* 16).

1980 January

In examining his predilection for accidents, Paulsen admitted, "I break things—arms, legs—all the time," evidence of his reckless curiosity (Lodge, 2012). He rescued Cookie, a starving husky, who returned the favor after her owner fell under ice. Before she pulled the sled team to his aid, he thought, "All these bubbles are my life and there it goes" (Grant, 1996, 18). By setting a pine tree on fire with fuel from his kerosene stove, he dried his clothes while standing in a sleeping bag.

1982 December

To enter the 1983 Iditarod, the author raised $14,000 with the aid of citizens of Bemidji, who sponsored raffles and dances. He made an eight-day drive in a 1960 Chevy truck to transport sled dogs to Trapper Creek in south central Alaska. In the night, he tried to shield his animals from moose attack by swinging an ax. A personal encounter with a moose cow cost him two molars and a cracked rib.

1983

Paulsen earned an Iditarod belt for finishing 42nd out of 73 racers over the 1,153-mile track to the Arctic Circle. For financing, he agreed to send any writing about the race to Richard Jackson, editor of Bradbury Press, who admired his story "The Deer" in a 1982 issue of *U.S. Catholic.* The sledding ordeal, encompassing 17 1/2 days from Anchorage northwest to Nome, Alaska, over spruce forest, rivers, and tundra, allied him with his 15 dogs and bonded him for life with Cookie, the leader. The event nearly cost him two toes to frostbite, yet left him feeling safer than he had in childhood.

Following the success of *Winterkill,* Gary specialized in fictional and semi-autobiographical studies of children and youth under duress. Driving and sleeping in a Chevy Chevette with his border collie Roop, the author traveled to juvenile halls and prisons, ate lunch in public school cafeterias, and narrated his adventures to rapt students. One listener demanded proof of authenticity by asking, "Wait a minute, are you real? And are the slides real, or is this some TV jive?" (Carey, 1996).

Messages poured in from distressed kids, especially the children of alcoholics, to "tell me things they won't tell their parents" (Barron, 1993, 28). From kid lingo and the observations of school librarians, he learned to speak directly to the audience in young adult cadence and vocabulary, filling in details from his nightmarish boyhood and giving hope to the troubled. He concluded, "I've found they're smarter than a lot of adults and they're honest" (Golden, 1999, ix). To meet their interest and thought patterns, he emphasized primary concepts and colors.

Paulsen introduced motifs of hard farm labor within the patriarchal family line in *Popcorn Days and Buttermilk Nights,* a preliminary survey of Carley and his uncles that recurred in *The Winter Room.* Carley's story features the alienated teen's "big-city snot pride" and paranoia, especially his suspicion that "neither of my uncles wanted me" because of his reputation for senseless window breaking and arson (Paulsen, *Popcorn,* 7, 6). The writer also perused a troubled spirit in *Dancing Carl,* an account of Carl Wenstrom, a B-17 pilot damaged by World War II. The author won an American Library Association (ALA) Best Book award and scripted a dance video on Minnesota Public TV. Set in McKinley in northeastern Minnesota, Carl's story contrasts realistic exploits with the torpor of school, "which is more or less just always there" (Paulsen, *Dancing,* 7).

1984

With *Tracker,* the author examined the emotional coil in 13-year-old John Borne, whose grandfather, Clay Borne, faces death from cancer. Essential to coming of age are the boy's immersion in daily farm chores and his venture into stalking a doe, a feat that Paulsen accomplished in his teens. The work won a second ALA Best Book citation and an award from the Society of Midland Authors for its depiction of youth maturing in the Midwestern outback.

1985

A second Iditarod race left Paulsen adrift on an ice floe until a floatplane rescued him and transported his dog team to Nome, Alaska. He described high winds that blew the huskies back to the sled: "After that, they were kind of demoralized. They didn't want to do it" (Pemberton, 2005, 10).

1986

Dogsong, a Zen-like bestseller, earned Paulsen his first monetary success. He exulted, "Suddenly, I'm getting five-figure royalty checks" (Morris, 1999, K6). He achieved the first of three Newbery Honor Awards plus a Parents' Choice Award, a Children's Book of the Year, Children Study Association of America citation, and Volunteer State Book. The plot depicted the 14-year-old Inuit Russel Susskit fleeing technology in his village by arming himself with a lance for subsistence hunting and guiding a dog team into the surreal past. The flight from modernity reduces him to foraging for food for himself and Nancy, a pregnant runaway who gives birth to a stillborn child.

June

A less successful experimental work, *Sentries* alternated segments about seven disparate lives. At the heart of the allegory lies an elder's query, "Are you whole?" (Miller, 1988, 6). According to Anne Connor, a reviewer for *School Library Journal*, a nuclear blast destroys the hopes of four teens, but the novel doesn't fully implement the title or the theme of tender ambitions.

1987

Paulsen completed his classic survival narrative, *Hatchet,* a day-by-day summation of a boy's ordeal in the Yukon. In spartan prose, the writer composed eight pages during his second Iditarod. Thrice rejected for print, the edgy story burst on the YA scene with a vigor and personal distress long lacking in literature for young readers. Paulsen later admitted, "It struck some nerve that I still don't understand, and that has made it one of my favorite books" (Gale, 1997, 24). The verisimilitude convinced the staff of *National Geographic* that protagonist Brian Robeson really existed.

The author pursued the saga for the next 16 years, earning a Newbery Honor, a Maud Hart Lovelace Book Award, citations from Flicker Tale Children's Books and Sequoyah Children and YA Books, a Golden Archer, and merit from William Allen White Children's Books, Dorothy Canfield Fisher Children's Book citation, a *Booklist* Editor's Choice, and state awards from Virginia, Ohio, Iowa, Indiana, and Georgia. That same year, he published *The Crossing,* a dual psychological study of mestizo beggar Manny Bustos and Sergeant. Robert S. Locke, an alcoholic veteran of Vietnam. The novel achieved Paulsen's fourth Best Book citation from ALA for characterizing an orphan's effort to cross the Tex-Mex border from Juaréz into El Paso.

1987 winter

The emergency landing of a Cessna 406 bush plane in Alaska from 3,000 feet gave Paulsen a jolt. Another incident on ice 90 miles out of Nome the next winter made him appreciate the expertise of bush pilots.

1988

From immersion in isolation, Paulsen turned experience in northwestern Minnesota into grist for *The Foxman*. The wintery tale depicted a young boy's friendship with a recluse, a scarred storyteller and survivor in 1916 of the Battle of Verdun. The intense study of a broken warrior satisfied the author's longing "to go inside of somebody's mind" (Miller, 1988, 6). Publisher Richard Jackson accounted for the psychological push: "I think he's very drawn into the whole subject of salvation—not Christian, but life salvation. In most of the books there is a thread of someone who's just at the brink of not being saved" (Miller, 1988, 6).

The Island won ALA acclaim for perusing the emotional and spiritual fine tuning of Wil Neuton via self-isolation on an island in Sucker Lake near Pinewood, Wisconsin, a voluntary imitation of Henry David Thoreau's retreat to a hut on Walden Pond, Massachusetts. Unlike the Brian Robeson series, Wil's story yields what critic Edwin J. Kenney terms "a meditative novel that subordinates, indeed practically stops, external action to concentrate on the reflections of a 14-year-old boy" (Kenney, 1988, A30). Simultaneous with YA publications, Paulsen issued *Murphy's Gold,* a second adult Western in the *Murphy* series.

1988 March

The Paulsens moved from the north woods to a farm outside Becida, Minnesota. Prosperity and a loan from the Veterans Administration enabled them to buy a washer and dryer and furnish their farmhouse. A recycled hog barn became Ruth's studio. Because of a recruiter's wooing of son Jim into the army, Paulsen called and threatened: "If you call again, it's personal. It won't be the Army. It will be you and me" (Miller, 1988, 6)

1989

The Voyage of the Frog, a novelized version of Paulsen's short story "Lost at Sea" for the November and December 1988 issues of *Boy's Life,* attained accolades from *School Library Journal, Parenting, Learning,* ALA, and the International Reading Association (IRA). The narrative depicted the commitment of 14-year-old David Alspeth to release his Uncle Owen's ashes in the Pacific Ocean. An encomium to the boy's skill at logic and introspection during a nine-day exploit, the novel earned the admiration of *Kirkus Reviews* and *Publisher's Weekly. Inkweaver* professed less approval, giving a rating of 80 percent for presentation and completion, but only 60 percent for plot and characters. A less famous work, *The Madonna Stories,* featuring nine short works, carried a dedication to the author's wife Ruth. Woven into aspects of love and coitus, he incorporated brief flashes of war, "death camps and genocide and clinical killing and My Lai and Cambodia" (Paulsen, *Madonna,* 37).

Public reception of *The Winter Room* contributed to the writer's acclaim for storytelling, including a book of the year listing in *Parenting* and an ALA award. Terse to the point of a fierce curtness, the text honors Norwegian-American settlers who incorporate the energies and drive of 11-year-old Eldon and his 13-year-old brother Wayne in operating a north Minnesota farm. Momentous to the author's style is the place of Uncle David's talk-story to the honing of a younger generation devoid of immigrant ambitions.

1989 September

For its rugged milieu and sense impressions, *The Winter Room* won Paulsen's second Newbery Honor citation along with laurels from the Judy Lopez Memorial.

1990s

Paulsen took up sailing the North American west coast and South Pacific. Of his reintroduction to the sea, in *This Side of Wild,* he exulted that he "[came] to know—to know—how small a part of everything I really happened to be.... And I realized we are never quite alone" (Paulsen, *Side,* x, xi). He motored 9,000 miles from New Mexico to Fairbanks, Alaska, and back on his Harley, stopping overnight at Jack London's cabin, built in 1898 on the North Fork of Henderson Creek south of Dawson City. Paulsen also lived on the coast in a 1979 relic sloop: "I ripped out all the amenities so it's not anybody's idea of genteel" (Scott, 1996, 12).

While satisfying his yearning for a sea adventure, Paulsen issued an adult western, *Dirk's Run,* followed by a sequel, *Dirk's Revenge.* He wrote while planning a voyage on his 31-foot cutter *Reunion* from the Sea of Cortez around Cape Horn and typed the final manuscript of *Caught by the Sea* on his laptop. Of his random itinerary, he remarked, "For me, the destination is unimportant" (*ibid.*).

1990

After the author ran dogs for nine years, he suffered an angina attack in Boston's Logan Airport. He had to adopt a new diet and give up dog sledding, but he kept Cookie, his arthritic lead dog and pal. Paulsen continued his obsessive writing, sometimes 20 hours a day. By verbalizing pictures in his head, he typed scenarios at a speed of 100 words per minute.

Hatchet appeared on film under director Werner Herzog's title *A Cry in the Wild,* starring Jared Rushton as Brian Robeson. Paulsen completed *Canyons* and *The Boy Who Owned the School,* tales of misfortune in the 19th-century West and contemporary injustice. He outlined the Iditarod in the memoir *Woodsong,* which he dedicated to Cookie, his beloved "sisterdog" (Fine, 2000, 84). He based the story on his daily Iditarod journal, the first ever recorded by a contestant. The work won an ALA award.

1990 June

Paulsen's family histories, like Joseph Bruchac's *Bowman's Store,* relished the warm, loving relationship with grandparents. He retrieved memories of his Norwegian grandma in *The Cookcamp,* a lyrical tale that contrasts the energetic singer of Norwegian lullabies and feeder of work crews with a five-year-old's efforts to aid a road building project. *Publishers Weekly* called the story spellbinding and the equal of *The Winter Room*; *School Library Journal* compared its simplicity and depth to Patricia MacLachlan's *Sarah, Plain and Tall.* It received notice from ALA and preceded an intense autobiographical tale, *Alida's Song.* Like *The Quilt,* the third in the trio, the action reprises Scandinavian culture among hard-living, hearty-eating farm folk and their influence on the narrator's boyhood. *Publishers Weekly* described the overt affection of the clan as "Waltons-ish" ("Alida's," 1999, 95).

Simultaneously, both *Parents* and IRA honored *The River; Woodsong* won applause from the Society of Midland Authors, Minnesota Books, Western Writers of America, and *Booklist* Editor's Choice for detailing Paulsen's experiences with the environment. The author's *The Monument* scored another ALA Best Book and an American Bookseller Pick of the Lists. In part for its unusual handicapped heroine, Rachael Ellen "Rocky" Turner, the novel won kudos from *VOYA, Kirkus Reviews,* and *School Library Journal. Publishers Weekly* panned the book for pedantry.

1990 October

The Mountains & Plains Booksellers Association in Park City, Utah, awarded Paulsen a $500 purse for juvenile fiction, which he donated to literacy programs.

1992

The Paulsens resettled once more in south-central New Mexico, where Ruth gained more natural light for her paintings and Gary crisscrossed the desert on a Harley. At their 200-acre ranch at La Luz in the Jicarilla Mountains, he chose an adobe hermitage 40 miles from White Oaks. In a milieu shared with snakes, deer, elk, mountain lions, and wild turkeys, he began training horses. Without mushing to invigorate him, he traversed the Bighorn Mountains of Wyoming, where he explored the terrain on his packhorse Blackie and mare Merry. For income, he submitted articles on mushing to *Reader's Digest* and *Lands' End* and led pack-trips at high elevations. The relocation failed to satisfy his urge for adventure.

The writer explained his decision to live on the edge of civilization, "I can't live in towns anymore.… I don't have anything against individuals. But the species is a mess" (Sides, 2006, B7). In a busy year, he completed his Duncan "Dunc" Culpepper series. For solace from the outdoors, he slept on the porch.

Paulsen relived a mid–World War II holiday in *A Christmas Sonata,* set during his residence with his mother in Minneapolis. His interest in family secrets imparted both suspense and accomplishment in *The Haymeadow*, the story of a summer trial for 14-year-old John Barron, son of a curmudgeon rancher, as lone herder for 6,000 sheep. The book earned Paulsen another ALA commendation and the Spur Award from the Western Writers of America as well as kudos from *Publishers Weekly, The Bulletin,* and *Booklist.* Susan Knorr, a reviewer for *School Library Journal,* disagreed, declaring that the action narrative suffered from jerky pacing and abrupt shifts. *Kirkus Reviews* concurred with Knorr about the packing of adventures with a bear, rattlesnake, skunk, coyotes, flooding, stampede, and accidents into so small a time span.

1992 September

To a question of favorites by interviewer David Gale, writing for *School Library Journal,* Paulsen picked his adult pastoral *Clabbered Dirt, Sweet Grass,* a survey of the uniqueness of the seasons, as his most artistic accomplishment to date. Of its tender appeal, Barry Potyandi, in a book critique for the *Calgary Herald,* acclaimed the work "a mellow evocation of that lost time" when farming dominated settlement of the plains (Potyandi, 1995, B14)

1993

Paulsen turned from raw realism to deadpan humor for *Full of Hot Air: Launching, Floating High, and Landing* and lyricism for *Dogteam*, a winsome picture book that Ruth illustrated. The latter idyll achieved an IRA citation for its appeal to beginning readers. He also published the bilingual *Sisters/Hermanas*, a gynocentric evaluation of the beauty myth and its devastation of girls' self-image. The story dramatized an unexpected mall encounter of Rosa with Traci, a pair of disparate 14-year-olds who trade on budding sexuality to achieve their ambitions. Of its honesty, he admitted, "I'm probably going to get in trouble for the book, but ... this is something I wanted to say" (Metella, 1993, D6).

Sisters/Hermanas attained the finals for a PEN Children's Literature Award. In *Wilson Library Bulletin,* reviewer Frances Bradburn remarked on Paulsen's fearlessness in tackling such powerful narratives. Disagreeing with the positive review in *Kirkus Reviews,* Sally Estes, writing for *Booklist,* dismissed the novel as "pretentious and self-consciously Hemingwayesque" (Estes, 1994). Ann Welton, a reviewer for *School Library Journal,* criticized the didactic tone and an uninspired Spanish translation. Alerts to preachy moralizing recurred the next year in reviews of *The Tent,* the story of the reclamation of Corey, a pulpit huckster reminiscent of Sinclair Lewis's Elmer Gantry.

October 29, 1993

Paulsen declared *Harris and Me: A Summer Remembered* one of his easiest narratives and one of the rawest. Named a National Education Association's top 100 books for children and winner of awards from ALA and *Booklist,* the story recapped Paulsen's purchase of pornography from a Manila street vendor and a summer in the 1950s with the fictional Harris Larson, an actual daredevil cousin named Harlan. In a rural setting, the boys stage G.I. Joe combat in a pigsty and imitate Tarzan swinging from a barn loft.

1994

While refitting a battered 44-foot sloop at Ventura Isla Marina in California, Paulsen prepared to cross the Pacific Ocean in autumn. Meanwhile, he reprised his dog racing adventures in *Winterdance: The Fine Madness of Running the Iditarod.* Writing on a discarded table in the basement, he dramatized slavery in *Nightjohn.* The author's abrupt redirection into African American history earned honors from ALA and the IRA Children's Book Council and praise from *Reading Teacher, Knowledge Quest,* the Minneapolis *Star Tribune,* and the *Washington Post.* With the royalties from Russian translations of his works, he began supporting a Russian orphanage.

May 17, 1994

As a literary invitation to the young outdoorsman, the writer completed *Father Water, Mother Woods: Essays on Fishing and Hunting in the North Woods.* His nonfiction won the Jeremiah Ludington Memorial Award, which honored his commitment to educational paperbacks. That summer, he lived at a marina in Ventura, California, and wrote on the *Felicity,* a 38-foot sloop. During a run to Hawaii, he captured a sighting of six orcas "longer than my home" (Buchholz, 1995, 28). To Randy Lewis, an interviewer for the *Los Angeles Times,* he explained the lack of leisure in his days: "I believe in what I do, and I just work" (Lewis, 1994, E6).

1995

For *Call Me Francis Tucket,* the novelist returned to the daring motifs of his 1968 western *Mr. Tucket,* boyish adventures rife with insights into plains tribes and culture.

By dramatizing the naiveté and good-heartedness of a lone frontiersman crossing the Oregon Trail from Missouri in June 1847, the text epitomizes American and native faults during the settlement of the West, particularly tribal animosities and white lust for land and gold. An author's note shifted tone and genre to essay to outline millennia of occupation by First Peoples. Additions to the series included *Tucket's Ride, Tucket's Gold, Tucket's Home,* and *Tucket's Travels,* an omnibus collection of the five-book saga.

Paulsen garnered positive reactions to *The Rifle*, a reflective biography of a real weapon that patriot John Byam fired at the British during the American Revolution. The author guided the text toward the warping of American values and the irresponsible handling of guns: "They're horrible. People do not understand that firearms are not toys; they're weapons—they are for killing" (Goodson, 2004, 55). He extended sympathy to children at risk of shooting deaths by gangbangers and classified adult thrill hunters as models of arrested development. The compelling story earned respect from the New York Public Library, a Regina Medal from the Catholic Library Association for distinguished contribution to children's literature, and a Notable Children's Trade Book in the Field of Social Studies.

A multicultural title, *The Tortilla Factory* introduced Paulsen's thoughts on science-based topics. By following the corn cycle from tillage to the "clank-clunking" mixing machine to the finished tortilla, he honored a Mexican food icon of health and culture (Paulsen, *Tortilla,* n.p.). His wife Ruth's elegant drawings enhanced the lyricism of a folk food cycle that earned a Children's Book-of-the-Month Club selection and listing by American Booksellers.

1996

Upon receiving treatment for a blocked artery was the source of cardiac distress, Paulsen directed a late mid-life crisis into riding horseback in Wyoming and biking on a Harley 5,000 miles round trip from New Mexico to Alaska, the subjects of *Pilgrimage on a Steel Ride.* The city-by-city itinerary covered St. Paul, Bismarck, Calgary, Edmonton, Dawson Creek, Whitehorse, the Yukon, and Fairbanks. An anonymous critic for *Kirkus Reviews* gave the interior monologues a so-so grade for disjointed transition, but admitted that the author is capable of "nice entertainment" ("Pilgrimage," 1997). When the book returned to print under the title *Zero to Sixty: The Motorcycle Journey of a Lifetime,* a *Playboy* reviewer called the odyssey "a perfect way to travel light" (Paulsen, *Zero,* cover). The *New York Times Book Review* added, "A helluva ride" (*ibid.*). More tributes derived from the *Washington Post* and *Nashville Tennessean.*

Realizing "I had a 26-year-old brain and a 52-year-old butt," Paulsen abandoned the adult audience and channeled his craft into print and audio works aimed at pre-pubescent readers, the ones most open to challenging ideas (Scott, 1996, 12). In addition to publishing *Project: A Perfect World,* an adventure tale about a mad scientist, he adapted *Nightjohn* for a Hallmark/Disney TV film based on the life of 12-year-old Sarny, a slave on a Southern plantation a decade before emancipation. For historical background, he searched the National Archives for chattel diaries. Within the year, he completed a sequel, *Sarny: A Life Remembered,* which carries 19th-century violence into the era of Ku Klux Klan night riding. Of its passion for educational freedom, Maureen Conlan, a reviewer for the *Cincinnati Post,* stated: "There's an aquifer that feeds Paulsen's stories, made up of intensity, compassion, hatred of oppression—and a belief in stating the bald truth" (Conlan, 1995, B-1).

February 17, 1997

In Washington, D.C., the American Library Association conferred on Paulsen the annual Margaret Alexander Edwards Award for lifetime achievement in YA literature. Specifically, judges saluted his perusal of physical and psychological survival motifs in *Dancing Carl, Hatchet, The Crossing, The Winter Room, Canyons,* and *Woodsong.* The committee chair lauded him for "quiet introspective memoirs" and "crazy courage born of adversity" ("1997"). Paulsen received a $2,000 purse and a lasting place among classic American writers. He shifted themes in *The Schernoff Discoveries,* an amusing take on the 14-year-old hero, Harold Schernoff, and his hit-or-miss applications of scientific method.

1997 June

In an interview with David Gale for *School Library Journal,* Paulsen identified art as the common solution to world problems. He remarked that "the life that we get is a wonderful thing. It appalls me how people waste it" (Gale, 1997, 24).

1997 August

Upon accepting the Anne V. Zarrow Award from the Tulsa Library Trust, Paulsen returned the $5,000 purse to the library for buying books.

1998

A paean to ordinary warriors, *Soldier's Heart: A Novel of the Civil War* required research into a four-year conflict and details of battle plans and weaponry from the early 1860s. In "The True Face of War," issued in spring 1999 in *Riverbank Review,* he recalled drawing on evening of poker in an army barracks with chain-smoking veterans "letting me see the true face of what most of them called The Job" (Paulsen, 1999, 26). The historical fiction earned a book of the year plaudit from *Publishers Weekly,* a *Booklist* Top of the List for Youth Fiction, and a salute from *New York Times Book Review* critic Henry Mayer for being a "stark, utterly persuasive novel of combat life in the Civil War" (Mayer, 1998, 40).

Paulsen's wife illustrated the author's autobiography, *My Life in Dog Years,* a premature farewell to the sport of mushing, which he returned to in 2007. He based the memoir on "The Last Great Race," a story he published in the March 1994 issue of *Readers' Digest.* He expanded the tale to book length while sailing the Canadian coast of British Columbia. For *The Transall Saga,* he recapped the adventures of 13-year-old Mark Harrison, a desert camper who travels a beam of light to another planet.

1998 February

Eschewing television, Paulsen sat out a winter in San Diego harbor repairing his boat *Felicity.* Because of *El Niño,* he could not sail the Pacific between Hawaii and coastal California.

1999

The author pounded out manuscripts on his laptop while sailing from Fiji to Tonga on an ocean he described as "the biggest wilderness in the world" (Creager, 1999, 4.). He teamed with his wife for an idyllic picture book, *Canoe Days,* which *Publishers Weekly* called a prose poem. For the bands of color and sunlit waters, reviewer Barbara Scotto, writing for *School Library Journal,* lauded the collaboration of writer and artist. *Kirkus Review* termed the effects tranquil, idyllic, and luminous in its survey of "Sunfish under lily pads living in cool green rooms, watching for water bugs to make a lunch" (Paulsen, *Canoe*).

2000

On a pragmatic theme, *Worksong,* versified by Paulsen and illustrated by his wife, examined reasons for jobs in entertainment, service, skilled crafts, and the helping professions. *Publishers Weekly* admired the gentle words and pictures; *School Library Journal* praised the lyrical survey for turning children's attention to essential forms of work and the satisfaction the jobs give laborers. A militaristic fantasy, *The White Fox Chronicles,* won applause from Elizabeth Elsbree, a reviewer for *School Library Journal,* and Gillian Engberg, a critic for *Booklist,* for appeal to reluctant readers. In the same year, the author returned to his youth in North Dakota for *The Beet Fields: Memories of a Sixteenth Summer*, a graphic memoir of a sociological conundrum—the child parenting the needy adult. Implied in the Gary character's departure from home, an unhealthy relationship with his mother forces him to escape potential incest. He admits the hard truth, "he had to run" (Paulsen, *Beet,* 20).

January 23, 2001

The author's autographical accounts in *Guts: The True Stories Behind Hatchet and the Brian Books* revealed episodes that inspired his award-winning, child-pleasing works.

2002

Paulsen achieved listing among ten outstanding American YA authors.

2003

As a gesture to single moms, the author wrote *The Glass Café (or the Stripper and the State; How My Mother Started a War with the System That Made Us Kind of Rich and a Little Bit Famous*), the story of Al (for Alice), a mom who performs at the Kitty Kat Club. Obviously comic from the start, the novel generated controversy at Carolina Beach, North Carolina, in late December 2012, when a parent, Tabitha Bachert, demanded that the public library censor the novel. She objected to the subject of exotic dance for her eight-year-old's reading.

2003 April

The author planned a 22-day sail from California to Hawaii and from there 25 days to the Cook Islands, the home of South Pacific Maoris.

2004 January

In Washington State, Paulsen joined fellow mushers at the Spokane Shriners' Hospital for the three-day Ikidarod, an opportunity for handicapped children to ride on a sled pulled by huskies.

2004 April

In April, the writer took his sailboat to Hawaii to ready it for a run around Cape Horn.

2004 fall

At age 65, Paulsen alternated scrutinizing a desert milieu rife with rattlers, bears, and mountain lions with breeding and running 50 sled dogs at his 40-acre ranch north of Willow in south-central Alaska. He occupied a two-story log house and protected his pack from moose with a .357-magnum pistol. His release of *The Quilt* returned to autobiography linking Gary at age six to a loving Norwegian-American community. *Kirkus Review* identified the poignant memoir as an ode to Grandma Alida, a character he referred to in *The Beet Fields* and reanimated in 2015 in *This Side of Wild.*

2005

Following the futuristic settings of *The White Fox Chronicles* and *Time Benders,* Paulsen created *The Time Hackers*, a sci-fi mystery reflective of the blazing techno-marvels in Orson Scott Card's *Ender's Game* saga. The use of holograms enabled Paulsen to introduce historical figures, from Jesus to Beethoven. More significant to the author's fans, the theme warned the unwary of what reviewer James Blasingame termed "the ever-escalating thrill of more and more realistic-looking fantasy video games" (Blasingame, 2006, 544).

February 14, 2006

A fictional arena for one of Paulsen's favorite characters, *Molly McGinty Has a Really Good Day* follows a persnickety journal keeper to Our Lord of Mercy Middle School for her Grandmother Irene Flynn's visit for Senior Citizen Day. Although *School Library Journal* and *Booklist* lauded the author for his accurate glimpses of middle school life, *Publishers Weekly* scolded the author for turning the loss of Molly's notebook into slapstick, a cruel trick on an orphan needing structure.

2006 March

With 23 new dogs purchased in Idaho, Paulsen returned to Alaska to make his third run of the Iditarod. To interviewer James Blasingame, he confided, "I thought I'd gotten dogs out of my system some 14 years ago, but all it took was one ride on a friend's sled to realize that the dogs were in my blood and I had to get back to them" (Blasingame, 2004, 271). He quit the competition in the 80th mile outside Nome after smashing into a gate and cutting himself on the raw edge of a pipe.

2006 June

The author revisited adolescence with *The Amazing Life of Birds: The Twenty-Day Puberty Journal of Duane Homer Leech*, a source of "the kind of humor you have right before you cry" (Woodman, 2006, 26). Maria B. Salvadore, in a review for *School Library Journal,* praised "laugh-out-loud lines and self-effacing humor" (Salvadore, 2006). More kudos from *Booklist, Publishers Weekly,* and *VOYA* centered on the author's fresh take on the anatomical thoughts that puzzle the puerile Duane, who substitutes the word "elbow" for the body parts that dominate his dreams and secret thoughts.

2006 August

The Legend of Bass Reeves: Being the True and Fictional Account of the Most Valiant Marshal in the West mapped in historical fiction the life of a former slave who became a sharpshooting federal deputy marshal. Paulsen chose a real hero as opposed to epic figures like Jim Bridger and Kit Carson, who have passed from real accomplishment into myth. However, much of the background material falls short of accuracy, especially identification of the Five Civilized Tribes, a summation of Oklahoma terrain, and knowledge of the Osage.

August 1, 2007

The pervasive theme of mushing resumed in Paulsen's writing in *Puppies, Dogs, and Blue Northers,* a biography of Cookie, the author's cherished, judicious lead dog. Of her unexpected mating with Rex, the author refers to the union as "God making puppies," which arrive 65 days later in mid–January (Paulsen, *Puppies,* 5). For the memoir's affection, *Publisher's Weekly* labeled it a love story. *Kirkus Reviews* declared the motif "domestic companionship until Cookie's blessedly peaceful death" ("Puppies," 1996). The loving commemoration of the author's great-hearted husky won two ALA commendations and a *Publishers Weekly* Best Book of the Year.

September 11, 2007

At the Children's Humanities Festival, Paulsen won the *Chicago Tribune* Prize for Literary Achievement. Book editor Elizabeth Taylor explained the young adult fascination with true-to-life adventure tales: "Adolescents everywhere are easily caught up in the excitement and emotion" ("Gary," 2007).

October 13, 2007

Paulsen delivered the key address in Sauk Centre, Minnesota, at the Sinclair Lewis writing conference. His works won a Parents' Choice citation.

March 24, 2009

A tale of the self-starting hero in a summer idyll, Paulsen's *Lawn Boy* earned from reviewer Charles McGrath the description "a Horatio Alger story for the hedge fund era" (McGrath, 2007). For "sounding exactly like a 12-year-old," the farce received awards from Texas and New Mexico, National Council for Social Studies, and ALA (*ibid.*). The action places an anonymous preteen native of Eden Prairie, Minnesota, in the enviable role of get-rich-quick entrepreneur. Abounding with serendipity, the plot buoys the day job of lawn mowing with some astute outsourcing to illegal laborers and profiteering in the coffin market. The character recurred in 2010 in *Lawn Boy Returns,* which features the theme of bullying.

2010

Publication of *Lawn Boy Returns* continued the author's writing focus on young boys from unassuming milieus. The 12-year-old "financial prodigy" faces labor issues while operating a $480,000 lawn business. For its unique take on exploitive capitalism among children, critic Lilijana Burcar charged the author with exonerating investors for overworking and underpaying migrant Hispanics. Nonetheless, the Oklahoma Library Association presented Paulsen a Sequoyah Book Award, selected by Oklahoma school pupils.

June 8, 2010

A salute to the native problem solver blessed with eidetic memory, Paulsen's *Mudshark* matched a boy sleuth with a psychic parrot.

2011

With *Liar, Liar,* Paulsen compounded humor and meaning, producing episodes that both entertain and perplex as the protagonist struggles to quash an ignoble habit. While sailing his sloop on the Pacific, the author developed Kevin Spencer, the comic braggart and foil of the protagonist of *Lawn Boy.* Kevin recurs in *Flat Broke: The Theory, Practice and Destructive Properties of Greed; Crush: The Theory, Practice and Destructive Properties of Love; Vote: The Theory, Practice, and Destructive Properties of Politics;* and *Family Ties,* an effort to unite a fractious family. Although the series lacked the spontaneity of Paulsen's classics, the novels achieved high ratings from *Booklist, School Library Journal, Kirkus Reviews,* and the *New York Times.*

January 11, 2011

An honest depiction of war, *Woods Runner* evolved from a concept that Paulsen developed after seeing a memorial obelisk to six Revolutionary War casualties from New Hampshire. In 1776, Samuel Lehi Smith, a 13-year-old western Pennsylvanian, weathers the colonial revolt against the Redcoats as well as insurgent Iroquois, Hessian mercenaries, and dysentery. Sam admires the patriot underground that attempts to throw off the rule of England's George III, but longs to return to the woods, his everyday sanctuary. The novel won a Parents' Choice citation and readers' choice selections by eleven states.

January 25, 2011

A touching summer idyll and salute to altruism, *Notes from the Dog* placed Finn and teen friend Matthew in the company of Johanna, an adult suffering from breast cancer. The novel flourished in print and audio CD editions.

August 9, 2011

With the rollicking collusions of Reed Hamner, Riley Dolen, and Henry Mosley in *Masters of Disaster,* Paulsen accounted for the temptation of extreme sports and dicey challenges to young males. The text collected three adventure tales previously published in *Boys' Life*—"Henry Mosley's Last Stand," "Breaking the Record," and "The Night the Headless, Blood-Drinking, Flesh-Eating Corpses of Cleveland (Almost) Took Over the World."

2012

In its 25th year, *Hatchet* continued to soar in popularity and achieved sales above four million copies. Critics began to cite the adventure title among American classics.

September 11, 2012

A trio of novellas, *Paintings from the Cave* reprised Paulsen's focus on creativity, dogs, and the relief of solitude and fear through art and camaraderie. On a more disturbing note, the author abandoned his ventures into the woods for children's struggles in urban jungles, a cacophony he had introduced in *Woods Runner* in colonial New York. In place of the outdoors, his text builds on 21st-century anxieties about a dope pusher notching a tongue with his knife and empathy for a boy Dumpster diving for a coat and three winos frozen during a cold night. The author's tone and atmosphere veer away from hope in nature and teamwork to cynical reflections on a survivor who saves himself by abandoning education and constantly fleeing stalkers, "'Cause you stop, you're done" (Paulsen, *Paintings*, 14).

2013 January

Teaming with son Jim Paulsen, an elementary school teacher, sculptor, and closet writer, the author began a two-year project writing *Road Trip*, a rescue motif told in human and canine voices by Ben and Atticus, his border collie. A narrative sure to appeal to at-risk readers, the quest novel varied adolescent drollery with wry dog philosophy. *Publishers Weekly* admired the father-son fellowship for its realism and humor.

January 7, 2015

Paulsen followed *Road Trip* with a companion work, *Field Trip*, featuring a pro-hockey tone and pro-dog atmosphere heightened by Atticus and Conor, a rescued puppy. The successful collaboration disproved Gary's previous choice to work alone. Of the partnership-by-email, he quipped, "Writing together seemed like an easier thing than sculpting together" (Lodge, 2012).

September 14, 2015

Shortly after publishing *This Side of Wild: Mutts, Mares, and Laughing Dinosaurs,* Paulsen received a nomination for the National Book Award for YA literature. A detailed memoir of animal encounters colors *This Side*, which details his crafting of a bow and arrows from willow, cane, and "tied-on chicken feathers" (Paulsen, *This Side*, 5). He wrested comedy from memories of broken arms and ribs and "seemingly impossible—an arrow self-driven through my left thumb" (*ibid.*).

2016 September

The author's skill at passing earth wisdom to the young found a voice in *Fishbone's Song*, an allegory that features a patient Kentucky hermit who builds resilience and respect in an unnamed foster son. A zanier source of kid philosophy energized *Six Kids and a Stuffed Cat,* a play set during a tornado drill in a school bathroom. Through what critic

Eden Ross Lipson identifies as "hard work, luck, and travails," the writer stands a chance of rising to the height of classic authors James Fenimore Cooper, Esther Forbes, and Mark Twain (Lipson, 2000, B7).

Source

"Alida's Song," *Publishers Weekly* (31 May 1999): 94–95.
Barron, Ronald. "Gary Paulsen: 'I Write Because It's All I Can Do,'" *ALAN Review* 20:3 (Spring 1993): 27–30.
Blasingame, James. "Books for Adolescents," *Journal of Adolescent & Adult Literacy,* 48:3 (November 2004): 269–273.
_____. "The Time Hackers," *Journal of Adolescent & Adult Literacy* 49:6 (March 2006): 543–544.
Buchholz, Rachel. "The Write Stuff," *Boys' Life* (December 1995): 28–29, 53.
Carey, Joanna. "A Born Survivor Joanna Carey Meets the Engaging Best-selling American Author Gary Paulsen," *The* [Manchester] *Guardian* (28 May 1996).
Conlan, Maureen. "A Writer with Stories to Fill Two Lifetimes," *Cincinnati Post* (5 April 1995): B-5.
Creager, Ellen. "View from the Outside the Wilderness Resonates for Children's Author," *Detroit Free Press* (13 April 1999): 4.
Estes, Sally. "Sisters/Hermanas," *Booklist* 90 (1 January 1994): 816.
Fine, Edith Hope. *Gary Paulsen: Author and Wilderness Adventurer.* Berkeley Heights, NJ: Enslow, 2000.
Gale, David. "Gary Paulsen," *School Library Journal* 43:6 (June 1997): 24.
"Gary Paulsen Awarded 2007 Chicago Tribune Prize for Young Adult Fiction," *PR Newswire* (11 September 2007).
Golden, Bernice. *Critical Reading Activities for the Works of Gary Paulsen.* Portland, ME: Walch, 1999.
Goodson, Lori Atkins. "Singlehanding: An Interview with Gary Paulsen," *ALAN Review* 31:2 (Winter 2004): 53–59.
Kenney, Edwin J., Jr. "The Island," *New York Times* (22 May 1988): A30.
Larking, Kate. "Haunting Tale of Deceit," *Calgary Herald* (11 September 2004): ESO5.
Lewis, Randy. "He Owes It All to Librarians and Dogs," *Los Angeles Times* (31 July 1994): E6.
Lipson, Eden Ross. "A Children's Author Joins the Immortals," *New York Times* (20 June 1986): A31.
Lodge, Sally. *Q&A with Gary Paulsen and Jim Paulsen.* http://www.publishers weekly.com/pw/by-topic/authors/interviews/article/55019-q-a-with-gary-paulsen-and-jim-paulsen.html, 2012.
Lynch, Amanda. "Gary Paulsen," *Children's Book Review* (26 January 2009).
Mayer, Henry. "The Boys of War," *New York Times Book Review* (15 November 1998): 40.
McGrath, Charles. "Lawn Boy," *New York Times* (12 August 2007).
Metella, Helen. "I Write the Way I Used to Run," *Edmonton Journal* (31 October 1993): D6.
Miller, Kay. "Suddenly Fame and Fortune," [Minneapolis] *Star Tribune* (10 July 1988): 6.
Morris, Anne. "An Inch Ahead of the Fireball," *Austin American Statesman* (7 March 1999): K6.
Moss, Meredith. "Novelist's Life Is In, Out of the Woods," *Dayton Daily News* (5 February 2004): E1.
Nickelson, George. *Gary Paulsen.* New York: Trumpet Club, 1993.
Pemberton, Mary. "Writing, Mushing Are Man's Twin Passions," *Whitehorse Star* (1 April 2005): 10.
"Pilgrimage on a Steel Ride," *Kirkus Reviews* 65:12 (3 November 1997).
Potyandi, Barry. "Warm Embrace of Pastoral Life Is Long Lost," *Calgary Herald* (24 June 1995): B14.
Price, Rodney. "Harley Journey a Rough Ride," *Rocky Mountain News* (30 November 1997): E3.
Salvadore, Maria B. "The Amazing Life of Birds," *School Library Journal* 52:10 (October 2006): 166.
Scott, Caroline. "Gary Paulsen," [London] *Sunday Times* (21 July 1996): 12.
"Sentries," *Kirkus Reviews* 54 (1 April 1986).
Shadle, Laura Smith. "Author Uses Own Life Experiences in Teen Novels," [Spokane, WA] *Spokesman Review* (2 February 2004): B1.
Sides, Anne Goodwin. "On the Road and Between the Pages, an Author Is Restless for Adventure," *New York Times* (26 August 2006): B7.
Winton, Tim. "Boy's Life His Own World War," *Los Angeles Times* (21 March 1993): 1.
Woodman, Tenley. "Acclaimed Author Takes on Awkwardness of Adolescence," *Boston Herald* (19 June 2006): 26.

Genealogy

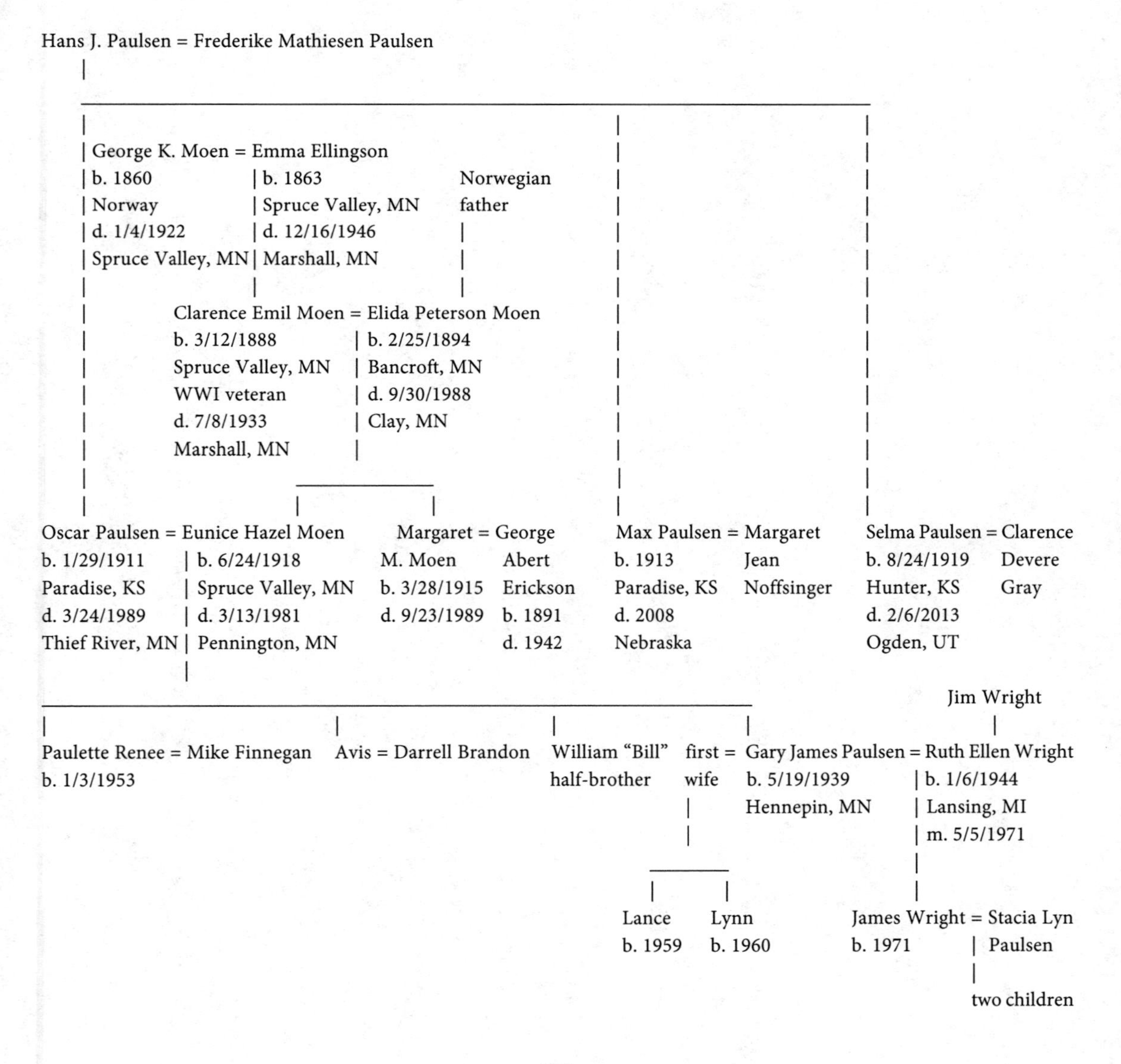
Hans J. Paulsen = Frederike Mathiesen Paulsen
George K. Moen = Emma Ellingson
b. 1860
Norway
d. 1/4/1922
Spruce Valley, MN
b. 1863
Spruce Valley, MN
d. 12/16/1946
Marshall, MN
Norwegian
father
Clarence Emil Moen = Elida Peterson Moen
b. 3/12/1888
Spruce Valley, MN
WWI veteran
d. 7/8/1933
Marshall, MN
b. 2/25/1894
Bancroft, MN
d. 9/30/1988
Clay, MN
Oscar Paulsen = Eunice Hazel Moen
b. 1/29/1911
Paradise, KS
d. 3/24/1989
Thief River, MN
b. 6/24/1918
Spruce Valley, MN
d. 3/13/1981
Pennington, MN
Margaret = George
M. Moen
b. 3/28/1915
d. 9/23/1989
Abert
Erickson
b. 1891
d. 1942
Max Paulsen = Margaret
b. 1913
Paradise, KS
d. 2008
Nebraska
Jean
Noffsinger
Selma Paulsen = Clarence
b. 8/24/1919
Hunter, KS
d. 2/6/2013
Ogden, UT
Devere
Gray
Jim Wright
Paulette Renee = Mike Finnegan
b. 1/3/1953
Avis = Darrell Brandon
William "Bill"
half-brother
first =
wife
Gary James Paulsen = Ruth Ellen Wright
b. 5/19/1939
Hennepin, MN
b. 1/6/1944
Lansing, MI
m. 5/5/1971
Lance
b. 1959
Lynn
b. 1960
James Wright = Stacia Lyn
b. 1971
Paulsen
two children

Gary Paulsen
A Companion to the Young Adult Literature

accomplishment

Gary Paulsen is an admirer of achievement, whether the professional conduct of a black deputy U.S. marshal in *The Legend of Bass Reeves;* the wood-chopping strengths of Uncle David, a Norwegian lumberjack in *The Winter Room;* or the self-control of reformed prevaricator Kevin Spencer in *Liar, Liar.* Characters often comment on surmounting challenge in boasts and description, as with Cornish McManus's admiration for his self-crafted flintlock in *The Rifle* and Coyote Runs's survey of some 140 horses on "a great raid, a raid they would speak of for years around the fire" (Paulsen, *Canyons,* 63). Mark Harrison, survivor of interplanetary transport by a mysterious beam of light in *The Transall Saga,* rewards himself for a deft arrow shot with a primal chant: "I—am—the—best. I—am—the—killer—of—the—terrible—Howling—Thing," a foreshadowing of his creation of a vaccine for the Ebola virus in adulthood (Paulsen, *Transall,* 44). Of a personal record, in *Pilgrimage on a Steel Ride,* Paulsen remains humbler than his fictional braggarts: "I have accomplished more than I ever thought I would. Certainly more—considering the rough edges of my life—than I deserve" (Paulsen, *Pilgrimage,* 3). The overt modesty explains the frequent chagrin and lack of braggadocio in his memoirs.

The author credits persistence for favorable outcomes. For 13-year-old woodsman Samuel Lehi Smith in *Woods Runner*, determination guides his northeastern quest from the Pennsylvania frontier to New York City to release his parents from British custody at a sugar mill. In the company of a mentor, Scots tinker/spy Abner McDougal, Sam listens to sound advice about entering a British enclave to seek two adults among 5,000 prisoners of war. Abner anticipates Sam's dogged plotting and logic with a rural simile: "You're pushing at this, ain't you? … Kind of like a root hog, digging at it" (Paulsen, *Woods,* 106). The image characterizes Sam's success at reuniting his family, as well as his assistance to Morgan's Rifles as a marksman and medic during the rest of the Revolutionary War. Paulsen's creation of the young liberator implies a model for colonists and American Independence.

Unlike the success of Sam at outfoxing Redcoats, in *The Crossing,* Paulsen ponders one of his broken soldiers. A satisfying military achievement eludes the career of Sergeant Robert S. Locke and leaves him guilt-ridden and grief stricken for the comrades he couldn't rescue from the Vietnam War. A shedding of regret and a merger with spirits of the dead seem his only means of escaping mental anguish and a daily retreat into beer and scotch. Like a mystic bridge, his mirror reflects a face true to the military code. Out of sight, qualms fester in his brain. By defending the orphan Manny Bustos, an undersized picaro in Juárez, Mexico, Locke ironically achieves his release through martyrdom. Thus, the Santa Fe Bridge at El Paso, Texas, enables one crossing to actualize another crossing into peace. Paulsen ennobles the pyrrhic victory as heroic and selfless. Simultaneously, new hope for the would-be immigrant lies in Locke's wallet, which can fund Manny's exodus from street squalor to a land of promise.

ACHIEVEMENT IN ACTION

The accomplishments of young characters like Sam and Manny recapture the author's boyhood joys in autonomy and solo subsistence in the outdoors, two activities that Paulsen shared with Francis Alphonse Tucket, the plainsman of the five-part Tucket series. In reprising the pride of snagging a panfish in *Hatchet,* memory revisits a surge of pride in his throat at what Brian Robeson "had done. He had done food" (Paulsen, *Hatchet,* 119). Brian returns to the thought with deeper consideration in *The River,* where he concludes, "Everything man has always been or will be, all the thoughts and dreams and sex and hate and every little and big thing" depends on food (Paulsen, *River,* 41). The statement illustrates Paulsen's belief that "when children are under extreme duress, they become incredibly strong" and equal to the challenges before them, both envisioned and unexpected (Paulsen and Nickelson, 1993).

The author's pro-child priorities, particularly in *Tracker, Brian's Return, The Foxman,* and *The Voyage of the Frog,* acknowledge the value of one-on-one mentoring and experience with nature. Paulsen symbolizes accomplishment by John Borne's touching a deer, Brian Robeson's revisiting past terrors in central Canada, the unnamed narrator's stalking a fox, and David Alspeth's sailing the Pacific Ocean alone to scatter Uncle Owen's ashes. The hands-on method makes up for the irrelevance of educational institutions to youth in need of self-confidence and of psychological and emotional support. Thus, John gains the self-confidence to face his grandfather's death from cancer, Brian elects to aid other survivors by reliving his perils, the Foxman's young friend finds the courage to honor the old war hero with a funeral pyre, and David withstands a storm and nine days at sea by retrieving lessons imparted by Uncle Owen.

In consideration of sports competitors, Paulsen tempers avid hero worship, which he claims has become an American religion. In repeated references to school sports, he credits the coach with influence superior to that of classroom teachers. In *The Island,* the author typifies Wil Neuton's athletic ambitions: "I wanted to be a jock for a long time," particularly for the appeal of athletics to girls (Paulsen, *Island,* 16). In an unforeseen face-off in *Brian's Return,* the text demeans the value of contact sports for endorsing senseless violence, the source of Brian's fight with Carl Lammers. Instead of the usual fist-to-fist slamming, Brian experiences "an automatic reaction" and becomes "animal-boy," a fugue state that sends him back to the mythic woods to conquer his enemy by the rules of the wastelands (Paulsen, *Return,* 13). In an illuminating moment, Brian accepts his spiritual dissociation from urbanite to survivalist: "It's what I am now" (*ibid.,* 22). Paulsen's appended note exonerates Brian for his transformation: "Once you have seen the horizon, have followed it, have lived with nature in all its vicious beauty, it is impossible to come back to 'normal' life" (*ibid.,*

113). Of his own pilgrimage to self, the author concludes, "I will go again—always, as Brian must always go" (*ibid.*, 115).

Analysts Jim Powell and Nancy Lafferty note that Paulsen favors scenarios of home, farm, and the outdoors, but details little of institutional school time, a central issue among illiterate slaves in *Nightjohn* and *Sarny* and among freedmen in *The Legend of Bass Reeves*. In *The Schernoff Discoveries*, the author pictures Mrs. Johnson's class as uninspiring and gym teacher Wankle as the "football coach—Nazi beast," who enjoys sadistic ridicule of geeks (Paulsen, *Schernoff*, 6). Similarly, in *Time Benders*, Zack Griffin yawns and parodies Mrs. J "like a chipmunk with glasses" while "wasting his time in her class" (Paulsen, *Benders*, n.p.). In *Brian's Hunt*, Brian accepts his boyhood error of "simply getting by, trying to learn just enough to pass the tests and never really *knowing* anything" (Paulsen, *Hunt*, 9). His acknowledgment indicates maturity in the 16-year-old that he hadn't displayed at age 14 in *Hatchet*.

The negativity toward classroom learning expresses Paulsen's childhood belief that hands-on training serves him best, a philosophy he shares with proponents of the Montessori method and with biology instructor John Homesley in *Canyons*. For Wil Neuton, the protagonist of *The Island*, remaining in Madison, Wisconsin, ensures that he can identify "which teachers were dorks and which weren't," a negative image that recalls his distaste for Mr. Musovich (Paulsen, *Island*, 7). Wil relives a gym teacher's assignment of 12 sessions of lifting weights for five minutes. Cleverly, the teacher builds a pattern of daily exercise that encourages muscle memory and habit strength. To atone for lying about obeying the teacher, Wil begins lifting weights when the gym is empty. He admits, "I must have lifted over twelve tons for that one small lie" (*ibid.*, 30).

A more bizarre setting, a school bathroom during a tornado drill in *Six Kids and a Stuffed Cat* provides the rudiments of a play featuring honest childhood reflections on where and how they learn. During a discussion between students Jordan and Avery about wit, Jordan notes the importance of amenable behavior to faculty: "It doesn't pay to be subversive in middle school" (Paulsen, *Six*, 88). The statement speaks directly to the difficulties of kids like Paulsen and his nonconforming characters, who are prone to aberrant behaviors. Of the outcome of divergent thinking, the author poses the example of cave dwellers in Lascaux, France, who painted animal figures and a human hand outline on the walls during the Pleistocene Age: "Signing the work with pride, with knowledge … that he or she of the hand is the one who made it.… An idea" (*ibid.*, *75*).

Dash and Daring

In a 2010 interview, Paulsen named aerospace and farm work as his introductions to basic know-how, a topic he develops in the autobiographical *Harris and Me*. For *The Cookcamp*, he relives his arrival at age five from Chicago by train to Pine, Minnesota,. Lacking a father figure at home during World War II, he observes Carl, driver of the farm truck, who uses a crescent wrench to repair a slipping belt. Attacks on the mechanical problem result in typical male self-congratulation, consisting of swearing, grunting, spitting in the dirt, and slamming down the hood. Carl completes the scene with blasphemy, "She's tight now, by God," followed by an apology to the lone female for his crudeness (Paulsen, *Cookcamp*, 18). The text broadens Carl's abilities by picturing large hands lifting the exhausted boy from the cab and carrying him into the house. The duality of an awkward male with mothering skills softens a macho image and honors Carl for being well-rounded.

The coping skills that enabled the adult Paulsen to adapt to harsh situations fill his writing, as with the equestrian talents of Amos Binder and Dunc Culpepper in *Cowpokes and Desperadoes,* who achieve mastery of their horses in minutes. Dogsledding outranked the author's earlier influences with life-saving crafts by forcing him to be innovative. For winter wear, he emulated Inuit style by making mukluks and parkas, which shielded him from frostbite at 60 degrees below zero, an ingenuity he gives to the protagonist in *Brian's Hunt.* Equally detailed, the seagoing acumen of eighth-grader David Alspeth in *The Voyage of the Frog* begins with day sails with his Uncle Owen to Catalina. As inheritor of the *Frog,* the boy takes stock of his sloop, determines how to proceed onto the Pacific Ocean, and completes a difficult errand, spreading Owen's ashes out of sight of land. The dual physical and emotional triumph epitomizes the author's belief that physical success triggers and fosters inner growth.

See also music.

Source

Paulsen, Gary, and George Nickelson. *Gary Paulsen.* Trumpet Club, 1993.

Powell, Jim, and Nancy Lafferty. "Tracking Adolescent Responses to Cancer" in *Using Literature to Help Troubled Teenagers Cope with Health Issues.* Westport, CT: Greenwood, 2000.

adaptation

Paulsen celebrates the power of the human spirit to cope with dissolution, loss, and peril, the controlling theme in *The Crossing* of mestizo orphan Manny Bustos's search for relief in the U.S. from pedophiles and gang-style torment in Juárez, of Mark Harrison coping with a mystic jungle in *The Transall Saga,* and of Francis Alphonse Tucket's fleeing outlaws and Indians on the Midwestern plains in *Call Me Francis Tucket.* For Francis, learning to sleep in the open, observe silence, and remain on constant alert forces a mature awareness of plains hazards, from enslavers to buffalo herds. He deduces that danger "made it doubly important for [him] to be aware of what was coming to get time to react or hide" (Paulsen, *Call,* 72). A lengthy series of dangers in the company of frontier trader Jason Grimes, his mentor, in *Mr. Tucket* convinces the 14-year-old that a similar career in Western gadding and trading with the Pawnee does not fulfill his ambitions. The deduction attests to a boy who is beginning to think like a pragmatic adult.

In *Tucket's Home,* the title figure accepts a juxtaposition of good with bad as the typical state of the West. He basks in "a country so beautiful that [he] often had trouble believing it was real," but he recognizes that Comancheros, Hispanics who trade with the Comanche, "are plain mean and will kill you for your shoes" (Paulsen, *Home,* 4, 13–14). In a reverse adaptation, on return to the family, Francis must accustom himself to sleeping indoors in a safe place and adjust to the claustrophobic closeness of too many people. He admits, "At first it bothered him" to return to daily familiarity with his mother and father (*ibid.,* 183). His compromise with home reaches culmination from family meals, which end the monotony of killing and eating rabbit, deer, and buffalo each day and replaces pit fire cookery with a full menu of vegetables, bread, and sweets prepared by his mother and sister Rebecca.

On a more painful level, the author depicts the human knack for transforming desperation into hope, the theme of Carley's salvation from juvenile delinquency in *Popcorn Days and Buttermilk Nights* and the salvation of Carl Wenstrom, a veteran B-17 pilot emotionally damaged during World War II in *Dancing Carl.* For the salvation of Sarny, the protagonist of *Nightjohn* and *Sarny,* survival on a Southern plantation depends on defying the use of herself and Alice, a mental defective, as producers of slave babies to be sold to increase the wealth of greedy owners like enslaver Clel Waller. When her husband Martin dies, Sarny retreats to "a corner of the slave quarters and hated. Hated Waller, hated cotton, hated God," a negative mood that wearies and depletes her usual spunky demeanor (Paulsen, *Sarny,* 14). By the end of Sarny's story in 1930 at a Texas rest home, she lives at peace with old age, widowhood, and deafness and turns her hand to a long-term project, her teacher John's dream of a chronicle of American slavery composed by a black author. By transforming experience into history, Sarny avoids the emotional crippling of regret and vengeance.

Accommodating Destiny

As revealed in the heroism of Francis Tucket, Mark Harrison, and Sarny, Paulsen specializes in the efforts of young people to grapple with situations as immutable as kidnap, bondage, and war, the situation that sharpshooter John Byam encounters in *The Rifle.* In the foreword to *Father Water, Mother Woods: Essays on Fishing and Hunting in the North Woods,* the writer regrets an insidious evil—the waste of young lives in toxic households like his own nuclear family. He divides the "familial casualties" into two classes: Those who "stand and take it" and the ones who "cut and run," the choice of the displaced narrator in *Tiltawhirl John,* an escapist story based on the author's teen years (Paulsen, *Father,* xii). By basing a world view on the northwestern Minnesota rivers and forests, Paulsen becomes "self-fostering," his term for self-adaptive, a descriptor of characters as plucky and clever as Sarny, Tucket, Mark, Carley, and John (*ibid.*).

To interviewer James Blasingame, Paulsen affirmed that children like Sarny, Mark, and Manny are wonderfully malleable: "Young people flex and adapt. They don't miss what they never had and they live, wonderfully, in the moment" (Blasingame, 2004, 269). The author applied the dictum to his characters and himself. Instead of expecting schools, orphanages, and other government institutions to rescue him from desolation, he turned to lakes, rivers, and woods, the source of comfort for Tucket's orphaned charges, Billy and Lottie; for Brian Robeson, the survivor in the *Hatchet* series; and for the introspective Wil Neuton, a newcomer to the Wisconsin outback in *The Island.* More to the point, the survival rate of characters in *Woods Runner* commends the emotional hardihood of Anne Marie Pennysworth "Annie" Clark, an eight-year-old traumatized by the slaughter of her parents, Caleb and Martha Clark, during the American Revolution. Her adaptation to fostering by the Smith family begins with a sibling relationship with teen survivor Samuel Lehi Smith and a convenient symbiosis with his parents, Abigail and Olin Smith, who need a daughter to start a new family. On conveying Annie and the Smiths to safety, Sam is able to relax: "His parents and Annie would be safe now" (Paulsen, *Woods,* 158).

Adjustment over Time

From past experiences, according to Eden Ross Lipson, a critic for the *New York Times,* Paulsen achieves a personal and literary transformation—"the products of personal difficulty and stress, a narrative distillation of anguished experience," the subject he peruses in *Harris and Me* (Lipson, 2000, B7). Similarly, a misconceived self-rescue in *The Car* attests to the efforts of 14-year-old Terry Anders to replace missing parental guidance with the depersonalized instructions for building a kit car, a Bearcat. Instead of schooling and home time with a mother and father or a foster family, he substitutes driving; dreams of visiting his Uncle Loren in Portland, Oregon; and squalid companions—Wayne, Waylon, and Suze—amoral teens who live outside the law. The plot illustrates Paulsen's theme of misdirected boyhood enthusiasm and a lack-logic attempt to flesh out an empty life with meaning, a motif he returns to with the characterization of Jo-Jo the Dog-faced Girl in *Paintings from the Cave* and Daniel Martin in *Danger on Midnight River.*

At a pensive point in Paulsen's memoirs, he relives his runaway youth in *The Beet Fields,* a story set in North Dakota that he introduced in 1977 in *Tiltawhirl John.* Picturing the 16-year-old laborer thinning out every other beet with a hoe, the 1955 scenario draws queries from the boy about how "Mexicans always outworked him" (Paulsen, *Beet,* 4). For $11 per acre, the protagonist adapts to metal dinner plates secured to the table with a roofing nail, sandwiches from day-old bread for $1 a day, and sleeping in sheds on burlap sacks. Struggling against blisters, heat, and fatigue, he still lags behind Hispanic workers, who seem naturally to accommodate misery, "always so clean that their white clothes made his eyes hurt" (*ibid.,* 11). One elderly Latino summarizes the newcomer's slow acquisition of field wisdom: "You are new at everything. It is because you are young" (*ibid.*, 14). The comforting words suggest the unfamiliarity of a white boy with the sorrows indigenous to nonwhite migrants, who have long endured in the white world through ceaseless toils and sufferings.

See also Hatchet; loss; nature; parenting; *Tucket's Home.*

Source

Blasingame, James. "Books for Adolescents," *Journal of Adolescent & Adult Literacy,* 48:3 (November 2004): 266–273.
Lipson, Eden Ross. "The Dark Underbelly of Writing Well for Children," *New York Times* (8 July 2000): B7.
"Mr. Tucket," *Journal of Reading* 38:1 (September 1994): 70–71.

alcoholism

From bitter childhood exposure, the writer expresses an insidious form of mortality—the drawn-out torment of addiction, such as the reliance of Bill Flaherty on bingeing in Adams, North Dakota, in *The Beet Fields;* Carl Wenstrom's pocket bottle and Pisspot Jimmy's red face in *Dancing Carl;* and the intemperance of Wild Bill Hickok in *The Car* and of the people of Kaltag, Alaska, in *Winterdance.* For Clel Waller in *Sarny,* enslavement to intoxicants and gambling result in the breakup of black families, whose sale price saves Waller's plantation from bankruptcy. Clel's gradual decline hastens the erosion of plantation authority and profit. One old woman outlines the sot's deterioration: "Man takes a drink, drink takes a drink, drink takes a man," a proverb the author repeats in *Zero to Sixty* (Paulsen, *Sarny,* 15; *Zero,* 77). Mammy restates the concept in *The Legend of Bass Reeves* with "Too close to the jug," an apt description of "the mister" who owns her and her son Bass (Paulsen, *Legend,* 11).

More subtly, alcoholism infects Paulsen's literary households with unending stress and sorrow, a source of anguish for a Korean War survivor in *Fishbone's Song* and of Eunice and Oscar Paulsen in *Eastern Sun, Winter Moon, The Cookcamp, This Side of Wild,* and *My Life in Dog Years.* From a more personal slant, the author recalls his mother invading his bed in his mid-teems in *The Beet Fields* and the turning point in his independence that motivated a permanent rupture with a drunken mother and father who appeared in public "with piss running down his leg and puke on his shirt" (Paulsen, *Beet,* 23). A family cycle of intoxication in *Harris and Me* forces the Gary character into summer migration among relatives from home to home, a crap shoot that lightens his worries among the Larson household. The down side of constantly adapting to a new family and environment strikes the boy at summer's end, when returning home to "puke drunks" reminds him of the pattern of boozing and household violence that turns his parents into "vegetables most of the time" in a "Four Roses coma" (Paulsen, *Harris,* 7, 1). By examining the ambivalence of a preteen, Paulsen endorses the belief of Bill Broz, a critic for *ALAN Review,* that "owing to issues such as ... drug and alcohol abuse, among others, teens are growing in awareness and sophistication at an earlier age" (Broz, 2009, 77).

A Gnawing Canker

Paulsen, himself a recovering alcoholic and the son of drunks living in a confining apartment in Thief River Falls, Minnesota, amplifies the mental misery of self-medication for battle fatigue, the source of his story "The Madonna." In *Eastern Sun, Winter Moon,* the preschooler Gary recognizes some threat to home and self from the 1940s pop songs that draw his mother to the Cozy Corner. In her loneliness during World War II, she turns too willingly to drink and partners with strangers to swing tunes for lindying, a spirited street improvisation to jazz. When drunkenness diminishes her modesty, the boy observes too much touching, too close a dance for Eunice to perform with unknown males. He recalls additional dance scenes on board the transport ship to the Philippines that heighten his disillusion with his pretty, flirty mother.

Lacking adequate feeding by his drunken parents in Minnesota, in *Guts,* the memoirist relives the éclat of capturing and cooking his first fire pit meals, a task that the protagonist of *Mr. Tucket* and Samuel Lehi Smith in *Woods Runner* come to enjoy as their reward for woodsmen's skills. Sam applies the predictability of escapist carousing to prison sentries in New York City, where a poorly guarded door enables him to free his starving parents, Abigail and Olin Smith, from intemperate Redcoats. Anne Goodwin Sides, a journalist for the *New York Times,* accounted for Paulsen's personal and literary vigor as an overflow of negative stimuli: "too much anger, too much drink, too much emphasis on virility, too many wives, too much loneliness" (Sides, 2006, B7). He fits numerous fictional characters with the complex:

- Russel Susskit's Inuit father in *Dogsong*
- Uncle Owen, a cancer patient in *The Voyage of the Frog*
- Mr. Henderson, the wino in *A Christmas Sonata*
- Judith Eve, Jimmy, and military officers in *Fishbone's Song*
- Petey, an alley denizen addicted to Sneaky Pete wine in *Paintings from the Cave*
- Fred, the hard-drinking grain elevator owner in *The Monument*
- Alan Deerfoot, the tipsy boyfriend in *Sentries*
- Billy Honcho, the former Navajo chief turned street derelict in *The Night the White Deer Died*
- Jason Grimes and the Comanchero traders in *Tucket's Ride*
- five heavily armed outlaws in *Tucket's Home*
- old man Knutson, who sees Jesus in a peach tree in *Harris and Me*
- drunks frozen in a ditch or car during a storm in *Puppies, Dogs, and Blue Northers*

Paulsen intensifies description of some luckless children, such as Jo-Jo the Dog-Faced Girl in *Paintings from the Cave.* In recalling nightly bickering at home, she describes her parents as "drunk, blind drunk, mean drunk" until they slept it off (Paulsen, *Paintings,* 67).

Healing the Spirit

Paulsen depicts family addiction as a psychological syndrome blending Sigmund Freud's life urges with death urges, particularly the personal anesthetizing of war veterans like the Foxman, the protagonist in "The Soldier," and the two "elbows-keeping-them-from-falling-to-the-floor" drunks in *Zero to Sixty* (Paulsen, *Zero,* 46). The music and stage show of Juaréz strippers wrapped in live snakes at the Congo Tiki nightclub in *The Crossing* exploit befuddled soldiers, who vomit their evening's consumption in the alley. In a psychological miasma, Sergeant Robert S. Locke bears Vietnam's "true scars—the scars that covered other parts of his body and all of his mind and thoughts, the scars that were part of the drinking" (Paulsen, *Crossing,* 4).

The text depicts Locke as a victim of grisly memories of a combat massacre by AK-47s until Cutty Sark scotch numbs his brain. Stiff belts keep "the edges [from] coming sharper," an ongoing balancing act doomed to failure (Paulsen, *Crossing,* 84). At low points, he stumbles about Juaréz and relives the Vietnam War. In a post-war fog, "He suspected strongly that it meant he was not a true macho man" (*ibid.,* 32). Paulsen stresses Manny's altruism in relieving some of the veteran's loss of humanity from post-war regret that he couldn't save his buddies from combat deaths and can't rid himself of alcoholism.

Self-treatment for psychic pain offers limited anesthesia at the bullfights, where the sergeant "moved off inside himself," a release of his mirrored self for the voyeuristic "Fight wait. Death wait," which he shares with the bull (*ibid.,* 93). With empathy for a mestizo orphan, Manny Bustos, an undersized urchin, Locke envisions doom for both of them, a time when "the hawks will get us all" (*ibid.,* 106). The knife wounds that end the post-traumatic stress disorder of the troubled Viet survivor come as both menace and relief from alcohol cravings and flashbacks of war casualties.

Publishers Weekly accused *The Crossing* of overtaxing young readers with the soldier's adult syndrome, but both *Kirkus Reviews* and Rosie Peasley, a critic for *School Library Journal,* admired the stark crisis for ending on a glimmer of hope for the boy. In a critique for the *Boston Globe,* reviewer Stephanie Loer declared the writing "prose that is brilliant in the evocation of time, place, and character … a work of storytelling art" (Loer, 1988, 48). By validating the feelings of children persecuted in dysfunctional households, *The Crossing* uplifts readers by rejecting low self-esteem and despair and enhancing a sense of agency and forbearance of behavior disorders.

See also healing and death.

Source

Barron, Ronald. "Gary Paulsen: 'I Write Because It's All I Can Do,'" *ALAN Review* 20:3 (Spring 1993): 27–30.

Broz, Bill. "Memoir: Reading Life," *ALAN Review* 36:3 (Summer 2009): 59–64.

Kaywell, Joan F., ed. *Using Literature to Help Troubled Teenagers Cope with Abuse Issues.* Westport, CT: Greenwood, 2001.

Lacy, Meagan. "Portraits of Children of Alcoholics," *CUNY Academic Works* 46:4 (December 2015): 343–358.

Latrobe, Kathy. "An Introduction to Ten Outstanding Young-Adult Authors in the United States," *World Literature Today* 76:3 (2002): 68–73.

Loer, Stephanie. "A Satisfying Depression Era Tale," *Boston Globe* (21 February 1988): 48.

Schmitz, James A. "Gary Paulsen: A Writer of His Time," *ALAN Review* 22:1 (Fall 1994): 15–18.

Sides, Anne Goodwin. "On the Road and Between the Pages, an Author Is Restless for Adventure," *New York Times* (26 August 2006): B7.

ambition

Gary Paulsen writes frequently about his aims and those of his characters. His mastery of boyhood daring, the subject of *Harris and Me,* "The Case of the Dirty Bird," and *How Angel Peterson Got His Name: And Other Outrageous Tales about Extreme Sports,* accounts for fandom among the tween-to-teen set, especially males. Essential to an understanding of his massive body of work is a close analysis of his memoirs, beginning with *Eastern Sun, Winter Moon,* which focuses on Gary's residence in Manila at age seven. Compared to Eudora Welty's *One Writer's Beginnings* and Robert Newton Peck's *Weeds in Bloom,* Paulsen's autobiography avows his oneness with independence and self-direction in the woods. In *Guts,* he exults, "Hunting, along with fishing, was all I lived and breathed for, all I was or wanted to be" (Paulsen, *Guts*, 70). The circumstances suggest that, in view of his toxic home surroundings, thriving in the outdoors remained his sole option for actuating vigor and ingenuity.

In his prose, the theme of coming-of-age goals dominates the quest novel *Canyons*, in which 14-year-old Coyote Runs, an untried Apache brave, approaches his first raid over the Organ Mountains into Mexico as a time of action. In his view, "There was much to do," an understatement suggesting a sense of responsibility, fearlessness of the three-day ride, and organization in the budding warrior, who already understands tribal demands on adult males like Magpie and Sancta, the chief (Paulsen, *Canyons,* 6). With his idol before him, Coyote Runs anticipates "raids to take horses and a Mexican saddle with silver on it like Magpie had done" (*ibid.,* 4). With the rewards would come a new name, indicating that the teen warrior had entered manhood.

In another setting of the 19th-century zeitgeist, 15-year-old Charley Goddard, the true-life protagonist of *Soldier's Heart*, attempts a similar encounter with destiny. Unlike Coyote Runs, the Union enlistee with the First Minnesota Volunteers intends to greet manhood within skirmishes of civil war. In 1862, Charley meets immediate disillusion from the inescapable horrors of battlegrounds. Paulsen justifies Charley's abandonment of dreams by confronting the private with sipping from a creek a-swirl with blood, slaughtering horses for meat to feed hospital patients, and crouching behind a protective wall of cadavers encircling a field surgery to avoid the wind. A constant in the writer's motifs, Charley's quest for glory turns into a scramble for survival amid blazing artillery fire and a private reappraisal of unsophisticated ideals of masculinity. Disillusioned by warfare, he admits, "the parades were done and the dances were done and the killing—he thought of it as butchery more than killing—was at last done" (Paulsen, *Soldier's,* 97). Unfortunately for men like Charley, emotional distress supplants their aims with despair.

Adapting to Reality

Paulsen's soul-baring texts like *Canyons* and *Soldier's Heart* resonate with insights into his daunting childhood and his rebirth in manhood from divorced alcoholic and failed parent of son Lance and daughter Lynn into an adventure writer. Of the start of each new day at 4:30 A.M., in *Shelf Life: Stories by the Book,* he depicts as an all-consuming ache his intent to "change lives" through storytelling, an aspiration he shares with Vietnam veteran/author Tim O'Brien in *The Things They Carried* (Paulsen, *Shelf,* I). Notable among Paulsen's enduring convictions—beyond punctilious diction and skill at short, pithy statements—stands disdain for writers who court fame or wealth rather than truth. He explains his delight in "the loops and whorls of the story dance," the enticement of words on the page (*ibid.*). Upon receipt of his first acceptance letter, he celebrates approval beyond all other rewards, "not first love nor first hope nor first time never, no never like this" (*ibid.*)

The author's involvement in young adult aspirations permeates his narratives with individuals who teeter on the edge of the same faulty self-assessment that Paulsen made in his pre-teen years. In the alleys of Juárez, Mexico, the orphan Manny Bustos, a 14-year-old master beggar and thief in *The Crossing,* longs for a workable future, symbolized by the American dream flourishing across the Santa Fe Bridge in El Paso, Texas. In his fantasies, he sees himself employed and wearing "a leather belt with a large buckle and a straw hat with a feathered hatband," the superficial rewards of the North American success story (Paulsen, *Crossing,* 4). In the end, the new start in America awaits, but costs the life of

Manny's rescuer, Sergeant Robert S. Locke, who dies amid the realization of his own ambition to join his compatriots who died in combat.

Mixed Outcomes

In addition to broken soldiers like Coyote Runs and Robert Locke, Paulsen depicts American failures, especially people living on the edge of prosperity, the lot of Hispanic migrant workers in *The Beet Fields* and landscaping workers in *Lawn Boy.* In *Road Trip,* Duffy, the father, admits to son Ben Duffy a middle-class dilemma: "I can't continue existing as a soulless midlevel corporate drone," a description of misery at the upper end of success as vice president of an insurance firm (Paulsen, *Road,* 10). In the sequel, *Field Trip,* Ben has reduced his father's former title to "corporate pencil pusher," a similar debasement of desk work as the business mogul's concept of hell (Paulsen, *Field,* 1). In place of office stagnation, Mr. Duffy resurges with vigor and a new determination to rebuild decaying residences into livable homes. His enthusiasm passes to Ben in hopes he will "explore opportunities, broaden your interests" (*ibid.,* 13).

In contrast to Mr. Duffy's middle-class goals, Paulsen peruses a variety of eccentric employment. The raffish existence of vagabond performers informs *Tiltawhirl John,* the author's take on a social dichotomy of carnies Billy, Wanda, and T-John, who snag and fleece their marks. The con artist's creed intrigues the 16-year-old farm boy until a sordid knife fight and T-John's murder of the rival Tucker insert realism. When the moribund victim slides into unconsciousness, the narrator realizes that he disapproves of the carnival milieu: "When he finally hit the ground and goobered and was dead I knew I wasn't a carny" (Paulsen, *Tiltawhirl,* 125). By learning in action outside the schoolroom, he internalizes a graphic lesson in framing goals and forming his own code of conduct.

On a more esthetic plane, Paulsen shifts to the nature and purpose of art in *The Monument, The Rifle, Sentries,* and *The Island.* Perhaps as therapy for limping on a fused knee, Rachael Ellen "Rocky" Turner, the orphaned protagonist of *The Monument,* turns to design, much as Peter Shackleton composes music in *Sentries* and Wil Neuton in *The Island* develops sketching, painting, journal keeping, and interpretive dance into paths to self-awareness and contentment. In a reflection on the latter novel, *New York Times* book critic Edwin J. Kenney cast doubt on the appeal of Paulsen's cerebral themes to young readers uninitiated into spiritual quests. From a different perspective, for *English Journal,* education expert Steven Vander Staay envisaged the search for meaning as a normal expectation of growing up. He championed works that dramatize the three phases of coming of age, beginning with separation from community, living on the margin while completing rites of passage, and returning wholly adult to society to quicken individual potential.

See also music; *The Rifle.*

Source

Davis, James S. "Memoir: Reading Life," *ALAN Review* 36:3 (Summer 2009): 7.
Kenney, Edwin J., Jr. "The Island," *New York Times* (22 May 1988): A30.
Vander Staay, Steven. "Young-Adult Literature: A Writer Strikes the Genre," *English Journal* 81:4 (April 1992): 48.

The Beet Fields

A frank, but stirring contribution to Paulsen's autobiographical writings, *The Beet Fields* opens in 1955 when he crossed the threshold of manhood. At age 16, the Gary character leaves home in a cramped apartment to labor with itinerant farm hands in North

Dakota. The math seems straightforward—$11 pay for hoeing an acre of beets, which took him three days to thin. Missing from the sums are hidden charges for hoes, gloves, and meals. When he sinks into torpor at the unrelenting rhythm of farm work, "an hour could have passed, a minute, a day, a year" (Paulsen, *Beet,* 7). The mindless chopping of every other beet shoot acquaints him with his hands and body and with the merciless economics of peonage, a destiny akin to the severed beet tops wilting in the sun.

Central to the opening scenario, the author builds contrast between a stingy, racist farm wife doling out fly-blown peanut butter sandwiches and the affable Mexican women, who pat out tortillas with a joyous cadence to fill with whatever mixture simmers in the communal pot. Opposition between races intensifies from the mean-spiritedness of the landowners and the great-hearted generosity of fellow field workers, who offer the Gary character two burritos, the equivalent of a feast for a hungry boy. The meal becomes an introit to belonging. Paulsen blends the welter of teen initiation into predictable and unconventional desire, which he introduces in the dark-eyed beauties on the hoeing team, his drunken mother's groping for him in the night, and the farm wife's lust for the smell of Mexican workers' clothes.

Life in the Raw

Paulsen places the Gary character in a folk society that relishes life passages. The boy witnesses joking, laughter, and a birth in the field, a common event for laboring class Hispanics who expect no medical care or intervention in their struggles. During an evening fandango, he drinks in the natural flow of gendered circles throbbing to the beat of guitar and the twang of a harmonica. Intense dance introduces him more intimately to female dresses clinging to sweaty breasts. The night's entertainment segues neatly into his first love, Lynette Flaherty, and a family crisis, the binge that keeps Bill Flaherty at Pete's Place in the town of Adams until after 2:00 A.M. The boy's hopes destroyed, he leaves Bill's employ without another glimpse of Lynette.

Paulsen builds on the concepts of real and perceived injustice by picturing the Gary character stripped of his money and jailed by a corrupt deputy sheriff. As obstacles mount up, the boy becomes adept at on-the-spot fabrication, a talent for making up names and relationships that he shares with Mark Twain's Huckleberry Finn. The Hungarian dishwasher's sudden death by flying pheasant and broken windshield glass produces a darkly hilarious dilemma, eased when Hazel offers a ride northwest to Clinton on the border of Ontario. Picaresque episodes infuse the mundane with the outré, notably, Hazel's plating of a lunch sandwich in honor of her son Robert, a soldier killed in World War II. At the story's climax, the boy concludes, "Home? … He had no home. Not anymore" (*ibid.,* 93).

The Long Escape

Patty Campbell, a critic for *Horn Book,* admired the style of Paulsen's teen reveries for being "honed down to bone-simple words and rolling Hemingway cadences" (Campbell, 2001, 132). For the protagonist, escape from gritty short-term housing leads to more predicaments as well as acts of kindness, the unexpected good deeds that rid the novel of outright cynicism. At his separation from Hazel, he feels "some loss he didn't understand," an inkling of oneness with a kind stranger who treats him to lunch after he washes his hands and bows his head for grace (*ibid.,* 110). In leaving Hazel on the midway and joining the carnival, he spends a week acquiring "carny rules, carny thoughts, carny lives," a whole cosmos away from oiling a swatter, climbing rafters, and the slaying of pigeons for the cook pot (*ibid.,* 125).

Paulsen enhances the stripping of the Gary character's innocence by introducing him to Taylor, a savvy, amoral carny with the look of a pro—ducktail hair, low-slung Levis over bare buttocks, and unfiltered cigarettes rolled in a T-shirt sleeve à la the James Dean look of the mid–1950s. The grand finale—the boy's loss of sexual innocence in Ruby's bed and his interest in a slick military recruiter's spiel—begins ridding him of false impressions and stereotypes and teaching him the rudiments of character. Of the lengthy death of his naiveté, Leigh Fenly, a critic for the *San Diego Union-Tribune,* contemplates a child "blown by a freezing wind, from one kind of pain to another, all of it probable and scarring," especially enlistment in the infantry (Fenly, 2001, 5). Despite complaints to school boards about crude language and impromptu sex, Claire Martin, a reviewer for the *Denver Post,* applauds Paulsen for sticking to stark realism.

Source

Campbell, Patty. "A Spyglass on YA 2000," *Horn Book* 77:1 (January/February 2001): 131–136.
Davis, Gina. "A 2nd Book to Return to Carroll High Schools," *Baltimore Sun* (12 January 2006): B-2.
Fenly, Leigh. "Just for Kids," *San Diego Union-Tribune* (1 March 2001): 5.

belonging

Bemused by the Greek concept of *philios,* Paulsen composes on myriad personal topics that reflect the fragmentation of his childhood and a dearth of affiliation with others at home or in school or community. Kevin Spencer, protagonist of *Family Ties,* summarizes Paulsen's faith that "People like to feel they belong somewhere," a need dating to prehistory and reflected in the protagonist's sisterhood with the three Marys in *Molly McGinty Has a Really Good Day* and in the Gary character's bonhomie with Mexican migrants in *The Beet Fields* (Paulsen, *Family,* 2). In the introduction to *Paintings from the Cave,* the author states his personal experience with need for place and welcome: "I was one of the kids who slipped through the cracks," his admission of disaffiliation and withdrawal (Paulsen, *Paintings,* ix). The absence of a place to anchor and a family to belong to turned him into a champion for rootless, unwanted children.

Many of the writer's autobiographical themes brood over the result of growing up without human warmth and protection. To gain the strength of a nuclear family during his father's army service throughout World War II, at age five, Gary lived in a cook trailer with his maternal grandmother, Alida Peterson Moen, the central figure in *The Cookcamp, The Quilt,* and *Alida's Song* and a pleasant dreamscape in *The Island.* The retreat freed him from a dismal Chicago apartment opposite the elevated train and his mother's introduction of "Uncle Casey," her live-in lover. Once liberated from an unprincipled family arrangement, Paulsen acclaims a child-friendly environment in the northern woods that clasps the boy in affection and security, if only for the summer. In adulthood, he continues to reflect on his grandmother, a sturdy mother figure.

Finding Inclusion

The author's fictional characters incur similar vicissitudes of acceptance, an adjustment problem eating at the contentment of Tim Harrow, a conservative gun fanatic in *The Rifle.* For the house guest in *The Foxman,* a perception that "I kind of fit in" nurtures sensations of a union with others (Paulsen, *Foxman,* 37). By February, the boy admits that farm life with Uncle Harold and Aunt Mildred seems "maybe even better than home" (*ibid.,* 89). However, in *Popcorn Days and Buttermilk Nights,* the contrast between Minneapolis and a country farm at first scares Carley, a citified juvenile delinquent who is unused to rural penury. The differences between Chicago and the work camp magnify the emptiness of an urban home, which Paulsen typified in *Paintings from the Cave* as "heres and nows that are cold and ugly and raw and cruel and vicious, with little to no hope" (Paulsen, *Paintings*, x).

The Cookcamp introduces young Gary to sensations of security—a hearty, nourishing diet of home-cooked potatoes, meat with gravy, stew, biscuits, and oatmeal and Grandma Anita's soft Norwegian songs and scent of lavender. "I'll always be here," she promises her "little thimble" (Paulsen, *Cookcamp*, 30, 25). Like the disparate "sugar and cinnamon and dough and juice and apples" that come together in her pies, a fond gathering of road builders—Carl, Sven, Altag, Nels, Harvey, Emil, Ole, Pete—forms a great-hearted union, where talk "flowed together and made one long sound" (*ibid.*, 55). Rather than blame the boy's mother for alienating him, Alida mutters imprecations at wars and men and "the cities that take the girls," leaving children to estrangement and disaffection (*ibid.*, 75).

Paulsen turns the wartime syndrome into drama in *Sarny* and *Woods Runner*. In the latter, Hessian bayonets slay Caleb Clark and his wife Martha, leaving unparented eight-year-old Anne Marie Pennysworth "Annie" Clark. In a two-sided reception, Abigail Smith, a neighboring victim of arson and imprisonment during the American Revolution, rekindles her mothering spirit: "Then she's our daughter.... From now on, as good as blood" (Paulsen, *Woods*, 149). By promptly adopting Annie as her own, Abigail's proposal earns her husband Olin's agreement to expand the Smith family tree into the Clark-Smith genealogy:

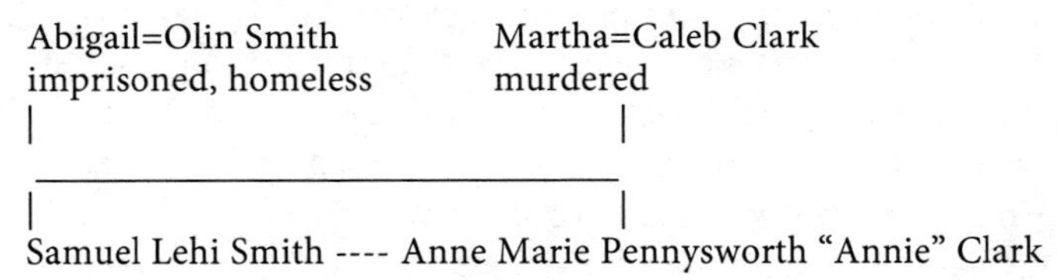

The newly formed household exemplifies the benefits to child and adults, both of whom satisfy the nesting instinct.

Post-war Distress

More to the point of child alienation, *Eastern Sun, Winter Moon* follows Gary from a fatherless wartime home among grouchy neighbors in Chicago to a transport ship from San Francisco through Honolulu and Okinawa to Manila. On departure, for comfort, the boy grips only a stuffed pet named Dog, a pathetic designation for a toy friend. The weeks-long voyage introduces a naive child to the smutty talk of military men shooting craps and playing seven-card stud. Without background on the dangers of child molesters, Gary tries to interpret the pummeling of a pedophile by angry sailors in what reviewer Tim Winton referred to as "the exclusive world of men below decks" (Winton, 1993, 1). The boy receives little amplification from his defenders or his mother of the pervert's crime. Paulsen depicts Gary as a lone island among adults who interpret events without explaining to him how and why they monitor his safety.

The out-of-kilter remainder of the writer's childhood in the Philippines extenuates his inability to understand adult behaviors in an army compound surrounded by threat of Huks and jungle snakes. Left to the care of servants Maria and Rom for two years, the boy develops no sense of place or identity in Manila amid the refugees, bombed-out streets, and rusted detritus of World War II. Instead of gaining parental basics at home, he evolves into a sneak and liar who bandies lewd language—cocksucker, tits, son of a bitch, nigger, cunt, fuckerfart—and spies on his drunken mother and her seduction of Sergeant Ryland. Gary reveals in *Harris and Me* the purchase of "art" photographs that a Manila street vendor calls "dourty peectures" (Paulsen, *Harris*, 6). By the Paulsens' departure for the U.S. on December 31, 1948, young Paulsen has set no pattern of family intimacy or loyalty with the two adults who determine the remainder of his coming of age.

Finding a Haven

Paulsen reprises his boyhood alienation in public school among peers who sport trendy 1950s outfits and ducktail haircuts. Because of parental neglect, he has to earn cash to purchase clothing by selling rabbits and fish. In *Shelf Life: Stories by the Book*, he elucidates his faulty notion that belonging to a group required the "right clothes," a common misconception of impressionable teens (Paulsen, *Shelf*, 3). He imagines that a better wardrobe "might somehow lift me from my wretchedly unpopular social life" (*ibid.*). To secure money, by night, he haunts bars to sell newspapers and hustles drunks for spare change, but his enterprises fail to guarantee the peer acceptance he craves. The author restructures his rescue by his grandmother in *Alida's Song*, a story of a budding juvenile delinquent from Chicago and his acceptance and stabilization among Norwegian farm laborers Gunnar and Olaf. The combination of ethnic oneness and rescue from urban sleaze begins the reclamation that Gary craves.

In a reflection on tough times in a splintered family, Paulsen recalled, "There was no machinery then to help—no foster home, no welfare" (Goodson, 2004, 54). His struggles return regularly to a respite—his joy in nature's extremes. Wilderness scenes become the controlling atmosphere of fictional escapes, particularly David Alspeth's sea venture in *The Voyage of the Frog* and the forest solitude of 13-year-old Pennsylvania woodsman Samuel Lehi Smith in *Woods Runner*, runner Brennan Cole in *Canyons*, and farm boy and hunter John Borne in *Tracker*. With ebullience in *Woodsong*, Paulsen celebrates "the raw-cold joy of going again and again inside the diamond that is northern winter," a form of retreat into the blue-cold far from human entanglements (Paulsen, *Woodsong*, 78). However, escape leaves unstable his understanding of familial relationships and trust.

Much of Paulsen's precarious upbringing undergirds fictional loners. For a unique dilemma, Francis Alphonse Tucket in *Mr. Tucket*, the first novel of the Tucket pentad, must scramble to stay alive after abduction by Pawnee along the Oregon Trail and pursuit by Comancheros in *Tucket's Ride*. Although nagged by memories of his parents and sister Rebecca, in *Tucket's Gold*, he discovers hospitality among the Pueblo: "He had found a new kind of peace here and loved life in the village" (Paulsen, *Gold*, 85). The young frontiersman clutches at the welcome, healing from snakebite, and a reprieve from the cyclical hazards of the American plains. Paulsen's theme indicates that hard traveling in the open takes its toll on Tucket, endearing him to a Native American enclave.

Reclaiming the Young

The writer's historical fiction characterizes the worst of being "rejected and abandoned, unloved and unlovable," the epitome of parental desertion in *The Car* and Southern bondage in *Nightjohn* and *Sarny* (Paulsen, *Paintings*, x). Even in slavery, Sarny and Delie, her foster mother, retreat to the quarters for nighttime reunions, shared food, and whispered conversation and prayers. Paulsen reprises the motif of out-of-sync characters in multiple books, locating pathos in Manny Bustos, the mestizo orphan in Juárez, Mexico, in *The Crossing*; the pariah Jo-Jo the Dog-faced Girl in *Paintings from the Cave*; and the handicapped artist Rachael Ellen "Rocky" Turner, a reclaimed orphan in *The Monument.* Two of his prime characters—Brian Robeson in *The River* and Wil Neuton in *The Island*—learn from experience with fame that notoriety in the media turns ordinary boys into freaks and misfits. Both teens must accept a modern truth—that dissociation from traditional society obligates them to rely on their inner strengths and to thrive forever away from cities. Of the characters' fictional plight, Paulsen confessed his own dilemma with withdrawal from home into seclusion: "I have spent years trying to change back and cannot do so" (Moss, 1999, E3).

In one of the author's best received historical fictions, a perverse sense of belonging burgeons in Charley Goddard, the 15-year-old enlistee in the First Minnesota Volunteers in *Soldier's Heart.* As a goad to bloodlust and an inhibitor of cowardice, in 1862, his fellow recruits exonerate their numerous war crimes by reminding themselves of the sins of "Southern crackers," the Johnny Rebs of the Confederate side (Paulsen, *Soldier's,* 16). The sense of loyalty to a cause abruptly wilts at the Battle of Bull Run in Manassas, Virginia, where Charley, amid smoke and carnage, views all soldiers—Union and Reb—as members of humanity. By the time he suffers a severe wound at Gettysburg on July 3, 1863, he anticipates belonging among the dead, who lie blissfully uninvolved in enmity, strife, and suffering. The tragic death-in-life of a traumatized veteran dramatizes the crushed spirit of one of Paulsen's irretrievable broken soldiers.

From a less menacing perspective, the theme of alienation unsettles a court remand in *The Foxman* and a battered boy in *Winterkill,* in which his boozed-up parents "can't stop until they're drunk and mean and dumb" (Paulsen, *Winterkill,* 62). Estrangement also dominates *Harris and Me: A Summer Remembered*, Paulsen's tribute to the mystique of boyhood bonding. In the latter, the main character, an unnamed 11-year-old Gary character living far from cruel sots, achieves a niche for himself after sheriff's deputy Orlo "dumped" him into the household of the affectionate Uncle Knute, Aunt Clair, Glennis, and a mischievous cousin, nine-year-old Harris Larson (Paulsen, *Harris*, 2). On his final day of summer as an observer of a rollicking household, the narrator rebels: "I had come to belong here, wanted to be here, thought of this as home" (*ibid.*, 152). Essential to the visitor's distress lies his loss of adopted siblings, Glennis and Harris, and of an intimacy tinged with freedom to be himself.

See also The Beet Fields; Brian's Return; Harris and Me; parenting; trust.

Source

Goodson, Lori Atkins. "Singlehanding: An Interview with Gary Paulsen," *ALAN Review* 31:2 (Winter 2004): 53–59.
Ley, Terry C. "The Monument," *English Journal* 83:3 (March 1994): 90.
Moss, Meredith. "'Hatchet' Author to Appear," *Dayton Daily News* (14 March 1999): E3.
Winton, Tim. "Boy's Life His Own World War," *Los Angeles Times* (21 March 1993): 1.

Brian's Hunt

For *Brian's Hunt*, the urgent 2003 sequel to *Hatchet,* Paulsen incorporates more destruction and death than in earlier parts of the series. In retrospect, the novelist favored Brian Robeson as a steady, sensible character he would rely on in a crisis. On a par with Russel Susskit in *Dogsong,* the spunky Grandma Alida in *The Cookcamp,* and Irene Flynn in *Molly McGinty Has a Really Good Day,* Brian, at age 16, has a knack for coping with disasters as small as choking mosquitoes and gnats and an irksome skunk who moves in next door and as vast as a plane crash over water in the Canadian outback or killing a bear, a challenge he reprises in the adventure novel *Grizzly*. He recognizes that contemplation of his first trip to Canada at age 14 helped him grow. As a result of immurement in the wild, he learned the sounds and ways of forest denizens and managed subsequent difficulties by rehearsing how to confront danger.

In late summer, Paulsen reintroduces his protagonist to a retreat from urbanism into "country to see, natural country that man had not yet ruined," an authorial intrusion stating Paulsen's beef with modernism (Paulsen, *Hunt,* 8). The action draws on the terrors of a bear attack and the mutilation and deaths of the boy's Cree friends, David and Anne Smallhorn, whom Brian buries. The story incorporates a female alter ego, Susan Smallhorn (Kay-gwa-daush), a fellow survivalist whose reputation for bravery causes Brian to consider initiating a friendship with a lover of the wild. Susan's orphaning by the bear and the wounding of a Malamute dog force Brian to accept a role as medic as well as communicator with a Mountie to unite Susan with relatives in Winnipeg.

Learning from Jeopardy

In the face of so horrific a loss, Brian realizes that his survival in the wilderness requires forbearance and serenity—"[waiting] patiently, controlling his breath, waiting" (Paulsen, *Hunt,* 57). Self-mastery enables him to direct action to the most essential needs, especially repairing his clothes and moccasins, stitching up the 18-inch rip in the dark-haired malamute's side, and locating Susan by identifying and following her tracks. From reliance on inner resources, he identifies change as a permanent state in the human mind. He convinces himself that he is equal to the challenge of hunting a rogue bear that had tasted human flesh, but he regrets that he must destroy it.

Paulsen develops the bear hunt into a valuable gestalt. By thinking of himself as prey, Brian accepts a humbling, edifying vision of humankind as part of the animal kingdom—"sharks, fever-bearing mosquitoes, wolves and bear, to name but a few" (Paulsen, *Hunt,* 103). The mental image enables him to joke about aggressors who think of him as dinner because they "simply did not get the memo about how humans are superior" (*ibid.*). In the afterword, the author states, "We don't like to think of ourselves as prey—it *is* a lessening thought—but the truth is that in our arrogance and so-called knowledge we forget that we are not unique" (*ibid.*).

A Changed Man

In the novel's development, the author compounds the view of Brian's growth and maturity. He implies a moment of sanctity in the act of cooking and eating meals, which is as close as Paulsen comes to worship or prayer. In a gesture to the universe on a par with Native American deference to Mother Earth, Brian says "Thank you … thank you again" for a meal of northern pike, a gift from nature that nourishes and sustains him (*ibid.,* 58). The comment implies a natural progression of humankind from appreciating nature and its bounty to reaching out to a creator, whom Brian does not attempt to identify by dogma or creed.

The variance in critical evaluation parallels the reception of Paulsen's works from a host of points of view. Paula Rohrlick, a reviewer for *Kliatt,* focused on the Cree couple's dismemberment and clouds of flies fouling the wounds rather than Brian's more meditative moments in burying Anne and erecting crosses over the graves. Overall, she classified the story as gripping and gory. Conversely, Kathy Holubitsky, a critic for the *Edmonton Journal,* upbraided Paulsen for anthropomorphizing the bear as a devil, the obverse of A.A. Milne's cuddly Winnie the Pooh.

Source

"Dear Gary Paulsen," [Saint John, N.B.] *Telegraph-Journal* (21 May 2008): D11.
Fine, Edith Hope. *Gary Paulsen: Author and Wilderness Adventurer.* Berkeley Heights, NJ: Enslow, 2000.
Gallo, Don. "The Promise and Seduction of Sequels," *English Journal* 94:4 (March 2005): 124–128.
Golden, Bernice. *Critical Reading Activities for the Works of Gary Paulsen.* Portland, ME: Walch, 1999.
Turvey, Shannon Lee. "The Trouble with Sequels," *Vancouver Sun* (23 May 1998): I10.
Wenger, Laurie. "Books for Building Circle of Courage: Independence," *Reclaiming Children and Youth* 8:1 (Spring 1999): 56–57.

Brian's Return

Paulsen appeases curious fans by rewriting the motifs of *Hatchet* from a divergent angle. He sets *Brian's Return*, another sequel excerpted in *Boy's Life,* on an 80-acre lake on June 3 of his fifteenth year. Age and maturity make a significant difference in the boy who previously panicked at crash landing in central Canada with no hope of rescue. A review in the *Hartford Courant* contrasted the action-packed *Hatchet* to the evenly paced *Brian's Return* for the "meatier philosophical thread holding it together" (Wergeland, 1999, F4).

The plot of *Brian's Return* revisits the famed survivor's skill at the nuts and bolts of outdoor living, for example, at lighting a birch bark fire to diminish blackflies, deerflies, and horseflies and at bear-proofing a camp. Reflecting over the past months, Brian scoffs at his notoriety in the press and at city life among shallow teens who prefer video games and malls to the outdoors. In place of trivial group excursions with his peers, he prefers packing necessities with an eye toward need, e.g., "Repair kit with a piece of glass cloth and epoxy resin. Light life vest … a plain belt ax.… A fabric military-style belt to carry the knife and hatchet" (Paulsen, *Return,* 51–52). To escape being a misfit, he chooses a reunion with the wilderness as a permanent separation from civilization and a way to shape a satisfying future.

A Peaceful Isolation

In a scan of the outback that had once terrorized him, the protagonist satisfies deep yearnings for the peace of creation. A confident loner, he contemplates the horizon, the prehistoric Inuit who first viewed the northern lights, and Indians of the U.S. Great Basin of the Southwest. Paulsen retains the occult concept of medicine in the appearance of Billy, a wise old Canadian Indian, who leaves Brian a rawhide loop adorned with two amulets, a crow feather and deer tail. Symbolically, the two elements of nature ally animals of the air and ground. In the words of book critic Kari Wergeland, Brian discovers his reflexes "finely tuned from warding off four-footed predators during his unexpected stint in the woods" (Wergeland, 1999, F4). He restates his understanding of killing to eat and opines, "Only man hunted for sport," an obvious intrusion of the authorial voice to condemn thrill slaughter as a masculine indulgence (Paulsen, *Return*, 3).

Reviving Brian's satisfaction in becoming part of the environment are mice that create tunnels to a burrow and labyrinth under bent grass covered with snow. In thinking over the mouse community, Brian ponders his inability to fit in with less experienced teens and his fight-or-flight response to Carl Lammers in a brutal fight at Mackey's Pizza Den. Unlike trained boxers, Brian strikes with the heels of his open palms, which bruise Carl's eyes, ribs, and stomach. Returned home in handcuffs by the police, Brian finds himself unable to express to his mother how wariness and self-protection in the wild had taught him to retaliate without mercy.

LEARNING FROM LOSS

Interaction with Caleb Lancaster, a counselor, surprises Brian with the man's blindness, which occurred three days after a headache. The unforeseen handicap summons from Brian a philosophy of the outback as unvarying as a fox snatching up mice for food. Before accidentally impaling his right upper thigh with a broadhead arrow, Brian reminds himself of the outdoorsman's dictum "expect the unexpected," which he repeats for emphasis (*ibid.*, 52). Paulsen inserts an authorial extension about planning for the worst and being glad that it doesn't happen. Key to the passage lies the writer's reminder of the difference between real nature and fiction, a timely proviso for readers of *Boys' Life*.

The author validates Brian's hardihood as being "possessed by the wild" and its "vicious beauty" and predicts, "It is not possible for him to be truly normal again" (*ibid.*, 111, 113). By paddling a canoe into the wasteland, Brian ponders the appeal of William Shakespeare's *Romeo and Juliet* and has a mystical encounter with Billy, who admires hunting in the old way, without a gun. After Billy slips back into the surroundings, Brian elaborates on a lucid principle—"I am where I belong and I belong where I am," a tenet similar to Buddhist patience and insight into travail (*ibid.*, 107). The comfort of fitting in as an outdoorsman and survivalist rings true to the epiphanies of philosopher Ralph Waldo Emerson, who stated: "What lies behind us and what lies ahead of us are tiny matters compared to what lives within us." In a salute to the author's musing on Brian's thoughts and beliefs, *Publishers Weekly* described the tone of Paulsen's pilgrimage novel as confident and persuasive.

Source

"Dear Gary Paulsen," [Saint John, N.B.] *Telegraph-Journal* (21 May 2008): D11.
Fine, Edith Hope. *Gary Paulsen: Author and Wilderness Adventurer.* Berkeley Heights, NJ: Enslow, 2000.
Gallo, Don. "The Promise and Seduction of Sequels," *English Journal* 94:4 (March 2005): 124–128.
Golden, Bernice. *Critical Reading Activities for the Works of Gary Paulsen.* Portland, ME: Walch, 1999.
Turvey, Shannon Lee. "The Trouble with Sequels," *Vancouver Sun* (23 May 1998): I10.
Wenger, Laurie. "Books for Building Circle of Courage: Independence," *Reclaiming Children and Youth* 8:1 (Spring 1999): 56–57.
Wergeland, Kari. "'Hatchet' Author Tells Civil War Tale," *Hartford Courant* (2 March 1999): F4.

Brian's Winter

In *Brian's Winter*, a novel excerpted in the February and March 1996 issues of *Boys' Life*, the author appeased fans by changing the original story of Brian Robeson's marooning. He resets the initial crash of the bush plane, but omits a radio signal summoning outsiders to Brian's position in central Canada. For maximum drama, Paulsen removes the rescue that ends the marooning with intervention by a *deus ex machina*. The restructuring alters both mood and atmosphere of a riveting challenge to boyhood logic and self-control.

With a sophisticated perspective for one so young, Brian accepts the earthly axiom that "Nothing that lived, nothing that walked or crawled or flew or swam or slithered or oozed—nothing, not one thing on God's earth wanted to die" (Paulsen, *Winter*, 10). The transcendent coming-to-knowledge underscores an adult-level affirmation of mortality. From more tenuous experiences with death, he remains alert to danger from a bear, wolves, a moose, and increasing cold, which could kill him from hypothermia. By Thanksgiving, he can eat hump meat and red berry sauce with a grateful heart and feel fortunate in his bounty. He muses, "How many times would he have to defend himself," an existential consideration of the daily threats to all fauna (*ibid.*, 43).

Humorous episodes lighten the mood, particularly the skunk that threatens to spray Brian. He jokes to himself, "I've got a pet skunk who's a terrorist ... a little robber ... a roommate with a terminal hygiene problem" (*ibid.*, 43, 44). While observing the animal's movements from its den, he names it Betty, a droll reference to his aunt. The humor broadens after a bear "took a full shot of skunk spray," a "gagging smell" that the bear seems to identify from past experience (*ibid.*, 60). The vignette implies a strength in Brian's character from light-heartedness and abilities to laugh at the unknown and learn from his mistakes.

Old vs. New

To expound on Brian's sources of insight, Paulsen incorporates the reverence of First Peoples for traditional medicine, a mystic supremacy or supernatural force over harsh weather, bad luck, sickness, accidents, loss, or foes. For tribal nurturance, a shaman or medicine man summoned primitive powers by donning a magic headdress or mask, smoking a peace pipe, dancing and chanting, analyzing natural phenomena or birds, or shaping a meaningful pattern in colored grains or symbols painted on tent fabric, buckskins, face, chest and arms, or the side of a horse. By propitiating traditional symbols, such as that found in the deer head in the fork of a tree and in Brian's "medicine arrow," the priest secured for humans the benevolence of Mother Earth for counsel, protection, wellness, and spiritual comfort (*ibid.*, 30). Brian replicates the ancient protocol by laboring to improve his archery and by touching his arrow for good luck.

In Brian's mental "visits" to the outside world during his 68 days marooned in south central Canada, a fear of madness grips him (*ibid.*, 13). Unused to solitude, he welcomes two male wolves as friends and concentrates on facts that he had gained from reading or from experience fletching arrows or tightening his snowshoes. As an antidote to fear during the howling winter winds, he focuses on logical solutions to problems and accepts his troubles as normal obstacles requiring a constant series of responses. The text remains in problem solving mode until Brian happens on a Cree family, David Smallhorn and his wife and children. David salutes Brian for "[looking] like one of the old-way people," a compliment to the boy's adaptation to ancient Inuit survivalism (*ibid.*, 132).

Critical Analysis

Experts dispute the success of Paulsen's rewrite. The theme of a changed attitude poses questions for the reader and Brian: "How can I leave this solitary beauty? How can I be in the world again?" (Fine, 2000, 95). The author poses the predicament as a natural outgrowth of human metamorphosis, the change that alters the heart and soul after any apotheosis. Critic Shannon Lee Turvey, a reviewer for the *Vancouver Sun*, noted that the sequel seemed drier because "the level of excitement is diminished" by extensive philosophy (Turvey, 1998, I-10).

Despite the more cerebral subject, scrutiny by Gary M. Salver for *ALAN Review* praised humorous elements, including Betty the skunk, whom Salver compared to E.B. White's Templeton the Rat in *Charlotte's Web*. Shirley B. Ernst, in a critique for *Language Arts*, took a more theoretical tack in citing the author for demonstrating how creativity could generate variant conclusions to the original dilemma, a beneficial reminder to the young of their innate abilities. Author Don Gallo concluded in *English Journal* that the success of Paulsen's sequel lies not in re-plotting, but in reader response to his storytelling style and the appeal of the main character, whom young adults enjoy and admire.

Source

"Dear Gary Paulsen," [Saint John, N.B.] *Telegraph-Journal* (21 May 2008): D11.
Ernst, Shirley B. "Brian's Winter," *Language Arts* 74:7 (November 1997): 566.
Fine, Edith Hope. *Gary Paulsen: Author and Wilderness Adventurer.* Berkeley Heights, NJ: Enslow, 2000.
Gallo, Don. "The Promise and Seduction of Sequels," *English Journal* 94:4 (March 2005): 124–128.
Golden, Bernice. *Critical Reading Activities for the Works of Gary Paulsen.* Portland, ME: Walch, 1999.
Jacobson, Ann. "Paulsen Revisits Bush in Finale of 'Hatchet' Series," *South Bend* [Ind.] *Tribune* (14 March 1999): F6.
Turvey, Shannon Lee. "The Trouble with Sequels," *Vancouver Sun* (23 May 1998): I-10.
Wenger, Laurie. "Books for Building Circle of Courage: Independence," *Reclaiming Children and Youth* 8:1 (Spring 1999): 56–57.

Call Me Francis Tucket

At age 15 in the fast-paced *Call Me Francis Tucket*, the protagonist feels educated in the ways of Indians and the plains. Treating the universal theme of journeys and the quest, the year's exposure to freedom on the plains lures Francis Alphonse Tucket from Eastern acculturation to a less hidebound lifestyle. At the opening of book two of the Tucket pentad, he relaxes "at the edge of the world" and anticipates "seeing over the next hill, some need" (Paulsen, *Call,* 1, 5). Automatically attuned to sights and sounds, he rides out alone in search of his family. With confidence to "free range" on the "endless grass" comes peace and self-determination from not having to explain himself or his actions (*ibid.,* 2, 65).

Paulsen looks through the boy's wondering glance at a buffalo stampede, wagons fording a stream, and the grandeur of America's open land, the draw that pulls seekers over the Oregon Trail, which wagons have rutted down to bedrock. Critics Rebecca M. Giles and Karyn W. Tunks, in an analysis for *The Councilor,* applauded the blend of history with a made-up character for "effectively [weaving] history into fiction … within an authentic historical setting" (Giles and Tunks, 2014, 15). The experts agreed that the result is "useful background knowledge that forms the foundation for future learning" on such disparate topics as vigilantism, orienteering, and child labor (*ibid.,* 16).

In a style "stark and barebones without stylistic pretensions," Paulsen unfolds Tucket's trial and error episodes with the ease of a natural storyteller, a quality that makes *Call Me Mr. Tucket* a worthy choice for reading aloud (Salvner, 1996, 16). A review in *Publishers Weekly* admired the adventure tale for salting episodes with details of pioneering, which range from hunting deer along the wagon trail to skinning a buffalo bull. With warnings of gopher holes and rattlesnake buzzes, the text upgrades Tucket's survival instincts with keen observation, a skill the boy shares with the protagonists of *Tiltawhirl John* and *The Voyage of the Frog* (Salvner, 1996, 16). His views of the banditry of Dubs and Courtweiler, the serene expression of a cadaver, and the austere beauty of the prairie offers a lens through which to glimpse the mid–1800s flurry of westward travel and a source of period vocabulary, such as watercourse, hobbles, scabbard, frock coat, and possibles bag, the source of Tucket's venison jerky and other necessary travel goods.

Adult Identity

In the company of the despicable duo of Courtweiler and Dubs, Tucket takes on a period identity as "a true child of the frontier," an ironic prediction of his logic and tracking ability (Paulsen, *Call,* 20). The smarmy dialogue of two grifters and Tucket's plan to shoot them at their camp contrasts the boy's tender dreams of beans and ham hock, a symbolic meal ladled up by his mother, who adds a loving touch, a chunk of butter. Paulsen's juxtaposition of boyhood care with a fireside scramble for his rifle vivifies the new Francis

Tucket, a grown man capable of fending for himself against lawlessness. The bold declaration, "I *will* shoot you," becomes Tucket's manifesto against intimidation (*ibid.*, 41).

Nature seems to conspire against Tucket and the foundlings, Lottie and Billy, who choke and sneeze on dust. When the storm washes away wagon tracks, Tucket becomes lost "and rode, and rode, and rode" (*ibid.*, 47). More lethal, the children escape the "water sickness," a revealing name for cholera, because the settlers push them out of a wagon train to prevent spread of contagion (*ibid.*, 58). At a significant pass in Tucket's quest, he accepts not only his own survival but that of the two refugees, who receive no mercy from Ellville, Johnson, McIntire, and Peterson. With the sense of a seasoned veteran, Tucket realizes that his future travels "would have to be taken a step at a time" (*ibid.*, 61).

Verbal Pacing

Paulsen's narrative excels at alternating styles of dialogue, from the stilted English of the two thieves and the blunt orders of armed men from the wagon train to the unschooled offers at the ramshackle trading post of swapping bacon for rifles and a mule. By selecting a mute, thumb-sucking boy and his sister Lottie with her persistent blather as a source of comedy, the author varies a bleak journey westward with a moment of humanity. He halts Lottie's fear of savages "cutting me open and eating my heart out" by declaring a hungry Indian band "people, just like us, looking for food" (*ibid.*, 69, 72).

In the resolution, the novel makes a handy summary—"captured by the Indians, beaten, escaping, living with Jason Grimes, trapping, blizzards"—to explain tensions and motivation that keep Tucket on the move and taking stock of his options (*ibid.*, 95). Janice del Negro, a book critic for Booklist, regretted Paulsen's use of a hasty falling action and plot resolution. Stephen Cvengros, in a critique for the *Chicago Tribune,* gave the novel three out of four stars because "The flat ending leaves too many questions" (Cvengros, 1995, 2). Conversely, for the reprise of traditional Western lore in a series of cliffhangers, *Journal of Adolescent & Adult Literacy* proclaimed the novel "rollicking" (Lesesne and Buckman, 1995, 34). Publishers Weekly declared the adventure series a "knock 'em, sock 'em ripsnorter" (Paulsen, *Call*, cover).

See also Mr. Tucket; Tucket's Gold; Tucket's Home; Tucket's Ride;

Source

Cvengros, Stephen. "Review: *Call Me Francis Tucket,*" *Chicago Tribune* (4 July 1995): 2.
Giles, Rebecca M., and Karyn W. Tunks. "Read the Past Now! Responding to Historical Fiction through Writing," *The Councilor* 75:1 (2014): 15–22.
Lesesne, Teri S., Rosemary Chance, and Lois Buckman. "Books for Adolescents: Journeys: Traveling Toward the Unknown," *Journal of Adolescent & Adult Literacy* 39:4 (December 1995–January 1996): 332–336.
Salvner, Gary M. *Presenting Gary Paulsen.* New York: Twayne, 1996, 16.

Canyons

Paulsen's literary duet contrasts the first raid of Coyote Runs, a 14-year-old Apache brave of the Horse Mesa band, with a wretched camping trip requiring Brennan Cole to discipline seven eight-year-old boys in the desert north of El Paso, Texas, at Dog Canyon, New Mexico. Set 126 years apart, from October 21, 1864, to 1990, the parallel narratives intersect after Bill Halverson tells a story to his young campers about the ghosts of Apaches killed by the U.S. cavalry during the Indian Wars. The introduction of supernatural elements anticipates Brennan's discovery of a skull left in the canyon from the execution of an Indian boy by a shooting close to the forehead. For the mystic union of the dual protagonists, Lin McCracken, a critic for the *Colorado Springs Gazette-Telegraph,* and Rhonda Stansberry of the *Omaha World-Herald* declared *Canyons* the best children's book of 1990.

The action follows the scattered sense impressions and hopes of the Apache horse rustler, who relies on spiritual medicine to save him from pursuing cavalrymen named Daneley, Doolan, O'Bannion, and Rourke. Paulsen's face-off between the Indian boy and four white adults elicits the prayer of Coyote Runs, "Take me, spirit, take me now quickly before, before, before" (Paulsen, *Canyons,* 77). Over 126 years later, the plea resounds in the mind of Brennan, who, at 3:00 A.M., seems to shapeshift into the doomed apprentice raider. Telepathic possession by the dying Apache seizes Brennan, "with him, in him, around him," compelling him to risk committing a crime by concealing and guarding the damaged skull of Coyote Runs, "a boy like him" (*ibid.,* 81, 90). Paulsen indicates that coming-of-age trials surpass in import any differences in race, upbringing, and belief systems.

Intuitive Cognizance

Through presentiment and dreams, Brennan shares identity with the Apache victim and dances in a vision to drumming, a steady rhythm suggesting the synthesized heartbeat of the boys. The sequence of animal identities—an eagle, a snake, and a straw-colored horse—introduces Brennan to medicine phantasms, which precede the sight of a girl walking away in a mist. Through repeated otherworldly episodes, he admits that "a thing takes over my thinking," a vague explanation of his empathy with Coyote Runs (*ibid.,* 113). The data supplied by Tibbets, a pathologist, intensifies the boy-to-boy identity, causing Brennan to exclaim, "I am not me," a declaration of full accession to an ancient doppelgänger (*ibid.,* 121).

Urgency shapes a gritty investigation that begins with skull examination and moves on to historical data from newspapers and letters. As Brennan enlightens himself with 19th-century eyewitness accounts, he absorbs the overriding atmosphere of "violence … the engine that seemed to drive the West," a prelude to the Vietnam War that educated medic John Homesley and his historian friend Ted Rainger (*ibid.,* 136). In sympathy with Brennan's tears for Coyote Runs, Homesley murmurs, "Things never change," a conclusion that emerges from the medic's on-site treatment of wounded soldiers and civilians (*ibid.,* 149). The shared perusal of brutality calls to mind John Donne's sermon, "And therefore never send to know for whom the bell tolls; it tolls for thee," a charge to the individual to accept union with all humankind.

Man-to-Man Sleuthing

At the core of *Canyons,* Paulsen stresses two factors: the need of Brennan for a father and his ability to "[know] things without knowing how," an inquiry of the heart shared by the two boys (*ibid.,* 161). Intuitive coaching from Coyote Runs follows Brennan into the desert, guiding his stick against snakes and informing him of the value of yucca stalks to quench thirst. With the support of Homesley and Brennan's mother, Brennan empowers himself through symbolic knowledge and trust. Drawing on what reviewer Dick Richmond calls "friends separated by a century," Brennan outflanks pursuers and harkens to an inner compulsion to complete the quest of Coyote Runs (Richmond, 1991, G-3).

The narrative achieves fruition by heeding the Native American faith in human reunion with the earth. By reaching the square medicine place at the top of the canyon, Brennan satisfies an obligation to reconnect Coyote Runs with his ancient forebears. The channeling of a murdered spirit grows insistent, then leaves Brennan empty and sorrowful, like wind blowing through a hollow reed. Critic Judith B. Rosenfeld, writing for the *Baltimore Sun,* deduced that "Paulsen draws comparison, not only with the two boys, but with the evil, senseless cruelty of the execution of the Indian boy and the violence of this era" (Rosenfeld, 1990, G-8). For his on-target theme and depiction of prescience, Paulsen won the 1990 Mountains and Plains Booksellers Association Regional Book Awards.

Source

Durichen, Pauline. "Review: *Canyons*," *Kitchener-Waterloo Record* (16 February 1991): H6.
McCracken, Lin. "Awards Honor Women Writers, American Indian Themes," *Colorado Springs Gazette-Telegraph* (13 October 1991): F-4.
Richmond, Dick. "'Friends' Separated by a Century," *St. Louis Post-Dispatch* (19 September 1991): G-3.
Rosenfeld, Judith B. "Canyons," *Baltimore Sun* (8 November 1990): G-8.

coming of age

Paulsen admires plucky youth and courts their readership because "They're still whole" (Miller, 1988, 6). He believes that children enter adulthood through an unavoidable wasteland, whether urban or rural, the motif of the Minneapolis delinquent Carley's visit to his Uncle David and Aunt Emily in *Popcorn Days and Buttermilk Nights,* the embarrassing thoughts of Duane Homer Leech about puberty in *The Amazing Life of Birds,* and Nicholas O'Connor's setting his hair on fire to impress Kimberly Klein in *Molly McGinty Has a Really Good Day.* For the Gary character in *The Beet Fields,* grasping manhood means letting go of childhood treasures, including his bike and shotgun, but clinging to memories of Thanksgiving meals with his grandmother.

The act of separation from childhood tests individual strengths. In *The Rifle,* Richard Allen Mesington in his mid-teens envisages an idealized future when "there are no, absolutely no goals that he could not achieve" (Paulsen, *Rifle,* 82). In contrast, the house guest in *The Foxman* summarizes the missteps of growing up by regretting that maturing "has to jerk your guts out and just about wreck you" (Paulsen, *Foxman,* 96). Wil Neuton, a disillusioned girl watcher in *The Island,* echoes that cynicism when he realizes that Cindy, his ideal girl, would not notice "if I got run over by a truck in front of her house" (Paulsen, *Island,* 43).

Of the children who encounter a welter of vivid feelings, the author asserts, "And once they start, once they see that horizon, they can't go back" (Creager, 1999, 4). The "horizon" of adulthood mystifies several of his characters, particularly Wil Neuton, the Thoreauesque loner of *The Island,* and Janet Carson, the dreamer who aids a derelict Indian in *The Night the White Deer Died.* Paulsen turns the horizon into a no-man's-land of crude questions and awkward moments in *Harris and Me* with Harris Larson's penchant for candor. He snorts to his know-it-all older sister, "How the hell am I supposed to know things if I don't go ahead and ask them?" (Paulsen, *Harris,* 7). For Harris's friend, the Gary character, puberty makes a hard hit at the end of age 12, when growing teens give up Gene Autry movies to pursue "dancing or in the front of the saloon necking" (*ibid.,* 123).

For Francis Alphonse Tucket, protagonist of the Tucket series, receipt of a Lancaster .40 caliber rifle for his 14th birthday in *Mr. Tucket* betokens a step toward maturity. His father presents the gift shortly before the boy's abduction by Pawnee and a harrowing series of adventures that essentially yank Francis into manhood. The boy's chutzpah in stealing war chief Braid's horse earns from the elder Standing Bear the description "one go-getter of a young warrior" (Paulsen, *Mr.,* 57). Paulsen's commiseration with tween and teen dilemmas like Tucket's and ingenious escapes from danger accounts for his ongoing visits to classrooms, libraries, and juvenile halls and his replies to anguished letters asking "What do you do when it's bad? When it gets really, really bad?" (Paulsen, *Paintings*, x).

Maturing in Fiction and History

Paulsen's prediction of the irrevocable demise of childhood proves true of a future deputy U.S. marshal in *The Legend of Bass Reeves* and of 13-year-old Samuel Lehi Smith in *Woods Runner,* a Pennsylvania frontiersman. During the early months of the American Revolution, Sam rescues his parents from imprisonment by Redcoats in a New York City sugar mill. On the escape back to the wild, his mentor, tinker/spy Abner McDougal, alerts him to a change in family rapport. Because of the weakness, malnutrition, and trauma suffered by Abigail and Olin Smith, Sam must become the adult, the decision maker. "You're so different. Grown.... You ... know things," his mother states, acknowledging the change in "New Samuel" (Paulsen, *Woods,* 149, 150). As the former food provider, the youth slips easily into leadership, a child parenting role that the author encountered in early boyhood.

In Paulsen's historical fiction, a chilling advance into manhood grips Charley Goddard, a farm boy and impulsive Civil War enlistee in *Soldier's Heart.* Charley's biography yields a cautionary tale about the broken soldier based on facts from the 1860s. The narrative follows the 15-year-old for four years, dramatizing a gung-ho facade that disintegrates during battlefield slaughter at the battles of Bull Run and Gettysburg. Susan Faust, a critic for the *San Francisco Chronicle,* described the volunteer's unenviable position in a Union battle line "more grotesque than glorious" (Faust, 1998, 8). Snatched into manhood, Charley loses his idealism and yen for adventure as he plods into his final years with the despair of a beaten elder.

The Hazards of Growth

In addition to the historic Charley, the author surveys a broad range of childhood mishaps and provocations on the individual route to adulthood, as with Jason and Jeremy Parsons's response to threats to the family ski lodge in *Thunder* Valley, the orphaning of the narrator and relocating her with grandma Irene Flynn in *Molly McGinty Has a Really Good Day,* and Jacob Freisten's penchant for disastrous scientific experimentation in *The Boy Who Owned the School.* Jacob expects ridicule by self-important athletes, who descend "like sharks smelling blood if they saw (him)" to "poke or jerk or punch or shoulder-hit" him (Paulsen, *Boy*, 3). As an antidote to catastrophe in "death row," his term for the jock locker area, Jacob chooses to go unnoticed, a pose that the author himself adopted during his inglorious school experience (*ibid.*). In class, Jacob prays, "Disappear me.... Disappear me, now," a suggestion of the protagonist's discomfort on Senior Citizen Day in *Molly McGinty Has a Really Good Day* and Paulsen's solution to boredom and apathy in class by retreating to the woods (*ibid.,* 13–14).

For less explicable downturns, the author depicts socioeconomic change, a threat to the dynastic pride of 14-year-old Wyoming sheepherder John Barron in *The Haymeadow* and of 14-year-old Russel Susskit, the discontented Eskimo boy in *Dogsong.* Paulsen places in Russel's internal dialogue his most candid self-evaluation: "Father, I am not happy with myself" (Paulsen, *Dogsong,* 9). Disillusioned with his father's modernized ways, Russel camouflages a distaste for Christianity, snowmobiles, and cigarettes. He confides, "Something is bothering me," an intangible vexation that his father diagnoses as a normal restlessness of the teen years (*ibid.*, 10). Russel turns to the mentoring of Oogruk, a wise elder and fount of reassurance. The pattern replicates the motif of the old advising the young, a common thread of world literature that Paulsen endorses.

In comic mode in *Masters of Disaster,* Paulsen lampoons the lack-logic of energetic, imprudent boyhood. Henry Mosley's gang plans a Friday-to-Sunday bush adventure along the river with "no food, no matches, no shelter: nothing" (Paulsen, *Masters,* 26). By emulating pioneer forefathers, Henry extols survivalism as though a plunge into danger confirms virility, a belief that 14-year-old Coyote Runs espouses to his mentor Magpie in *Canyons* and the camper Thatcher approves in the story "People Call Me Crazy." To lessen fears in Henry's best friends, Reed Hamner and Riley Dolen, Henry diminishes the possibility of pain in his followers and suavely promises, "Definitely no blood" (*ibid.,* 6). Comedy emerges from the trio's unfamiliarity with the outdoors and from the naiveté of boys ill prepared for emergencies.

Accepting Death

On a more serious level, the author amplifies the first confrontation between youth and mortality as an essential rite of passage, the release of Sarny from childhood and bondage as a slave breeder in *Nightjohn,* for Coyote Runs during his discovery of "large medicine" during an Apache raid in *Canyons,* and for 13-year-old Manny Bustos, a Mexican beggar, from the grip of street crime and pedophiles in *The Crossing* (Paulsen, *Canyons,* 61). For 14-year-old John Barron in *The Haymeadow,* his father's use of the word "rot" to describe terminal cancer in Tink, a revered ranch hand, generates a fearful image almost beyond words (Paulsen, *Haymeadow,* 20). Without experience, John faces a June-to-September replacement of Tink as guard to 6,000 sheep grazing in the high country. In stream of consciousness, his mind turns to possible dangers from "the mountains and the coyotes and the bears and and and" (Paulsen, *Haymeadow,* 21). The unexpected assignment epitomizes Paulsen's stress on unforeseeable stepping stones from childhood to adult duties, a motif he reprises in *Sentries* and *The Foxman.*

In additional works—*The Voyage of the Frog, Hatchet, Tracker,* and *Notes from the Dog*—pubescent characters encounter unexpected reminders that death awaits all living things and sometimes leaves the young in charge before they are ready. For 14-year-old Brian Robeson in *Hatchet,* survival requires capturing and slaughtering fish, birds, and small animals for food, the natural annihilations that sustain life. By the time that Brian reaches age 16 in *Brian's Hunt,* he welcomes change as a normal part of manhood and a sign of readiness for adult challenges. In *Notes from the Dog,* Johanna's courageous, selfless defiance of breast cancer involves her teen friends in collecting funds for medical research, a positive redirection of sorrow. In more personal assaults by loss, protagonists in *The Voyage of the Frog* and *Tracker* accept the finality of a mentor's death that empowers mature outlooks on their own ambitions.

See also The Island; mentors; maturity; *Mr. Tucket; Soldier's Heart.*

Source

Creager, Ellen. "View from the Outside the Wilderness Resonates for Children's Author," *Detroit Free Press* (13 April 1999): 4.
Faust, Susan. "Young Soldiers Face War's Horror," *San Francisco Chronicle* (25 October 1998): 8.
Golden, Bernice. *Critical Reading Activities for the Works of Gary Paulsen.* Portland, ME: Walch, 1999.
Miller, Kay. "Suddenly Fame and Fortune," [Minneapolis] *Star Tribune* (10 July 1988): 6.

dogs

A devout dog lover and respecter of their vitality and temperament, Gary Paulsen honors canines, whose atavistic instincts, he declares, "take you back 30,000 years" (Moss,

2004, E1). Jane Austin, a critic for the [Fort Worth] *Star-Telegram* chortled that calling Paulsen a "dog person" is "like saying Godzilla is grumpy" (Austin, 1999, E-8). The author believes that residing with dogs is "mandatory for decent human life," a credo he shares with Jo-Jo the Dog-faced Girl in *Paintings from the Cave,* with the Smallhorn family and their malamute in *Brian's Hunt,* and with Oogruk and Russel Susskit, promoters of mushing in *Dogsong* (Paulsen, *My Life,* 2). In readying teams for three Iditarod runs in *Woodsong,* the author sleeps with his team in outdoor pens and "becomes as tough and wild and dirty and innocent as they are" (Thompson, 1995, 11). In an interview with Valerie Giles for the *Prince George Citizen,* the author reverences canines for their *joie de vivre:* "To know them and be with them is an experience that transcends—a way to understand the joyfulness of living and devotion" (Giles, 2005, 13). The commendations rise above the level of loving house pets to a tribute for the merits of working animals.

Pacing his travels in accordance with lope speed, in *My Life in Dog Years,* Paulsen begins admiring "a beauty he saw and took into himself but could not explain," a source of wonderment and identity with quadrupeds (Paulsen, *My Life,* 63). In fiction, Russel, the Inuit teen in *Dogsong,* fills husky bellies with "deer meat, rich guts and stomach linings," a meal to give his huskies power and drive (Paulsen, *Dogsong,* 102). To reward the team before feeding himself, he selects pieces three times larger than a human fist. The first person experiences of Russel and the author reverence a transcendent oneness with dogs, "that little hot worm deep inside us all that, no matter how damaged and broken we are, still allows us to respond to … the love that a good dog gives" (Paulsen, *Paintings,* x). The author's faith in the human ability to reciprocate canine adoration suggests pairings with dogs that reclaim depressed, feeble, and dispirited individuals, particularly veterans, the disabled, and prisoners.

Rescuer and Rescued

The *Ottawa Citizen* ribbed the author for being a "sucker for a furry face" ("Washed," 1998, E6). He expressed his lifestyle as possession by border collies and mixed-breed rescues, the inspirations that he termed "friend-pets" (Paulsen, *Paintings,* ix). His first pet, a black dog he named Snowball, he liberated from hungry villagers in the Philippine mountains; Corky, a small mixed poodle, he salvaged from the pound. He treasured hunting with Ike, a black lab, and lauded Dirk, a homeless mutt who rescued Gary from the stalker Happy and his gang of bullies in *My Life in Dog Years.*

During a three-year-plus army hitch, the author relieved the stress of building warheads by confiding in a Weimaraner. To interviewer Mary Pemberton, a journalist for the *Whitehorse Star,* Paulsen summed up the appeal: "With dogs, you are never alone" (Pemberton, 2005, 10). The writer typified loss of a favorite animal buddy in *The Island,* where Wil Neuton remembers the death of Fred, "hit by a car … broken and dead and gone; all of the … laughter gone with the going of Fred" (Paulsen, *Island,* 105). As a relief from mourning his lost pet, Wil admires a serene small dog at a gas station.

The Haymeadow expresses the author's regard for border collies Billy, Jenny, Peg, and Pete, who collect and move 6,000 sheep during summer grazing with barks and little nips. Like keenly drilled soldiers, Billy and Peg direct the front of the herd. The text details the guidance of dogs for cornering the pack: "Jenny and Pete kept the edges of the long, gray, fuzzy mass within the road and between the fences" (Paulsen, *Haymeadow,* 51). When a ewe leads a band off the lane, Jenny and Pete reroute the strays into the mass. At the height of threat, the dogs collaborate in driving off a bear that mauls 16 sheep. The narrative credits the herd dogs with "[remembering] from year to year what to do," responsibilities that the collies embrace with more enthusiasm than John Barron, the reluctant teen-age shepherd (*ibid.*). Because of their dedication to herding, the four border collies become four-legged mentors to John.

The author's commitment to raising and running sled dogs requires his attention to canine health, stamina, and nutrition in Canadian-bred animals whose fervency he compares to serial killers. For his first Iditarod in 1983, he monitors shipments of dog food and worms Cookie, his lead canine, to restore her wellbeing. In *Woodsong,* Paulsen's love for Storm, a brindle, slant-eyed wheeler, results in terror in the dog owner when blood squirts from the dog's anus. The damage to Storm's intestines results from Paulsen's use of dry dog pellets, which incorporate indigestible ground corn that lacerates internal linings. Storm's refusal to be sidelined enlightens the author on a canine instinct for sledding: "It was part of his life, the drive to be in the team and pull, then nothing else mattered," even the dwindling of stamina from blood loss (Paulsen, *Woodsong,* 20).

Anthropomorphic View

While running his first sled pack, Paulsen recognized his bonding as much more than a man's companionship with dogs—rather, it became a symbiosis with the team. He rejoiced at howling, a prompt from the husky most eager to join the line, and at the "manic insanity to it that infected the whole kennel" (Paulsen, "Wolfdreams," 22). In rapture at a moonlit run, he sank into the silence "like being pulled by a silent steam ghost up through the moonlight" (Miller, 1988, 6). In a mystical reverie, he determines that "Someone, Some One had to be thanked," an indebtedness to an unidentified creator god that the author shares with Brian Robeson in *Brian's Hunt* (Beckman, 2004, 1). With an enigmatic gratitude for his dog team, in the foreword to *Clabbered Dirt, Sweet Grass,* he experiences "a kind of prayer every time I ran them" (Paulsen, *Clabbered,* xii).

Through sensory telegraphy of touch and hearing, Paulsen harmonized with the "round sound that is so eerie and hauntingly beautiful" (Paulsen, *Puppies,* 36). Like the blind elder Ulgavik in *Dogsong,* without clear visibility, he could run the team because "what the dogs saw came back up through the sled," an enigmatic reference to tactile and aural impressions (Paulsen, *Dogsong,* 20). At the end of a run, the huskies in *Dogteam* lope home gleeful and pleased to share their joy. By picturing their ebullience, Paulsen hoped to refute "the biblical silliness about humans having dominion over the earth," his diminution of humankind to equality with beasts (Thompson, 1995, 11).

The writer identified sophisticated motives and behaviors in his pack. Storm, his clever wheeler in *Woodsong,* develops a flair for teasing and trickery by hiding a teammate's bootie and burying a ladle and a hat in snow. Obeah and Duberry, who save Paulsen from death from a gash in his knee, earn his regard for their "great, old knowledge … something we had lost," a suggestion of Carl Jung's collective unconscious, a cognizance of symbolic archetypes shared within a single species (Paulsen, *Woodsong,* 29). Of daily communion with the pack, Paulsen determined that dogs possess great-heartedness: "Animals open their lives up and make us a part of them" (Lynch, 2009). In Storm's last hours, the author repays the husky's generosity by setting the failing body east, a gesture of rapport and empathy with animal instinct.

Living with Dogs

While residing in the wild, Paulsen concluded, "I think that dogs offer the only form of unconditional love that's available to humans," a belief he shares with writer Kate DiCamillo, author of *Because of Winn Dixie* and Louis de Bernières's *Red Dog* (Lodge,

2012). He enfolds the toddler Richard Allen Mesington in the love of his pal Sissy in the novel *The Rifle.* Of the advance from jealousy to devotion with the birth of the family's first baby, Paulsen invests Sissy with "the bond of obligation that connects dogs—and especially collies—to humans" (Paulsen, *Rifle,* 73).

The author has kept a half dozen house dogs and some 70-husky teams, who taught him the elements of mushing and the distinctive smells of the trail. Running alongside the sled, he exulted in sharing kinesics, "the same flow across the tundra," a unified movement that allied his body with the canines (Paulsen, *Woodsong,* 122). Their howls introduced him to the "come back" song, which summoned Paulsen to rejoin the pack; their sit-down strike communicated disapproval of human foolishness and misdirection (*ibid.,* 32). He praised the canines for rescuing him from a fall under a horse in Colorado and for yanking him out of 12 feet of icy water. According to *Father Water, Mother Woods,* after bow-shooting a doe, he experienced "the first moment of true doubt; doubt that would plague him the rest of his life, moral doubt, growing doubt, doubt that ended childhood" (Paulsen, *Father,* 177). Out of honor and respect for his teams and their place in all animal life, he gave up killing with iron-jawed traps, arrows, or rifle and began eating only vegetables.

For *Winterdance: The Fine Madness of Running the Iditarod,* the author differentiated between hearthside lapdogs and the 15 Canadian huskies that included alpha female Cookie, wheeler Storm, troublemaker Devil, and rivals Columbia and Olaf. From haphazard runs and upsets, he advanced to sleeping in the dog lots, establishing his place in the pack, and selecting the best runners for leaders and wheelers, the stoutest of the line. For feedings, he collected slaughterhouse offal and outdated meat from grocers, ground it for freezing, and thawed the mass for feedings. The constant focus on sled dogs changed his sleep cycle, causing him to awaken in anticipation of their needs for food, water, bedding, shoulder massage, and examinations of paw pads for damage. Rather than humanize canine behaviors and responses, he honored them for preserving primordial instinct "through their genes and the habits that they try to teach one another" (Dar, 2015).

Training required year-round running of teams into the bush, whether pulling sleds over snow or wheeled carts and a car frame over dry ground in summer. He came to know his animals as "wonderful, wild, doggy folks" with "personalities and likes and dislikes and humor and anger and great heart and spirit" ("Iditarod"). Still green at the sport of mushing, he spent eight weeks in Anchorage milling around dogsledding stars to pick up vital tips on getting the most out of a team and protecting each runner from harm. In a 2010 interview, he classed husky teams as the true athletes of the Iditarod and chose Cookie as the husky whom he most identified with, trusted, and relied on.

Canine Adoration

To recreate the purity and dedication of animals, Paulsen incriminates the Southern agrarian use of dogs as stalkers and despoilers of runaway slaves such as Jim and Alice, victims nearly eaten alive by Clel Waller's killer hounds in *Nightjohn.* In a different mood, the author salutes the welcoming of the smiling farm dog in *Tiltawhirl John,* who "looked so jolly he could have been a giant Santa Claus" (Paulsen, *Tiltawhirl,* 21). The author relives his union with dogs in the introduction to *Puppies, Dogs, and Blue Northers* as "singular ... one in all things" (Paulsen, *Puppies,* n.p.). He praised their "unassuming Love" as "the most dedicated and pure of any" (*ibid.*). For humor, he subtitled the work "Reflections on Being Raised by a Pack of Sled Dogs" and evolved diction that Mollie Bynum, a reviewer for *School Library Journal,* applauded as "direct and often nostalgic" (Bynum, 1996, 130). He dotted his folksy texts with a menagerie of four-footers: the black and white dog at the butcher shop in *The Crossing;* Scruff, the kidnap victim in *Dunc and Amos Go to the Dogs;* the sled husky Ortho in *Winterdance;* Jake the farm dog in *The Quilt;* the unnamed female malamute in *Brian's Hunt*; and Suzy, the exuberant ranch collie in *Cowpokes and Desperadoes.*

In 2013, the writer joined his son, Jim Paulsen, in voicing a pair of novels from the human and canine perspective of Ben and his father Duffy and of Conor, the rescued pup in *Road Trip.* With the sequel, *Field Trip,* completed in 2015, the duo depict the 15-year-old border collie Atticus, the witty commentator, as a pet that "understands my priorities" (Paulsen & Paulsen, *Field,* 4). Ben views the breed as "a control freak with paws ... to keep everyone in their world in check" (Paulsen & Paulsen, *Road,* 3). Paulsen's tribute generalizes that "Dogs never lie or cheat, and their default setting is love" (*ibid.,* ix). He lists dignity, honor, and humor among their attributes, all of which canines reinforce in their owners. More archetypal is the sled team in *Dogsong,* which critic James Blasingame salutes during a grueling vision quest as "the engine that drives [Russel's] exploration into the heart of his own cultural heritage" (Blasingame, 2007, 87). The analyst corroborates Russel's reverence of Oogruk's kennel as sacred, a veneration of dogs that guides Paulsen's animal tales.

See also Iditarod.

Source

Austin, Jane. "The Best Doggone Pooches, Vampire Bunnies and Extreme Survival Tips Are Contained in the Fall's Best Books," [Fort Worth] *Star-Telegram* (14 September 1999): E-8.
Beckman, Rachel, James Chryssos, and Candice Hahm. "Talking with Gary Paulsen," [Long Island, NY] *Newsday* (27 April 2004): 1.
Blasingame, James. *Gary Paulsen.* Westport, CT: Greenwood, 2007.
Bynum, Mollie. "Puppies, Dogs, and Blue Northers," *School Library Journal* 42:7 (November 1996): 130.
Dar, Mahnaz. "'This Side of Wild': A Conversation with Gary Paulsen," *School Library Journal* (13 October 2015).
Giles, Valerie. "Quotable Quotations," *Prince George Citizen* (27 June 2005): 13.
"Iditarod Race Across Alaska," eacher.scholastic.com/activities/iditarod/top_mushers/index.asp?article=gary_paulsen.
Lodge, Sally. *Q&A with Gary Paulsen and Jim Paulsen.* http://www.publishers weekly.com/pw/by-topic/authors/interviews/article/55019-q-a-with-gary-paulsen-and-jim-paulsen.html, 2012.
Lynch, Amanda. "Gary Paulsen," *Children's Book Review* (26 January 2009).
Miller, Kay. "Suddenly Fame and Fortune," [Minneapolis] *Star Tribune* (10 July 1988): 6.
Moss, Meredith. "Novelist's Life Is In, Out of the Woods," *Dayton Daily News* (5 February 2004): E1.
Pemberton, Mary. "Writing, Mushing Are Man's Twin Passions," *Whitehorse Star* (1 April 2005): 10.
Thompson, Laura. "It's a Dog's Life," [London] *Sunday Times* (5 march 1995): 11.
Turvey, Shannon Lee. "The Trouble with Sequels," *Vancouver Sun* (23 May 1998): I10.
"Washed by the Wave," *Ottawa Citizen* (1 February 1998): E6.

fear

Paulsen portrays fear as an archetypal reaction to anything larger than or more powerful or threatening than the individual, as with the armed Comanche in *The Legend of Bass Reeves,* a coiled rattlesnake in *The Beet Fields,* and Redcoat officers targeted by patriot sharpshooter John Byam in *The Rifle.* During the nine days solo at sea experienced by eighth-grader David Alspeth in *The Voyage of the Frog,* terrors range from killer whales, a shark attack, and a close call with an oil tanker to a major storm. Other sources of fear haunt the mystic reveries of Janet Carson in the ethereal dream-story *The Night the White Deer Died,* prevent Thatcher from crossing a bridge over deep water in "People Call Me Crazy," and undermine the self-confidence of Air Force Major Toni McLaughlin after she is shot down in a Blackhawk III helicopter in *The White Fox Chronicles.*

To disseminate fear among plantation field hands in *Nightjohn,* slave owner Clel Waller brandishes a whip and pistol and breeds flesh-hungry hounds for retrieving and maiming Jim and Alice, two runaway slaves. Even after General Robert E. Lee and the Confederate army surrender to General Ulysses S. Grant on April 9, 1865, at Appomattox, Virginia, in *Sarny,* the sequel, night riders threaten the title character's right to operate a freedmen's school. With her characteristic bravado, Sarny states, "We can't … let a little thing like fear put us back" (Paulsen, *Sarny,* 146). Her pluck derives from a lifetime of grappling with terrors that lie beyond a slave's ability to vanquish.

Adult mentors relieve the qualms of displaced youth such as Carley, a summer visitor to Uncle David and Aunt Emily in *Popcorn Days and Buttermilk Nights;* Caleb Lancaster, the counselor of Brian Robeson after the boy's arrest for assault in *Brian's Return;* and the protagonist of the five-book Tucket series, Francis Alphonse Tucket, who searches the Oregon Trail for his missing parents and sister Rebecca until his reunion with them in *Tucket's Home.* For the mestizo orphan Manny Bustos, an undersized beggar and thief in *The Crossing,* companionship with Sergeant Robert S. Locke introduces the boy to an adult soldier seized by fear. In sobriety, Locke, a traumatized veteran, relives the terrors of Vietnam: "The smell that had a copper taste and the copper taste that became fear" (Paulsen, *Crossing,* 32). The narrative enlarges on the sergeant's final showdown against three knife fighters and a chain wielder, an exaggerated choreography that ends fear in both Manny, the survivor, and Locke, the martyr.

Paulsen's rapport with other Viet vets supplies multiple views of the fighter's regrets for surviving when others died, the crux of post-war malaise in the damaged protagonists of *The Foxman* and *Dancing Carl.* In the story "Stop the Sun" for the January 1986 issue of *Boys' Life,* the author amplifies for protagonist Terry Erickson his father's memories of a nighttime ambush in a Vietnam rice paddy. The veteran's remorse relives combat priority: "We could never get low enough, and you could hear the rounds hitting people," including his buddy, Pete Kressler, and the rest of the Americans who leave Terry's father the only living insurgent (Paulsen, "Stop," 38). Of his chance escape from slaughter while hiding under the remains of a corpse, the veteran weeps, "I died. Inside where I am—I died," his summation of an experience so dreadful that it vanquished the mortal parts of him (*ibid.*).

Historic Clashes

In the heart-clenching revelations of the American Revolution in *Woods Runner,* Paulsen introduces 13-year-old Pennsylvania hunter Samuel Lehi Smith to another kind of stalking and slaughter, the predations of Iroquois and Hessian mercenaries who abet the Redcoats. Throughout the next year, the boy suppresses fear by relying on forest lore and camouflage to avoid confrontations with armed men. Although traumatized by the job of burying nine massacred and scalped villagers, Sam forces himself to trust in logic and grit to achieve his aim. A sudden engagement with a British officer on the road south toward Philadelphia forces the youth to fire on his first victim "just beneath the chin, killing him instantly" (Paulsen, *Woods,* 156). Again, rational evaluation of warfare lessens Sam's qualms and enables him to settle his parents, Olin and Abigail Smith, with a foster daughter, eight-year-old Anne Marie Pennysworth "Annie" Clark, and return to the eight-year fight for independence as a medic and sharpshooter with Morgan's Rifles.

The juxtaposition of coming of age with unnerving events and people in the 1860s reaches a gripping peak in *Soldier's Heart,* where maggots and corpse bloat disfigure horses and men left on the battlefield. For 15-year-old Charley Goddard, an enlistee in the First Minnesota Volunteers, the Civil War is too anarchic, too murderous to comprehend. At

Manassas, Virginia, the game-changing Battle of Bull Run on July 21, 1861, persecutes him while the infantry fights in an amorphous hell: "Death was everywhere, nowhere" (Paulsen, *Soldier's*, 21). The sounds of bullets sundering the air seem inconsequential until Charley views his comrade Massey's decapitation by cannon fire. In *English Journal*, reviewer Ken Donelson concluded that Charley's contemporaries die "in fits and starts, especially in the mind and the soul" (Donelson, 1999, 148). The reality of slaughter fuses fear with anger, plunging the enlistee into manic "slashing, clubbing, hammering, jabbing, cutting," a mental fugue akin to a robotic madness, precipitating post-war angst (Paulsen, *Soldier's*, 84).

Fear in Multiple Genres

In a survey of humankind, Paulsen dates frightful experiences to birth. In the epigraph preceding Chapter 1 of *Dogsong*, he recites an Eskimo nativity poem that names fear as the original reaction of a newborn to the atmosphere outside the womb. The author identifies childhood terrors that resonate from his earliest memories, particularly his mother's killing of a potential pedophile in a Chicago alley and the Japanese incineration of Filipino prisoners of war with flamethrowers in *Eastern Sun, Winter Moon*. In fiction, he details apprehension on Jacob Freisten's approach to class in *The Boy Who Owned the School;* "fear and confusion etched on … faces" of victims in *Captive!;* and in Wil Neuton's dread of flight in a 50-year-old seaplane in *The Island*, when he is "so scared he couldn't blink his eyes and was afraid that he would wet" (Paulsen, *Island*, 105). The loss of physiological control reduces the victims to an infantile state, reprised in the quavering of a small race of primitive people before backpacker Mark Harrison in *The Transall Saga*.

As described by Eden Ross Lipson, a book critic for the *New York Times*, "Transforming early childhood stress can take many forms," from comedy to allegory to verse to memoir (Lipson, 2000, B7). A Mexican field worker in *The Beet Fields* uses a phobia of ridicule as a fulcrum for nudging the Gary character into catching and killing more pigeons for dinner. In the autobiographical scenes of *The Cookcamp*, Paulsen relives his amplified fantasies at age five, when he perches on a bench in the depot at Pine, Minnesota, and weeps while awaiting his grandmother, Anita Halverson. Panic suits the atmosphere—a lone railroad station, dark woods, and abandonment far from his mother's Chicago apartment. The text swamps boyhood imaginings with the arrival of a Norwegian grandma who smiles with her eyes. The author blends in wisps of memory of "Uncle Casey," the live-in lover who makes coital "sounds" with the boy's mother and who grasps the child's hand "hard, really hard," a suggestion of abuse that the five-year-old and his alert grandmother recognize as progressive bullying (Paulsen, *Cookcamp*, 48). Symbolically, Anita does battle with Gary's fears by swatting flies.

The author returns to autobiography with *The Quilt*, which details the Gary character's introduction at age six to childbirth in a house devoid of men. While he plays with Jake, a yard dog, in the Minnesota farmyard of Kristina Jorgenson, she retreats to an upstairs room with Grandma Alida and Martha, the immigrant Norwegian midwife. The rigors of labor and delivery occur out of sight, but petrify Gary with "a deep, grunting, ripping sound that turned into a piercing shriek and ended in panting murmurs" (Paulsen, *Quilt*, 46). He deduces that Kristina's cries and commentary from the other women are forbidden to males. At a tense moment, Paulsen quips, "Roy Rogers and the Sons of the Pioneers would not have to hear them" (*ibid.*, 68).

Retreating to the yard to pet Jake, Gary fails to make sense of the communal birthing. As labor continues, Norwegian-speaking women continue to snack on lefsa and stew and to joke about Kristina's "hard work" (*ibid.*, 34). They drink scalding coffee and bake bread while more shocking outbursts deepen his anxiety. Paulsen's scenario dramatizes mysteries of the female world that lie outside a boy's understanding of adult womanhood. Rather than contemplate the rigors of childbearing, he anticipates a man's life of fishing, hunting, and leaving home to fight wars. Lack of information compounds his alarm, a boyhood plight that the author pities.

CONTRASTING MILIEUS

Out of empathy for earthly life, Paulsen wrestles with loneliness and the bestial trepidation of an creature's being hunted and eaten for food, especially while the heart still beats, a possibility he vivifies in *Guts*. For *This Side of Wild,* he quails at solitude: "I was alone, some kind of strange dread of that dark band of spruce and that bears, or any other animal, could stand there and watch" (Paulsen, *Side,* 23). In *Woodsong*, he relates a sudden encounter with a doe fleeing brush wolves and details the anatomical reaction to fear: "Something coppery about it, a metallic smell mixed with the smell of urine and feces" (Paulsen, *Woodsong*, 4). The frantic flight of the doe over bad ice and her death from flashing fangs epitomize for the author the mortal struggle of all creatures for mercy.

With *Paintings from the Cave,* the author shifts atmosphere from beasts in the wild to stalkers and persecutors in city streets and alleys echoing with police sirens. By arming gangbangers Blade and Petey for the hunt with knives and glocks that produce notched tongues and gunshot wounds, Paulsen intensifies panic for Jake, a victim overwhelmed by metropolitan bugbears. Without backup, he has no choice but to "hide in the basement in the day. Stay low" (Paulsen, *Paintings,* 4). The trio of novellas varies urban settings, besetting Jo-Jo the Dog-faced Girl with social ouster and Jamie with homelessness and hunger. Jo-Jo dreams "she couldn't get to her bedroom with the dresser pushed against the door fast enough" (*ibid.*, 73). Jamie copes with a compounded fear of "hungry, cold, dirty or sick to death of wondering where we're going to sleep tonight," the complex terrors of ghetto children (*ibid.*, 114). For each refugee from fear, the texts propose stop-gap comfort in art, books, and protective dogs, all solaces to Paulsen in his autobiographies.

See also Nightjohn.

Source

Bookman, Julie. "Paulsen's Tale Gets to 'Heart' of the Civil War," *Atlanta Journal-Constitution* (9 January 1999): E5.
Donelson, Ken. "Soldier's Heart," *English Journal* 89:2 (November 1999): 147–148.
Lipson, Eden Ross. "The Dark Underbelly of Writing Well for Children," *New York Times* (8 July 2000): B7.

female persona

Paulsen has stated his admiration for women for devoting their adult lives to study and growth and for being "better than men on all levels" (Miller, 1988, 6). The types of admirable women includes these:

- Aunt Clair, the kind cook and assuager of hurts in *Harris and Me*
- female road workers in Canada, whom Paulsen observes in *Pilgrimage on a Steel Ride*
- Nikki, the bold equestrienne in *Escape from Fire Mountain*
- Susan Smallhorn (Kay-gwa-daush), the intrepid Cree tracker in *Brian's Hunt*
- the hippie giving birth in a cemetery in "The Madonna"

- the grandmother who serves a Thanksgiving meal in *The Beet Fields*
- Katrina M. "Tina" Zabinski, the genuine pal of Kevin Spencer in *Crush* and *Family Ties*.

His compliment to female strength fits the mother of Francis Alphonse Tucket, who dreams of "a pot of beans on the stove" in *Call Me Francis Tucket*. For family delectation, his mother typically placed a fatty ham hock and "cooked [it] to perfection" (Paulsen, *Call,* 34). In *Tucket's Home,* he reunites with his parents and sister Rebecca after his abduction by Pawnee and near murder by Indians and outlaws. Rebecca cooks for him; his mother confers maternal welcome with visits to him at night to smooth his hair and "kiss him on the forehead, touch his cheek" (Paulsen, *Home,* 83). At first, her tenderness vexes Tucket, but the actions comfort him from long travels on the American plains by duplicating the motherly ministrations he knew in infancy.

Although the writer is capable of creating such admirable characters as Ms. Diamond, the state social worker in *Flight of the Hawk;* Peggy Ollendorfer, the champion wrestler in *The Amazing Life of Birds;* and spunky photographer Robin Waterford in *Skydive!*, he favors male protagonists like John Barron, the 14-year-old shepherd in *The Haymeadow;* Pennsylvania gunsmith Cornish McManus in *The Rifle;* Inuit musher Russel Susskit in *Dogsong;* and Brian Robeson, hero of *Hatchet*. Paulsen blames his gender for bias. In the introduction to *Molly McGinty Has a Really Good Day,* he explains, "I was a boy and I did boy things—still do, since I'm what might be called an old boy" (Paulsen, *Molly,* Foreword). The admission agrees with the views of critics that Paulsen writes boy-pleasing works, including outdoor adventures for *Boys' Life* and *Scholastic Scope*, male grit in *Grizzly,* treasure hunting in "The Case of the Dirty Bird," and interplanetary travel in *The Transall Saga*.

In defense of the opposite gender, Paulsen characterizes standout girls and women for their cheer, goodwill, grace, charity, and noble spirits, particularly these:

- Mammy, who insists women be buried with dignity in *The Legend of Bass Reeves*
- Leeta, the language tutor to Mark Harrison in *The Transall Saga*
- the attractive Karla Tracey in *Notes from the Dog*
- Al, the stripper at the Kitty Kat Club who defends son Tony in *The Glass Café*
- Brennon Cole's mother in *Canyons*, a single parent like Al
- Nancy, the girl-woman who gives birth unattended in *Dogsong*
- Grandmother Aggie, the genial cook for grandson John Borne in *Tracker*
- the mother figure of Aunt Emily, who sets a "plate on the table when she sees [Carley] coming" in *Popcorn Days and Buttermilk Nights* (Paulsen, *Popcorn,* 27).
- Old Maria, who feeds the mestizo orphan Manny Bustos an occasional free tortilla and roasted chicken in *The Crossing*
- Sarah Thompson, the tough sidekick of Will Little Bear Tucker in *The Legend of Red Horse Cavern*
- Bobbie Walker and Cousin Alex, partners defying the mischievous Bledsoe brothers in *Hook 'Em, Snotty!*
- Lottie, the endearing chatterbox of *Tucket's Gold* who eventually marries Francis Alphonse Tucket in *Tucket's Home*
- the war orphan, eight-year-old Anne Marie Pennysworth "Annie" Clark, in *Woods Runner,* who is "ready to do what had to be done" (Paulsen, *Woods,* 96)
- Abigail Smith, the harried survivor of arson and prison who accepts Annie Clark as a daughter "as good as blood" (*ibid.*, 139).

In urban scenarios, the author notes girls' ability to ignore obnoxious male peers, the social situation in *The Schernoff Discoveries, Cowboys and Desperadoes,* the Dunc and Amos series, and *Masters of Disaster.* In more serious settings, females cope well in a manless milieu, particularly pregnant war widow Kristina Jorgenson and the lone Norwegian Grandma Anita Halverson in *The Quilt.* From his maternal grandmother, Paulsen learned that "maybe the male side is crushed because I didn't make it, but I can also have compassion. I can try to understand my failure and I can try to learn from it" (Barron, 1993, 27).

In reflections on the 1940s and 1950s, memories of Paulsen's maternal grandmother dominate recreations of early boyhood, causing him to adore her "more as a mother than his own mother" (Paulsen, *Alida,* 14). In references in *The Winter Room* and *The Island* and in her first appearance in his memoir *The Cookcamp,* Grandmother Anita Halverson—the fictional alter ego of Alida Peterson Moen—subdues terrors in the five-year-old protagonist from Chicago by smiling with her eyes, exuding the scent of lavender, and stroking his hair. In *This Side of Wild,* he reveres her for being "wonderful, all-knowing" (Paulsen, *Side,* 62). A parallel figure in *Alida's Song,* Mrs. Torku, slips the boy three hot rolls from the bakery to "take the chill out of the air," a physical misery akin to the spiritual withering he endures at home (Paulsen, *Alida,* 10). Both nurturers depict the quiet assurance of mothers, the essential figure missing from Gary's early years.

Central to her role as rescuer of a grandson, Alida's attentiveness translates small details about "Uncle Casey" into a mental warning of child abuse and potential pedophilia in the boy's daily existence with his mother's live-in lover. *English Journal* reviewers Allen Pace Nilsen and James Blasingame, Jr., declared, "Gary Paulsen has a heart of gold and is a big teddy bear, but he turns into a grizzly bear if he thinks kids are being mistreated or disrespected" (Nilsen & Blasingame, 2009, 15). Out of patience with her daughter, Alida swats flies with a vengeance and scribbles a heated letter to the mother for neglecting the five-year-old while romancing her lover. The gracious, fun-loving Grandma Anita becomes a prototype for the red-haired grandmother in *Lawn Boy Returns,* in which she thrills at boxing lessons and charms fight officials. Like other wise elders on Paulsen's character list, she offers advice on human support systems: "If you have good friends, you can consider yourself truly wealthy" (Paulsen, *Returns,* 21). The aphorism counters her grandson's pervasive interest in profiteering from capitalism.

Gender Traits

Paulsen honors females for their mercies toward needy people, the tie that binds the dreamer Janet Carson to the derelict Navajo Billy Honcho in *The Night the White Deer Died,* Eunice Moen Paulsen toward hungry islanders who survived World War II in Okinawa and Manila in *Eastern Sun, Winter Moon,* and Irene Flynn to an orphaned granddaughter in *Molly McGinty Has a Really Good Day.* The appearance of Johanna in *Notes from the Dog* pinpoints an open-hearted stranger who moves directly toward Dylan, a smiling border collie. She welcomes Finn, the protagonist, and his friend Matthew for being "dog people and Dylan fans" (Paulsen, *Notes,* 8). As though detecting their need for better nutrition, she courts them with roast beef sandwiches, potato salad, watermelon, lemonade, and cookies. More important than food, she nourishes their spirits with ideas and activities that take them out of their mental fug and into hopeful, upbeat collaboration with raising donations for cancer patients.

The writer's regard for women reaches a pinnacle in his bondage novels, *The Legend of Bass Reeves, Nightjohn,* and *Sarny.* In an interview for Twayne publishers, he remarked, "Women are inevitably emotionally tougher than men. I want to understand their kind of toughness, and so feel that I must write about it" (Salvner, 1996, 79). For deputy U.S. marshal Bass Reeves, his mammy instills the ethics that guide his lengthy career as a frontier law officer. She explains, "Ain't no man your master. Not now. Not ever" (Paulsen, *Legend,* 4). Similarly, Sarny's first-person account of separation from her enslaved mother at age four relates foster mother Delie's haphazard method of marking time annually on notched sticks. The first 12 serrations warn girls of "the troubles," a folk term for menarche and the transformation of a child field hand into a potential breeder, the fate of the simple-witted slave Alice (Paulsen, *Nightjohn,* 16). The term captures the dread of losing innocence to a system of propagation that ranks nubile girls among farm mares and dairy cows.

Sarny's introduction to a ditch school elevates her status from beginning breeder to alphabet teacher, a noble rescuer of her people into her 80s. By 1930, the protagonist of the sequel *Sarny* advances to storykeeper, the spokeswoman for Stanley, Martin, and other slaves who died from the brutality and privations of agricultural bondage and the racial violence of night riders. Sarny recognizes the doggedness in women who "could learn at night even after working in the day" (Paulsen, *Sarny,* 9). She takes pride in being "the one to live and live and write it all down," Paulsen's salute to the role of female storytellers and historians in recording slavery's past and honoring its survivors (Paulsen, *Sarny,* 5).

Character Selection

The author explained his rationale for choosing young female protagonists like Katrina M. "Tina" Zabinski, the girlfriend who lives in the daydreams of Kevin Spencer in *Vote;* Susan, the loyal friend of Wil Neuton in *The Island;* Helen Swanson, the female ideal of Carl Wenstrom, the troubled World War II flying ace in *Dancing Carl;* and Clara, the sweetheart and widow of colonial gunsmith Cornish McManus, whom the British hang in *The Rifle.* In each instance, male figures long for sympathetic female companions, especially deathbed comforters like Anna in "The Killing Chute"; the sexually savvy Ruby, a carnival stripper in *The Beet Fields;* and the female survivors telling life stories in "The Library." According to an older woman, Grandmother Alida, the prototype for the nurturer in *The Cookcamp, The Island, The Quilt,* and *Alida's Song,* Paulsen needs a respite from the military and can restore purpose and joy in his life by marrying. Alida stresses, "It is the best thing for you—for a man—to be married" (Paulsen, *Alida,* 3). The author's faith in matrimony emerges from his respect for Alida's satisfying union with Clarence Moen and the birth of nine children and for Paulsen's experience with his third wife, artist Ruth Wright Paulsen, a partner in his creative efforts.

In Paulsen's canon, girls bring out courage and vision in males, such as the would-be hero Amos Binder, love interest of Melissa Henson in *Amos Gets Famous,* and 13-year-old Katherine "Katie" Crockett, instigator of a search for her missing father in *Curse of the Ruins.* At their best, for example, librarians and an understanding fourth grade teacher in *Shelf Life: Stories by the Book* and the Norwegian matriarch Pearl in *The Quilt,* women inspire decorum, compassion, and right thinking in both genders. To David Gale, an interviewer for *School Library Journal,* the logic of *The Monument* hinges on gender differences that set Rachael Ellen "Rocky" Turner apart for her sensitivity to idealist Mick Strum: "A young girl would be more affected artistically, I think, by a visiting artist than a young boy would" (Gale, 1997, 24). Paulsen's faith in females remains steady throughout his works as anchors for fitful, less rational males, especially Bonnie, the lover of Officer Nuts Duda in *Winterkill.*

Gender Contrast

In less prominent roles, sedate girls heighten the contrast to rambunctious boys seeking the attention of females. In *Masters of Disaster,* Marci Robbins's prissiness differs from the misdirected yen of males who "do not have enough mystery in [their] lives" (Paulsen, *Masters,* 58). She lacks enthusiasm for Henry Mosley and Reed Hamner's ill-conceived night in the school cafeteria Dumpster. She wishes the males luck with "um, the whole odor thing you've got going here," a polite allusion to the boys' indifference to sanitation and hygiene (*ibid.*, 46). At an "aha" upsurge in Reed's developing maturity, he realizes that following Henry's leadership toward danger and "doing things that ... make me smell" are counterproductive to social intercourse (*ibid.*, 76). For incidental humor, the author implicates the male principal, who tacitly abets prepubescent daredeviltry with "a wink and a handshake" (*ibid.*, 101).

For comedy in *The Boy Who Owned the School*, Paulsen turns the prim female into a rival, forcing on her brother layered injustices and misfortunes. Jacob Freisten's 17-year-old sister ranks so high at home with her parents that she rates a grand suite, a sporty red car, and allowance five times that of her brother. In contrast to her cosmetic surgery and dermatological treatment for blemishes, Jacob gets "braces that hummed" when he passes through the library security device (Paulsen, *Boy,* 11). The imbalance of parental valuation of daughter over son serves the author as a fulcrum on which to mount drollery.

See also food; *Sarny.*

Source

Barron, Ronald. "Gary Paulsen: 'I Write Because It's All I Can Do,'" *ALAN Review* 20:3 (Spring 1993): 27–30.
Belden, Elizabeth A., and Judith M. Beckman. "Torn Up and Transplanted," *English Journal* 80:2 (February 1991): 84–85.
Gale, David. "Gary Paulsen," *School Library Journal* 43:6 (June 1997): 24.
"The Glass Café," *Journal of Adolescent and Adult Literacy* 49:3 (November 2005): 227–234.
Miller, Kay. "Suddenly Fame and Fortune," [Minneapolis] *Star Tribune* (10 July 1988): 6.
Nilsen, Allen Pace, and James Blasingame, Jr. "Getting Up Close and Personal with Living Authors," *English Journal* 98:3 (January 2009): 15–21.
Salvner, Gary M. *Presenting Gary Paulsen.* New York: Twayne, 1996, 79–133.

food

Near starvation and undernourishment influence much of Paulsen's writing, perhaps because, in childhood, his neglectful parents failed to provide the basics for him—a stocked pantry, regular cooking, and nutritive table service for a nuclear family. Fictional scenarios often brim with edibles:

- bowls of gift food that a primitive tribe gives backpacker Mark Harrison in *The Transall Saga*
- meaty smells that draw Carley to Aunt Emily's cookstove in *Popcorn Days and Buttermilk Nights*
- Aunt Clair's welcoming rhubarb pie and Glynnis's syrupy pancakes for breakfast in *Harris and Me*
- a high-fat diet for Commander Sidoron in *The White Fox Chronicles*
- pigeon meat and tortillas with beans to satisfy migrant workers in *The Beet Fields*
- cornbread flavored with bacon drippings and honey in *The Legend of Bass Reeves*
- roast buffalo hump with brown gravy and boiled potatoes in *Tucket's Home.*

In *Pilgrimage on a Steel Ride,* the author admires the adaptable menus of Mexican cooks. He describes their choice of simmering large potfuls of beans "with any animals we could catch thrown in," including squirrels and woodchucks, and sharing the stew with guests in open-hearted hospitality (Paulsen, *Pilgrimage,* 84). The alliance of pot-luck with generosity in his writings accounts for the visual and spiritual motif of family love shared thrice daily at the table.

In the memoir *Alida's Song,* the author parallels affection with the coffee-dunked sugar lump that the title character tucks under her tongue. The act symbolizes the slow, steady spread of sweetness from a grandma who offers family meals, understanding, and dependable mothering, elements missing from her grandson's home. During the musings of Finn, the narrator in *Notes from the Dog,* about his smiling border collie Dylan, the boy reveals elements of parental neglect. In a comment on scrambling eggs and buttering toast for Dylan, the boy concludes, "You always feel better when you do something nice for someone you love," a suggestion of the Greek *agape,* the kind of attention he lacks (Paulsen, *Notes,* 10). The statement bears the gentle wisdom of the ancient moralist Aesop, who declared in "The Mouse and the Lion" that no act of kindness, however small, is ever wasted.

In contrast to his early childhood meals in Thief River Falls, Minnesota, Paulsen's description of Russel Susskit's breakfast in *Dogsong* discloses the Eskimo preparation for winter with fishing and the hunting of caribou, deer, and seals. Cached outside icehouses, the meat remains frozen for lopping with a hatchet or ax, a chore that Russel performs for his father and wise old Oogruk, a village elder. From sautéing in oil, the pieces pass directly to the mouth, where the diner slices free each bite with the semicircular ulu, a catchall cooking and sewing tool. Russel's father reminds his son, "We do not eat it raw anymore" because of "small things in the meat to make you sick" (Paulsen, *Dogsong,* 9). As a model of cultural shift, Paulsen relates the change in Eskimo meals by evaluating the need for thorough cooking, a white man's adaptation to prevent trichinosis and other parasites from raw or semi-raw flesh.

Other texts use snacks and meal planning as evidence of the times and the state of the economy, especially Mammy's overview of Mexico as a place where people eat beans and tortillas in *The Legend of Bass Reeves* and John Byam's hasty bites of bread as he draws a bead on Redcoats in *The Rifle.* Isaac's spruce and pine needle tea in *Woods Runner* dramatizes the use of a homemade drink that frees Pennsylvania colonists from dependence on British tea, a taxable commodity imported by the East India Company to enrich the English monarchy. By contrasting hunks of roasted ox on the trail with condiments—maple sugar, butter, jelly, gravy, cream, apple butter—at Caleb and Martha Clark's house, the author indicates that protagonist Samuel Lehi Smith has lucked into a prosperous spread. At a thrilling moment in the rescue of his parents, his father, Olin Smith, chews a beef sandwich and gulps milk laced with rum before declaring that the gift food "is life itself" (Paulsen, *Woods,* 139). The strengthening of Olin through high-fat, revitalizing meals requires Sam to shoot a raccoon to replace lean, stringy venison. The management of Olin's rehabilitation attests to Sam's progression to child-parent of his own mother and father.

To suggest the exigencies of wartime rationing, in *A Christmas Sonata,* the memoirist describes his mother serving fried potatoes and Spam, a low-end canned pork product popularized during World War II by Hormel Foods. On the train from Minneapolis to Uncle Ben and Aunt Marilyn's farm in December 1943, mother and son eat liver and onions with mashed potatoes and rolls, the cheapest entree on the menu and the easiest on the mother's pocketbook. Paired with Aunt Marilyn, Gary's mom joys in cooking *lefsa,* a Norwegian flatbread heated on a griddle and sprinkled with sugar. For Christmas, the family enjoys soup with dumplings and potato sausage, suggestions of wartime rationing of fresh produce and meat.

Food as Solace

Paulsen's memoirs depict eating as an antidote to anxiety, fear, and loneliness, a solace to the five-year-old in *The Cookcamp* who welcomes bottled milk and a sack lunch on the train containing a jelly biscuit and grapes. Alone at his destination, he nibbles a sugar doughnut while waiting in a depot. Observing a road-building crew in the cook trailer and their consumption of pie, biscuits, syrup-soaked pancakes, and coffee with sugar and condensed milk builds the boy's regard for his Norwegian grandma, Anita Halverson, a confident feeder of working men. After the comforting repast, the laborers round out their pause from labor with snoose, a pinch of pulverized tobacco tucked into the lower lip, a hands-free form of savoring nicotine. The respite dramatizes the need for ample, flavorful repasts during the grueling highway project connecting Minnesota with Canada.

In a more frugal wartime setting, sailors of a U.S. transport vessel in *Eastern Sun, Winter Moon* have little to gain from the rationing of staples, which reduces breakfast to "scrambled powdered eggs fried in grease with two pieces of dry toast, a small bowl of oatmeal with milk mixed from powder that still had lumps in it and no sugar" (Paulsen, *Eastern,* 39). The contrast of galley menus with cookcamp spreads ennobles Anita for her foresight in understanding the power of food to raise spirits. Less hopeful, the pouring of slops into buttermilk in a trough in *Nightjohn* epitomizes the depths of human bondage, which deems the worth of Delie, Sarny, Alice, John, and other slaves on a par with farm beasts.

In *The Quilt,* communal birthing enmeshes Norwegian-American women in a kitchen festival of flatbread, stew, and scalding coffee. Frequent snacking counteracts the shrieks of lone farm wife Kristina Jorgenson, who withdraws upstairs with Gary's grandmother and Martha the midwife to give birth to a first child. In the midst of a gynocentric milieu, the six-year-old enjoys reassurance and a stomach filled with honeyed and buttered bread. In innocence, he ignores the tense midwifery and declares, "He had never eaten food that tasted so wonderful" (Paulsen, *Quilt,* 29). The comment reveals a child who allows the sensory pleasures of food to deflect the sounds of a two-day labor in childbed.

The Food of Fiction

Like the Gary character, the lone child in *The Quilt,* hasty eating becomes a temporary reprise from poverty for Manny Bustos, the orphaned mestizo in *The Crossing* and the pioneering protagonist in *Call Me Francis Tucket* and from solitude on the mountain for 14-year-old John Barron in *The Haymeadow* and a forest hermit in *The Foxman.* The lone shepherd accepts the limited fare of ranch hands, who consume without complaint sandwiches of canned meat without mayonnaise or butter and dinners of canned beef stew or chili with crackers and cups of coffee, all evidence of isolation far from a well-stocked pantry. More important for his June-to-September post, John plans to supply fodder for his horse Spud, sweet grass for the cattle, and dry dog food for border collies Billy, Jenny, Peg, and Pete. In contrast to the needs of animals, John gulps down viscid eggs fried in lard and squashed into cold hash heated in the can, which he "ate without looking" (Paulsen, *Haymeadow,* 33). The ranch hand Cawley summarizes the situation in terse range lingo: "Can't have nothing much fresh," a statement that captures the bleak seclusion and scanty fare of the high country herdsman (*ibid.*, 36).

In detailing the parental abandonment of 14-year-old Terry Anders in *The Car,* a popular road narrative, the author relives the dietary choices of a deserted boy, who lacks peanut butter and bread for toast while he builds a kit car. In its place, he coats sugary cereal with more sweetener, a food more filling than nourishing. A dinner of frozen TV meals and a lunch meat sandwich at 3:00 A.M. perpetuate the use of food to tide him over until he can locate something better. The make-do rations echo Paulsen's memories of sharing Ritz crackers with Dirk, the stray he adopts in *My Life in Dog Years,* and the meals of Finn in *Notes from the Dog,* who snacks on pretzels and juice while his father studies at the library. In futuristic surroundings, Paulsen supplies Mark Harrison with lizard jerky, fire bugs, unidentified mush, and tree rock juice in *The Transall Saga,* a wobbly blend of survival lore with sci-fi.

Dream Snacks

For the Brian Robeson saga, Paulsen's dream sequences of submarine sandwiches, pizzas, hamburgers, fries, malts, and chocolate shakes in *Hatchet* connect the 14-year-old New Yorker with a past security based on a wealth of sustenance, a fantasy he shares with Tucket's imagery of beans and ham hocks. Brian imagines, "A mental picture of hamburger, the way they showed it in the television commercials.... Rich colors, the meat juicy and hot" (Paulsen, *Hatchet,* 48). As his stomach churns and growls, he ponders, "What had he read or seen that told him about food in the wilderness" (*ibid.,* 56). Past menu choices seem luxurious in comparison with the spartan stomach fillers—fish, raspberries, fool birds (grouse), turtle eggs, crayfish—that he gleans from the wilds of south central Canada. After locating unidentified berries, Brian proves true the Roman philosopher Cicero's aphorism that hunger is the best sauce, but he encounters digestive upset from unfamiliar fruit, which he calls gut cherries.

As canny as archetypal humans, Brian outpaces animals with planning for future needs: "Food first, because food makes strength" (Paulsen, *Hatchet,* 158). By stocking a pond to keep fish for later meals, he reduces anxiety, the stress that threatens him with hysteria. His fright of starvation generates an axiom about nature: "The fish he had been eating all this time had to eat, too" (*ibid.*, 168). Brian's generalized thinking precedes more opinions about sustenance in the wilderness. He recognizes the flavor and texture that cooking imparts to raw panfish, grouse, and rabbits. By sharing inklings from ancient ancestry, he eludes self-pity and unites mystically with cave man, a Jungian theory of the collective unconscious, which reverences the accumulation of instinctive knowledge within the species during human evolution. After recovering packaged food from the sunken Cessna 406, Brian appreciates the wonder and variety of stew and peach whip, which he shares with Cree tracker David Smallhorn, the first human to encounter Brian in the wild. Paulsen's touch of grace honors all civilization for the human refinement of bestiality with generosity.

In *The Schernoff Discoveries*, Paulsen revisits food in the wild with a brief mention of fresh carp smoked over an ironwood fire and a pubescent boy's enthusiasm for a breakfast of Pepsi-soaked peanuts. With less enthusiasm in *Guts*, he recalls sharing a nest of turtle eggs with his lead dog Cookie. While she devours the leathery spheres and their mucilaginous contents, he struggles to keep down a taste and slime reminiscent of rotted vaseline. On a more pleasant note, he details purifying water for drinking and stone-boiling rabbit meat or fish in a birch bark cone, a method advanced by Native Americans. The narrative compounds instructions for open pit cookery with descriptions of planks and spits as alternatives to pots and pans. His favorite style, pit roasting, jogs memories of some of his tastiest outdoor repasts, including the broiling of a buffalo hump: "It was a grand feast," a reflection of the prehistoric discovery of tenderizing meat with fire, a skill he reprises in *Father Water, Mother Woods* and *Tucket's Travels* (Paulsen, *Guts*, 147).

FOOD IN THE CITY

At his most pessimistic, Paulsen fills the days of Jake in *Paintings from the Cave* with urban scavenging for something to still his gut rumblings, a visceral gnawing echoing the author's memories of hunger in North Dakota migrant camps in *Tiltawhirl John* and *The Beet Fields*. The stark choices of Jake's aunt and Layla's mom reduce menu planning to lunch meat on week-old bread and economy-sized cans of beans, a cheap form of protein. Layla cadges leftovers from fast food boxes that drunks leave behind. For more filling dinners, Jake shoplifts supplies from Skinny Tony's store and skims change from pockets and purses. The desperation diet reveals a common plight of the ill-fed underclass.

Like characters from Walter Dean Myers's ghetto fiction "The Treasure of Lemon Brown," Jake admits to hopelessness: "I take what I can find" (Paulsen, *Paintings,* 19). Through voyeurism, he stares at diners, and "can almost touch the smell of food," a model of synesthesia rife with fantasy and frustration (*ibid.,* 23). Jake's work for Blade, a job at the felonious end of the survival pile, tends to involve street kids selling weed, using drugs, and prostituting themselves, the worst of urban ills. Susan M. Harding, in a review for *School Library Journal,* praised Paulsen for pairing slum children's undernourishment and heartache with redemption.

See also female persona

Source

Harding, Susan M. "The Cookcamp," *School Library Journal* (1991).

Harris and Me

For a humorous respite with the Larson family, Paulsen sends his troubled Gary character at age 11 out of a citified element on an episodic adventure. In 1950, the unnamed protagonist arrives at a rural oasis set in the forest outside Pinewood in north central Wisconsin, a haven as safe from parental abuse as a fortress. The narrative depicts agrarian life as though farm folk lack experience with technological advances, such as the automatic milking system on Susan's family's farm in *The Island*. By viewing the kitchen table and dance floors by Coleman lanterns and watching an isolated movie reel at a "Gene Autry binge," the Larsons seem as dimwitted a bunch of rubes as a Li'l Abner cartoon strip (Paulsen, *Harris,* 100).

The boy is fortunate to find pal Harris, parent surrogates like Uncle Knute and Aunt Clair, and an older sister like Glennis who "smiled with her whole face" (*ibid.,* 6). After studying Harris's antics for two weeks, the protagonist gains insight into what his second cousin is plotting. Over Harris Larson's *modus operandi* hovers his nemesis: "Rules. Every time you turn around there's something you can't have or something you can't do" (*ibid.,* 74). His scorn of order sets the tone and direction of the summer catastrophes, which at times threaten life and limb. Harris intensifies the comedy by demanding to his daily dupe, "When's the last time I was wrong?" (*Ibid,* 93). The Gary character has to admit, "I had to do it, whatever it was he wanted to do" (*ibid.,* 101).

FANTASY FUN

Less controlled in imagination than the farm hand Louie's carved diorama of a miniature winter logging camp, Harris's literal mind devises the disasters that begin as boyish fun, as with the firing of a banty chicken out of a stovepipe with an inflated inner tube and increasing the velocity of a bicycle with a washing machine motor. Hyperbole governs

Paulsen's wayward narrative, which embroils the boys in a pancake-gobbling struggle and imaginary World War II attacks on enemy Japs, which plunge both Harris and his visitor into pigsty muck. From tackling sows, the boys progress to acting out the story of Tarzan in the lost land of dinosaurs with the granary-to-barn loft "Tarzan Leap" (*ibid.*, 68). For animal characterization, the author assigns names to eccentric farm creatures—Minnie and Gertie the sows, Buzzer the lynx cat, and Ernie the "manic rooster," who threatens kamikaze attacks (*ibid.*, 58). Integral to mishaps, the protagonist's gullibility and belief in Harris's logic leaves him vulnerable to blame, injury, dirtying or tearing his clothes, and pain.

For the sake of a laugh, the author overworks coarseness, notably, Harris's bruised groin from a leap onto Bill the plow horse and gaping bib overalls that reveal a lack of underwear for the trip to the "Lumberjack Lownge" (*ibid.*, 84). Louie's unseemly gorging on farm meals precedes a night of guzzling beer and urinating on himself before Knute hauls him to the truck. Paulsen cites Harris for naming green puke as a symptom of "mad croup" and for tormenting a frog anally with a straw, a caper that brought complaints of animal abuse from a parent in Arlington Heights, Illinois, in 2006 (*ibid.*, 8). Nonetheless, Sue Engel, a book critic for the *Wausau* [Wisconsin] *Daily Herald*, applauded the substantial plot and "strong comedic value" (Engel, 2015, 5).

Family Belonging

At a crisis of action, Paulsen upends slapstick comedy to remind the reader that farm and stock work is dangerous, potentially deadly. The loss of Uncle Knute from a broken hand and Aunt Clair to drive him to the doctor in Pinewood informs the Gary character that taking their places requires exhausting labor. Nearly as disastrous as agricultural accidents and unwieldy bulls, the narrative introduces Elaine Peterson, a girl who sends the Gary character into a mute tailspin at a community dance. The *coup de grâce*—the electrical charge from a stock fence that convulses Harris's body—repays him for sabotaging the brief courtship with Elaine, but launches a new wrangle about the loss of two pornographic photos to Louie. Despite parental appeal in mid–December 1997 to ban the book in Battle Mountain, Nevada, the wacky farce remained available to junior high readers.

In the estimation of critic Meagan Lacy, the Gary character "is fully transformed, able to recognize himself as someone who matters and belongs to a family" (Lacy, 2015, 362). The narrative leads him to a view of himself as part of the Larson clan, "like I was home" (*ibid.*, 140). While viewing Louie's diorama, "A strange feeling came over me, seeing the figure" of himself working on the farm (*ibid.*). He anoints his coming to knowledge with tears and begins to think well of himself. Paulsen illustrates the value of long distance communication with Harris's letter and package, love gifts that extend summertime brotherhood. Reviewer Elizabeth MacCallum, in a critique for the Toronto *Globe and Mail*, declared that the book "reveals not only a writer that I had underestimated, but a book that may become a classic" (MacCallum, 1994, C17).

Source

Engel, Sue. "'Bad Feeling' Offers Some Slapstick Fun," *Wausau* [Wisconsin] *Daily Herald* (3 September 2015): 5.

Lacy, Meagan. "Portraits of Children of Alcoholics," *CUNY Academic Works* 46:4 (December 2015): 343–358.

MacCallum, Elizabeth. "Rude, Outrageous: An Ideal Book for Kids," [Toronto] *Globe and Mail* (5 February 1994): C17.

Hatchet

A tribute to the outlook, prudence, and quick-wittedness of teens, Gary Paulsen's provocative five-part Brian Robeson series bears elements of Jack London's blend of realism and urgent initiation into northern climes. Paulsen's Newbery Honor Award-winning text sets a standard for sparse, unlabored American prose on a par with Mark Twain's *Tom Sawyer* and *Huckleberry Finn* and Laura Ingalls Wilder's Little House series. The pentad—*Hatchet, The River, Brian's Hunt, Brian's Return,* and *Brian's Winter*—examines rudimentary logic and risk-taking devoid of adult guidance and control. Fans flock to the author's public appearances at libraries and schools and write letters asking about Brian's ability to feed and protect himself. While introducing young readers to name recognition of outstanding authors, the notoriety of *Hatchet* earned the author a six-figure income, freeing him from years of poverty and make-do.

Author Laurie Wenger explained that true independence like Brian's requires that he "possess and demonstrate personal power and control over things that matter," namely, food and safety among animals that roam the same territory, a quandary he shares with backpacker Mark Harrison in *The Transall Saga* (Wenger, 1999, 56). New York Public Library expert Elizabeth Bird put the concept in current parlance as "escapism for kids with helicopter parents" (Royte, 2013). An admiring educator accounted for the upward curve of Brian's success in the wild: "You can feel sorry for yourself as much as you want, but when you're done with that, you still have the problem to deal with. And I think kids can relate to that," a pragmatic aspect of the Hatchet series and its trial and error methods of sustaining life (Kelley, 2011). The author confided that he viewed solitude in nature with Brian's eyes because, "I'm really only about 14" (Jacobson, 1999, F6). The quip hints at deep-seated anxieties that vexed his own teen years, when he forsook a foundering home life to transform himself through seclusion alone in non-human nature. He, like the protagonist of *The Legend of Bass Reeves,* finds "joy in becoming part of nature" (Paulsen, *Legend,* 97).

Staying Alive

For background on Brian's suspenseful stranding in the North American wilderness, the author, Brian's alter ego, drew on years of the woodcraft, foul weather, and foraging in authentic wilderness with hand-made weapons, a skill he returns to in *The Legend of Bass Reeves*. Throughout his career, he recounted his exploits in short stories and novellas such as *Danger on Midnight River,* the Tucket series, "Lost at Sea," and *The Transall Saga*. As a result of Paulsen's familiarity with theme, topic, and setting, *Hatchet* required only four months of writing to achieve verisimilitude. Speaking through Brian's interior monologues, the novel intrigues the reader with the boy's candor about setbacks, mistakes, and triumphs.

For the grueling tests of a tenderfoot's reason and experience over a rapid descent in a two-seater Cessna 406 from 7,000 feet and a 54-day ordeal in south central Canada, reviewer Elizabeth Royte tweaked the five novels as "loners-in-nature sufferfests" (Royte, 2013). With less admiration, critic Edwin J. Kenney, writing for the *New York Times,* relegated boyhood adaptation to a wasteland and its demands to "a rather conventional macho ethos" (Kenney, 1988, A30). Young readers continue to confute both critiques by identifying with Brian, his multiple face-offs against the outback, and a mystic salvation that Stephen Fraser, writing for the *Christian Science Monitor,* called a "spiritual resurrection" (Fraser, 1987, B-5).

The fictional survivor reminds himself "There were these things to do," a litany of actions that ward off depression and prevent dismay or longing for home, even though his parents' divorce has shattered the original threesome (Paulsen, *Hatchet,* 103). With surprising self-awareness, he values "waiting, and thinking and doing things right," a pattern that sustains him in *Hatchet* and again in *Brian's Hunt* (*ibid.,* 141). With a childlike internal chant, Brian rewards himself for self-sufficiency: "I can get food and I know I can get food and it makes me more" (Paulsen, *Hatchet,* 148). A boost to his self-confidence comes from memories of Mr. Perpich, an English teacher who advised students to value themselves as sources of survival. The uplift enables Brian to deflect the initial effects of shock and panic and to bag a moose, from which he drags the front, ribs, and hump meat back to his camp. In the final scenario, elements of subsistence that he retrieves from the Cessna fuselage nullify food problems by equipping the protagonist with freeze-dried meals, utensils, cookware, and butane lighters.

Adapting and Changing

The 13-year-old protagonist voices Paulsen's empathy for contemporary children who suffer repressed anger and regret over divorce and visitation rights. To Brian, the legal term for habitation invoked "fights and yelling, lawyers … and the breaking and shattering of all the solid things," an allusion to home and the family circle (Paulsen, *Hatchet,* 2–3). The emotional onslaught burdens him with a secret beyond his understanding: he recognizes that adultery terminates the affinity of his mother for her former husband. In a critique for the Kingston, Ontario, *Whig-Standard,* Maureen Garvie applauded the "simplicity and immediacy that keep the palms wet with tension, and what Brian learns about himself in the process strikes a responsive chord" (Garvie, 1988, 1).

Essential to Brian's coping with an adult impasse, self-sufficiency during nearly seven weeks in the wild at an elevation of 4,000 feet changes him from child to contemplative, tough-minded man who embraces inner awareness, harmony with the outdoors, and a mature self-worth. In the words of author biographer Edith Hope Fine, Brian "stumbles, learns, and grows," a motif that Paulsen's novel shares with Stephen Crane's *The Red Badge of Courage* and James Vance Marshall's *Walkabout* (Fine, 2000, 78). Analyst Frances Ward Weller, a book critic for the *Los Angeles Times,* lauded the main character for being "bright, gutsy, and ultimately able to laugh at his own ineptness" (Weller, 1987, 6). Astute and confident, he has learned to trust his own criteria of self-approval. His ingenuity and self-discovery influenced Paulsen's creation of other characters, especially 13-year-old Samuel Lehi Smith, the lone forest explorer in *Woods Runner;* a physically and emotionally scarred survivor of the Battle of Verdun during World War I in *The Foxman;* and Daniel Martin, an unlikely rescuer of teasing peers in *Danger on Midnight River.*

See also food; survival.

Source

"Dear Gary Paulsen," [Saint John, N.B.] *Telegraph-Journal* (21 May 2008): D11.
Fine, Edith Hope. *Gary Paulsen: Author and Wilderness Adventurer.* Berkeley Heights, NJ: Enslow, 2000.
Fraser, Stephen. "Adventure Stories: Exciting Tales of Challenge and Survival," *Christian Science Monitor* (6 November 1987): B-5.
Garvie, Maureen. *"Bookstand,"* Kingston, Ontario, *Whig-Standard* (30 January 1988): 1.
Jacobson, Ann. "Paulsen Revisits Bush in Finale of 'Hatchet' Series," *South Bend* [Ind.] *Tribune* (14 March 1999): F6.
Kelley, Annie J. "Gary Paulsen: A Book Can Change a Life," *Battle Creek* [Michigan] *Enquirer* (11 February 2011).
Kenney, Edwin J., Jr. "The Island," *New York Times* (22 May 1988): A30.

Royte, Elizabeth. "Grumpy Old Man and the Sea: Adventures with Gary Paulsen," https://www.outsideonline.com/1919481/grumpy-old-man-and-sea-adventures-gary-paulsen, 2013.
Weller, Frances Ward. "One Boy's Solitary Fight for Survival," *Los Angeles Times* (12 December 1987): 6.
Wenger, Laurie. "Books for Building Circle of Courage: Independence," *Reclaiming Children and Youth* 8:1 (Spring 1999): 56–57.
Wergeland, Kari. "'Hatchet' Author Tells Civil War Tale," *Hartford Courant* (2 March 1999): F4.

healing and death

Paulsen's sensitivity to physical forces tinges his writing with sharp life/death moments, the fatal crossover that results from the crushing of Harvey's arm in the story "The Cook Camp" and the autobiographical novel *The Cookcamp,* the Gary character's fall from barn rafters in *The Beet Fields,* and the threat to soldiers of the Continental Army from dysentery in *The Rifle.* The runaway slave treated for wolf bite with a cauterizing iron by the Creek rescuer named Peter in *The Legend of Bass Reeves* at first misidentifies fainting as a moribund state and proclaims it "not bad at all" (Paulsen, *Legend,* 91). The author also individualized needs in Uncle David's broken heart at the death of his wife Alida in *The Winter Room*, destitute female worshippers in *The Tent,* Wil Neuton's yearning for isolation in *The Island,* and Gunnar's cleft palate and speech defect in *Alida's Song.* Edging closer to mortality in the latter, Paulsen words his boyhood thoughts on underage driving at night and fantasizes suicide by pistol, a pervasive image among depressed teens, who picture themselves being mourned rather than lying inert in a coffin.

The writer's knowledge of first aid and medical care ventures from treatment for poison to assuaging blunt force trauma, particularly the broken arm of Uncle Knute in *Harris and Me,* Mark Harrison's insect bites in *The Transall Saga,* and flashbacks to Wendell's gut wound in "The Madonna." Paulsen's subplots in *Tucket's Home* actualize the Pueblo use of a poultice to prevent snakebite from killing Francis Alphonse Tucket; similarly, experience as a medic in Vietnam informs John Homesley of the shape and destructive power of a rifle shot to the head in *Canyons* and the efficacy of a Murphy drip against shock. Of Billy's father's death from cholera, a common plight of pioneers on the Oregon Trail in *Call Me Francis Tucket*, Francis learns that "The man had gone off to die alone to protect his children, although leaving them alone in the prairie was close to a death sentence" (Paulsen, *Call,* 59). In *Woods Runner,* the first conflict introduces Samuel Lehi Smith's near demise from the blow of an Iroquois war club until Coop, a poorly educated woodsman, applies a poultice of tobacco juice and spit. Subsequent close calls elucidate Paulsen's belief that all living beings cling to the raw edge of existence, especially vulnerable children.

Death in Life

For the historical fiction in *Woods Runner,* Paulsen refers directly to dehydration from dysentery during the American Revolution and, for civilians, emotional survival of the trauma of raids, capture, imprisonment, and arson. To the wounded refugees whom teen outdoorsman Samuel Lehi Smith and Scots tinker/spy Abner McDougal pass on the road to New York City, gifts of laudanum and bandages offer some comfort, but no hands-on treatment or first aid. More essential to surviving the War for Independence, Sam's kindness and understanding extends to Anne Marie Pennysworth "Annie" Clark, an eight-year-old witness of bayonet stabbings of her parents, Martha and Caleb Clark, and begins the child's healing from loss. Undiscerned by Sam lies the simultaneous relief of his own sorrow and worry, which he palliates by concentrating his efforts on rebuilding his malnourished father, Olin Smith, with adequate protein and protecting the little girl, a repeat of the dual rescue motif in *The Crossing*.

The author examines the anticipation of death as the onset of grief, such as Anna's comfort of a victim of a bone tumor in "The Killing Chute" and Coyote Runs's visualization of a corpse and the realization that "Magpie was a body" in *Canyons* (Paulsen, *Canyons*, 71). For 13-year-old John Borne in *Tracker*, the mysteries of the advanced age and approaching demise of Grandfather Clay Borne from cancer stymy the boy's usual enthusiasm for farm work. Doctors fail to halt the disease with "tests and more tests and ... chemicals and knives" (Paulsen, *Tracker*, 4). While musing over the buck and two does John had killed in previous Novembers, he finds himself overcome with weeping at thoughts of his grandfather's imminent loss from an incurable wasting disease. In *Using Literature to Help Troubled Teenagers Cope with Health Issues*, educators Jim Powell and Nancy Lafferty confirm John's need to ponder the immutability of death, a reality that typically bewilders the immature mind during late childhood and the early teen years. Unfortunately for the young, families may be so deep in grief that they fail to reduce dread and trauma for children.

Paulsen, a proponent of mentoring, emphasizes the wisdom of age that enlightens John Borne on the yin and yang of mortal existence and the inseparability of life from death. John concludes about mortality: "It was just a thing that *was*" (*ibid.*, 86). As a lesson in mystery, Grandfather Clay states, "The best joy and beauty are the kinds that are unplanned" (*ibid.*, 26). After a transcendent moment tracking a doe, the boy realizes that living would not be beautiful and majestic if there were no death to render life precious. For the story's grasp of defining moments, Barbara Erickson, a reviewer for *Journal of Adolescent and Adult Literacy*, affirmed the novel's verbal impact by identifying it as an ideal read-aloud along with Paulsen's *The Monument, Canyons,* and *The Crossing.*

Befriending the Sick

The motif of friendship with the terminally ill recurs in Paulsen's works, both fictional and history-based, as with the impromptu nursing skills of Lucy and Sarny among wounded soldiers after a late Civil War skirmish in *Sarny* and the protagonist's love for the doomed World War I veteran of the Battle of Verdun in *The Foxman*. In the story "The Liberty Ship" and the memoir *Eastern Sun, Winter Moon,* the author dramatizes from a six-year-old's perspective a bout of chicken pox, seasickness, and the rapid rescue of plane crash victims, women and children who tread water in the path of sharks. Unable to tear his eyes away from carnage, Gary watches his mother and Corpsman Harding perform triage, choosing which gashes to sew and which to leave to certain bleed-out. Meticulous details particularize the use of a saw to lop off splintered limbs and his mother's mastery of a syringe to administer morphine and bandages to cushion wounds. The three-day marathon of treating shark victims elevates both Eunice Paulsen and Harding for their bravery and redeems the wayward mother in the boy's estimation.

The writer's concern for cancer patients informs *The Haymeadow,* in which a rancher chooses to solace his ailing employee Tink, leaving to son John Barron the old ranch hand's former post as up-country herder of 6,000 sheep. In *Notes from the Dog,* Johanna, a chemo patient with no hair, shares love with Finn and Matthew, emotionally needy boys. The hypothesis that charity begets charity results in a campaign to raise $10,000 for breast cancer research, a method of enabling the boys to repay Johanna for her affection. More poignant for the author, the aging and death of his revered lead dog Cookie dominates *Puppies, Dogs, and Blue Northers,* a fitting obsequy for Paulsen's most trusted husky. In each instance, the human acceptance of mortality attests to compassion as well as maturity and self-knowledge.

See also alcoholism.

Source

Barron, Ronald. "Gary Paulsen: 'I Write Because It's All I Can Do,'" *ALAN Review* 20:3 (Spring 1993): 27–30.
Cummins, Amy. "Border Crossings: Undocumented Migration between Mexico and the United States in Contemporary Young Adult Literature," *Children's Literature in Education* 44:1 (March 2013): 57–73.
Loer, Stephanie. "A Satisfying Depression Era Tale," *Boston Globe* (21 February 1988): 48.
McCaleb, Joseph L. "Story Medicine," *English Journal* 93:1 (September 2003): 66–72.

history

Paulsen flinches at the extremes of history. In *The Legend of Bass Reeves,* his most virulent chronicle, he quails at Native American stories of violence, "some parts … so horrible they are virtually unprintable" (Paulsen, *Legend,* 70). In fiction, he cultivates a jarring, compelling awareness of history by viewing events from the perspective of ordinary people, particularly these:

- Kristina Jorgensen, a new mother and World War II widow in *The Quilt*
- Uncle David, a blacksmith in *Popcorn Days and Buttermilk Nights*
- Sergeant Robert S. Locke, a career soldier and Vietnam veteran in *The Crossing*
- the crew of a B-17 in *The Rock Jockeys*
- day laborers in *Working*
- a trapper and World War I veteran in *The Foxman*
- Mammy, slave and single mother in *The Legend of Bass Reeves*
- Corey, the evangelist in *The Tent*
- Coyote Runs and the Apache raider Magpie during the Indian wars in *Canyons.*

At an everyday moment in Hazel's life in *The Beet Fields,* the palpable anguish of her son's death in the Pacific war hovers over the lunch table, as real to her as his photograph.

For "Stop the Sun," a story of post-traumatic stress disorder in the January 1986 issue of *Boys' Life,* Paulsen depicts protagonist Terry Erickson's attempts to understand his father's post-war syndrome. Reading Vietnam War history offers him no clue. Terry concludes, "It was all numbers, cold numbers, and nothing of what had *happened*" (Paulsen, "Stop," 36). The complaint epitomizes the author's insistence that young people need more realistic books to animate their heritage and to vivify events, especially wars. Educators Rebecca Giles and Karyn Tunks agreed that "the more details children have about how people of the past lived, the better prepared they are to see connections between themselves and those who lived long ago" (Giles and Tunks, 2014, 16).

For background, Paulsen conducts the same style of investigation to learn true inklings of character, particularly soldiers in *Sentries,* Scandinavian immigrant farmers in *The Winter Room,* and the group decisions of primitive societies in *The Transall Saga.* The author poses as models of valor the historical decisions of Magellan, Lord Nelson, the mountain man Jim Bridger, trapper Jeremiah Johnson, Civil War generals, and the 20 mushers who ran the initial Iditarod in January 1925. In the plot of *Curse of the Ruins,* the author depicts an archeologist, Professor William Crockett, as a scholar sensitive to New Mexican Indian beliefs about their prehistoric ancestry at the abandoned community of El Debajo. Of the organic method of research, the writer explains, "I pick up a book here or there or see a documentary or talk with an expert in the subject, and my curiosity about the one area of study and discovery always leads to another" (Lynch, 2009).

In contrast to his years of failing at formal education, Paulsen typifies as more effective a curiosity-driven personal inquiry, the impetus for Tag Jones's dive into the sunken Spanish galleon in *The Treasure of El Patrón,* the crash of a B-17 bomber over Devil's Wall in *The Rock Jockeys,* and the exploration of the Devil's Hammer, a tavern owned by pirate George Bonney in "The Case of the Dirty Bird." For Amos Binder in *Culpepper's Cannon,* trying to learn history in class is as ephemeral as "water through a funnel," a testimonial to Paulsen's disdain for textbook readings (Paulsen, *Culpepper's,* 3). Even worse than classroom lecture, Amos hates American history under Mr. Trasky, who instructs by assigning papers. On the effort to outline notes for an essay, Amos expresses his lack of direction with a question: "So now what do we do?" (*ibid.,* 2). Clueless about study methods and purpose, Amos speaks for Paulsen a childhood protest of boredom and misdirection by public school educators.

Realism in YA Literature

Of ineffective efforts to instruct children, Paulsen warned in an interview with Stephanie Zvirin for *Booklist:* "Not telling the truth is doing an enormous disservice to our young people," a theme he illustrates with a preventable firearm death in *The Rifle* (Zvirin, 1998, 864). He introduced the effects of Revolutionary War trauma early in *Woods Runner,* after 13-year-old Samuel Lehi Smith encounters the devastation of Iroquois arrows and tomahawks and Hessian bayonets on western Pennsylvania villagers in 1776. Within the first 24 hours of a raid, by recovering nine bodies and burying them, the boy recognizes in himself signs of psychological change in a heart "torn and gutted and forever changed" (Paulsen, *Woods,* 50). The rapid shift from sorrow to rage prepares Sam for an international war and its hellish erasure of homes and colonists by cold-blooded mercenaries.

In balance, the author introduces Coop, a backwoods patriot who heals Sam's concussion with spit and tobacco juice, and tinker/spy Abner McDougal, another rescuer who helps the boy evaluate a plan for retrieving his parents from imprisonment in a sugar mill in New York City. With the aid of an anachronism, Abner characterizes George III as crazy, a symptom that didn't emerge until 1788, more than a decade after the onset of the American Revolution. From the Scotsman's perspective, the war began in Boston because colonists are "sick of being treated like livestock" (*ibid.,* 113). Paulsen also relies on a Dickensian device, the unlikely encounter of Sam with his mother, Abigail Smith, amid the 5,000 prisoners and a swirl of Redcoats in New York. A period fact, the drunkenness of sentries, enables Sam and Abner to plot the extraction of Abigail and Olin Smith from a starving mass of prisoners of war.

Personal research of the American Revolution and subsequent wars enhanced Paulsen's knowledge of post-traumatic stress disorder. For Charley Goddard's biography, *Soldier's Heart,* the writer sought letters and diaries from the Minnesota Historical Society containing the infantryman's original words. The writer dedicated himself to full disclosure of Civil War atrocities by studying the butchery caused by "a musket, a bayonet, and a cap-and-ball handgun … [and] a four-inch cannon" (Zvirin, 1998, 864). In reference to positive reviews of his historical fiction, he declared, "the real credit goes to Charley.… He gave everything he could for his country" (*ibid.*). Student awareness of the historic volunteer and vicarious participation in his life provide reference points and background knowledge for later appreciation of the salvation of the Union.

Readying himself to clarify the background of an actual person and free the story of myths and stereotypes, the writer studied the role of marksman John Byam in the Revolutionary War as background for *The Rifle* and the terrors of piloting a B-17 bomber during World War II for *The Rock Jockeys* and *Dancing Carl.* To flesh out a personal dimension of bondage, Paulsen scrounged for data on Deputy U.S. Marshal Bass Reeves and dedicatee Sally Hemings, Thomas Jefferson's mistress. Her meager history precipitated slave interviews and characterization of Mammy, John, Delie, Alice, and Sarny, the frameworks for *The Legend of Bass Reeves, Nightjohn,* and *Sarny.* For *Mr. Tucket,* a prairie survivor traveling from Missouri on the Oregon Trail, the author's preparatory reading encased the historical significance of Standing Bear, a Ponca chief from Omaha, Nebraska, and mountain man Jim Bridger, a trapper in the far west to the Great Salt Lake, and summarized the differences in the sensibilities and territorial worldview of the Sioux, Crow, Kiowa, and Pawnee. The effort rebutted generalization of participants in the Indian Wars as innocent whites and evil Indians.

The author allows his narratives to range over an expanse of U.S. history. A post-war approach explained the wounding of soldiers in Vietnam, the focus of a combat survivor's panic attack at a mall in the story "Stop the Sun." For *The Crossing,* Paulsen accounts for changes in the self-doubting career soldier Sergeant Robert S. Locke, a battlefield survivor who blames himself for his comrades' deaths. In *Mudshark,* Paulsen honors libraries as the source of such historical details as post-traumatic stress disorder, "the answers to all things, to everything," even causes of the hurts and self-anesthetizing that follow warriors like Locke, Dancing Carl, and the Foxman into peace time (Paulsen, *Mudshark,* 18). The intensity of Paulsen's probing suggests his attempts to understand his warrior father, Colonel Oscar Paulsen, and the hostility and violence that destroyed their family.

Western History

The writer reached a height of historical accuracy in *Nightjohn* and *Sarny,* pre–Civil War reflections on the anguish of laboring as field hands and breeders for greedy enslaver Clel Waller, who unleashes dogs that chew alive the runaways Alice and Jim. For the redemptive value of emancipation, Paulsen contributes *The Legend of Bass Reeves,* a biography hyperbolized with an authorial claim that Reeves was "the most valiant marshal in the West" (Paulsen, *Legend,* subtitle). Limiting the Wild West era to 60 years, from 1830 to 1890, the introduction lists Buffalo Bill, Wyatt Earp, Wild Bill Hickok, Billy the Kid, and Butch Cassidy and debunks the writings of Ned Buntline and the hype on all five Western heroes before distinguishing the career of Reeves as "honest and honorable" (*ibid.,* n.p.). Similar in locale and danger to Charles Portis's *True Grit,* the biography sets a boundary between outlawry in Oklahoma, then known as Indian Territory, and law and justice in Fort Smith, Arkansas, the jumping-off place for the fictional Rooster Cogburn and actual U.S. marshals patrolling the western frontier. Paulsen articulates the narrative with credible details from newspaper accounts—Comanches, Texas Rangers, Winchester rifles, outlaws, and Isaac Parker, the Fort Smith hanging judge who economized by executing six felons at one time.

For all Paulsen's scholarly efforts and good intentions, critics have questioned the authenticity of his reprises of past events. *Kirkus Reviews* thought highly of the Reeves biography and suggested basing a film on the story. However, the same journal's survey of *Fishbone's Song* charged the author with glamorizing the moonshine trade and with misrepresenting elements of the Whiskey Rebellion. On the subject of migrant labor, Liljana Burcar, a book critic for *Jeunesse,* characterized Paulsen's views in *Lawn Boy* as simplistic to the point of turning field workers into grinning Uncle Toms content with exploitation. On a more positive note, Karen Coats, in a critique for *Bulletin of the Center for Children's Books,* praised the writer for embedding tales with "gems of oral history and enduring lessons" (Coats, 2016, 89).

See also legend; *The Legend of Bass Reeves; Nightjohn; The Rifle; Sarny; Soldier's Heart;* Timeline of Historical References; *Woods Runner.*

Source

Bartky, Cheryl. "An interview with Gary Paulsen," *Writer's Digest* 74:7 (July 1994): 42–44.

Burcar, Lilijana. "(Global) Capitalism and Immigrant Workers in Gary Paulsen's *Lawn Boy:* Naturalization of Exploitation," *Jeunesse* 4:1 (Summer 2012): 37–60.

Coats, Karen. "Fishbone's Song," *Bulletin of the Center for Children's Books* 70:2 (October 2016): 89.

Giles, Rebecca M., and Karyn W. Tunks. "Read the Past Now! Responding to Historical Fiction through Writing," *The Councilor,* 75:1 (2014): 15–22.

Lynch, Amanda. "Gary Paulsen," *Children's Book Review* (26 January 2009).

Robertson, Judith P. "Teaching about Worlds of Hurt through Encounters with Literature: Reflections on Pedagogy," *Language Arts* 74:6 (October 1997): 457.

Zvirin, Stephanie. "Gary Paulsen," *Booklist* 95:9–10 (1 January 1999): 864.

humor

Anecdotal mirth colors much of Paulsen's episodic writing, as with the husky Cookie's becoming "romantically involved" with Rex in *Puppies, Dogs, and Blue Northers;* the capitalization of "Something Important" to designate adult arrogance in *The Island;* and the cry "Die you commie jap pigs" as Harris Larson leaps into a pigpen in *Harris and Me* (Paulsen, *Harris,* 39). The author enjoys smirking at fools and himself in what *Publishers Weekly* called "acerbic insecurity masking humor," the purpose of a nosebleed in *Six Kids and a Stuffed Cat* and the catapulting of Francis Alphonse Tucket over the head of a stolen Pawnee pony in *Mr. Tucket* ("Six," 2016). In a review of *Winterdance* for the *Chicago Sun-Times,* Dolores Flaherty and Roger Flaherty approved the "novice musher's account of his training, … a blend of discovery and wry humor [that] ruthlessly mines the possibilities for self-deprecation offered by the combination of ignorance and obsession peaking in absurdity" (Paulsen, *Winterdance,* 19).

On a broader scale, Paulsen laces his canon with incidental humor, as with the 16-foot Kevlar canoe named "The Raft" in *The River* and fear of "Beans + Dylan = Killer Farts" in *Notes from the Dog* (Paulsen, *Notes,* 18). Both *Harris and Me* and *The Island* contain outtakes from dialogue to precede each chapter, as with Jim Neuton's belief that football players ended up "either selling cars or running insurance agencies" (Paulsen, *Island,* 16). His son Wil builds on the stereotype of the grazing teenager by picturing his jaw unhinged and the "contents of the refrigerator [tipped] into his mouth" (*ibid.,* 134). For Duane Homer Leech, protagonist of *The Amazing Life of Birds,* the sight of a zit on his forehead reminds him of a "suppurating wound," the type of hyperbole common to acne-conscious teens (Paulsen, *Amazing,* 16). The self-torment worsens from a face that looks "like I tried to kiss a rotary mower" and, on the next page, with the self-deprecating epithet "Doo-Doo the Zit Boy" (*ibid.,* 16, 17).

The writer exploits the competitive streak and treasure quest for his zany fictional Amos Binder and Duncan "Dunc" Culpepper in *Coach Amos* and the story "The Case of the Dirty Bird." In the latter, the plot opens on a "skuzzy parrot" that mimics advertising for GE refrigerators, a 1962 Chevrolet Impala, Brylcreem hair tonic, Ipana toothpaste, Old Gold cigarettes, and Chef Boyardee spaghetti and meatballs (Paulsen, "Case," 32). Catastrophe from an explosion in a tunnel filled with gunpowder left over from the Civil War causes no more harm than Amos's singed eyebrows, but precipitates his parents' droll discussion of "shipping him to the Arctic" (*ibid.*). The exasperation of a harried mother and father echoes the motif of other Paulsen tales as harum-scarum as *Molly McGinty Has a Really Good Day, Field Trip,* and *Zero to Sixty: The Motorcycle Journey of a Lifetime.*

Teen Illogic

The author salts his adventure tales with wry exaggeration. In satiric classroom scenes, he jokes in *Time Benders* that Jeff Brown circles test answers without reading the questions. In reflections on school pecking orders, Paulsen describes the discomfiture of Niles Strand in *The Island* for offending a spiteful football center and tweaks the surmise of Jacob Freisten, a shrinking misfit in *The Boy Who Owned the School,* that "hell was made for jocks," the muscle-bound football heroes who make his life miserable (Paulsen, *Puppies*, 2; *Boy*, 4). For *Dunc's Halloween,* the author parodies pubescent appetites and eating habits with Duncan Culpepper's sampling of leftovers in the fridge. Without closing the door, Dunc "polished off a pound of potato salad, half a meat loaf, and a full bowl of macaroni salad. And he was still hungry" (Paulsen, *Halloween,* n.p.). In *The Schernoff Discoveries,* the protagonist shoots a grouse and cooks it by instructions listed in *Field and Stream.* Improper carcass cleaning and questionable table manners reduce the hunter to chewing grouse and "[spitting] shot half the night" (Paulsen, *Schernoff,* 27). Subtler jests emerge from the talk of youth, such as the orphan Lottie, a motor-mouth in *Tucket's Ride,* and Willy Taylor in *Dancing Carl,* who anticipates maturing "without getting dumb" like most adults (Paulsen, *Dancing,* 11).

In *Masters of Disaster*, Paulsen wrests comedy from mention of the "Night of the Living Sludge" spent in a Dumpster amid "microscopic crawly things" (Paulsen, *Masters*, 41, 52). The outlandish ambitions of protagonist Henry Mosley and his two best friends, Riley Dolen and Reed Hamner, turn exhibitionism into potential broken bones from trying to set a "world record for the most forward airborne somersaults on a bike" (*ibid.*, 12). Paulsen pads the text with the tracking of Reed by his screams, Ace bandages, cries of "Call 9-1-1!," and reminders of "the vinegar and baking soda incident in the garage," a veiled implication of mishaps in the trio's past (*ibid.*, 22, 30). Paulsen's choice of plausible escapades with available trappings enhances authenticity, the benchmark of critical approval. The result is popularity among at-risk students. One media specialist declared, "Gary Paulsen is the go-to author for students who say, 'I don't like to read. You can almost always get them hooked on one of Gary Paulsen's books," in part because of veritable narrative and frequent humor (Kelley, 2011).

On droller subjects, such as Reed Hamner's achievement of altitude in an airborne bike competition, Paulsen glorifies boyhood shenanigans—soaring at 47 feet from the Batsons' roof, bouncing on a diving board, and flipping over a pool while counting to "two-Mississippi in his head" (Paulsen, *Masters,* 21). The feat is a testimonial to foolhardy, enterprising males seeking capers producing "pain and blood," essential proof of masculine verve (*ibid.,* 6). Henry aggrandizes the plan as unprecedented in "a guy our age" (*ibid.,* 13). At a pivotal moment in evolving logic, Reed, the gang's dupe, categorizes the proposal as "doing stupid things just to get their stupid name in a stupid record book," an example of Paulsen's skill at verbal repetition for effect (*ibid.*, 18).

Textural Comedy

In a limp effort at situational witticism, Paulsen strays from his original fictional method in later works, particularly the red hen pecking eight-year-old Anne Marie Pennysworth "Annie" Clark's toes and her stifled "talker" during an uneasy silent trudge through western Pennsylvania in *Woods Runner.* Like the tobacco spit encrusting beards of tinker/spy Abner McDougal and Matthew, the riverboat captain, Louie's body filth and crude belching and slurping in *Harris and Me* revive the raillery toward an unsanitary curmudgeon. Of the author's judicious, sometimes raunchy diction, Elizabeth MacCallum, a reviewer for Toronto's *Globe and Mail,* deemed the language "sardonic and absurd" (MacCallum, 1994, C17). She characterized juvenile japes as inane slapstick, a style of fun lost on politically correct adults: "So dead-on, so disrespectful of social propriety and order, so laced with bad language and unacceptable prejudices, that it's bound to be banned in exactly the places where it is most needed" (*ibid.*). Her analysis exonerates Paulsen for breaching adult boundaries and burrowing into the mindset of tweens and teens.

Paulsen at times overworks facetiousness, for example, the group laugh at Dr. Mark Harrison's lack of hardihood in *The Transall Saga.* In *Rodomonte's Revenge,* a banal genetics quip pictures the villain as a "computer-generated pituitary case" conceived by a VCR and a Game Boy (Paulsen, *Rodomonte's,* n.p.). The author salts *The Time Hackers* with one-liners as ineffective as "They don't like it if you miss homeroom even if you're dead" (Paulsen, *Time,* 2). In addition to death jokes, the hijinks of Dorso Clayman and Frank Tate involves the boys in a prurient search for pornography in the form of "anatomical studies" of Cleopatra, Helen of Troy, and Nefertiti (*ibid.*, 6, 25). Although *Kirkus Reviews* raved at the levity and Diana Pierce okayed *The Time Hackers* in a review for *School Library Journal,* Cindy Welch informed *Booklist* that the scanty plot and complex science seemed too mature for tween readers.

In *Pilgrimage on a Steel Ride,* the author cranks up the scale of humor, as with the reek of garlic-eating Chinese soldiers during the Korean War that warns a U.S. night patrol of a Communist raid. He turns jest on himself as both army veteran and adventurer and manages a chuckle at "four million mosquitoes [that] found me" and sneers at RV drivers as "road-ignorant old [farts]" (Paulsen, *Pilgrimage,* 161, 142). On the light side of ridicule, he admits that he belongs in the "old fart" category, in part because of his late-in-middle-age investment in a used Harley-Davidson for motoring the 10,000 miles from New Mexico to Alaska and back. In a second swipe at his biking skills, Paulsen concedes that "a set of training wheels wouldn't be out of line" (*ibid.,* 148). The self-skewering quips personalize his witty quest tale while down-playing any accolades for his prowess.

See also Harris and Me.

Source

Flaherty, Dolores, and Roger Flaherty. "When Gary Paulsen Went Utterly Mad and Ran the Iditarod," *Chicago Sun-Times* (26 February 1995): 19.

Kelley, Annie J. "Gary Paulsen: A Book Can Change a Life," *Battle Creek* [Michigan] *Enquirer* (11 February 2011).

MacCallum, Elizabeth. "Rude, Outrageous: An Ideal Book for Kids," [Toronto] *Globe and Mail* (5 February 1994): C17.

"Six Kids and a Stuffed Cat," *Publishers Weekly* 263:8 (22 February 2016).

Iditarod

Paulsen's recounting of the 1,153-mile race from Anchorage to Nome, Alaska, engulfed the competitor and his team in what critic Laura Thompson called "the indestructible, mysterious magnitude of North America" (Thompson, 1995, 11). Enthrallment in the wild introduced to his style in *Winterdance, Ice Race,* and *Dogsong* an eerie impressionism that he termed "primitive exaltation" at the symbiosis between musher and dog ("Gary," 2010). The annual contest dates to January 27, 1925, when twenty mushers relayed a 20-pound cylinder of vaccine from Anchorage to Nome to stave off a diphtheria epidemic that devastated Inuit children. Traveling along the icy Yukon River in blizzard conditions before Norwegian gold prospector Gunner E. Kaassen, the lead dog Balto, a black and white Siberian husky, pulled the sled 54 miles. On February 2, Kaassen passed the relay to Leonhard "Sepp" Seppala, a Norwegian driver for a mining firm, and his lead dog Togo, another Siberian husky. Coordination of human and canine efforts established an esprit de corps that invested the competition for years to come.

During a run on the historic trail in spring 1983, Paulsen conducted an inward search and tapped into obscure rivers of self. Like a Taoist exegesis, his writing answers unfathomable questions and produces a formless, wordless notion of being truly *homo sapiens*. He assured Caroline Scott, an interviewer for the London *Sunday Times,* that the effort was transformative: "You go back 10,000 years in your mind and body. You don't sleep right ever again" (Scott, 1996, 12). After advancing some 20,000 feet over the Alaska Range, he experienced a union with the cosmos: "I felt this tap on my shoulder. I turned around, and it was the sun" (Buchholz, 1995, 53). The warmth left him feeling "part of the sun," an association that stimulated joy and energy (*ibid.*).

On the Trail

In *Ice Race,* the author reiterated historical admiration for Balto and Togo. Over a half century after the first Iditarod, he chose Wilson as lead dog. Paulsen identified in his huskies "a kind of core toughness. It isn't macho and it's not phony" (Metella, 1993, D6). During winter practice, he remained busy "feeding dogs, taking care of dogs, taking care of their feet, each foot on twenty dogs, eighty feet, every hour changing booties" (Paulsen, *Pilgrimage,* 40). In warm weather, he replicated the rigors of 18-hour winter runs by training his team first to pull an old Schwinn bicycle, then a wood cart and a car chassis over dry ground. Of the athleticism of his team, Paulsen declared, "The Iditarod is not really a sled race, nor a race of people, nor of money, nor of macho idiocy, nor of feminine strength, nor intellect, nor bravery. It is a dog race … the base of the equation is dogs" (Jensen, 1999, 11). After the initial run and an unscheduled halt in a blizzard on the Bering Sea, a selfless cheering of canine heart dominated his writing.

For the maiden run, Paulsen planned for on-the-trail needs. He packed light with extra harness line and safety gear, headlamp batteries, clothing, a thermos and Walkman, and plenty of meat for himself and his charging team. In the description of Randy Lewis, a journalist for the *Los Angeles Times,* the author made a "Keystone Kops–like leap out of the starting gate" (Lewis, 1994, 1). Then, on departing the starting chutes in Anchorage at some ten miles per hour, he missed a turn and misdirected other mushers. Journalist Susan Stevens reported: "Wilson ran wild around Anchorage, leading Paulsen and all 140 feet of dog team through the city's neighborhoods past astonished homeowners for four hours" (Stevens, 2002, 1). Fortunately for his writing of *Winterdance,* self-skewering humor endeared him to fans, who cheered for the fumble-footed underdog.

Paulsen recouped by replacing the half-wild Wilson with Cookie, a sustained leader. Along the route to the Rhone and Yukon rivers, over Happy Canyon switchbacks, and into the 20-mile Rainy Pass, he saw caribou, wolves, and moose, which he described as large as "a Buick with legs" (Paulsen, *Woodsong,* 62). He and his pack braved dogfights, shock, rigor, sleep deprivation, and frostbite from cold as low as -83 degrees. For energy and warmth, he drank tea and consumed protein burgers formed from meat and raisins and thawed on a portable stove. His balance of details with impressions intrigued both adult and teen adventure readers, establishing his place as a master of a broad nonfiction genre packed with comic asides, notably, "I was unofficially voted the least likely to get out of Anchorage" (Lewis, 1994, 1).

Learning from Dogs

For two and a half weeks on the trail with stops every 60 miles, the author shot 750 slides and kept writing in longhand his reactions to the race. Running in view of Mount McKinley, he experienced hallucinations of an Inuit elder and an apotheosis of the canine spirit. He recalled, "It's so much more than people know. You enter a state of primitive exultation. You are never normal again. It's an astonishing thing that happens to you" (Stevens, 1991, 1). At trail's end, he wanted to go on.

The satisfaction of narrating the competition in *Wintersong* preceded a sequel, *Winterdance: The Fine Madness of Running the Iditarod,* a classic of extreme sports. The plot describes the author's growing love of mushing and a realization that his experience running teams in Minnesota readied him for a larger dog pack and professional competition. Because of cardiac disease that caused his collapse in Boston's Logan Airport, he gave up competitive trail running, sighing, "God, I miss it. I really do" (Lewis, 1994, 1). In place of the natural, primal thrill of mushing, he turned to second best—sailing.

In *Puppies, Dogs, and Blue Northers,* Paulsen reflects on his memories of dogsledding and identifies females like Cookie as the cagier leaders and males like Rex as the stronger pullers. He relishes teams that are "quiet, wonderfully silent, when they run; mile after mile in soft winter nights," a scenario he returned to in the picture book *Dogteam* (Paulsen, *Puppies,* 3). A series of verbs—yip, bark, keen, scream, whine, wheeze, growl, harmonize—particularize husky songs that owners identify immediately in a cacophony of up to 800 dogs. For its tender regard for huskies, the *Chicago Sun-Time* approved Paulsen's memoir for its warm, pristine, and touching presentation of love and respect for animals.

See also dogs.

Source

Buchholz, Rachel. "The Write Stuff," *Boys' Life* (December 1995): 28–29, 53.
"Gary Paulsen In-Depth Written Interview," https://www.teachingbooks.net/interview.cgi?id=91&a=1, 2010.
Jensen, Joyce. "From Fences to Fast Getaways, the All-Time All-American Greats," *New York Ties* (6 November 1999): 11.
Lewis, Randy. "He Owes It All to Librarians and Dogs," *Los Angeles Times* (31 July 1994): 1.
Metella, Helen. "I Write the Way I Used to Run," *Edmonton Journal* (31 October 1993): D6.
Scott, Caroline. "Gary Paulsen," [London] *Sunday Times* (21 July 1996): 12.
Stevens, Susan. "Adventure Author Gives Audience Wild Ride," [Arlington Heights, Illinois] *Daily Herald*] (14 March 2002): 1.
Thompson, Laura. "It's a Dog's Life," [London] *Sunday Times* (5 March 1995): 11.

integrity

From the beginning of his writing career in young adult literature, Paulsen realized the need for truth-telling child literature, an awareness that guided his grim scenes in the historical novel *The Legend of Bass Reeves* and in the cautionary tale about firearms in *The Rifle*. He stated, "It's the only place where you can be realistic and have it accepted as art" (Carey 1996). He resolved, "I couldn't lie" because children respond to honesty, such as the danger of farm work around bulls in *Harris and Me* and the initiation of the Gary character into coitus in *The Beet Fields* (Levy, 2002, E1). His bargain with the truth produced insights into juvenile delinquency in *Winterkill* and *Popcorn Days and Buttermilk Nights,* bullying in *Captive!* and *Danger on Midnight River,* parental favoritism in *The Boy Who Owned the School,* single mothers in *The Glass Café* and *Canyons,* and families divided by divorce in *Notes from the Dog, Hatchet,* and *The River.*

Honest dialogue and glimpses of stoicism and child soldiery yielded hair-raising adventure stories and historical fiction about young people embroiled in the American Revolution, Oregon Trail, Mexican War, Indian Wars, U.S. Marshal service, and Civil War that refused to flinch at bloodshed. In the words of Indian trader Jason Grimes, rescuer of the protagonist in *Mr. Tucket,* "Kinda keep the air clean around here, if we talk straight" (Paulsen, *Mr.,* 35). As mentor to 14-year-old Francis Alphonse Tucket, Grimes insists that speaking the truth avoids trouble. On an intrinsic level, Wil Neuton, protagonist of *The Island,* lives a Shakespearean verity from *Hamlet,* "To thine own self be true." Faithful to his inner drive, he refuses to abandon a savvy path to self-discernment, even when his parents call in a counselor to diagnose his sudden hermetic behavior.

Critics approved of Paulsen's straightforward narratives for dispensing wisdom, such as the grandmother's advice to Kristina Jorgenson about brave widowhood and single motherhood in *The Quilt* and Magpie's preparation of Coyote Runs for his first Apache raid in *Canyons.* Ian Chipman, a reviewer for *Booklist,* applauded *Woods Runner* for the political balance of "scalping bands of Iroquois, pillaging squads of mercenary Hessians, and a few hardy, helpful rebels, … the sobering realities of the Revolution," all elements in the eight-year colonial separation from British authority (Chipman, 2010, 72). Chipman concluded that Paulsen's setting of frontier combat at the Pennsylvania homesteads of 13-year-old Samuel Lehi Smith and eight-year-old Anne Marie Pennysworth "Annie" Clark redefined heroism as a blend of coping and endurance. Through realism, the author introduced readers to the role of young patriots in the chancy war that preceded national independence of the U.S. from England.

Character Elements

Paulsen's historical fiction of the colonial era establishes a human need for faith and self-reliance, the backbone of character. By introducing Sam to a network of spies, tinker and peddler Abner McDougal indicates the value of men like Micah the farmer and Matthew the riverboat captain, whom the boy "can trust … with your life," an allusion to shifting loyalties during the War for Independence rather than a hyperbole (Paulsen, *Woods,* 125). Without lengthy consideration, Matthew agrees to provide a home for Annie Clark if Abner and Sam "get scragged," a euphemism for "killed" (*ibid.,* 126). The ease of life-sustaining pledges reveals overt qualities in people who fight on the colonists' side. In thanks for brotherhood, in 1779, Sam returns to the war as rifleman and medic for Morgan's Rifles because "I owe," a reference to the reciprocity of aid to those in need (*ibid.,* 160).

For *The Legend of Bass Reeves,* the author declares that the famed slave-turned-deputy U.S. marshal "was honest and honorable, and just flat tough.… He rejected countless bribes" (Sides, 2006, B7). The description rings true of Paulsen. New York Library children's librarian Margaret Tice acknowledged the author's authenticity because "he's always lived his life on the edge and survived true adventures" (*ibid.*). In an evaluation for the *Cincinnati Post,* Maureen Conlan celebrated the author's values: "It's not so much that he writes about them as that he lives them and his observations and writing spring from that" (Conlan, 1995, B1). For his purity of purpose and dedication to troubled youths, readers flock to his appearances at book stores and schools.

Of the post–Vietnam war era in *The Crossing,* the author progressed to more complicated urban realities on the Tex-Mex border. In a drunken stupor, army sergeant Robert S. Locke deals truthfully with a complex face-off at the Santa Fe Bridge between authorities of Juárez, Mexico, and El Paso, Texas. While dragging 13-year-old Manny Bustos, a mestizo sneak thief, away from an alley, Locke must defog his brain to satisfy official inquiries about the abduction. To a local policeman, Locke adapts the truth of the theft of his wallet from his pocket to a benign tale of a boy guiding him to the bridge. The police officer, an experienced questioner, concludes "All people lie about all things all the time," a jaded response to an on-the-spot fabrication (Paulsen, *Crossing*, 55). For Manny as well, there is no time for integrity in a place where cooks sell burritos with meat reputedly chopped from beasts in the bullring and hungry children's lives count for little more than amusement for thugs and sexual predators.

Contemporary Settings

In a graphic view of children of the über rich, *Sisters/Hermanas* contrasts Rosa, an illegal immigrant like Manny from Mexico City, with the coddled Traci Barrancs, daughter of a well-heeled elitist. The mother's advice for success hinges on a snobbish view of female aspirations:

> To marry money. To have a wonderful, successful life with a fancy home and drive a Mercedes and have servants and travel all over the world--- to the clean places, of course, not the dirty ones, none of the messy places like India or Africa or China or South America [Paulsen, *Sisters*, 26–27].

By vaunting appearances over reality, Mrs. Barrancs sets up Traci for a pursuit of pleasure and privilege and disappointment in a vapid beauty myth based on eternal youth. Paulsen returns to the theme of wisdom in *Six Kids and a Stuffed Cat*, in which a close setting in a school bathroom provides what *Publishers Weekly* called "opportunities for thought and conversations about self-honesty, stereotypes, and making friends in unexpected situations" ("Six," 2016).

From his increasingly risky challenges to self and stamina, Gary Paulsen surmised much about his motivation and values, the inner workings of the spirit that permeate the story of Mark Harrison in *The Transall Saga*. In *Winterdance: The Fine Madness of Running the Iditarod*, the writer pushes himself so close to the edge in a 17.5-day race over the Alaskan outback that he achieves a breakthrough in introspection. He prioritizes facets of his life in the Minnesota wilds with wife Ruth Ellen Wright and son Jim and resolves to avoid money grubbing and social climbing. By rejecting materialism, greed, and technological advances, he chooses the straightforward path blazed by philosopher Henry David Thoreau in *Walden*: "Our life is frittered away by detail. Simplify, simplify." During Paulsen's rehabilitation from cardiovascular disease, his unaffected household proved both satisfying and salubrious to his heart.

Integrity crops up frequently in the author's descriptions of historical and fictional characters, as with the reformed fibber Kevin Spencer of *Liar, Liar,* boys curious about Santa Claus in *A Christmas Sonata,* and Charley Goddard, the idealistic teen in *Soldier's Heart* who lied about his age to enlist in the First Minnesota Volunteers at the onset of the Civil War. For self-sacrifice, John, the title figure in *Nightjohn,* intercedes for Mammy, who bears the lash for teaching the alphabet. By confessing his part in educating Sarny, he accepts the prescribed punishment—the lopping of his middle toes. His nobility emerges the next night, when he increases Sarny's skills to H, the eighth letter, evidence that alphabet lessons will continue to enlighten slaves despite threats of dismemberment. An historical model of commitment, John's courage empowers Sarny to devote her distinctive voice to an unflinching history of slavery and resistance.

See also Sarny.

Source

Carey, Joanna. "A Born Survivor Joanna Carey Meets the Engaging Best-selling American Author Gary Paulsen," *The* [Manchester] *Guardian* (28 May 1996).

Chipman, Ian. "Woods Runner," *Booklist* 106:9–10 (1 January 2010): 72.

Conlan, Maureen. "A Writer with Stories to Fill Two Lifetimes," *Cincinnati Post* (15 April 1995): B1.

Edmonds, Arlene. "Deltas Open Festival with Discussion about 'Nightjohn,'" *Philadelphia Tribune* (13 November 1998): D1.

Levy, Paul. "One for the Books," [Minneapolis] *Star Tribune* (30 October 2002): E1.

Sides, Anne Goodwin. "On the Road and Between the Pages, an Author Is Restless for Adventure," *New York Times* (26 August 2006): B7.

"Six Kids and a Stuffed Cat," *Publishers Weekly* 263:8 (22 February 2016).

The Island

Lacking his usual brio, Paulsen treads unsteadily into realism with *The Island.* He opens the novel about a lone spot in Sucker Lake near Pinewood, Wisconsin, with a nonfiction explanation of variations in earth's crust during the Pleistocene or Ice Age, a link centering humankind in a vastly old cosmos. The move 160 miles north from Madison to Pinewood jolts the Neuton family and impels Wil to seek peace and harmony on a horseshoe-shaped blip of land. The author builds contrast between the boy's need for a haven and the father's loopy "back-to-the-land" projects, which vary from growing cauliflower and chinchillas for profit to Neuton's Pinewood Berry Farm, a source of quality "berries, straw, razz, and blue" (Paulsen, *Island,* 41). At length, Wil escapes household discontent and loses himself in the mysteries of heron life.

NEUTON GENEALOGY

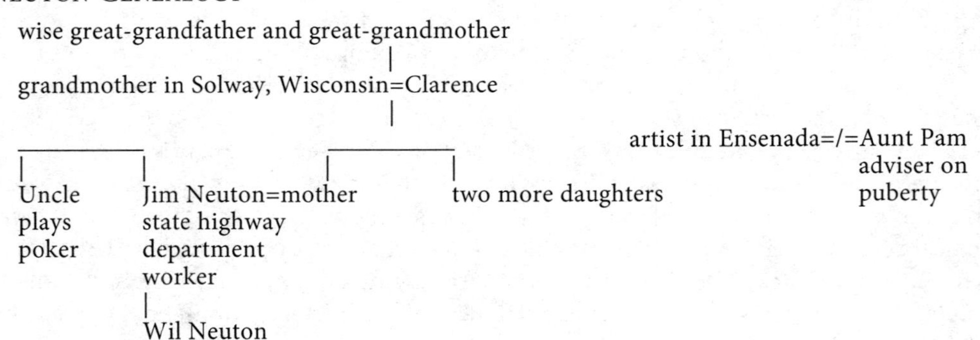

At a decisive point in his maturation, Wil comes to treasure an island that "had become a big deal" (*ibid.,* 57). Key to his absorption in nature lore is the stillness that precedes "[letting] his mind roll," a form of immersion in "a second of rightness" that the author echoes in his autobiographical memories in *Caught by the Sea, Dogteam,* and *Woodsong* (*ibid.,* 49). By studying a heron devouring a frog, the boy knows a "satisfaction that there could be mystery like that" (*ibid.,* 50). Contrasting the transcendence of a serene day of divergent thinking, Paulsen juxtaposes a TV program featuring a talking, singing, dancing car, "an awful show" that exemplifies the author's disdain for ignorant media entertainment (*ibid.,* 57).

Learning from Observation

Paulsen uses Wil as a model of logic based on observation, especially his delight in "rain tracks," sunfish, and the belief that "it took lots of solutions to solve just one problem," a conclusion he shares with backpacker Mark Harrison in *The Transall Saga* (*ibid.,* 101, 76). An unattributed critique in the *Hutchinson* (Kansas) *News* stated that the author set out to prove "that knowledge and peace can be found in nature ... can calm us and help us think straight," a simplistic analysis of a complex psychological situation ("In Defense," 2010). In the cafe in Pinewood, Wil acquires more from music when he can't hear the lyrics. In the farmers gathered for morning coffee, he recognizes a primitive strength covered by cracked, dirty skin and blended into voices discussing rainfall on crops. At dinner, he epitomizes the sounds of his parents' voices when they discuss the setbacks of residing in a place as outback as Pinewood. Wil dubs the tense discussion "cobra questions" and recognizes when his mother's "voice was a little too controlled, too tight" (Paulsen, *Island,* 71, 128). The lack of interest of Jim Neuton and his wife in their son's rapture in the island increases Wil's need to escape the house and camp out for a few nights in solitude, "almost ... as if he were coming home" (*ibid.,* 79). Ironically, the parents diagnose his retreat as neurosis rather than mental health.

The protagonist's skill at trial and error mirrors projects that Paulsen apparently dredges up from boyhood, including studying how fast bluegill learn about nibbling toes and baiting an ant hill with the remains of canned stew, an experiment that Mark Harrison replicates in *The Transall Saga.* By bracing a rowboat with driftwood into a lean-to and building a fire pit, Wil readies himself for a mental trial—meditation by thinking of "a wonderful, peaceful blankness" (*ibid.,* 81). The result, a dreamscape of his grandmother, recalls the author's adoring relationship with his Norwegian grandmother, Alida Peterson Moen, in *The Cookcamp, The Quilt,* and *Alida's Song.* By experimenting with a character study and mixing watercolors, Wil validates the arts:

To paint.
  To write.
    To know.
      To be. (*ibid.,* 99).

The growth of humanistic creativity informs him of greater spiritual depths and excites his curiosity about nature.

Perspective on Life

At the novel's climax, Wil's abrupt decision to move to the island seems far-sighted, but stirs fears in his parents of drugs, sex, and cults. His dread of "somehow [losing] what I am" anticipates the realization that "they wouldn't understand" (*ibid.,* 116, 126). Their sniping reminds him of a three-character play, "Bickerbits," that dramatizes the generational divide between parent and child and a resulting sadness. With a deft segue, the author simulates the virulent quarrel with the glimpse of a snapping turtle charging a sunfish, a symbol of human dissension and a token strong-over-weak vision. Susan's arrival with paints and pencils restores Wil's tranquility. More significant to views of parenting, her family accepts Wil and his need for natural beauty as an exemplar of "somebody who had the light on him" or "one of the thirsty ones," a canny explanation of his need to observe more of the island (*ibid.,* 145, 147).

Philosophical after his fight with Ray Bunners, a stereotypical lunkhead, Wil develops regard for individual perspective along with the stirrings of desire for Susan. He has the maturity to face his father nonviolently and to explain a need to "fill the empty places" (*ibid.*, 160). The fractious conclusion yanks Wil out of isolation and harmony into print and electronic media and into his father's admiration. The simple resolution of a coming-of-age episode earned tepid responses from Colby College teacher Edwin J. Kenney Jr., in a critique for the *New York Times Book Review* and even less enthusiasm from the *Bulletin of the Center for Children's Books.* With more appreciation for the Thoreauesque retreat into self, Paulsen biographer and critic Gary M. Salver summarized the story as "an effort to step back from [reality], to examine and understand its essential nature" (Salvner, 1996).

See also ambition; storytelling.

Source

"In Defense of Getting Outdoors," *Hutchinson* [Kansas] *News* (20 April 2010).
Lounds, Sue. "St. Johns Students Earn Honors in Writing Contest," *Lansing State Journal* (2 June 2013).
Salvner, Gary M. *Presenting Gary Paulsen.* New York: Twayne, 1996.
Vogel, Mark, and Anna Creadick. "Family Values and the New Adolescent Novel," *English Journal* 82:5 (September 1993): 37.

kenning

Paulsen's titles lean heavily on kenning—*Winterkill, The Haymeadow, Dogsong, Winterdance, The Cookcamp, The Foxman,* and *Woodsong*—a transformative wordplay that stimulates his oeuvre with precise imagery and vitality. The composite figures of speech, according to specialist Jonathan Davis-Secord, produce "a deeply allusive simile compressed into a single compound word or phrase" (Davis-Secord, 2016, 19). Paulsen turns the tropes into literary insights, as with these models:

- moneywood and winterstories in *Clabbered Dirt, Sweet Grass*
- smell-scrub in *Popcorn Days and Buttermilk Nights*
- Sunacres in *Sarny*
- ache-joy, kicked-pushed, and shit-kid in *The Beet Fields*
- whole-life-night in "Rape"
- own-love-tough in *Tracker*
- heady-musk-flush in "Aunt Caroline"
- sisterdog in *Woodsong*
- day-heat and smell-feel in *The Island*
- winternight, dogcold, and dognight in *Dogteam.*

The one-word metaphors that derive from Viking poesy suit the raw atmosphere and impromptu style of mythological and eighth-century heroic narrative. The Icelandic *Edda* and Anglo-Saxon *The Seafarer* date to the wandering harper or storyteller, who mesmerized audiences with creative synonyms called "kenning," from the Old Norse verbal for "knowing." Examples enhance pictorial accuracy, as with "breast-care" for sorrow, "last-words" for eulogy, "cold-grains" for hail, "twilight-spoiler" for dragon, "worth-memory" for honor, "all-tide" for forever, and "chest-locker" for breast. *Beowulf* alone contains 1,070 such compounded tropes from the gleeman's wordhoard.

In modern times, wordplay flourishes in a range of expressions as disparate as "skydance" and "heartlight" in film and music, "wishwell" and "wife-loss" in modern poetry, "pigskin" and "B-ball" in sports, "whiteout" in weather forecasting, and "washday"" and "babyland" from genial advertising jingles. In 1953, fantacist J.R.R. Tolkien revived Scandic word splicing in *The Lord of the Rings* with the name Grima Wormtongue and in *The Homecoming of Beorhtnoth* with "troll-shape" and "hell-walker." Irish lyricist-translator Seamus Heaney vivified the concept of a skeleton with the two-element kenning "bone-house" and an "iron-flash" to indicate a clash of swords.

So too does Paulsen engineer semantic devices, significantly, the merged nouns for "dogsister" and "dogmother" in *My Life in Dog Years,* "thought-idea" and "thought-grow" in the epilogue of *Six Kids and a Stuffed Cat,* "scutpuppy" in *Notes from the Dog,* and "dream-run" in *Dogsong* to express the hallucinogenic effect of guiding huskies along the trail. The 13-year-old sled runner in "Wolfdreams," a story in the February 2017 issue of *Boys' Life,* intuits from the galloping "night-ghosts, moon-ghosts" that stream alongside his sled a welter of "thought-words," an introduction to his unvoiced instincts. For the title *Cowpokes and Desperadoes*, Paulsen taps Western American flair for graphic compounds, as found in "roundup," "gunslinger" and "cutthroat." At a fearful moment in a cardiac test in *Winterdance,* Paulsen can "smell-taste" the "copper-blue" of death (Paulsen, *Winterdance,* 254).

For a more lyrical, playful effect in the picture book *Dogteam*, Paulsen applies repetition and alliteration to "did you did you did you did you" and a visual string of kennings:

> They come alongside in the moonlight, moonwolves, snowwolves, nightwolves, they run with us, pace the dogs, pace our hearts and our lives and then turn, turn away in the blue dark [Paulsen, *Dogteam*, n.p.].

The coupling of Paulsen's kenning, repeated roots and consonance, and the conceit of pacing hearts magnifies the nocturnal beauty that the narrative spiritualizes. Before the team reaches home, the *tour de force* passage returns to gentle humor with "dogsmiles, doglaughs," a personification of the canine display of human merriment (*ibid.*). For the dog master, the exercise constitutes a "dance. Through the trees, in and out" as "they fly away and away and away," a coordinated effort graceful in its traversing of the snow-decked landscape (*ibid.*).

Paulsen's wordcraft flaunts a cavalier attitude toward merging elements into tropes, as with Jacob Freisten's fantasy of hospitalization from "car-foot," the result of being run over by a vehicle in *The Boy Who Owned the School,* and the "white-blink of arctic ice," a hint at snow blindness in *Shelf Life: Stories by the Book* (Paulsen, *Boy,* 16; *Shelf,* 6). By eliding words—farm wife Kristina Jorgenson's plaintive "dowhatwillIdowhatwillIdo" in *The Quilt* and "thoughttrue" and "timewhen" in the Korean War veteran's storytelling in *Fishbone's Song*—the author characterizes a surreal elision in the main characters' thought processes. At his most incisive dramatizing, Paulsen makes multiple use of the name Nightjohn. For both title and main character, the compounded noun creates a dual meaning: the black-skinned wanderer depends on darkness to conceal his ditch-school, a make-do classroom lighted by glowing pine knots. The metaphoric night of human bondage ends in 1863 with the Emancipation Proclamation, but the African American story lives on in John's pupil, Sarny, whose aged hands record the struggle to thwart the enslaver.

Source

Davis-Secord, Jonathan. *Joinings: Compound Words in Old English Literature.* Toronto: University of Toronto Press, 2016.

legend

The place of myth, folklore, talk-story, story-song, and chronicle in Paulsen's philosophy falls between extremes as historic as King Tut in *Time Benders* and Norwegian immigration in *The Winter Room* and as unlikely as a firebird in *Flight of the Hawk* or a giant prehistoric beast in *The Creature of Black Water Lake*. The author tackles the dividing line between legend and biography with his commentary on Pennsylvania gunsmith Cornish McManus in *The Rifle* and on a black deputy U.S. marshal in Indian Territory in *The Legend of Bass Reeves*. In the latter, by differentiating for readers the novelized portion of historical fiction, the author accounts for episodes that fill in the gaps in a remarkable Western hero. Educator Janis Flint-Ferguson, in a book review for *Kliatt*, recommends classroom application of "the discussion of truth and legend that Paulsen presents," such as the ingenuity of Dr. Mark Harrison, formulator of a vaccine for the Ebola virus in *The Transall Saga* (Flint-Ferguson, 2006, 12).

For the orphan Manny Bustos, a scrawny mestizo urchin in *The Crossing*, the legendary agility of Manuel the prizefighter fades to second place beside Juárez hero Pancho Villa, the hit-and-run raider who shot up the Mexican border town in April and May 1911 in defiance of oppressive wealth of hacienda owners. The boy envisions "all the horses coming in abreast and the men firing and Pancho in front with his large sombrero and the silver pistol" (Paulsen, *Crossing*, 63). Just as Paulsen pictures Manny fantasizing about renaming himself Pancho in honor of the peasant juggernaut, the writer flaunts history and literary studies of explorers Kit Carson, Captain Cook, and Jim Bridger and the Yellow Rose of Texas, a famed tauntress reputed to have distracted General Santa Anna during the Battle of San Jacinto on April 21, 1836. In admiration for past voyagers, warriors, and freedom fighters, Paulsen discounts the modern reliance on electronic truth, which tends to turn valiant figures into video game caricatures like those in *Rodomonte's Revenge* and, to a lesser degree, in *The Seventh Crystal*.

With more realism in *Woods Runner*, Paulsen speaks of the hunters, trappers, settlers, and natives who disappear on the dense Pennsylvania frontier, a legendary vanishing of a few "gone to the woods" in the style of Daniel Boone (Paulsen, *Woods*, 5). One such backwoodsman, whom the boy studied when he was ten, fidgeted in the company of buyers in a store before gliding way on silent moccasins "to become part of the forest" to escape prying eyes (*ibid.*, 6). The apocryphal tone of the exodus foreshadows Samuel Lehi Smith's naturalistic love of solitude and mastery of game trails and roads. His skills lead him out of danger in New York City, which the British commandeer during the American Revolution. Paulsen reprised the horrors of wartime in "Stop the Sun" and *The Foxman*, in which storytelling by elders informs youth of gallant episodes, epic battles, psychological stress, and the tragic waste of human life.

Over a unique metaphysical genre, Paulsen perused the elusive nature of memory. He created the story of 15-year-old Brennan Cole in *Canyons*, an intuitive teen who rescues a centuries-old skull of the teen Apache raider Coyote Runs from ignominy and secures it on sacred ground. A compelling story, Paulsen's novel turns a psychic experience into a glimpse of American crimes against First Peoples. With more history as a basis, the author honored a black deputy U.S. marshal in *The Legend of Bass Reeves*, a forgotten Western hero who inspired "no epic films or drums or music, no last words or sweeping eternal thoughts. He was there. And then he was gone" (Paulsen, *Legend*, 137). The image reflects the ephemeral nature of heroism, which lingers in the eyes of witnesses before its metamorphosis into cautionary tale, patriotic lore, or epic novel or film.

Instinctive Lore

To retrieve the fading past, the author paints broad swaths of antiquity unbounded by human time keeping. In *Dogsong*, a fusion of present reality with a mammoth hunt by prehistoric Eskimos, he questions the source and magnetism of shamanic truths. Enshrined in the memories of the elder Oogruk reside "songs for all of everything," an Inuit lyric tradition that villagers have largely abandoned (Paulsen, *Dogsong*, 16). Randy Bush, a reviewer for *CU Commons*, cites a theory that such traditional myth derives, not in response to trivial problems, but from a subconscious unease with pettiness and insignificance, the ills of the present. Out of a visceral need for worth and consequence, mythographers like Oogruk frame narrative that affirms the bare bones of creation. Bush compares the boy musher Russel Susskit, Oogruk's pupil, and his transcendental moments to the visions of Black Elk, the Oglala Lakota priest and author of *Black Elk Speaks,* North America's first scripture.

Paulsen's respect for the lore of First Peoples permeates *The Legend of Red Horse Cavern* and *Woodsong.* Of a stirring dog run, the latter text incorporates three poetic lines from the Navajo beautyway, a ritual liturgy that blesses a seamless unity of all creation, which the author repeats in the story "The Grotto." In the visionary myth of *The Night the White Deer Died,* dreamer Janet Carson relives the legendary past in ephemeral reveries that both enthrall and terrify her. Elizabeth MacCallum, a reviewer for the Toronto *Globe and Mail,* found these attempts at metaphysics unconvincing. In her opinion, the motif of the recurrent night images that prophesy the death of Billy Honcho become "a cliche-ridden, unconvincing account of a victimized noble savage and an over-sensitive modern kid" (MacCallum, 1990, C20).

The author returned to the lyric Navajo beautyway chant in *This Side of Wild: Mutts, Mares, and Laughing Dinosaurs*, concluding, "All around me is beauty" (Paulsen, *This Side,* 7). The cadence, calming in its simplicity, cherishes earthly reality as certainly in current times as it did in the dim past. At a more pensive incident in *Guts*, Paulsen characterizes the human species' loss of intuitive wisdom from immersion in television and the Internet: "We have grown away from knowledge, away from knowing what something is really like, toward knowing only what somebody else *says* it is like" (Paulsen, *Guts*, 53). He refers to such secondhand information as drama rather than reality.

Generating Tales

Permeating Paulsen's works, moments of legend formation mark illustrations of how and why folklore emanates from everyday experience, as with Samuel Lehi Smith's wordless encounter with a genuine frontiersman in *Woods Runner* and the stories of Great-Grandfather Barron's refusal to travel on foot or to own sheep in *The Haymeadow.* As reviewed by Neil Scotten for the *Edmonton Journal,* the latter novel debunks "the 'old man' myth," a holdover from Homeric epic and the Western code heroes dominant in John Wayne films (Scotten, 1992, B4). By placing the protagonist in parallel dilemmas of marauding coyotes and bears, Paulsen stresses the inherent valor in all youth, whether armed with their grandsire's Colt .45 or not.

Legend suits the tenor of Paulsen's two-book study of plantation slavery. In a first-person narration in *Nightjohn,* the child Sarny notes that people ruminate over the appearance of John, the mythic literacy instructor at Clel Waller's plantation, who arrives shackled and naked. Two suppositions—John was summoned by witchcraft or sent by God—endow the story with the murky beginnings of a legend or hagiography, the lore of sainthood. Whatever the provenance of the slaves' instructor, John walks into their milieu in front of Waller's horse: "Beautiful. So black he was like ... marble stone," an allusion to classic sculpture as bold as the Greek Charioteer at Delphi or Michelangelo's David in Florence, Italy (Paulsen, *Nightjohn,* 28). John's audacity startles Sarny, who can't imagine why he ran to freedom in the north and reverted to danger in the plantation South to open the "hidey-schools" that help others learn (*ibid.*, 57). Boosting his significance, rippling whip scars cover his back, evidence of martyrdom to the hazardous lawlessness of instructing the illiterate.

For *The Rifle,* the author focuses on colonial sharpshooter John Byam, a woodsman and volunteer in McNary's Rangers during the first five years of the Revolutionary War from 1776 to 1781. Like the juxtaposition of Great-Grandfather Barron with his Colt .45 in *The Haymeadow*, Byam's firearm sets the focus and tone of his biography. The plot accounts for legends of the infantryman and his flintlock, which won considerable acclaim for gunsmith Cornish McManus. Like the premise of horror tales, the story advances to Byam's demise from dysentery during the Revolutionary War and the shelving of the famed rifle in Sarah's attic, Paulsen's suggestion of the waning of vainglorious gun worship in American history. The narrative advances to subsequent owners and rifle users and to the suffering, depression, and death that ruin their lives and curtail their promise. At the book's violent conclusion, the unforeseen shooting death of 14-year-old Richard Allen Mesington leaves for young readers the conundrum of accidental misfirings of guns and the heart-rending aftermath.

See also history; *The Legend of Bass Reeves; Nightjohn.*

Source

Durichen, Pauline. "Review: *Canyons*," *Kitchener-Waterloo Record* (16 February 1991): H6.
Flint-Ferguson, Janis. "Review: The Legend of Bass Reeves," *Kliatt* 4 (July 20006): 12.
MacCallum, Elizabeth. "What We Need to Know about Natives," [Toronto] *Globe and Mail* (17 November 1990): C20.
Scotten, Neil. "A Feel-Good Story in a Simple World," *Edmonton Journal* (4 October 1992): B4.

The Legend of Bass Reeves

To inform young readers of the integrity and pluck of a peerless deputy U.S. marshal, Paulsen's three-part historical novel revives from legend black lawman Bass Reeves. With Gothic detail about Colt firepower, gut wounds, and relay stations for changing brands on stolen stock, the narrative introduces readers to the West at the height of out-of-control crime. Similar to the birthing of calves that begins Robert Newton Peck's *A Day No Pigs Would Die,* the initial scene places Bass near a cow in labor and describes a Southern superstition that canids can predict the future. Because a coyote warns Bass that "Things will change," he ponders the tangle of rules that "keep the colored down," lower in position and worth than their white owners (Paulsen, *Legend,* 6, 10). By novel's end, Paulsen proves that the change is beneficial to Reeves, Oklahoma, and the American frontier.

For authenticity, Paulsen inserts technical and period jargon—span of mules (pairs), full house (a pair plus three of a kind), swamper (laborer), get down on (dislike), worked out (crippled by labor), Jesus stick (sharpened throwing weapon)—and dialect terms as stark as "got a mad on for" to explain Comanche anger, "suckin' on something sour" for moody, and "cross fingers and spit on the ground" to seal a promise (*ibid.*, 26, 27). Through aphorism and example, Mammy educates Bass in "town manners," a form of subservience expected of blacks in communities like Paris, Texas (*ibid.,* 41). In addition to looking down while addressing whites, the boy masters the "darky shuffle," an aimless foot slide suggesting a nonthreatening witlessness (*ibid.,* 78). Because all parts of his coming of age aid him when he enters the U.S. marshal service, *Publishers Weekly* called the novel articulate and effective ("Legend," 2006, 76).

A Racial Mix

Paulsen's five-page history of federal government relationships with Native American tribes veers from narrative to rant directed at the injustice of the Indian Removal Act of 1830 and the Trail of Tears eight years later. His overly negative assessment of Indian Territory pictures a hellish terrain where "the tribes measured the distance in blood, in bodies" of members lost during a forced march from traditional lands to settlement in Oklahoma (Paulsen, *Legend*, 72). Contributing to the chaos of installing the Chickasaw, Creek, Cherokee, and Choctaw (not Cree) on unlivable land, criminals turn the expanse into a thieves' den where "life was unbelievably cheap" (*ibid.*, 73). The writer's sensationalized account of tribal deracination precedes Bass's arrival in Oklahoma at a perilous point in American frontier settlement. His native savvy along with wisdom from Mammy and Flowers saves him from risky encounters with whites.

Key to characterization in his late teens, Bass's memory and conscience set him apart from the savagery that prevails in Indian Territory. He defines himself as both a fleeing slave and man killer, but reveals his humanity in reflections on the Comanche torment of the Garnett girls and the Indians' skinning of a wagoneer at "Torture Bluff" (*ibid.*, 87). Remaining on the move for months, he turns his observations of gang hideouts and heavily armed marauders into an education in detective work. The teenager's climactic rescue of four-year-old Betty Two Shoes from wolves underscores Bass's homesickness for Mammy and an inner need for family, which the Creek offer at their sod hut in 1841. However, rather than stagnate, he spends the next 22 years running a ranch and "always studying, always learning" (*ibid.*, 103).

The Reeves Lineage

[N.B. Recorded names and dates vary from the author's data.]

Basse Washington
|
Parilee Washington Stewart=unnamed mate
b. 10/16/1821 in Tennessee
d. 1/28/1915 in Van Buren, Arkansas
|
Bass Reeves=Nellie Jennie Foreman Reeves
b. 7/1838 in Van Buren, Arkansas | b. 1840 in Texas
d. 1/12/1910 in Muskogee, Oklahoma | d. 3/19/1896 in Fort Smith, Arkansas
|
Bennie H.=Tess=/=lover
b. 1880 d. 1894
d. 1958

Robert and George A.
b. 1866 b. 1870
Newlan, Edgar, and William
1873 1876 1877–1942
Homer and Bass, Jr.
1882–1903 1887–1901
=Winnie Sumter Reeves
widowed boardinghouse keeper
b. 1861 in Oklahoma
m. 1900
|
Estella Sumter
b. 1887

Sally, Harriet, and Alis Mae,
b. 1864 b. 1868 1880–1966
Lula
1881–1899

LATE CAREER

Reeves's hardihood and perseverance and his skills at disguise and horsemanship direct his success as a U.S. lawman from May 10, 1875, to November 16, 1907, and as constable of Muskogee, Oklahoma, from 1907 to 1909. Living among Indians and monitoring the reckless banditry of outlaws and rustlers, he manages 3,000 apprehensions and 14 killings without the aid of a deputy. By seizing ten felons and shooting another two in one arrest, he earns from Judge Isaac Charles Parker of Fort Smith, Arkansas, the nickname "bargain-basement deputy" (*ibid.*, 110). Paulsen focuses details of shootouts by visualizing the marshal's search for Bob Dozier, Tom Story, and Jim Webb, all horse thieves and murderers:

- Bass killed Jim Webb in June 1884 near the Sacred Heart Mission in the Arbuckle Mountains of Oklahoma, where the dying killer offered the marshal his weapon and scabbard out of regard for the lawman's expertise.
- At the Delaware Bend Crossing of the Red River on the Texas-Oklahoma border in 1889, Bass outshot horse thief Tom Story in a draw-down.
- In 1891 in the Cherokee Hills of central Oklahoma, Bob Dozier, a serial killer, fell to Bass's Colt shot to the chest after the marshal pretended to be dead.

With the eye of a camera, the author follows hand and torso motions as Bass in action gets the most out of a stallion, two backup horses, a Colt .38–40, and a rifle.

Paulsen turns the tracking of 22-year-old Bennie Reeves into a poignant falling action. As marshal and father, Bass maintains personal integrity and holds his son to a high standard of obedience to the law. Just as Mammy insisted on adherence to slavery codes, the lawman makes Bennie accept responsibility for murdering his unfaithful wife Tess. The text enwraps the manhunt in the respectful compliments of others for Bass's honesty and toughness. *Bulletin of the Center for Children's Books* issued a review by Elizabeth Bush casting doubts that the lawman lacked "a few warts himself" and insists that serious readers "may have little patience with this fanciful account" (Bush, 2006, 89). Conversely, John Peters, a book critic for *Booklist*, declared the novel an "engrossingly told tale [that] fills in the unrecorded youth of an unjustly obscure historical figure" (Peters, 2006, 75).

Source

Burton, Art T. "Lawman Legend Bass Reeves: The Invincible Man Hunter," *Wild West* 19:5 (February 2007): 50–57.
Bush, Elizabeth. "The Legend of Bass Reeves," *Bulletin of the Center for Children's Books* 60:2 (October 2006): 89.
"The Legend of Bass Reeves," *Publishers Weekly* 253:30 (30 July 2006): 76.
Peters, John. "The Legend of Bass Reeves," *Booklist* 102 (1 June 2006): 75.

literacy

Paulsen writes convincingly of the benefit of literacy to the individual and promotes the concept that "Ignorance never works" (Lewis, 1994, 1). The idea comes full circle with a preventable shooting death in *The Rifle* and with Mark Harrison's need for a second language in *The Transall Saga*. In *The Island,* the author studies the yearning of Wil Neuton for experience in the wild. Like a professional biologist, Wil reaches for his notebook and, with the zeal of artist Jean-Jacques Audubon, records lasting impressions of a blue heron swallowing a frog. Repeatedly, Paulsen tells fans and journalists about the librarian who introduced him to recorded thoughts. To Joanna Carey, a journalist on staff of the Manchester *Guardian,* he exulted: "She gave me my brain. She gave me writing which I love. She gave me all the things I am now. She gave me the whole world. God, this lady was so neat!" (Carey, 1996).

Although his reading skills lagged behind his age group, at age 13, the author quickly evolved into a passionate bibliophile. In his canon, he portrays the need for word knowledge among slaves. From a practical standpoint, ignorance deprived bondsmen of understanding of the law, commerce, and religion. As Paulsen explains in *The Legend of Bass Reeves,* "No slave was allowed to read, so how could they know all the rules … [that] filled books that he couldn't read?," which includes the symbols of mathematics and games of poker (Paulsen, *Legend,* 9). To right the wrongs of bondage, Bass chooses flight, becoming a hunted man on his way to a real career. For counting cattle, he uses his fingers to add up to "fives … and fives of fives," a hand-based arithmetic system that dates to prehistoric herders (*ibid.,* 53). To succeed in law enforcement, he has "somebody read the warrants to him" (*ibid.,* 115).

For *Nightjohn,* the author lauds methods that circumvent the Southern slave's ignorance of numbers, words, and maps. He depicts primitive record keeping in Mammy's notched sticks, a system equivalent to saw-toothed beams, the Nez Perce string balls, and knotted "talking ropes" of the quipu, the Quechuan time-keeping method created in the South American Andes after 1100 B.C.E. Through the words and example of John, the literacy teacher, the author equates competence with letters and numbers with human dignity and self-assurance. John explains to Sarny, "To know things, for us to know things, is bad for them," a contrast between literacy and bondage, a foul system doomed to failure for dehumanizing preliterate black Africans (Paulsen, *Nightjohn,* 39).

Paulsen implies that slaves who can interpret words on paper are more likely to rebel against white corruption and demand human rights. In the sequel, *Sarny,* John's star pupil glories in comprehending biblical passages and in helping readership to "spread like fire in dry grass," an allusion to the withering plantation system during the abolitionist era (Paulsen, *Sarny,* 10). Essential to the upsurge of hope in the early 1860s are scraps of newspapers, which Sarny and her fellow slaves scour for information about emancipation and the Civil War. From totaling the names of the dead at Gettysburg, Sarny concludes that editors can lie to shape favorable opinions. Logic eases her fears that the Confederate army is winning the war. The opening of Sarny's Riverside School starts a groundswell in New Orleans, a center of post-war opportunity for freedmen.

The Educated Mind

In other works of historical fiction, the writer identifies the traits of the self-educated, as with Isaac, the hermetic frontiersman in *Woods Runner.* Employing Western Pennsylvania dialect, Isaac states his preference for evergreen tree infusions over "furriner tea from outside," his reference to English tea imported by the East India Company under a British tax, a cause of the American Revolution (Paulsen, *Woods,* 14). Out of courtesy to Abigail Smith, Isaac adds, "But thankee, missus" (*ibid.*). Paulsen amplifies the fact of meager colonial education with the backwoods lingo of Isaac and Coop and the limited training of Anne Marie Pennysworth "Annie" Clark, an eight-year-old war orphan. Annie excuses her faulty reading comprehension as a failure to fit letters into words, her term for advancement to Gestalt perceptions—from alphabet training to spelling and word recognition.

Paulsen dramatizes the role of language in enriching lives and behaviors of characters, as with the partial bilingualism of the Mexican orphan Manny Bustos, the illiterate mestizo beggar in *The Crossing,* and the multiple lingual skills of Norwegian-American women in *The Quilt.* For 13-year-old Samuel Lehi Smith, protagonist of *Woods Runner,* reading takes the place of institutional schooling. Because his parents, Abigail and Olin Smith, value literacy and the arts, they read aloud to him in their cabin west of city amenities. By the time that Sam can read, he thrills to "the joyous romp of words on paper" and consumes the family's books and those of other settlers in the valley (*ibid.,* 9). He intends to know more of the world and satisfy his vivid imagination. A parallel teen, 15-year-old Charley Goddard, protagonist of *Soldier's Heart,* has little classroom education, but enough to supply his mother with letters about basic training at Fort Snelling, Minnesota. His historic descriptions of army life among the First Minnesota Volunteers preserve the misconceptions of a teenager about boy soldiery.

The author promoted 21st-century literacy by publishing *Shelf Life: Stories by the Book,* an anthology producing funds for the ProLiteracy Worldwide effort, a global advocacy launched in Syracuse, New York, in 2002. Introducing the collection, he exulted in empowerment: "Words are alive—when I've found a story that I love, I read it again and again, like playing a favorite song over and over" (Paulsen, *Shelf,* 166). With reverence born of trust, he declared books life savers for expanding his horizons beyond battling alcoholic parents in a dismal apartment in the worst part of a northern Minnesota town to an immersion in mysteries, adventure, and history.

Into adulthood, Paulsen remained a devotee of free reading. In a witty fillip in *Culpepper's Cannon,* the author chortles at Dunc Culpepper for questioning his friend Amos Binder's literacy, to which Amos replies that he reads to attract girls. In the short story "Wolfdreams," Paulsen lauds a 13-year-old who reads during a two-hour bus ride to school, a daily journey he shares with Paulsen's son Jim. After witnessing student disgruntlement at being forced to read the same book as the rest of the class, the writer took offense at coercion. He stated that an individual's comprehension is self-correcting and declared, "Reading becomes attractive to kids when options are given to them" (Ward, 2012, 131).

Fictional Bibliophiles

In the introduction to *The Winter Room,* Paulsen reverenced the dual role of publishers and bibliophiles: "If books could have more, give more, be more, show more, they would still need readers" (Paulsen, *Winter,* 3). His memoir *The Cookcamp* distinguishes the desire for stories in early childhood with five-year-old Gary's mesmerism by picture books and Donald Duck comics. Harris Larson, a so-so reader in *Harris and Me,* scarfs up comic books, reveling in a story of Tarzan and "[filling] in the gaps by deductive reasoning based on the graphics" (Paulsen, *Harris,* 61). For *Tucket's Home,* the text provides a map of the U.S. frontier from 1857 to 1849 and calls on symbol interpretation of the legend as it applies to Western territories surrounding the Oregon Trail. The author's respect for first-person narrative like that of Francis Alphonse Tucket underscores admiration for personal composition, as with the main character's notebook in *Molly McGinty Has a Really Good Day* and for Grandma Alida Halverson's admonitory letters to her daughter in *The Cookcamp.*

For authenticity of research, Paulsen dignifies the writing that appeals to common folk, particularly *Farm Gazette,* the bible, and the book collection of Uncle David, an immigrant Norwegian farm laborer in *The Winter Room.* The author elevates to folk history a navigator's diary in *The Rock Jockeys,* in which Rick, J.D., and Spud piece together a gruesome coverage of cannibalism that followed the crash of a B-17 bomber. For the dog birthing scene in *Puppies, Dogs, and Blue Northers,* the author settles an anxious mind by sinking into Anthony Trollope's *The Pallisers,* a six-book saga about British aristocrats. The choice illustrates the bibliophile's broad choice of escapist reading.

EMPOWERING THE MIND

In an explanation of the human drive to read and write, the daring title figure from *Nightjohn* explains, "We all have to read and write so we can write about this—what they doing to us. It has to be written" (Paulsen, *Nightjohn,* 58). As a credo, John's resolve survives through his student Sarny, the chronicler still reading and writing at age 92. The slaves' advance from the alphabet to three-letter combinations—hid, fib, jab, had, big, bag—introduces pre-literate field hands to "how the words is to be looking and how the words is to be sounding," a simplified description of visual and aural vocabulary (*ibid.,* 60). Debbie Abilock, editor of *Knowledge Quest,* summarized the training as "the politics of reading," an empowerment of an otherwise lost generation (Abilock, 2002, 7).

Upon learning how slaves studied pilfered letters and mail order catalogs, Paulsen magnified the struggle for literacy as the keystone of freedom. He wrings pathos from the strictures against education for black children, who can't differentiate letters from numbers, and the inability of a reading teacher who has no background in lb., the abbreviation for pound. Even at a base level of understanding, both tutor and pupils risk loss of their thumbs, a possible reduction to the animal level of paws and hooves for Sarny's simple act of scratching "BAG" in the dirt (Paulsen, *Nightjohn,* 61). By fictionalizing the sufferings heightened by ignorance, Paulsen celebrates learning as a true emancipator. For his readers, he relies on the childhood ability to "step into somebody's shoes and see it from another perspective" (Kelley, 2011).

See also history; *Nightjohn; Sarny;* slavery.

Source

Abilock, Debbie. "The Politics of Reading," *Knowledge Quest* 30:3 (2002): 7.
Carey, Joanna. "A Born Survivor Joanna Carey Meets the Engaging Best-selling American Author Gary Paulsen," *The* [Manchester] *Guardian* (28 May 1996).
Kelley, Annie J. "Gary Paulsen: A Book Can Change a Life," *Battle Creek* [Michigan] *Enquirer* (11 February 2011).
Lewis, Randy. "He Owes It All to Librarians and Dogs," *Los Angeles Times* (31 July 1994): 1.
Robertson, Judith P. "Teaching about Worlds of Hurt through Encounters with Literature: Reflections on Pedagogy," *Language Arts* 74:6 (October 1997): 457.
Ward, Barbara, Terrell A. Young, and Deanna Day. "Crossing Boundaries: Genre-Blurring in Books for Young Adults" in *Teaching Young Adult Literature Today.* Lanham, MD: Rowman & Littlefield, 2012.

logic

Paulsen's protagonists demonstrate both native intelligence and a knack for reasoning, for example, Cody Pierce's suggestion in *The White Fox Chronicles* that Major Toni McLaughlin suck on a pebble to overcome thirst, Malcolm "Mallard" Westerman's attempt to solve a series of kidnappings in *The CB Caper,* and the Gary character's rapid mastery of carny shilling in *The Beet Fields.* In transport by a mystical shaft of light, Mark Harrison, protagonist of *The Transall Saga,* tests his experiences to differentiate between hallucination and reality. Quickly, he determines, "Okay, I'm in another world, possibly on another planet" (Paulsen, *Transall,* 8). With the cool reason of Brian Robeson in the *Hatchet* series and of biology teacher John Homesley in *Canyons,* Mark talks himself through bizarre encounters with the buffalo creature and snakebite and prepares for a long residence by making a two-level treehouse and stocking it with edibles and a spear. The text projects two decades in Mark's future, when his deductive skills result in a vaccine for the Ebola virus, a validation of the logic he developed in the wild.

In models of detection and strategy, the author creates puckish humor from situations in "Speed Demon," a story excerpted in the January 23, 2006, issue of *Scholastic Scope;* the Amos and Dunc series; and *Mudshark.* Lyle Williams, the protagonist of *Mudshark,* enjoys Death Ball, an amalgam of soccer, football, wrestling, rugby, and mudfighting, which the school principal bans because of "Certain Insurance Restrictions and Prohibitions Owing to Alarming Health Risk" (Paulsen, *Mudshark,* 2). In "Speed Demon," Paulsen applies kid logic to humor. In an exaggeration about flat land, protagonist Carl "Angel" Peterson ruminates that "you could probably roll a bowling ball from northern Minnesota to Montana without half trying" (Paulsen, "Speed," 18).

Droll examples of skewed reasoning permeate the hilarious farm capers in *Harris and Me* and the ongoing antics of the Amos and Dunc series. After a serious skid into a dining room chair in *Dunc's Doll,* Amos's mother applies grease to his head to release it from a wedge between the two bottom rungs, a more sensible plan than Dunc's intent to distract a guard dog with hamburger and pepper. For *Dunc and the Scam Artists,* stuffing "the most Oreo cookies inside his mouth without crunching them" relieves the tedium of babysitting (Paulsen, *Scam,* 1). In a show of exaggeration, Paulsen reveals the competitors at the cusp of eleven Oreos "going for twelve," an unlikely accomplishment in a normal mouth (*ibid.*).

Life-Saving Reasoning

More pertinent to survival, Paulsen's writing portrays life-defining savvy in his keenest characters. The deputy U.S. Marshal in *The Legend of Bass Reeves* applies a knowledge of horse stamina during the tracking of Jim Webb, a vicious horse thief and murderer. John, the wandering slave tutor in *Nightjohn,* coats his leather shoes with lard and pepper to throw off packs of vicious hounds from a human scent. The application of practical knowledge increases the success of resistance, as with Mammy's whispered prayers inside the kettle and Delie's notching of sticks to estimate children's ages and the approach of breeding duties. In *Sarny,* the sequel, the protagonist confides how she outwits enslaver Clel Waller by pretending to cooperate with enforced breeding, but secretly convincing potential mates to lie about their sexual relations with young girls. The subterfuge enables Sarny to survive the onset of the Civil War and facilitates her new start in New Orleans as organizer of a freedmen's school.

Reasoning empowers other of Paulsen's survivors to avoid serious hazards, a necessary skill as gunsmith Cornish McManus crafts his most accurate firearm in *The Rifle.* For Andrew "Andy" Carson Hawkes III in *Flight of the Hawk,* the sudden appearance of "Uncle Harvey" raises questions about a relative who never received mention before Andy's father's death in a diving accident off Bermuda. Like Andy, Jeremy Parsons in *Thunder Valley* doubts spurious claims that Grandpa has sold the family ski lodge to Timothy Ryland Enterprises because the sale violates predictable character pride in business success. Because the ski business dominates the family's lifestyle, reasoning assures Jeremy that "it was unbelievable that his grandfather could have done this thing" (Paulsen, *Thunder,* 13). For his take-charge approach to a kidnapping and garage fire, his twin, Jason Parsons, compliments him: "Hey, you sound like a natural-born administrator," an acknowledgment of innate talent in a brother (*ibid.*).

For 13-year-old Manny Bustos, a mestizo orphan in *The Crossing,* Paulsen dramatizes the alliance of desperation with guile. Plotting a way of traversing the Rio Grande from Juárez, Mexico, to El Paso, Texas, requires Manny's lengthy observation of illegal immigrants and the American border patrol. His plan involves waiting for U.S. officers to seize the first group, then he "could slide sideways down the river to the end of the lighted area and get across" (Paulsen, *Crossing,* 41). The fault in his scheme results in capture from behind by street thugs, a force he had not factored in. The failure of his maneuver illustrates the two-sided dangers of Texas authorities to the north and Mexican predators in the south, who prove too much for the 13-year-old to outsmart. Annoyed with himself, he regrets "crowing like a stupid young rooster" about the ease of sneaking into lower Texas (*ibid.,* 46). The text nullifies the gang with a *deus ex machina,* the help of Sergeant Robert S. Locke, who offers his wallet and his protection to facilitate Manny's escape.

Wartime Strategy

The author's sympathy with beleaguered youth like Manny reaches its acme in wartime situations, especially in *Woods Runner.* At an appalling turn in his family's homesteading, logic sustains Samuel Lehi Smith, a 13-year-old frontiersman in western Pennsylvania. Experience in the woods with orienteering and hunting enables him to estimate how to make an eight-mile run to the Smith cabin to identify the cause of a smoky fire. For a protection against branches, Sam turns his rifle into a shield, a clever use of technology in dense woods to ward off scratches and possible eye damage. Wisely, he chooses to alternate between jogging and an all-out run, a means of saving his wind and muscle power for the investigation to come, which he conducts in widening circles.

Paulsen admires Sam for both head and body sense, which enables him to tackle the man-size job of burying nine dead villagers and locating his parents in New York, a city of 25,000 people. From his mentor, tinker/spy Abner McDougal, Sam learns a truism: "Simple plans are best," a statement of action to free Abigail and Olin Smith from imprisonment in a Redcoat sugar mill and flee west across the Hudson River without assistance or loss (Paulsen, *Woods,* 133). Amid the uproar caused by coincidentally liberating 40 men from the mill, Matthew the boatman sets sail over the dark Hudson River before British guards can intervene. His comment projects optimism: "Fortune favors the well prepared," an allusion to a rainy night that obscures their mission and the milk, rum, and beef sandwiches that sustain the Smiths on safe passage to New Jersey (*ibid.,* 137). By detailing the caper, the author involves readers in actual colonial era hazards.

The Human Jungle

In addition to stories of wartime crisis, the author features youth applying logic to the complexities of human relationships, for example, Irene's search for a father for her unborn child in *Winterkill* and a son's perceptions of his father's post-traumatic stress disorder in "Stop the Sun." In *Dogsong,* 14-year-old Russel Susskit, an Inuit musher, realizes that he understands nothing of females because "he was not ready for women yet," an admission based on a sensible acceptance of the stages of growing up (Paulsen, *Dogsong,* 18). To gain a grasp on change in himself and his Eskimo village, he communes with elderly Oogruk and accepts the old man's ability to look past the physical to the spirit within. By following a husky team over an icy expanse, Russel encounters Nancy, a pregnant girl-woman, and facilitates the birthing and burial of her stillborn child. The application of reason suggests that Russel has advanced from teen misgivings to more mature responsibilities.

The cerebral control of the unknown results in less terror and more sensible approaches to dilemmas. Along the Oregon Trail in *Tucket's Gold,* Francis Alphonse Tucket stops his brain from speculation on the predations of Comancheros: "He did not want to think of what they would do with him if they caught him alive" (Paulsen, *Gold,* 8). By concentrating on eluding danger, he manages to save himself and two orphans, Billy and Lottie. Similarly, for Brian Robeson, protagonist of the *Hatchet* series, a patient analysis of crises enables him to work out solutions to foraging, fire building, mosquito infestation, and retrieving equipment from the sunken wreckage of a Cessna 406, a rationality that he shares with fictional survivors Wil Neuton in *The Island,* Daniel Martin in *Danger on Midnight River,* and the migrant workers in *The Beet Fields.* By jettisoning self-pity, Brian concludes, "That's all it took to solve problems—just sense" (Paulsen, *Hatchet*).

See also coming of age; *Hatchet;* maturity; *The River;* survival.

Source

Carey, Joanna. "A Born Survivor Joanna Carey Meets the Engaging Best-selling American Author Gary Paulsen," *The* [Manchester] *Guardian* (28 May 1996).
Kent, Susan I. "Saints or Sinners?," *Social Education* 63:1 (January/February 1999): 8–12.

loss

Paulsen's works pursue humanistic questions that he poses for young adult and grown-up readers, as with the outcome of a grotesque knife fight against predators that kills Sergeant Robert S. Locke in *The Crossing,* tribal mourning for the beating death of the warrior Tukha in *The Transall Saga,* and the arson that destroys Carley's reputation in *Popcorn Days and Buttermilk Nights.* From autobiography, the author tells of devastation of Okinawans and Manilans by bombs in *Eastern Sun, Winter Moon;* the return of the Gary character to drunken parents in *Harris and Me;* the death of Wendell from a stomach wound in "The Madonna"; and the declining health in "The Face of the Tiger" and *A Christmas Sonata* of Matthew, a fictional version of Gary's cousin Raleigh, who died in childhood of renal failure. A pattern from Southern history, the sale of Sarny's mother in *Nightjohn* initiates a lifetime of mother hunger and curiosity about the woman who survived Sarny's breech birth. The approach of menarche places Sarny in a cyclical plight, the result of Clel Waller's treatment of motherhood as a form of agrarian investment. For female support, Paulsen supplies Delie, a foster caregiver who fills in for the missing mom.

The author recounts episodes of sorrow by creating youngsters who have lost loved ones to sudden death, as with the death of parents in an accident in *Molly McGinty Has a Really Good Day,* Charley Goddard's horror at seeing his comrade Massey's head blown off by a cannon ball at the Battle of Bull Run in *Soldier's Heart,* and David Alspeth's grief at the demise of Uncle Owen, the skipper and mentor in *The Voyage of the Frog.* Other protagonists face economic impediments that strip them of home and familiar environment, the catastrophe in *Woods Runner* that introduces 13-year-old woodsman Samuel Lehi Smith to homelessness and a blow to the forehead by an Iroquois club at the onset of the American Revolution and the unforeseen fatal disease of John Byam, a soldier in McNary's Rangers in *The Rifle.* A parallel crisis in the life of Anne Marie Pennysworth "Annie" Clark costs her home and parents Caleb and Martha Clark, leaving Annie in Sam's care. His willingness to foster Annie ennobles him at a time when he longs to move quickly toward New York City to retrieve Abigail and Olin Smith from imprisonment by Redcoats in a sugar mill. Paulsen implies that Sam has personal reasons to identify with Annie, who expresses outrage at the bayonetting of her parents by Hessian raiders.

The onslaught of such obstacles endangers Coyote Runs during an Apache raid in *Canyons,* perplexes the young plainsman Francis Alphonse Tucket in *Tucket's Gold* when outlaws and Comancheros threaten his life, and stymies a slave family in *The Legend of Bass Reeves*. For the *Hatchet* saga, Brian Robeson ponders the collapse of his parents' marriage because of "The Secret" and evidence that his mother is concealing her lover, the blond man in the white shirt whom she embraces in her station wagon (Paulsen, *Hatchet,* 30). The result is a brutal loss of innocence. Upon Brian's return to civilization, the four sequels inform readers that he has also lost anonymity to media surveillance of his outdoor adventures, an annoyance he shares with Wil Neuton in *The Island*. The author depicts Brian and Wil in the late teens coping with change after change in their boyhood lifestyle, a gauntlet that beset Paulsen himself into manhood.

Coping with Change

On an ethnic level, the atrophy of native culture demoralizes Russel Susskit, the 14-year-old protagonist of *Dogsong,* who yearns for a traditional Inuit environment. By exchanging perceptions of modernization with the elder Oogruk, Russel verbalizes his despair at the absence of whales for hunting, the substitution of cooked meat for raw in the Eskimo diet, the influence of Christianity, and the loss of songs from Eskimo culture. Oogruk acknowledges the role of snowmobiles in destroying silence and confesses that old age robs him of edifying memories. Most troubling, "many of them are gone now," a permanent loss of village women and the songs of nature, an alteration that dispossesses Arctic life of ancestral satisfactions (Paulsen, *Dogsong,* 22).

Paulsen specializes in images of suffering, grief, and demise among characters like Russel Susskit, the musher in *Dogsong,* John Borne in *Tracker,* Janet Carson in *The Night the White Deer Died,* and Johanna in *Notes from the Dog*. In a summation, critic Bernice Golden poses the author's unframed question to the individual: "How can I respond to life's injustices yet still live a full life?" (Golden, 1999, v). In the author's most evocative prose, he revisits a childhood plight in *The Quilt,* a juxtaposition of birth with death set on a farm in 1945. In the afterglow of Kristina Jorgenson's successful delivery of a healthy son, named Olaf after his father and grandfather, unforeseen news plunges her into hysteria. The loss of her soldier husband in combat leaves her on a Minnesota farm to rear the infant alone. The author pictures a Norwegian-American sisterhood of quilt makers and the scraps of wedding dresses with "words embroidered in the middle" that sustain Kristina and the other quilters (Paulsen, *Quilt,* 58). More important to Kristina's survival, a pep talk by Gary's grandmother redefines the new mother's lot as a widow, farmer, and single mother.

Wisdom and Strength

At a nadir of narrative atmosphere and tone, Paulsen speaks through the grandmother, the alter ego of his own Grandma Alida Peterson Moen, the maker of Thanksgiving feasts in *The Beet Fields*. The author instills a female credo based on endurance. Through her scrutiny of experience, she condenses the cycle of human hurts into a series of ordeals that women must bear for the sake of their families. Like the numerous matriarchal burden bearers of literature—Ma Joad in John Steinbeck's *The Grapes of Wrath,* O-Lan in Pearl Buck's *The Good Earth,* the unnamed mother in William Armstrong's *Sounder,* and Marta Hansen in Kathryn Forbes's *Mama's Bank Account*—the grandmother toughens Kristina. The age-old feminist maxim directs thinking toward fortitude: "We are the strong ones, we have always been the strong ones" (*ibid.,* 79). Her assertion opposes the truism that males are the bulwarks, the soldiers who shield their loved ones.

The matriarch's speech restates the premise that quilt stories solace and inspire the Norwegian clan. Retellings perpetuate family traits as dependable as dogged persistence in a new land and an acceptance of homesteading's toil and hardship. By handling the beloved patchwork and relating past lore, women like Kristina reanimate female touchstones such as Pearl, the barren "pearl of great price" who sheltered and mentored other women's daughters with advice on coming of age, men, courtship, and marriage. The reintroduction of women to the Scandinavian viragos of the past ensures the clan that traditional strengths and joys will withstand the grief of loss.

See also healing and death; *Nightjohn; The Rifle;* war.

Source

Golden, Bernice. *Critical Reading Activities for the Works of Gary Paulsen.* Portland, ME: Walch, 1999.
Robertson, Judith P. "Teaching about Worlds of Hurt through Encounters with Literature: Reflections on Pedagogy," *Language Arts* 74:6 (October 1997): 457.

maturity

In works of archetypal fiction, Paulsen's breakthroughs in coming of age and adult thinking extend a brief, often unsatisfying acceptance of reality, particularly for the Gary character in *The Beet Fields,* for Wil Neuton in *The Island,* and for hiker Mark Harrison, a level-headed earthling transported to another planet in *The Transall Saga.* While pondering an approach-avoidance feeling for Susan, Wil "just accepted his feelings as they were and let them flow on" (Paulsen, *Island,* 44–45). In the outrageous experiments of the two cousins in *Harris and Me,* the author characterized the pilgrimage of the young out of childhood as "a kind of individualism or freedom" achieved by probing a physical or mental wilderness (Creager, 1999, 4). For some beginners, the way seems strewn with obstacles. Hard lessons become the fate of Sarny, a girl in the early bloom of womanhood in *Nightjohn;* the immigrant Rosa picking through the garbage dump in Mexico City in *Sisters/Hermanas;* and John Barron, the teen herder of 6,000 sheep in *The Haymeadow.* For each, the departure from childhood forces some reexamination of misconceptions. In *The Night the White Deer Died,* Janet Carson acknowledges "she was having trouble changing from a girl to a woman," a statement that applies to maturation of the author's perplexed protagonists (Paulsen, *Night,* 72).

Through third-person narration in *The Crossing,* the author examines the thinking of orphan Manny Bustos, a red-haired mestizo urchin who may not live to adulthood amid trolling gangs and pedophiles in the alleys of Juárez, Mexico. Manny's decision to escape poverty and perverts requires emigrating over the Santa Fe Bridge into El Paso, Texas. Paulsen reflects on the boy's past life in an orphanage and fantasies of success in the U.S. and applauds the necessary decisions that keep him alive. In contrast, the narrative juxtaposes Sergeant Robert S. Locke, a Viet veteran and drunkard no longer certain of his worth as a career soldier. The novel builds on strengths shared by the literary foils—Manny and Locke—but leaves life and death questions unanswered.

The Rewards

In the opening scenes of *Soldier's Heart,* Paulsen surveys an historic wartime threat to 15-year-old farm boy Charley Goddard, an enlistee in the First Minnesota Volunteers. Beguiled by romantic notions of glory, he is game for the fray. He fears that the Civil War will end before he can join the Union army and see "the big fuss," a boyish concept of combat (Paulsen, *Soldier's,* 5). To convince his widowed mother to agree, he summarizes his aim as leaving "to earn eleven dollars a month and wear a uniform," two redemptive elements of boy soldiery in spring 1861 (*ibid.*).

After the First Battle of Bull Run on July 21, 1861, Charley recognizes immutable eyewitness experience. As a veteran, he realizes that there is no way to help young Nelson grow up to meet the challenge of the next assault: "You couldn't say it. You had to live it," a mantra that Paulsen adheres to in his descriptions of both war and maturity (*ibid.*, 46). The author returns to the veteran's exposure to horror in *Guts,* in which Paulsen envisions "the thousand yard stare," a blank expression resulting from participation in carnage too wrenching, too awful to forget (Paulsen, *Guts,* 4).

The author's view of the passing of childhood impacts some of his most poignant characters, particularly the slave mother in *Sarny,* the delinquent Carley in *Popcorn Days and Buttermilk Nights,* and the outback survivors Francis Alphonse Tucket and Brian Robeson in the *Tucket's Home* and *Hatchet.* Shannon Lee Turvey, a reviewer for the *Vancouver Sun,* summarized the incipient manhood of Brian, the author's most famous outdoorsman: "He is an entirely different person—more observant, more appreciative of things he had previously taken for granted, and in much better physical condition" (Turvey, 1998, I10). Beginning with the shearing of the firing pin in his rifle in *Brian's Winter,* he accepts the need to replicate the original methods in *Hatchet* of surviving, warming, and feeding himself without the aid of firearms. In recollection of winter trials, he feels more in touch with his capabilities and less fearful of the unknown, a adult-size attitude shared by Sarny, Carley, and Tucket.

The Conundrums

Similar to evolving adulthood in the teen foursome, for John Borne, the troubled deer hunter in *Tracker,* an acceptance of the inexplicable opens his mind to spiritual avenues of exploring the universe. An apotheosis from walking down a doe and touching her riddles his thoughts with more puzzles that overlap glimpses of the vulnerable deer and Grandfather Clay Borne, who had only a few months to live. John muses, "It was not something he was sure he really understood himself," an acknowledgment of mysticism in human thinking (Paulsen, *Tracker,* 86). His existential musings on animal life and the cancer eating away at Grandfather Clay prepare John for an adult acceptance of the unknown as an essential, if baffling, part of life.

Paulsen's works illustrate how maturation figures in other lethal situations, as with a prisoner in a Mexican jail in the story "Rape" and John Byam's hasty introduction to fighting for the patriot cause in *The Rifle.* For Wil Neuton, the self-marooned Crusoe in *The Island,* solitude forces him beyond self "truly to see, to know and to be," a man-size inkling he shares with John Borne (Kenney, 1988, A30). Edwin J. Kenney, a book critic for the *New York Times,* explains the transformative power of islands like those in Mark Twain's *Huckleberry Finn,* Robert Louis Stevenson's *Treasure Island,* and William Golding's *Lord of the Flies:* "Islands, especially fictional ones, are magically suited by their isolation to reveal the potential hidden in all of us" (*ibid.*). Self-determination requires Wil's mind to become the island. According to literary critics Mark Vogel and Anna Creadick, the boy "must carve out his precepts even as he listens to advice from all sides" (Vogel and Creadick, 1993, 37). By shutting out confusing opinions, he frees his thoughts to survey unique needs and ambitions.

New Perspectives

Paulsen dramatizes perceptions of adulthood as flashes of insight, a significant educator of the unnamed house guest in *The Foxman,* Sue Oldhorn in *Sentries,* and Carley, a budding juvenile delinquent in *Popcorn Days and Buttermilk Nights*. For the unnamed protagonist in *Harris and Me*, a scan of home dysfunction boils down to dissolute parents who "drank Four Roses professionally," an addiction that turns them into "vegetables most of the time" (Paulsen, *Harris*, 1). For the anonymous protagonist of *Winterkill*, an analysis of police officer Nuts Duda boils down to pragmatism. After the boy survives a beating by Gib Nymen, Duda advises, "Just grow up. That's all you have to remember" (Paulsen, *Winterkill*, 38). The likelihood of a love-conquers-all conclusion shreds in nightmares. While dreaming of a marriage between Duda and brothel madam Bonnie, the boy surrenders hope for adoption by a loving family and an idyllic residence in the country. He shudders out of the dream in a sweat and recalls "It isn't a movie and it doesn't end that way" (Paulsen, *Winterkill*, 137). The acceptance of reality precedes Duda's ignoble death, the loss that obliterates the protagonist's magical thinking.

For the award-winning historical novel *Woods Runner*, Paulsen's Cooperesque view of a 13-year-old escapist Samuel Lehi Smith flees a settlement in western Pennsylvania to embrace the wild. Like frontiersman Natty Bumppo, hero of James Fenimore Cooper's Leatherstocking Tales, Sam realizes that "the more he was of the woods, of the wild, of the green, the less he was of the people … his skills and his woods knowledge set him apart, made him different" (Paulsen, *Woods*, 35). Armed with a flintlock rifle and skinning knife, he accepts responsibility for feeding his family with venison that he tracks, shoots, and readies for the table. The commitment satisfies his need to be useful.

On the negative side of growing up, the narrative illustrates Sam's acceptance of atrocity as the nature of battle. When the four-antagonist war worsens, he witnesses the burning of his home and graphic Iroquois, Hessian, and British inhumanities against colonists. Grim scenarios of arrow-slain and tomahawk-scalped settlers and the Hessian bayoneting of Caleb and Martha Clark, the parents of Anne Marie Pennysworth "Annie" Clark, press Sam toward vengeance. With a salute to the classic American novelist of *The Deerslayer*, Paulsen names Sam's friend Cooper and enables the boy to assist Coop in his final undignified moments, crouched over a latrine in the throes of fatal dysentery. As a member of Morgan's Rifles, Sam embraces manhood in opposing roles, as a sharpshooter and medic. The contrast enhances Paulsen's views on maturation as an acceptance of paradox.

See also coming of age; healing and death; mentors; *Mr. Tucket*.

Source

Creager, Ellen. "View from the Outside the Wilderness Resonates for Children's Author," *Detroit Free Press* (13 April 1999): 4.
Kenney, Edwin J., Jr. "The Island," *New York Times* (22 May 1988): A30.
Phillips, Anne K. "James Fenimore Cooper's Literary Descendants: American History for 21st Century Adolescent Readers," *James Fenimore Cooper Society Journal* (Fall 2015): 7–10.
Turvey, Shannon Lee. "The Trouble with Sequels," *Vancouver Sun* (23 May 1998): I10.
Vogel, Mark, and Anna Creadick. "Family Values and the New Adolescent Novel," *English Journal* 82:5 (September 1993): 37.

mentors

The staid pairing of an elder character with a novice takes on potency and direction with Paulsen's stress on self-discovery, a concept as old as the Greek motto "Know thyself." In *Woods Runner*, while 13-year-old outdoorsman Samuel Lehi Smith works out the logic of entering New York City to retrieve his parents from captivity by Redcoats in a sugar mill, he questions why Abner McDougal, a Scots peddler/tinker/spy, risks getting involved in a British stronghold of some 25,000 people. Abner's response explains how a difference in age sparks altruism in the mentor: "Until you get old you don't really start adding … up" past rights and wrongs (Paulsen, *Woods,* 107). The elder traveler adds, "I help them that needs it when I can," a folksy rebuff of outright heroism (*ibid.*).

Through unselfish acts, Paulsen supplies coaching for neophytes who need directing toward goals and expectations, the situation that helps master artisan John Waynewright turned Cornish McManus into a journeyman gunsmith in *The Rifle,* that the Gary character learns from the labors of Uncle Knute in *Harris and Me,* and that the motherless slave Sarny faces at age 12 in *Nightjohn.* Her receipt of maternal caution from Mammy and alphabet training from John set in motion a complete makeover, the subject of the sequel *Sarny.* Rushed into womanhood through the despicable plantation system of slave breeding, Sarny "smiled some for a time" at her secret knowledge of the alphabet letters A-H (Paulsen, *Nightjohn,* 82). Through self-confidence, she profits from marriage, motherhood, wisdom, and education. Ironically, she reaches age 94 before the combined tutelage produces a storyteller capable of chronicling the history of American bondage.

Other segments of the author's oeuvre line up adviser with advisee to express the necessity for sage guidance during abandonment of childhood:

mentor	***role***	***title***	***protagonist***	***locale***
Abner McDougal	Scots tinker	*Woods Runner*	Samuel Lehi Smith	west of NY
Billy Honcho	derelict Navajo Indian	*The Night the White Deer Died*	Janet Carson	Tres Pinas, NM
Buck	instructor	*Skydive!*	Jesse Rodriguez	Seattle, WA
Caleb Lancaster	counselor	*Brian's Return*	Brian Robeson	Canada
Carl	companion	*The Cookcamp*	five-year-old Gary	Pine, MN
Carl Wenstrum	traumatized B-17 pilot	*Dancing Carl*	Marsh and Willy	McKinley, MN
Clay Borne	grandfather, woodcarver	*Tracker*	John Borne	Grand Forks, ND
Coop	patriot volunteer	*Woods Runner*	Samuel Lehi Smith	western PA
Delie	childcare worker	*Nightjohn*	Sarny	Southern plantation
Dunc Culpepper	pal	*Amos and the Chameleon Caper*	Amos Binder	Des Moines, IA
Fishbone	hermit veteran of World War I	*Fishbone's Song*	foster son	Caddo Creek, OK
Francis Tucket	young frontiersman	*Tucket's Gold*	Billy and Lottie	Southwest
grandfather	companion	*Masters of Disaster*	Henry Mosley	Cleveland, OH
grandfather	lecturer and storyteller	*Sentries*	Sue Oldhorn	Minnesota
Grandma	adviser	*Lawn Boy Returns*	young entrepreneur	Eden Prairie, MN
Grandma	optimist	*Lawn Boy*	young entrepreneur	Eden Prairie, MN
Jason Grimes	one-armed trader	*Mr. Tucket*	Francis Alphonse Tucket	Black Hills, SD
Johanna	neighbor	*Notes from the Dog*	Finn Howard Duffy	—
John	slave teacher	*Nightjohn*	Sarny	Southern plantation
John Waynewright	master gunsmith	*The Rifle*	Cornish McManus	colonial PA
Laura Harris	prostitute	*Sarny*	Sarny	New Orleans

mentor	*role*	*title*	*protagonist*	*locale*
Magpie	instructor	*Canyons*	Coyote Runs	Organ Mountains, NM
Matthew	river boatman	*Woods Runner*	Samuel Lehi Smith	Hudson River, NY
old Mexican	migrant worker	*The Beet Fields*	Gary character	North Dakota
Mick Strum	teacher	*The Monument*	Rachael Ellen "Rocky" Turner	Bolton, KS
Nuts Duda	police officer	*Winterkill*	teen delinquent	Twin Forks, MN
porter	child tender	*The Cookcamp*	five-year-old Gary	Minnesota
Robert S. Locke	alcoholic army sergeant	*The Crossing*	Manny Bustos	Juárez, Mexico
Uncle David	blacksmith	*Popcorn Days and Buttermilk Nights*	Carley	Norsten, MN
Uncle David	farm worker	*The Winter Room*	Eldon and Wayne	Minnesota
Uncle Harold Peterson	farmer	*The Foxman*	unnamed boy	Minnesota
Uncle Knute	foster father	*Harris and Me*	Gary character	Pinewood, WI
Uncle Owen	skipper	*The Voyage of the Frog*	David Alspeth	Pacific Ocean
Uncle Smitty	companion	*Danger on Midnight River*	Daniel Martin	Camp Eagle Nest

A controlling motif in many instances, the oral instructions of wise mentors prove more immediately applicable and less tedious that formal lessons, a valuable trove to David Alspeth during nine days afloat in the Pacific Ocean in *The Voyage of the Frog* and to Apache warrior Coyote Runs on his first raid in *Canyons*. According to analyst Ronald Barron, Sergeant Robert S. Locke and Manny Bustos develop "a mutual friendship, bordering on a father-son relationship" akin to the mutual need of Jim and his 13-year-old rescuer in Mark Twain's *The Adventures of Huckleberry Finn* (Barron, 1993, 29). In a model of open-ended man-boy counseling, the title figure in *Fishbone's Song* asks his young friend, "We're all here because why, why?," a rhetorical question meant not for one-word answers but for a lifetime of contemplation (Paulsen, *Fishbone's*, 109).

Sources of Strength

With queries as confounding as the koans of Zen Buddhists, the author acknowledges the irrevocable impasse in some advancements toward adulthood. For Russel Susskit, the 14-year-old musher of *Dogsong*, ambition directs him to a dead end: "When he looked ahead he didn't see more, he saw only less" (Paulsen, *Dogsong*, 22). A session with the elder Oogruk reveals a valued village graybeard who seems to possess a knack for reading minds. Without words to inform him, Oogruk concludes that Russel fears the loss of tradition from noisy snowmobiles that drive away seals and whales. Using gentle counsel, Oogruk helps Russel interpret "the way things were now" since Eskimos no longer express their culture in songs (*ibid.*). On Russel's long sled route and during his stay in a snow cave, he profits from Oogruk's insistence that the journey is more important than the destination, a belief the old man shares with the Buddha.

An optimistic glimpse of mentoring derives from the tender care of young Gary by a nameless railroad steward in *The Cookcamp*. Throughout a lonely train trip from Illinois to Minnesota, the action features a five-year-old under the supervision of the porter. The anonymous train worker oversees toilet breaks, a box lunch with grapes and a jelly biscuit, and rest in a Pullman pull-down bed. The child's sleeplessness concerns the porter, who sings as a lullaby "Ole Josie, … a long song about a woman in New Orleans" (Paulsen, *Cookcamp*, 6). Visions of the nameless adult who wraps the boy in a blanket during a change of trains in Minneapolis anticipate the mothering that the child receives from his Norwegian grandmother, a singer of real lullabies.

Accepting Trials

Unlike sententious models of decorum, the author's works extend unceremonious invitations to dare, to test the brain, instincts, and muscles in competition with self and nature, a primary motif in *Popcorn Days and Buttermilk Nights* and *The Beet Fields*. From J.D., Paulsen's counselor in *Pilgrimage on a Steel Ride*, he receives terse provisos: "Never to sit with my back to a door or window, never to trust anybody I didn't love, and always take care of myself" (Paulsen, *Pilgrimage*, 79). Fictional advice frequently takes the form of aphorism, as with Grandfather Clay Borne's dictum to his grandson John in *Tracker*, "You worked a job to done," a brief bit of praise for the work ethic and thoroughness (Paulsen, *Tracker*, 12). By honoring farm chores, Clay instills in his descendant thoughts of "good things, of growing and rich things … a whole series of small beauties" (*ibid.*, 12, 14). By tempering outcomes, the author readies the youth to expect slight, but satisfying rewards for performing duties.

For more dangerous responsibilities, risk taking allows adolescents like Brian Robeson and Francis Alphonse Tucket to set their own limits within the parameters of worthy advice. In five historical novels—*Mr. Tucket, Call Me Francis Tucket, Tucket's Ride, Tucket's Gold,* and *Tucket's Home*—the author samples the migration west from Missouri over the Oregon Trail from the perspective of a 14-year-old abductee. After capture by the Pawnee, Tucket eludes the Indians and throws in with a one-armed trader, Jason Grimes, in a familiar boy-with-wise-elder motif. The customary Western scenario of advice from an experienced frontiersman elevates Francis to a quick learner who absorbs the necessities of survival, particularly straight shooting with his new rifle. At a turning point in Tucket's maturation, he recognizes diverse strands in Jason's philosophy—survival on the prairie and vicious retaliation against an enemy. Tucket wisely accepts the first and distances himself from murder and scalping, yet, in *Call Me Francis Tucket,* admits that parting from Grimes was like "his life had a hole torn in the middle of it," in spite of his "rough humor and final viciousness" (Paulsen, *Call,* 5, 91).

At Unalakleet on the Bering Sea, the author himself experiences the gravity of an elder in *Woodsong,* in which an Inuit invites Paulsen, an amateur runner of the 1983 Iditarod, to remain in Alaska, trade stories, and hunt seals. The old man puts the matter into a stark this-or-that choice: "Isn't it better this way than the way you live the other times?," an assumption based on the elder's observation of discontent in white people (Paulsen, *Woodsong,* 238). The ambiguous counsel proves useful to Wil Neuton in *The Island* and Brian Robeson of the Brian series. Both must flee media attention to relocate peace in the wild. In each case, the learner must make an informed decision by progressing beyond mentoring to self-direction.

See also coming of age; maturity; survival.

Source

Gregory, Kristiana. "Commodore Perry in the Land of the Shogun," *Los Angeles Times* (11 May 1986): 7.
Nappi, Rebecca. "Books That Mentor," *McClatchy-Tribune Business News,* (19 April 2009).
Salvner, Gary M. *Presenting Gary Paulsen.* New York: Twayne, 1996, 79–133.

Mr. Tucket

In five historical novels—*Mr. Tucket, Call Me Francis Tucket, Tucket's Ride, Tucket's Gold,* and *Tucket's Home* and an omnibus version, *Tucket's Travels*—the author surveys the Great Migration west of the Rocky Mountains over the 2,170-mile Oregon Trail. From the perspective of a 14-year-old abductee, Francis Alphonse Tucket, the venture offers an opportunity for autonomy, symbolized by his cherishing of a rifle, a gift from his father. At the height of westward travel from Missouri northwest to Oregon Territory from 1843 to 1855, some 1,000 immigrants like the Tucket family departed the East Coast for the Pacific shore. The Tuckets wisely chose oxen to pull their load from Missouri across Kansas. The animals were too slow and awkward to stampede or rustle, a common practice of disgruntled plains Indians who wanted to discourage white settlers. Of the racial divide, critic Michael Maschinot, in a review for the *St. Petersburg* [Florida] *Times,* notes that Paulsen's Pawnee "are neither stereotyped nor romanticized, but are complex people who pose a legitimate threat to [Tucket's] survival" (Maschinot, 1994, D-6).

In the estimation of Carol Otis Hurst, a reviewer in *Teaching Pre-K-8,* the good guys/bad guys motif suits the reading appetites of Paulsen's fans. At the onset of action, the kidnapping begins on June 13, 1847, a day after an apotheosis in Tucket caused by receipt of a Lancaster .40 caliber rifle for his birthday. The long gun becomes a symbol of manhood and independence for Tucket and other boys growing up in the West. While he lags behind his parents and sister Rebecca to target practice at buffalo chips, he falls into Pawnee hands. The boyish error in judgment of staying behind alone as well as his friendship with Ike and Max, irksome Quaker bullies who terrify girls with a garter snake, contrast the title, which suggests that Tucket will eventually mature to full manhood.

Ethical Standards

After seizure by seven Pawnee led by the harsh war leader Braid, Tucket observes the Native American concept of masculinity. Among testosterone-driven Indians and a scolding female who leashes him with a rope, insults quickly demoralize him for fighting like a girl. Paulsen stresses suspense by implying that Braid killed and scalped the blonde Rebecca and took her doll, a terror that heightens the danger and inspires Tucket's first attempt at escape. Movement to the northeast toward the Black Hills in Dakota Territory further demoralizes the boy, who knows that Ballard's wagon train journeys in the opposite direction. Yet, the text indicates that Tucket keeps an open mind about a "living river" of buffalo and the beauty of the territory, which he prefers to the Rockies (*ibid.,* 11).

The novel builds character contrast from eccentricities of trade and traders, who seem inured to Indian ways. Three weeks into captivity, Tucket eludes the Pawnee, steals a pony, and throws in with one-armed trader Jason Grimes in a familiar lad-with-wise-elder motif. As Tucket flees Braid's village, he falls off his mount. Because Tucket has learned to keep the North Star over his right shoulder and interpret trembling grass and footprints in soft dirt, his observations enable him to elude recapture. With boyish glee, he declares his revelry in plains adventure: "Never had he been so purely thrilled," a boy's view of the westering fever that gripped the country (*ibid.,* 30). Paulsen develops his jubilation in wilderness challenges and highlights his increasing resourcefulness as a natural talent of teenagers.

Personal Ethics

From his savvy mentor, Tucket learns to shoot fast and straight, palaver with the Sioux, trap beaver, stalk antelope, and "pull his load," Paulsen's gesture toward the American work ethic (*ibid.*, 82). The escapee concludes that "he'd come what seemed like a thousand years," an ethnic metaphor for eluding his parents' values and learning to think like the Pawnee and Sioux (*ibid.*, 76). The author remarks on Tucket's ability to focus by "[stiffening] his back and [trying] to remember something not related to where he was now" (*ibid.*, 56). The method of putting extraneous thoughts out of mind parallels the growing self-control of Brian in *Hatchet* and John Borne in *Tracker,* a necessity for the in-between years when childhood slips away.

Tucker perceives that the Pawnee "live by nature" and recognizes in his mentor an acculturation to the frontier: "He was of the prairie, the land, the mountains," which supersede human codified law and courtesies (*ibid.*, 50, 165). However, for Tucket, lawlessness has its limits. Grimes repulses the apprentice frontiersman by killing and scalping his enemy Braid, a savage act suited to beasts in the outback that *Kirkus Reviews* called unfortunate. The realization forces Tucket to prioritize his personal views on right and wrong, cut ties with the inhumane mountain man, and head west to rejoin his family in Oregon (Paulsen, *Mr.*, 166). The decision introduces self-determination at a turning point in Tucket's coming of age and sets the stage for the next four novels in the series, all occurring in the American Wild West. Educators Andi Stix and Marshall George recommended the book and its sequels for "integrating into the curriculum as a complement to traditional textbooks" to make studies relevant and interesting to tweens (Stix and Marshall, 2000, 25).

See also coming of age; mentor.

Source

Giles, Rebecca M., and Karyn W. Tunks. "Read the Past Now! Responding to Historical Fiction through Writing," *The Councilor* 75:1 (2014): 15–22

Hurst, Carol Otis. "Four Literature Webs You'll Be Glad to Get Caught In," *Teaching Pre-K-8* 26:1 (September 1995): 112.

Maschinot, Michael. "Journeys of the Spirit Series," *St. Petersburg* [Florida] *Times* (27 February 1994): D-6.

Salvner, Gary M. *Presenting Gary Paulsen.* New York: Twayne, 1996, 79–133.

Stix, Andi, and Marshall George. "Using Multi-Level Young Adult Literature in the Middle School American Studies," *Social Studies Journal* (Jan-Feb 2000): 25–31.

music

Paulsen's stories insert dance, melody, and singing at significant places, particularly in the titles *Woodsong, A Christmas Sonata,* and *Fishbone's Song,* a reference to a witty raconteur's blend of tune with oral communication called "story-song" and "song-stories" (Paulsen, *Fishbone's*, 17, 38). Melody suits unique characters—in the legless fiddler, the dog dancing to a crank organ, and a funeral band down the streets of New Orleans in *Sarny;* the flamenco chords strummed on a guitar by the title figure in *The Foxman;* and Mammy's crooning of "All my trials, Lord, soon be over" in *The Legend of Bass Reeves* (Paulsen, *Legends,* 15). For humor in *The Island,* the Wil Neuton sings "La, la" to dispel boredom at yard edging work and sneers at an album of country-and-western gospel hits sung to organ accompaniment "so drippy it almost drew flies" (Paulsen, *Island,* 41). In solitude on the island, he dances in imitation of a heron as a means of understanding bird life and meditates on a frog's "high-pitched trilling sound, a song … singing from his log, his place" (*ibid.,* 121).

In *This Side of Wild,* Gary's Norwegian grandmother turns his attention toward bird gifts: "Songs, for you and me, from them" (Paulsen, *This Side,* 62). Among Mexican workers in *The Beet Fields,* the blend of harmonica with guitar produces a folk fandango naturally suited to a summer night. For Billy Honcho, a derelict from the pueblo on the streets of Tres Pinos, New Mexico, in *The Night the White Deer Died*, playing the flute and intoning traditional Navajo chants bring him peace. Of the rain verse, he explains, "I sing the song because it has much beauty in it" (Paulsen, *Night,* 64). Paulsen implies that the structure of poetry reassures Billy after hours of wandering the town square in a drunken stupor.

During the summer 1861 Civil War mania that grips Winona, Minnesota, in *Soldier's Heart,* singing expresses partisan support for the Union. Charley Goddard, an impressionable 15-year-old, proves vulnerable to the hoopla. He readies himself for stereotypical manhood glorified by drumming, children's cheers, slogans, parades, and songs that "everybody and his rooster was crowing" (Paulsen, *Soldier's,* 1). More than six decades later for *Dancing Carl,* a plaintive post–World War II meditation on music infiltrates the atmosphere of the ice rink, "rolling through the ice—close to the sounds the whales make" (Paulsen, *Dancing,* 24). The rhythm and melody set the atmosphere and tone of Carl Wenstrom's emergence from post-traumatic stress disorder and unrequited adoration of Helen Swanson. At the story's emotive climax, Carl's dance speaks without words his fondness for a female beloved.

In other works, the writer interjects a subtler musical clue, for example, the harmonic Spanish conversation of field workers in *The Beet Fields,* the dance-pantomime for a primitive tribe in *The Transall Saga,* and the efficacy of "'shine" in turning frontier soldiers "to singing, maybe, foot shuffle dancing, telling good stories" (Paulsen, *Fishbone's,* 117). For the boy alone on the train in *The Cookcamp,* the porter's New Orleans blues lulls him to sleep. For Brian Robeson in *The River,* the loose slouch of the bush plane pilot with chin bobbing to cassette music relaxes a tense flight over the Canadian outback. While mushing huskies by night in *Dogteam,* the writer finds emotional release in the "highsoftshusshh-whine of the runners," a tone eliciting an unpremeditated merger with his huskies (Paulsen, *Dogteam,* n.p.). On a jollier note, father Gary and son Jim belt out "On the Road Again," an anthem for *Road Trip* "inspired by the country music stations" (Paulsen, *Road,* 110). In each instance, an automatic response places melody deep within a heedful mind.

On a more spiritual plane, Paulsen put his faith in the integrity of the soul's inner harmonics, such as the song of the aged Ojibwa grandfather in *Sentries* that replicates the flight of the arrow, the soft lyrics written by Milton Van Sickle in *Tiltawhirl John,* the drum dance that draws Brennan Cole into a tribal circle in *Canyons,* and the song that Kevin Spencer hears in *Family Ties* every time he thinks of Katrina M. "Tina" Zabrinski. With increased poignance, Paulsen permeates the suspense of *Woods Runner* with the hymns and lullabies of Old Bobby, a gravedigger who seems so "teched" that he scares off Iroquois marauders who "saw crazy people as graced by the High Power" (Paulsen, *Woods,* 45). A father states to his son Russel in *Dogsong*: "Sometimes words lie—but the song is always true," advice that leads Russel to self-reclamation via a revival of traditional values, such as the song that the old Eskimo Oogruk once used to summon whales to his harpoon (Paulsen, *Dogsong,* 11).

Music in Autobiography

The author seems drawn to the magic of music. In the earliest memories in *Eastern Sun, Winter Moon,* Paulsen refutes the beneficence that technology reputedly offers to rhythm and tune. For *Alida's Song,* the introduction to folk music of Alida Halverson's 14-year-old grandson—a teen version of Gary—lightens the few evenings they have free of exhausting farm work. In the parlor, Gunnar clacks rib bones against his knees while Olaf bows the violin. The boy expresses subconscious delight by "smiling and didn't know he was smiling" (Paulsen, *Alida,* 60). By challenging him to dance, Alida introduces her grandson to one of the dynamic pleasures men share with women. The author stresses the value of companionship, sacrifice, song, and dance as a countermeasure to the hard labor of milking cows and repairing fences. In a brief respite, "the heat and work of the day seemed to evaporate," leaving the grandson "wonderfully tired" (*ibid.*, 61).

Olaf's composition of "Alida's Song" sets in motion a Saturday night ritual—the community dance, a folk entertainment that Paulses reprises in *Harris and Me* with comic sounds "like cats fighting inside a steel drum" (Paulsen, *Harris,* 87). The more mellifluent music of *Alida's Song* features Olaf and Gunnar's fiddling and rhythm accompanied by accordion. Amid trays of sweets, venison, and fish and cold root beer and grape juice, neighbors "broke into a wild schottische," a popular rhythm among Bohemian farmers that influenced the Norwegian *gammeldans* (Paulsen, *Alida*, 80). The debut of Olaf's song honoring Alida and her deceased husband Clarence shifts the tone to sounds so sweet that the grandson imagines he sees the two lovers. The combined efforts of musicians and Alida's demonstration of steps embolden the boy to a mature partnering with girls and connecting with others, all "helping him to grow, to change, to find the world and himself" (*ibid.*, 87). In memories of Alida in *The Island* and *This Side of Wild,* Paulsen revered her cooking, stories, and treasury of the arts—Norse tales of "animals, telling tales of love and hate and joy and music" (Paulsen, *This Side,* 62).

The Incomparable Song

In contrast to his love of folk and traditional melodies and dances, the clangor of modern music repulses the author. He studies the use of a "four-horn-and-one-guitar band" in *The Crossing* as an inducement for sex and exploitation of drunken U.S. soldiers and tourists in Juárez, Mexico (Paulsen, *Crossing,* 33). Viewed by the orphan Manny Bustos, a mestizo beggar and thief, the Club Congo Tiki, a squalid Gringo dive, offers titillating girlie shows, which Paulsen reprises in the story "The Soldier." Semi-nude, the performers gyrate in exotic gambol down the runway to "brassy music, the loud grinding clanky music" (*ibid.,* 27). They enhance their allure with coiled snakes, a suggestion of the boy's captivity in a claustrophobic hellhole.

The writer resumes his study of contemporary music in *Sentries,* in which the rock band Ice Shackleton veers from commitment to composition into partying and snorting cocaine. As Paulsen observes through Dunc in *Amos's Killer Concert Caper,* musicians who "can't even write a real song" lose the respect of rock fans, who dismiss repetitious nonsense as "junk" (Paulsen, *Caper,* 1). The writer extends his criticism of noise-based rock in *Notes from the Dog,* in which "the music was so loud it was making my back teeth jiggle" (Paulsen, *Notes,* 109). Peter, the creative spirit of Ice Shackleton, wisely steers his thinking and labor away from pointless din and drugs to the greater good of his band, to "a new sound that had been kicking around in his head" (Paulsen, *Sentries,* 55). The narrative validates melodic composition that derives from true creativity.

Paulsen turns Peter's quest for a mesmerizing song into an heroic achievement. Like Sir Ernest Shackleton, the Irish explorer of the Arctic in 1901 whose surname he bears, Peter ventures beyond the shallow interests of teen groupies to a single beguiling ambition, the composition that will meld musicians with their audiences. The text elevates Peter's aims above the mediocre and lauds as a mark of ingenuity and persistence his pulse that unifies "the band, the crowd, Peter, the words, all the same" (*ibid.,* 163).

Source

Barron, Ronald. "Gary Paulsen: 'I Write Because It's All I Can Do,'" *ALAN Review* 20:3 (Spring 1993): 27–30.

Johnson, Nancy, *et al.* "Language of Music," *Reading Teacher* 53:7 (April 2000): 602–604.

Snodgrass, Mary Ellen. *Encyclopedia of World Folk Dance.* Lanham, MD: Rowman & Littlefield, 2016.

names

For people and animals, Paulsen selects names that aggrandize or intimate a broad significance, the purpose of Dylan, the dog of a Bob Dylan fan in *Notes from the Dog;* Scarhead, the battered bear in *Woodsong;* Buzzer, the domesticated lynx in *Harris and Me;* and the furtive Spot Johnnie in *Mr. Tucket.* Others enhance comedy or whimsy: Meany the policeman in *Dunc Gets Tweaked;* Mog and Zon in *The Seventh Crystal;* Girrk in *Amos and the Alien;* Joey Pow the prizefighter in *Lawn Boy;* Colonel Sodoron in *The White Fox Chronicles;* and Lightning Man in *Super Amos.* Sergeant Robert S. Locke's surname in *The Crossing* suggests his mental captivity by sorrow and addiction to beer and scotch. During the evolution of the American gun culture in the 1990s, Paulsen names an evangelical NRA fanatic Tim Harrow, a verb rich with grief and affliction, the result of gun mismanagement in *The Rifle.*

Paulsen selects names that imply character traits, as with the gentleness of Leeta and the barbarity of the Rawhaz cannibals in *The Transall Saga.* In memories of the dog Dirk, the author compares the snarling body guard to a pet alligator. Rex, the mate of Cookie in *Puppies, Dogs, and Blue Northers,* sires eight pups in a lordly seduction performed in sight of the author. With a tip of the hat to Harper Lee's classic Southern novel *To Kill a Mockingbird,* the author and his son Jim name the canine narrator in *Road Trip* Atticus, the first name of the fictional egalitarian Atticus Finch and the adjectival form of "Athenian," a reference to the cradle of Western democracy.

Human names reflect Paulsen's eye for detail, as with the corrupt heart of Corey in *The Tent* and the grousing of Duane Homer Leech, the protagonist in *The Amazing Life of Birds,* about not being "name-lucky" and wishing he could have been called "Steve, or Carl, or Clint" (Paulsen, *Amazing,* 8). To identify Oogruk, the wise mentor in *Dogsong,* Paulsen selects the Yupik word for bearded seal, an allusion to an inscrutable patriarch. For the 13-year-old protagonist John Borne in *Tracker,* the patronym hints at the burden of fear for his grandfather, Clay Borne, who suffers from terminal cancer, a source of mortality that recalls the "Earth to earth, ashes to ashes, dust to dust" of the Anglican funeral rite. A dual implication in *Nightjohn* for enslaver Clel Waller depicts him as walling in hapless plantation laborers and suggests "wallow" for his ignoble part in degrading and tormenting blacks with whip, pistol, and flesh-eating hounds. For a touch of grandeur in *Sentries,* the author chooses for Peter Shackleton the lineage of a 19th-century hero, a leader of three expeditions to the arctic, a pathless wasteland that demands daring and genius from its conquerors.

In *The Crossing,* Paulsen leaves Manny Bustos, a fatherless street waif in Juárez, Mexico, free to select among amusing stories and intriguing heroes for a given name. He delights in bearing the praenomen of Mañuel the prizefighter, a reflection of toughness absent in Manny's small frame. Still hungry for stature, the boy crosses Santa Fe Street near the bridge to El Paso, Texas, a symbolic roadway from "holy faith" to "the step," his escape route from orphanhood and terror of thugs and pedophiles. In a gauzy fantasy, he strolls the railroad and relives the bravery of Pancho Villa, a guerrilla warrior who led rebel liberators through Juárez in April and May 1911. By shooting bullets into hotel walls, Villa generated dash and romance as well as hope for peasants oppressed by hacienda owners. In a rhapsody of macho legend, Manny considers calling himself Pancho, a character Paulsen revisits in the story "The Soldier."

Evocative Names

Monosyllabic men's names—Spud and Rick in *Rock Jockeys,* Finn in *Notes from the Dog,* Blade in *Paintings from the Cave,* Buck in *Skydive!,* Andy Hawkes III in *Flight of the*

Hawk, Tag Jones in *The Treasure of El Patrón,* and Wheel, Dash, Goob, and Jay M in *Flat Broke*—attest to a masculine energy that dominates action in Paulsen's androcentric fiction. Professor William Crockett, the archeologist in *Curse of the Ruins,* carries the historic surname of frontiersman Davy Crockett, explaining the scientist's bravado and sensitivity to Indian culture. For different reasons, Pearl, the matriarch in *The Quilt,* bears a direct tie to Jesus's parable of the pearl of great price in Matthew 13:45–46. In contrast, the naming of Francis Alphonse Tucket for the Tucket series, the title figure's alliterated name in *Molly McGinty Has a Really Good Day,* and Woody "the Worm" Winslow in *Captive!* hint at humor and misadventure in the lives of anti-heroes. The author reserves some of his more parodic names for teachers, as with Mrs. Burnbottom, a science teacher in *Amos Goes Bananas,* and the social studies instructor Mrs. Wormwood in *Prince Amos.* For Mr. Trasky, the onerous American history teacher in *Culpepper's Cannon,* the unusual patronym implies a portmanteau word formed of "task" and "travesty," a silent rebuke of unimaginative assignments of research papers that bore students.

Names bear imaginative links, especially the hermit Fishbone in *Fishbone's Song* and Amos Binder, the devoted friend bound to Duncan "Dunc" Culpepper in *The Wild Culpepper Cruise.* The bookish title figure in *The Schernoff Discoveries* and psychologist Derek Holtzer and Wil Neuton in *The Island* model the scientific acumen of European mathematicians and of physicists Albert Einstein and Isaac Newton. Similarly, the Barron family, like feudal lords, manages prime land of the Wyoming high country in *The Haymeadow.* For humor in *Mudshark,* the author names the librarian Ms. Underdorf, a suggestion of her gullibility.

The questionable background of Jason Grimes, the one-armed trader in the five-book Tucket series, leaves in doubt the worth of his peripatetic life, in the style of Apollonius's beleaguered Greek navigator Jason and the Argonauts. The last name suggests Grimes's dubious value as a mentor to a 14-year-old loner on the Oregon Trail, particularly because of Grimes's bicultural vacillation between white man's law and the Pawnee tradition of clubbing and scalping. For a more pernicious character, the video game caricature in *Rodomonte's Revenge* implies an exotic villain. For comedy in *Masters of Disaster,* Paulsen identifies the Batsons' roof as the location of a batty escapade concluding in soaring from a diving board over a pool.

Historic Identification

For *Woods Runner,* set in western Pennsylvania in 1776, Paulsen selects men's and women's names that link colonial America to its Puritan past. The choices from the Old Testament—Isaac, Lehi, Ishmael, Micah, Caleb, Abigail, Abner, Ebenezer, Ben, Samuel—and Matthew and Martha from the New Testament signify a Bible-reading populace who honor their faith from birth in the naming of children. The narrative compounds the religious atmosphere with grace before meals and a cycle of altruistic acts to benefit refugees and needy strangers. Paulsen reprises the use of biblical names in *Tucket's Home* with Orson's men Caleb, Isaiah, James, and John, who "[head] west for the promised land in the golden valley," a reference to the group's utopian ideals (Paulsen, *Home,* 52). A similar ethnic unity dominates a military scene in *Tucket's Ride,* where a trio of Irish cavalrymen out of Missouri bear the names Brannigan, Flannagan, and O'Rourke, a patronymic acknowledgment of the role of the Irish in settling the American West. The lone outsider, William James Bentley the Fourth in *Tucket's Home,* denotes the dilettante British hunter named for a luxury car, the type of visitor to America who trolls the frontier for "a grand adventure" (Paulsen, *Home,* 9).

In token of a Scandinavian lineage, the author supplies American characters with Nordic names. His list includes:

- Tim Peterson in *The Island*
- Bill Halverson in *Canyons*
- Carl Peterson and Archie Swenson in *How Angel Peterson Got His Name*
- Carl Wenstrom, Pederson, and Marshall Knuteson in *Dancing Carl*
- Emil Peterson in *Popcorn Days and Buttermilk Nights*
- great-grandfather Karl and Kristina Jorgenson in *The Quilt*
- Gretchen in *This Side of Wild*
- Gunnar and Olaf in *Alida's Song*
- Oleson and Jacobsen in *The Beet Fields*
- Gunnar Pederson in *Clabbered Dirt, Sweet Grass*
- Gust Homme and Carl Sunstrum in *Winterkill*
- Lieutenant Olafson in *Soldier's Heart*
- Gustaf, Carl, Sven, Altag, Nels, Emil, and Ole in *The Cookcamp*
- Hans and Agile in *The Foxman*
- Harrin Olsen, Alen, Nels, Orud, Melena, Karl, and Siggurd in *The Winter Room*
- Jeff Dodsen in *Captive!*
- Johanna in *Notes from the Dog*
- Karl Elsner in *Tiltawhirl John*
- Kenny Halverson in *Lawn Boy Returns*
- Melissa Hansen in the Amos and Dunc series
- Mrs. Olsen in *Time Benders*
- Swen in *Father Water, Mother Woods*
- Uncle Knute Larson, the Halversons, the Severs kid, old man Knutson, and Harold, Clyde, and Elaine Peterson, in *Harris and Me.*

Paulsen transforms Grandmother Alida Peterson Moen into Anita Halverson, the fictional midwife who helps deliver the third Olaf to the Jorgenson family, a scene replicated by Mexican farm workers at a field birth in *The Beet Fields.* Additional ethnic ties betoken as First Peoples an assortment of figures:

- Betty Two Shoes in *The Legend of Bass Reeves*
- Billy Honcho, a defeated pueblo leader in *The Night the White Deer Died*
- Bird Dance, Braid, and Standing Bear, a Sioux who negotiates with whites in *Mr. Tucket*
- Kay-gwa-daush, an appealing teen girl in *Brian's Hunt*
- the Old One and William Little Bear Tucker, an Apache cave explorer in *The Legend of Red Horse Canyon*
- Iktah in *Tucket's Home*
- Red Horse in *Curse of the Ruins*
- Sancta and Magpie, the raider and trainer of the Apache youth Coyote Runs in *Canyons*
- Alan Deerfoot and Sue Oldhorn, a modern Ojibwa out of touch with her grandfather's traditions in *Sentries*
- the Smallhorn family, Cree wilderness dwellers in *Hatchet*
- three Pueblo—Kashi, Annas, and Two Toes–in *Tucket's Gold*
- Ulgavik, the blind Inuit musher in *Dogsong.*

Significant racial traits identify the Marias in *The Beet Fields;* Pasqual, the Hispanic labor organizer named for Easter in *Lawn Boy;* Stoney Romero, the lawn service organizer in *Canyons;* Bass and Flowers in *The Legend of Bass Reeves;* and Delie, Sarny, and Nightjohn, slaves bearing plantation designations in Paulsen's classic *Nightjohn.* Also living on society's periphery, the title figure in *The Foxman* intimates that residence in the wilderness strips him of humanity and substitutes animal traits. The protagonist endorses the unusual nickname "because people like the Foxman never need real names—what they are is more important" (Paulsen, *Foxman,* 7).

See also writing.

Source

Lewis, Randy. "He Owes It All to Librarians and Dogs," *Los Angeles Times* (31 July 1994): 1.
MacCallum, Elizabeth. "Rude, Outrageous: An Ideal Book for Kids," [Toronto] *Globe and Mail* (5 February 1994): C17.
_____. "What We Need to Know about Natives," [Toronto] *Globe and Mail* (17 November 1990): C20.

nature

Gary Paulsen values experience with flora and fauna in their natural settings as a cornerstone of his manhood, an element he applies to the sterling character of John Byam in *The Rifle,* to camper Brennan Cole in *Canyons,* and to the Gary character in *Harris and Me.* To George Nickelson, an interviewer for Trumpet Club, the author declared that he relished wilderness as "my bedroom, my living room, and my study" (Nickelson, 1993). The mystique evolved into a lasting magnetism that imbued *Woodsong, Dogteam, Guts, This Side of Wild,* and *Puppies, Dogs, and Blue Northers.* He explained, "The wilderness pulled at me—still does—in a way that at first baffled me and then became a wonder for me" (Paulsen, *Guts,* 71).

The author's respect for the sensory impressions of creation caused him to give up guns in favor of bow and arrow. He described how noise "kills the whole woods," robbing his jaunt into the forest of the undertone of small animals on the move, such as the tunneling mice that Brian Robeson views in *Brian's Return,* the foraging of ants in *The Island,* and Brennan Cole's awakening to the cry of a mountain lion in *Canyons* (*ibid.*, 75). In a brief reflection on nature's soothing effects, during the torture of Mammy in *Nightjohn,* the maternal victim turns her thoughts from thirst and manacles to birdsong, a commodity free to all, even slaves.

Like the writer himself, characters coalesce with the spirit of the wild, a particular release for delinquents in *The Foxman, Winterkill,* and *Popcorn Days and Buttermilk Nights.* The exposition in *Woods Runner* describes 13-year-old frontiersman Samuel Lehi Smith, a rural western Pennsylvanian, as "a child of the forest … [living] in two worlds," including the community of homesteads inhabited by his parents, Abigail and Olin Smith (Paulsen, *Woods,* 3). In a description of a perilous raid on the Smith cabin preceding the War for Independence and Sam's escape from psychic pain brought on by a tomahawk blow to the forehead during an Iroquois raid, the writer declares rivers and woods as sources of relief that cause no emotional pain. Of Paulsen's personal reflections on the outback, he adds, "The mountains will teach you and so will the sea. You learn fast" (Parmer, 2004, 3).

At insightful moments, the author's works look back on the emergence of *homo sapiens* from the wild, a thought that bolsters the Brian Robeson series. In *Brian's Hunt,* the protagonist reports on in-depth reading about edible fish and the slime that covers their bodies to prevent bacterial infection. Paulsen promotes an understanding of animals and primitive human existence for an organic reason: "We are really a part of nature and we don't know how to handle it" (Moss, 2004, E1). Reflecting on media survival shows, he dismisses TV versions as staged and "patently absurd" (*ibid.*). Of current obsession with screen time, he reviles the media as "horrible intellectual carbon monoxide" capable of destroying the younger generation and its perception of creation (*ibid.*).

The Real Outdoors

Like Jack London, Edgar Rice Burroughs, and Herman Melville, major literary idols from boyhood, Paulsen has no truck with the "golden sunset and rainbow" school of nature writing. Rather, he stresses how "nature ... shows you how things can be right, and the human species shows you how to do it wrong," an apotheosis to juvenile delinquent Carley in *Popcorn Days and Buttermilk Nights* and seeker Wil Neuton in *The Island* (Goodson, 2004, 54). At a brief glimpse of a buck, Wil values the sudden encounter for the lingering image, "the burned beauty of the picture in his brain" (Paulsen, *Island,* 45). The pictorial sensation "from another time" seems therapeutic to a teen who struggles to converse with his parents and with Susan, a girl his own age (*ibid.,* 46).

To Ann Goodwin Sides, an interviewer for the *New York Times,* the author characterized the natural impression of a blue heron swallowing a frog as magnetic. To satisfy Wil's lack of exposure to the wild, he feels "a great roaring thirst to know more of things" (*ibid.,* 47). From such experiences, Paulsen admits in *Pilgrimage on a Steel Ride* that, once introduced to sleeping outdoors, it is difficult for him to return to bedrooms. He adds, "If I can't see the sun or the sky I feel lost, emotionally, psychologically, and physically lost" (Paulsen, *Pilgrimage,* 156).

Integral to the author's joy in wastelands lies the transcendence of creation and its effects on the inner self—the draw of sunfish lurking under lily pads in search of water bugs in *Canoe Days;* the anticipation of carp, pike, and walleye fishing season in *Father Water, Mother Woods: Essays on Fishing and Hunting in the North Woods;* Justin's study of a she-bear in *Grizzly,* and John Borne's mesmerism by a doe in *Tracker.* For John the concentration required by deer hunting relieves him of worry about his grandfather's lethal cancer: "It came to him suddenly that he hadn't thought about his grandfather for nearly an hour" (Paulsen, *Tracker,* 50). Other characters experience breakthroughs in thought and personal philosophy. At a climax in the story "Wolfdreams" in the February 2017 issue of *Boy's Life,* the protagonist accepts visions of timber wolves as a predictable part of mushing because "they were part of it, part of the snow and cold and silence and lake and moonlight and dogs and me" (Paulsen, "Wolfdreams," 22). In terms of character response to myriad settings in *Canyons, Caught by the Sea,* and *Project: A Perfect World,* educator Bernice Golden summed up the pivotal question of Paulsen's life in the wilderness with a rhetorical question: "What is important in life and in nature?" (Golden, 1999, v).

Nature's Dangers

Akin to Alfred Lord Tennyson's depiction of "nature, red in tooth and claw," the dangers of honeycomb ice and the predatory side of rattlesnakes, mosquitoes, and sharks are self-evident. Paulsen's survival stories gravitate toward the "vicious beauty" of fauna, a quality captured in the stomping of Holt by a moose cow in *The Foxman,* the Gary character's snapping of pigeon necks in *The Beet Fields,* and the slashing and ripping of lambs by bear claws in *Grizzly* (Creager, 1999, 4). A flippant remark in *The Grass Easters* notes that bears care nothing about humans and "will dust you off, quickly if you get in their way," a mock-cheery description of a grisly demise (Paulsen, *Grass,* 12). With more regret, he characterizes the killing of a deer as a "loss of beauty; the end of a graceful thing" (*ibid.*, vii).

From a philosophical slant, the author accepts roughing it as the ideal. He remarks in *Woods Runner*, "It was a world that did not care about man" yet, to a frontiersman, cities could not offer "a more sensible way to live" (Paulsen, *Woods*, 11). At sight of wolves devouring a doe in *Woodsong*, the author marvels that he was viewing "some ancient thing I did not know any more than I knew what it was like to live in the Ice Age" (Paulsen, *Woodsong*, 7). He told Anne Morris, an interviewer in Austin, Texas: "You can have all your silly little plans, and a 40-foot wave will change your whole life," an admission that no survivalist can predict eventualities (Morris, 1999, K6).

The author's texts incorporate natural laws that derive from immutable needs, a constant thought in the mind of Mark Harrison among cannibals in *The Transall Saga*. In *Mr. Tucket*, the tough-talking mentor, Jason Grimes, observes to Francis Alphonse Tucket that nature "makes a she-bear gut you if you mess with her cubs," a defensive reaction of a mother quadruped (Paulsen, *Mr. Tucket*, 50). Conversely, the author justifies the need for killing animals to supply humans with food, a stance that calls for mutual respect between species. In the background of *Tracker*, John's grandfather, Clay Borne, repudiates sport hunting for fun and exonerates the spilling of animal blood only as an "act of turning a material resource into valuable food" (Powell and Lafferty, 2000, 79).

The Alert Nature Lover

Interviewer Elizabeth Royte pictured the author's milieu as "cruel or indifferent, a source of salvation or a potential killer" (Royte, 2013). Paulsen's frank depiction of frostbite, attack on a farm truck by a moose, snow blindness, and brush wolves devouring a doe informs young readers of the perils of living in the wild in extreme cold and isolation. For *Winterdance: The Fine Madness of Running the Iditarod*, he recounted a musher's horror at the goring of a lead dog by a moose. His setting of accidents within outdoor episodes reminds the naive of possible breakdowns of health and accidents as treacherous as a cracked knee and a fall through 12 feet of icy water. In a terse dismissal of nature's lack of mercy, he twice quipped, "Man proposes; nature disposes," a rephrasing of medieval religious writer Thomas à Kempis (Goodson, 2004, 55).

Requisite to Paulsen's speeches and fiction are wise observations concerning earth's fragility and the obligation of humankind to walk lightly and leave no damage on the trail, as displayed in the filth defiling the Rio Grande in *The Crossing* and the rusting war machines clogging Manila's countryside in *Eastern Sun, Winter Moon*. He warned of current profligacy: "We've somehow managed to design nuclear weapons. We've polluted one jewel of a planet. We're overbreeding at a rate that's frightening" (Lewis, 1994, 1). With similar gravity, in *Fishbone's Song*, the title figure counsels his foster son to become a steward of the land: "No tracks, not a wrinkle to show you were there. No waste. No want. No bother to nobody or no thing" (Paulsen, *Fishbone's*, 109). In the evaluation of Karen Coats for *Bulletin for the Center for Children's Books*, Paulsen "passes on his stories along with simple blues lyrics that distill the experiences into tight nuggets of hard-earned wisdom" (Coats, 2016, 89).

See also adaptation; Iditarod; mentors.

Source

Coats, Karen. "Fishbone's Song," *Bulletin of the Center for Children's Books* 70:2 (October 2016): 89.
Creager, Ellen. "View from the Outside the Wilderness Resonates for Children's Author," *Detroit Free Press* (13 April 1999): 4.

Golden, Bernice. *Critical Reading Activities for the Works of Gary Paulsen.* Portland, ME: Walch, 1999.
Goodson, Lori Atkins. "Singlehanding: An Interview with Gary Paulsen," *ALAN Review* (Winter 2004): 53–59.
Lewis, Randy. "He Owes It All to Librarians and Dogs," *Los Angeles Times* (31 July 1994): 1.
Morris, Anne. "'An Inch Ahead of the Fireball,'" *Austin American Statesman* (7 March 1999): K6.
Moss, Meredith. "Novelist's Life Is In, Out of the Woods," *Dayton Daily News* (5 February 2004): E1.
Nickelson, George. *Gary Paulsen.* New York: Trumpet Club, 1993.
Parmer, Janet. "Author on Tour Chronicling Life of 'Brian,'" [Santa Rosa, CA] *Press Democrat* (6 February 2004): 3.
Powell, Jim, and Nancy Lafferty. "Tracking Adolescent Responses to Cancer" in *Using Literature to Help Troubled Teenagers Cope with Health Issues.* Westport, CT: Greenwood, 2000.
Rodesiler, Luke, *et al.* "Teacher to Teacher: What Literature Related to the Environment and Nature Do You Enjoy Teaching?," *English Journal* 100:3 (2011): 27–29.
Royte, Elizabeth. "Grumpy Old Man and the Sea: Adventures with Gary Paulsen," https://www.outsideonline.com/1919481/grumpy-old-man-and-sea-adventures-gary-paulsen, 2013.
Sides, Anne Goodwin. "On the Road and Between the Pages, an Author Is Restless for Adventure," *New York Times* (26 August 2006): B7.

Nightjohn

An historical novel about dedication to freedom and the voracious love of words, Gary Paulsen's *Nightjohn* redirects his energetic prose toward black history in the cadence of oral story. The plot, set in 1848, replicates a real melodrama of enslavement's barbarisms in the American South some 13 years before the onset of the Civil War and 15 years before the Emancipation Proclamation. To David Gale, an interviewer for *School Library Journal,* the author stated that plantation owners "used to try to work a man to death by the time he was 26. By 26, they thought they had all the useful work they'd get out of him, and they would work him and starve him until he died" (Gale, 1997, 24). For that reason, the novelist chooses Sarny for the protagonist because female breeders had a longer life, a more profitable purpose, and less body-killing drudgery.

Paulsen sets the lingual stage amid the elided speech of the Uncle Remus South. The rhythmic dialogue, which literary analyst Judith P. Robertson terms "beautifully cadenced language of Black English," echoes Sarny's sense of belonging and unity in the quarters among black African survivors of agrarian bondage (Robertson, 1997, 457). Robertson applauds the narrative for dramatizing period facts and relevance to the present. *Sarny,* the sequel, enhances the sound of Southern dialect with the idioms "wet up" for cry, "fancy house" for bordello, and "passed over" for died (Paulsen, *Sarny,* 92, 1, 172). Like the Nordic sounds of Uncle David and Aunt Emily to Carley, a Minneapolis urbanist in *Popcorn Days and Buttermilk Nights,* slave era dialect confers credibility and a sense of membership in a cohesive, supportive extended family.

Critical Response

Critics gravitate to Paulsen's slave novel for its themes of integrity and ambition and for the contrast between the vulnerable orphan Sarny and her sadistic owner, planter Clel Waller. The narrative places in the title figure's words the real crime of illiteracy: "Words are freedom … 'Cause that's all slavery's made of. Words. Law, deeds, passes, all they are is words," a clarification featured in the film version, which stars Carl Lumbly as John. The enslaved teacher, a renegade with a sober dignity, pictures reading as a treasure that whites intend to keep for themselves.

Some reviewers, including Jane Horwitz at the *Washington Post,* identify supernatural elements in the novel, which turns Nightjohn into a mythic quest hero. Rosalind Bentley, on staff at the Minneapolis *Star Tribune,* noted a mystic power in teaching: "All he needs is dirt and a stick. Or a piece of coal and an ashen brick hearth in a slave-quarter shack" (Bentley, 1997, E-15). Reviewer Howard M. Miller, for *Reading Teacher,* expanded on the image: "Literacy becomes a rare and precious treasure, and the quest for this treasure brings with it great danger," both to resolute blacks and to acquisitive wastrels like Waller (Miller, 1998, 602). The spare narrative places Sarny at the raw edge of catastrophe for defying a bigot who profits from her ignorance and who intends to make more money from her offspring.

HISTORIC IDEALS

Paulsen links emancipation with a history of sacrifice and martyrdom. To the surprise of Mammy and Sarny, John espouses higher ideals than the typical plantation slave. He admits that he once fled north, then returned to teach reading and writing "a little here, a little there … in hidey-schools," a dodge to protect him and his students from repercussions (Paulsen, *Nightjohn,* 57). After Union bluecoats free Waller's plantation, 11 years after learning the alphabet, Sarny reflects on the gift of literacy from John, who "gave me reading so I could find my children" (Paulsen, *Sarny,* 64). The statement refers to scattered households and alludes to all black Americans as children in need of reclamation through education and opportunity.

According to commentary in *Knowledge Quest,* Judi Moreillon and Kristin Fontichiaro applaud *Nightjohn* for its dual models of perseverance, a shared trait between mentor and pupil. John's long-range purpose—beyond his own life and travels—is the compilation of a history of black African captivity in the New World, which he intends for black writers to record for the edification of future readers. The plan comes true in *Sarny,* when the aged storyteller follows the advice of grandson Carlisle to write her memories because "Someday people will want to read it, read it all" (Paulsen, *Sarny,* 4). According to the memoirist, a bit of John lives on in her grandson. The legacy ennobles learning as a chain linking black Americans over time into a greater cosmos. In the estimation of Pamela S. Carroll and Steven B. Chandler, writers for *Strategies,* the novel can "make textbook history come alive" (Carroll & Chandler, 2001, 36).

See also legend; literacy; *Sarny.*

Source

Atherton, Tony. "Literacy Fable Wrapped in Slavery Melodrama," *Calgary Herald* (16 June 1996): E5.
Bentley, Rosalind. "'Nightjohn' Offers Lesson to Remember," [Minneapolis] *Star Tribune* (6 June 1997): E-15.
Carroll, Pamela S., and Steven B. Chandler. "Sports-related Young Adult Literature," *Strategies* 14:5 (2001): 35–37.
Gale, David. "Gary Paulsen," *School Library Journal* 43:6 (June 1997): 24.
Miller, Howard M. "Victims, Heroes, and Just Plain Folks," *Reading Teacher* 51:7 (April 1998): 602–604.
Moore, Opal. "Tellers and Their Tales," *Washington Post* (13 June 1993): X-11.
Robertson, Judith P. "Teaching about Worlds of Hurt through Encounters with Literature: Reflections on Pedagogy," *Language Arts* 74:6 (October 1997): 457.

parenting

Paulsen's survey of parental duties and errors in judgment reiterates his own disorderly upbringing, a childhood nightmare reprised in drunken arguments in *The Beet Fields* and *Popcorn Days and Buttermilk Nights;* Corey, a tent preacher, tricking the gullible in *The Tent;* and a drunken mother knifing her son in *Winterkill.* In a mild example of child-adult conflict in *Project: A Perfect World,* Jim Stanton can do little more than pout at his father's move to Folsum, New Mexico, far from Jim's friends and a summer of league baseball, a painful break that recurs for Jim Neuton's family, who move from Madison to rural Pinewood, Wisconsin, in *The Island.* As a relief of household squabbling, Wil turns the Neutons' disconnect into a play, "Bickerbits." In a more painful locale in *The Car,* Terry Anders, a forsaken teen whose parents abandon him in Cleveland, Ohio, speaks wisdom acquired from years of observation. Of the traits of a self-absorbed mother and father, he summarizes, "They just aren't the types who make parents" (Paulsen, *Car,* 64).

The author revisits the themes of neglect and abuse in multiple settings and genres, including the farcical *Harris and Me,* which introduces a throwaway child to acceptance as a foster son of the hardworking Larsons and their rascal son Harris. The novel extols unconditional love to a boy who feels alienated and misplaced at home among alcoholics. According to *Globe and Mail* book critic Elizabeth MacCallum, amid slapdash, scampish antics, the episodes "achieve the impressive feat of outraging the prissy of almost every hue of today's socio-political-religious watchdogs," while appealing to participants in normal home uproar (MacCallum, 1994, C17). Her remark exonerates households for surface chaos if they espouse love and acceptance of their young.

The author's expertise at domestic compensation echoes in varied autobiographical and fictional situations, as with the household struggle with limited funds in *Lawn Boy,* Harv Kline's need to save money to educate his two children in *The Rifle,* and Kevin Spencer's exploration of marital intimacy by observing his parents in *Crush: The Theory, Practice and Destructive Properties of Love.* In *Field Trip,* Atticus, the dog narrator, divides the household power structure into two adults, "the boss and the real boss who smells like flowers," his term for Ben's mother, Mrs. Duffy (Paulsen, *Field,* 9). For rounders like Henry Mosley, Reed Hamner, and Riley Dolen in *Masters of Disaster,* lying to parents complicates the fallout from their shenanigans, particularly malodorous Dumpster diving. In a post-parental situation, John Borne's knowledge of his deceased parents in *Tracker* from the honest accounts of Grandmother Aggie requires imagination to recreate two people he scarcely remembers. In a reverse of John's longing for a living mother and father, Richard Allen Mesington's enjoyment of Christmas lights with his mother and dad in *The Rifle* precedes a stunning loss after he dies from a gun accident, leaving his parents deep in sorrow. In each situation, the emotional divide stirs longing for a reunion of the nuclear unit.

Eccentric Parents

For *My Life in Dog Years,* Paulsen outlines the significance of dogs, especially Snowball, Ike, Dirk, Caesar, Rex, and Cookie, in relieving his loneliness and guiding him in less literal ways than human mentors. By supplanting disaffection in Paulsen's post–World-War II stilt house in an army compound at Manila in *Eastern Sun, Winter Moon,* Snowball, a dog rescued from the cook pot, becomes a quadruped father replacing an army martinet who cares little for his six-year-old. The author rediscovered canine guidance over the winter of 1982–1983 after readying a husky team to compete in the Iditarod. As reprised in *Winterdance,* the lessons of limitless dog love compensate him for a childhood devoid of normal parental devotion.

Of the one-person parenting in *Canyons,* Paulsen dramatizes a maternal specialty: "The Mother Look. The what-are-you-up-to Mother Look" (Paulsen, *Canyons,* 93). In a comedic variation of Brennan Cole's predicament, the author wrests humor out of Tony's single mother Al (for Alice), a stripper at the Kitty Kat Club in *The Glass Café.* Although degraded for her career and charged with assault, child endangerment and mistreatment, and resisting arrest, she represents the author's image of the resolute mama who takes

Tony "to the doctor ... even if I'm a little sick" (Paulsen, *Glass,* 8). In addition to warning him about processed meats that "will make my liver rot before I'm sixteen," she defends her son against a host of accusers from social services and the police (*ibid.,* 12). *Audiobook* praised the novel's "fresh and funny exploration of motherhood" supervised by a mom that *Kirkus Review* called "intelligent, forthright, fiercely protective ... memorable" ("Glass," 2016; *Kirkus,* 2003).

Difficult Childhoods

The writer's exploration of child-rearing styles as disparate as Colonel Paulsen's and Al's encompasses an array of figures, from Mrs. Barrancs, a shallow, privileged divorcee in *Sisters/Hermanas,* to the affectionate grandma in *Lawn Boy* and the parents who extend welcome to Francis Alphonse Tucket in *Tucket's Home,* a satisfying reunion story ending a lengthy pentad. The motherly slave Delie, the plantation childcare provider, replaces Sarny's birth mother in *Nightjohn* and *Sarny.* At the depths of despair from her husband Martin's death at age 27, Sarny clings to Delie, who "sat with me, held me, cried with me and patted me on the side of my head," all nonverbal, tactile means of minimizing sorrow (Paulsen, *Sarny,* 14). By example, Sarny repeats the model in loving her own children, Tyler and little Delie. Thus, the pattern of maternal tenderness permeates subsequent generations and upholds Sarny after Clel Waller sells her son and daughter to settle gambling debts. In the chaos following liberation, she concentrates on finding her little ones, a family that keeps her sane and focused, and swells her household by adopting Tyler Two, a white toddler. Sarny's great heart expresses post-war tolerance and a rejection of vengeance toward the once-superior white race.

With some sympathy for adults, Paulsen unveils the coping mechanisms of troubled parents, for example, a stash of chocolate peanut butter candy that soothes Kevin Spencer's mother in *Crush,* worshippers seeking healing in *The Tent,* and sisterhood with the Welcome Wagon ladies in *Dunc's Doll.* In *A Christmas Sonata,* the narrator admits that the adult reply "We'll see" means no more than a retreat from truth until adults can formulate a better answer (Paulsen, *Sonata,* n.p.). For Abigail and Olin Smith, prisoners of war in *Woods Runner,* accepting coming of age in 13-year-old son Samuel Lehi Smith requires acknowledgment of his sudden progression to manhood and to protector of a household devastated by arson and imprisonment by Redcoats. For Catherine McLure Fruit Goddard, a real widowed parent of the protagonist in *Soldier's Heart,* obvious dissatisfaction in her son Charley's letters about military bootcamp grieves her. She encourages Charley to desert, a motherly solution to discontent that he disregards, perhaps because the army punishment for desertion is the firing squad. In both wartime settings, parents as well as their sons come to accept change, especially maturity and consequences of actions.

In *The River,* a *bildungsroman* of the *Hatchet* saga, as Brian Robeson wrestles with his parents' divorce, he internalizes the choices of his mother, Katie Robeson, to date her lover and of his father to remarry. In *Brian's Hunt,* Katie, a realtor who protects the famous son in the Brian series from intrusive reporters, maintains parental strictures even after he reaches age 16 and proves once more his ability to flourish in the wild. Unlike adapting to the woods, Brian's compromises with a fractured household grate more permanently on his psyche. The straightforward dramatization of a splintered family appeals to young readers who have themselves experienced shattered homes or who know peers who undergo the turmoil of blended families. Paulsen honors his fictional hero for accepting a grueling form of coming of age that develops maturity and adaptation to the dissolution of his nuclear family.

See also alcoholism; *The Island.*

Source
"The Glass Café," *Brilliance Audio* (2016).
"The Glass Café," *Kirkus Reviews* (1 June 2003).
MacCallum, Elizabeth. "Rude, Outrageous: An Ideal Book for Kids," [Toronto] *Globe and Mail* (5 February 1994): C17.

The Rifle

In a shattering a 217-year history of an object, Paulsen's historical novel *The Rifle* follows the people and events connected with an historic firearm from its design in 1768 and completion around 1776 into the late 20th century.

LINEAGE OF THE RIFLE

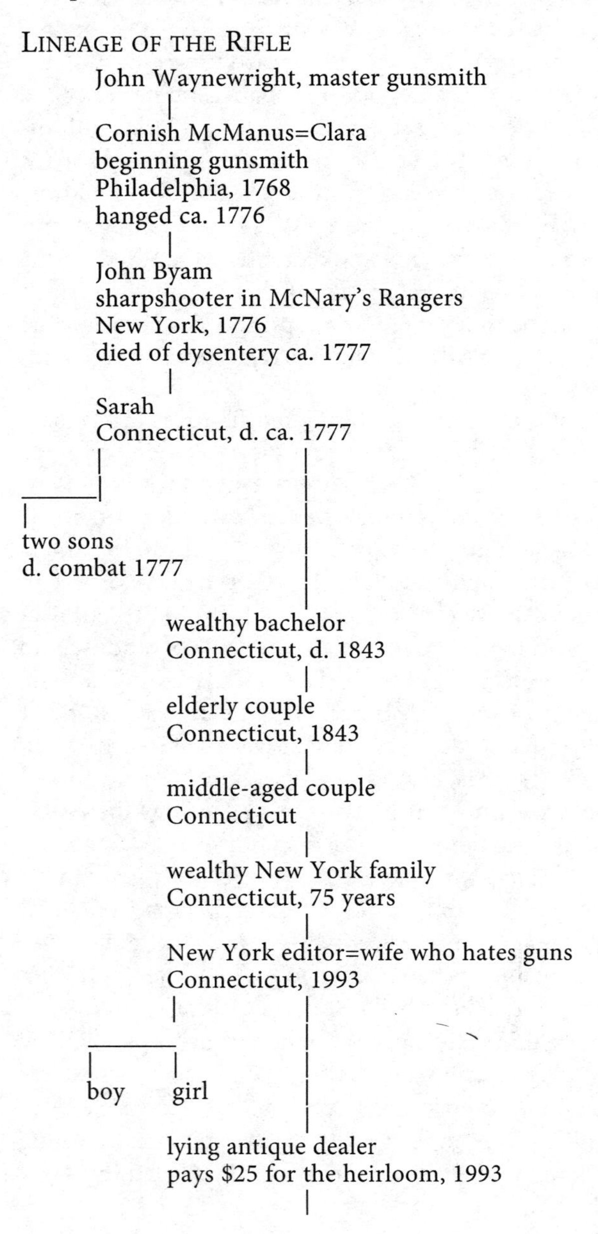

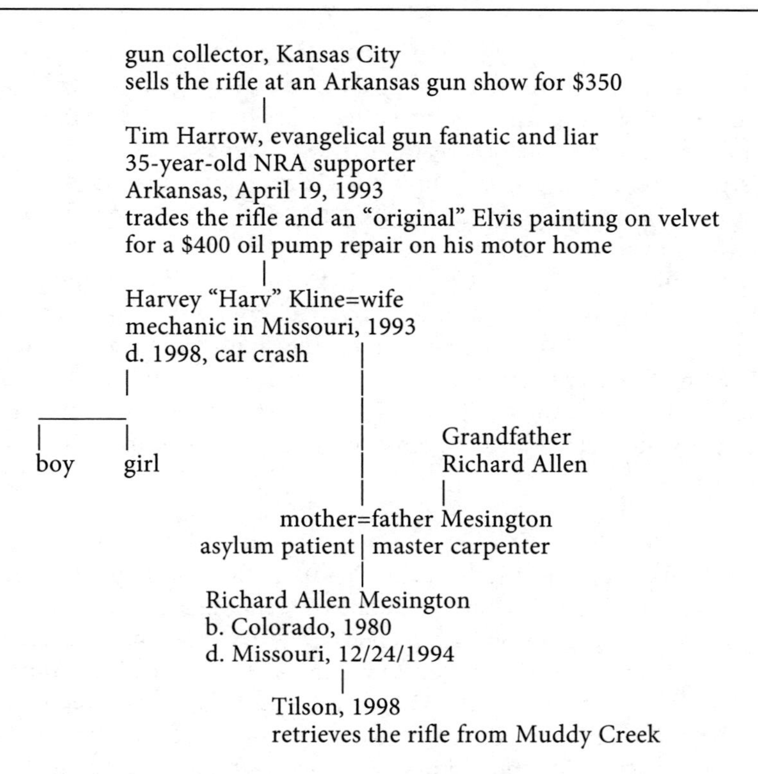

The introduction of gunsmithing depicts the production of a flintlock like other manufactured machinery. The text details the meaning of "sweet," an adjective reserved for a beautiful, technically accurate firearm that ensures food on the table and self-defense of the marksman (Paulsen, *Rifle,* 5). As a mystic element to the story, the author inserts a raw curly maple gunstock that "seemed to come alive," a scenario similar in tone and history to Michelangelo's first view of the marble from which, in 1504, he "freed" the statue of David (*ibid.* 8).

In contrast to its destructive blast, McManus's sweet flintlock firearm with its small .40 bore, comes together painstakingly slow by yellow candlelight with his use of exacting tools—draw-file, chisel, rasp, burr, ramrod, bore tube. Equally slow and measured, the choice of an owner leads the gunsmith to John Byam, a frontiersman who handles the long gun with reverence and understanding of the smaller bore. The text credits Byam with applying his unusually accurate rifle to sharpshooting against British officers, a target the enemy claims broke the laws of engagement. Simultaneously, Paulsen compares the love of the two men for gun artistry with McManus's adoration of Clara, his future wife, a motif that recurs in the last segment of the narrative with a boy's love for his dog Sissy. The untidy fusion of themes—the inertia of machinery with the vigor and fragility of a human body—anticipates the hanging of Bainbridge, whom Byam's marksmanship fails to save from a Redcoat noose.

Suspenseful Conclusion

Throughout six changes of ownership, the Connecticut residence, where the rifle remains in the attic, houses the carefully wrapped and greased firearm. For irony, Paulsen pictures a New York editor calling the gun "so … so American," a suggestion of differences in attitude from the 1770s to 1993 (*ibid.,* 51). In a brief survey of NRA fanatic Tim Harrow and his ilk, Paulsen creates a pattern of twisted logic connecting American constitutional rights with the aims of Christianity. Tim's arsenal of long guns, handguns, and military surplus firepower accommodates his conservative views of patriotism, "the American ideal," and the right to possess and use lethal weapons in self-defense (*ibid.*, 58).

Paulsen extends sentimentality—Byam's love for Clara, Harv's responsibility to educate his two children—to liberate gun victims of fault but not from their failure to view the flintlock as what journalist Dan Davis, on staff at the *Whitehorse* [Yukon Territory] *Star,* calls "essentially an instrument of death" (Davis, 2000, 33). By picturing Richard Allen Mesington as an admirable teen and his neighbors as friends preparing for Christmas Eve, the action establishes the sudden death as an accident precipitated by a single spark. Carrying the story forward four years, the text implies that Tilson, the next owner, who reclaims the flintlock from Muddy Creek, places the antique in murky territory, where a valuable collectible gains killing power once more after the owner decides to reload.

Defining Guns

The media issued varied opinions about the major themes, which question the wisdom of storing guns in homes. In an interview with *ALAN Review* writer Lori Atkins Goodson, the author clarified his purpose—to show an "insanely warped" attitude toward firearms, which have become "an epidemic" caused by the stunted maturity and misdirected pride of American gun enthusiasts (Goodson, 2004, 55). *Toronto Star* book reviewer Arlene Perly Rae declared: "*The Rifle* will shake the complacent among us out of our socks as Paulsen takes issue with the cliche: 'Guns don't kill people, people kill people,'" (Rae, 1996, L-16). Critic Davis concurs that the cautionary tale "makes a powerful statement about the dangers of unregulated gun ownership [and] certainly makes a strong case for responsible use" (Davis, 2000, 33). Of the story's impact, *Kirkus Reviews* summarized the impression in one word, "Unforgettable" ("Rifle," 1995, 17).

In an essay for *Voices from the Middle,* Paulsen detailed the source of *The Rifle.* His memory of a shooting death two decades earlier by a gun fan in the wrong yard infused his story with "what that brief moment with what a gun did, the lives it destroyed" (Paulsen, 2000, 64). His unusual amalgam of fine craftsmanship and service to the American Revolution with right-wing fanaticism and careless trading and sale underscores the danger of firearm purchases for the sake of investment in antique firearms, off-kilter philosophies, and home decoration. He stresses that, if a story like *The Rifle* "is based on real things, the truth comes out by itself" (*ibid.*).

Source

Davis, Dan. "Tales of Guns and Hunting Hawks," *Whitehorse* [Yukon Territory] *Star* (8 December 2000): 33.

Goodson, Lori Atkins. "Singlehanding: An Interview with Gary Paulsen," *ALAN Review* 31:2 (Winter 2004): 53–59.

Paulsen, Gary. "The Way Stories Dance," *Voices from the Middle* 8:1 (September 2000): 60–65.

Rae, Arlene Perly. "Poignant Story Grapples with Abuse at School," *Toronto Star* (3 February 1996): L-16.

Ralston, Jennifer. "The Rifle," *School Library Journal* 49:10 (1 October 2003): 98.

"The Rifle," *Kirkus Reviews* (1 September 1995): 17.

The River

In *The River,* the second book in the Brian Robeson saga, Paulsen's protagonist continues to value his own merit as a thoughtful outdoorsman, an identity he believes must be earned rather than taught. Marked by cliffhangers and suspense similar to those in *Hatchet,* the action features a survey of survivalism for a government school training soldiers and astronauts, a trial run that Brian attempts with only a folding knife and a hand-sketched map. Despite bacterial infection in his hands that require medical attention, he remains a confident woods dweller on the Necktie River, a flow 70 feet wide that becomes his sole avenue for escape and rescue.

Of the documented return to the stranding site in south central Canada, Brian admits, "It was strangely easy for him to get in the bush plane," despite the memories of crashing the small Cessna 406 over water and barely surviving (Paulsen, *River,* 15). Backed by psychologist Derek Holtzer, Brian defies his mother, realtor Katie Robeson, and lies that he will have a tent, rubber boat, first-aid kit, fishing gear, cook pots, and food to lessen danger. His companion admires Brian's ease as "something more going for you besides luck" (*ibid.,* 5). Hesitating to be candid with three strangers, Brian later admits to himself that he had "learned to accept things—his mother, the situation, his life, all of it" (*ibid.,* 11).

An Altered Approach

For the sequel, Paulsen takes a fresh, distinct detour from the original novel by adding deliberate obstacles. On exiting the floatplane, Brian orders Holtzer to abandon the supplies. The psychologist agrees to leave all behind except the radio, which ironically becomes unusable after lightning strikes a tree and Holtzer. Intending to recreate the hardships of his original 54-day trip, Brian re-acclimates to an experimental camp 100 miles east of the first crash site. The venture identifies verities that might help others survive the wilderness. In a review for the *Los Angeles Times,* analyst Michael O'Mahony declares the protagonist "two years older and eons wiser" (O'Mahony, 1991, 13). The statement implies instinctive advancement in Brian from the skittish boy he had been at age 13 to a 15-year-old capable of poling a balky raft 100 miles toward rescue.

Paulsen highlights in the protagonist a stalwart nature, something more than just luck to endure predicaments over "food, hunger, home, distance, sleep, the agony of his body" (Paulsen, *River,* 128). During Brian's original ordeal, discovering fire and hunting and cooking food had transformed him permanently, easing his anxieties. At age 15, he incurs a natural misadventure from the electrical jolt that plunges Holtzer into a coma. Brian resolves to evacuate him over rough waters to Brannock's Trading Post. O'Mahony summarizes the economical, fast-paced plot as "a taut ordeal of human ingenuity battling the eat-or-be-eaten canon of the wild," his overview of the crags, rapids, and marshes that slow the raft, leaving Holtzer thin, unfed, and dehydrated (*ibid.*).

Mixed Responses

In reference to success against all odds, Brian describes the altered self as "reborn in the woods," where he feels confident of striking fire from flint, predicting bad weather, and lashing eight poplar logs into a raft to ferry Holtzer to safety at a dock downriver (*ibid.,* 9). Unlike the surge of critiques lauding the second novel for its emphasis on orienteering to the trading post, a review in the Moncton, New Brunswick, *Times* lambasted Paulsen for describing raft building from fallen logs that seemed too perfect and a story line less intriguing than the original. In a more pointed critique for the Minneapolis *Star Tribune,* Jane Resh Thomas, a frequent doubter of Paulsen's acumen, charged the author with "[falsifying] reality, idealizing the power of human beings" like "superkid" Brian (Thomas, 1996, F-17).

Other critics sensed something new in Paulsen's sequel, beginning with Katie Robeson's charge that the idea is crazy and including Brian's abandonment of "recitification" to hear once more each birdcall, view the hills that line the Necktie River, and gauge the weight that the raft will hold. *Kirk's Review, Publishers Weekly,* and other literary surveys admired the terse language and energy of *The River,* which replicated the intensity, ingenuity, and authenticity of *Hatchet* by confronting the protagonist with new terrors in the wild. In advice to readers, Paulsen urged involvement like Brian's: "Get right into it, find out what's going on, and try to do it yourself" (Stetson, 1996, 7).

See also Hatchet.

Source

"Dear Gary Paulsen," [Saint John, N.B.] *Telegraph-Journal* (21 May 2008): D11.
Ernst, Shirley B. "Brian's Winter," *Language Arts* 74:7 (November 1997): 566.
Fine, Edith Hope. *Gary Paulsen: Author and Wilderness Adventurer.* Berkeley Heights, NJ: Enslow, 2000.
Gallo, Don. "The Promise and Seduction of Sequels," *English Journal* 94:4 (March 2005): 124–128.
Golden, Bernice. *Critical Reading Activities for the Works of Gary Paulsen.* Portland, ME: Walch, 1999.
O'Mahony, Michael. "The River," *Los Angeles Times* (30 June 1991): 13.
Stetson, Nancy. "Been There, Done That: Gary Paulsen Spreads the Words on Survival," *Chicago Tribune* (12 March 1996): 7.
Thomas, Jane Resh. "'Superkid' Aura Mars Paulsen's Latest," [Minneapolis] *Star Tribune* (16 June 1996): F-17.

Sarny

Sarny, Paulsen's most admired heroine, epitomizes the human yen to learn as a counteragent to sexual bondage, mother hunger, and torture. She belittles enslaver Clel Waller's breath—"White stink. Pig stink"—scorns his surname, and refuses to use it as her own patronym, "the back part of my name" (Paulsen, *Nightjohn,* 62, 15). Despite being "worked to the bone," the 12-year-old risks slave-era reprisal for studying the first eight alphabet letters with the tutor John (*ibid.,* 18). To impress on readers what lies at stake, Paulsen pictures Delie whipped to the bone and hanging from chains in the spring house.

Torment fails to quell Sarny's thirst for more learning. Even threatened with Waller's whip and chains, she grasps at letters and the three-letter words they form as though snatching life from a hopeless plantation enslavement. At the prompting of her teacher, she longs to extend that legacy into the future. Out of admiration for resisters like John and Sarny, Paulsen dedicated *Nightjohn* to Sally Hemings, the kept woman of Thomas Jefferson and mother of his biracial children.

Clever Resistance

Paulsen salutes empowerment in girls like Sarny—"tobacco girl"—who possesses more resilience and spunk than Pecola Breedlove, the pathetic victim in Toni Morrison's *The Bluest Eye* (*ibid.,* 51). Although shut out of communication among whites, Sarny uses weeding time beneath the manse windows as a source of eavesdropping on Margaret Waller and her sister Alaine (*ibid.,* 51). Although skimpily clad in the standard shirtdress or shift, a cloth quadrangle stitched at shoulders and sides, Sarny stands up to humiliation and disenfranchisement. By the time she masters seven letters, she can decipher "bag," thus making the connection between word and object, an epiphany she shares with Helen Keller in William Gibson's classic play *The Miracle Worker* (*ibid.,* 60).

In *Sarny: A Life Remembered,* set in 1930, John's star pupil recounts her autobiography from breech birth in 1836 and the magic of literacy that staves off worse harm than assignment to the breeding shed. Through reading and writing, she is able to forge passes and reads newspapers and the bible. The loss of husband Martin to overwork belabors the reflections of a former slave wife.

Sarny's Genealogy:

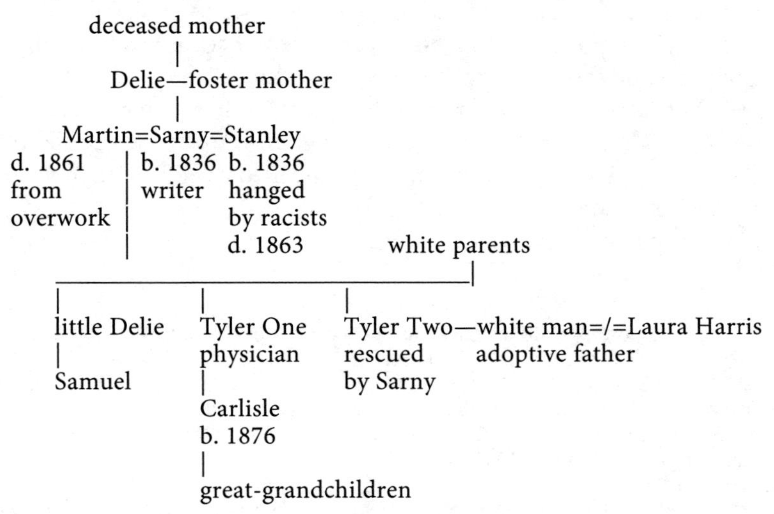

From locating her children's bills of sale, Sarny deduces that each bondsman has a market value like other luxuries in the capitalistic world. Like coins in the bank, slaves in the quarters assure the planter's wealth and foster his greed until Sarny outsmarts him. Critic Ellen Creager, a journalist for the Bergen, New Jersey, *Record*, surmised, "The penalty for learning is high, Sarny finds out, but the penalty for not learning is higher" (Creager, 1993, C-9).

In the resolution of the Civil War, Sarny makes her way to New Orleans in the carriage of Laura Harris, an octoroon courtesan who subverts sexual enslavement for her empowerment and personal enrichment. The women arrive on April 11, 1865, to a mansion equipped with ample food, luxuries, books, and the authority that Laura wields over lustful Louisiana males. A foil of the ogre Clel Waller, who loses his wealth by drinking and gambling, Laura becomes the *deus ex machina* who speeds Sarny toward a full and satisfying liberation from the past. Central to her rise, her children achieve freedom and hope for the future. The family acclimates to a genteel kind of manners, the submission of self to white power that Mammy teaches her son in *The Legend of Bass Reeves.*

Sarny's Gifts

Beyond enabling by Laura and her money, Sarny's twofold legacy rests on her founding of freedmen's schools in Louisiana and Texas and on the quality of her children's upbringing. Deaf and resigned to a retirement home near Dallas, Texas, at age 94, she continues to ponder fascinating words and to reflect on her husbands—Martin, who died "worked down and broke" in 1861, and Stanley, killed by night riders in 1863 (Paulsen, *Sarny,* 2). Paulsen's depiction of male vs. female strengths awards Sarny long life and productivity in contrast to her mates and to her tormentor, Waller, who expires from a gut wound inflicted by a Union soldier's bayonet.

Unlike the remarkable acclaim for the original story in *Nightjohn*, the sequel achieved less success because of its anticlimactic falling action during a less dramatic era of American history. A review in the *Ottawa Citizen* declared that *Sarny* lacked "visceral impact … magnitude and pervasiveness of the terrors and degradations faced by freed slaves" ("Sarny," 1998, E5). Jane Resh Thomas, a previous Paulsen critic, declared that "a litany of unremitting violence and cruelty ... seems self-indulgent" and considered the novel too horrendous for a child reader (Thomas, 1993, H-11).

Readers appreciative of Sarny found passionate themes to extol. Opal Moore, a reviewer for the *Washington Post,* claimed the slaves themselves as Paulsen's focus: "The true hero is neither NightJohn nor Sarny, but an enslaved people whose courage and cooperation protect NightJohn and the rebellious souls who would learn to read and free themselves" (Moore, 1993, X-11). With an eye toward subsequent clashes with whites in African American struggles, Alice Cary, a critic for *Children's Literature Review,* praised the historical novel as "a spare but riveting tale, tracing not only a compelling life but the story of civil rights in the United States" (Cary, 2003).

See also female persona; literacy; *Nightjohn;* slavery.

Source

Cary, Alice. "Gary Paulsen on the Go: Sleds, Motorcycles, and Sailboats," *Children's Literature Review* 82 (2003).
Creager, Ellen. "Two Tough Reads for Preteens," [Bergen, NJ] *Record* (22 April 1993): C-9.
James, Caryn. "To the Cabin of Slaves, a Gutsy Girl Brings Light," *New York Times* (1 June 1996): 13.
Moore, Opal. "Tellers and Their Tales," *Washington Post* (13 June 1993): X-11.
Robertson, Judith P. "Teaching about Worlds of Hurt through Encounters with Literature: Reflections on Pedagogy," *Language Arts* 74:6 (October 1997): 457.
"Sarny," *Ottawa Citizen* (15 March 1998): E5.
Thomas, Jane Resh. "Slavery Tale Piles on Description," [Cleveland, Ohio] *Plain Dealer* (4 April 1993): H-11.

slavery

Bondage in Gary Paulsen's writing focuses on the everyday cruelties to body and spirit epitomized by the primitive Tsook tribe, which enslaves hiker Mark Harrison in *The Transall Saga.* From a historical perspective in *Nightjohn, Sarny,* the Tucket series, and *The Legend of Bass Reeves,* the author presents Comanchero traders, dogs, a club and whip, hammer and chisel, pistols, branding irons, and the soul-killing travail on a Southern plantation that rose "on the backs of others" (Paulsen, *Sarny,* 56–57). In *Tucket's Gold,* the protagonist resolves to rescue two orphans, Billy and Lottie, from Hispanic villains to whom "Children meant real money because they could be sold or traded into slavery" (Paulsen, *Gold,* 3). According to Mammy, the parent and instructor of Deputy U.S. Marshal Bass Reeves, slaves must differentiate between the body and soul: "We got to do what we got to do 'cause of the white man's law. But that don't make no man your master in God's eyes" (Paulsen, *Legend,* 4). The bold declaration captures the courage of a woman whom the master won in an Austin poker game and regards as chattel.

For Charley Goddard, a Union recruit to the First Minnesota Volunteers in *Soldier's Heart,* seeing a black person in thrall to whites arouses insight into the harm of bondage. The yank of a white woman on her domestic alerts him to the absence of everyday freedoms as simple as watching an army on parade. He concludes it "strange to own a person" and wonders how war will change the social evil by freeing black people, who are an unquestionable "part of the South" (Paulsen, *Soldier's,* 15, 16). The narrative implies that these complex musings inflame citizens of the North and South and arouse controversy in U.S. and Confederate lawmakers.

In *Nightjohn,* the author reshapes bondsmen from submissive minions to subversives. The verbal resistance of the mean-spirited owner's slaves takes the form of rude names—"dog droppings and pig slop and ... horse crap," an early indication that bondswomen like Sarny revere the power of words to degrade the evil Clel Waller (Paulsen, *Nightjohn,* 14,

21). Pitted against the master's "dirt mean" shackles and bloodthirsty dogs, the backbiting seems a tepid reprisal until a wandering tutor introduces Waller's field hands to reading and writing (*ibid.*, 47). By elevating intellectual pursuits, John offers pride and a mental escape from unending labor, forced breeding, and trough feeding. The hope for freedom enables Sarny to cling to learning and to revere John for his sacrifices.

Treating the Surface

In the plantation South, the slaveholder of *Nightjohn* abases field workers through a variety of humiliations as cruel as tying the simple-witted slave Alice for breeding and whipping her with the belt from a cotton gin, a significant choice in an economy based on fiber. The author particularizes the sadism of Clel Waller, a plantation enslaver "pale white maggot ugly," for lashing Alice and hanging her in a spring house, a dual torment intended to demean her and sap her spirit (Paulsen, *Nightjohn*, 61). As an antidote, Mammy's healing root tea derives from folk cures based on natural remedies for pain and infection. After dogs chew Alice's chest, Mammy stitches the remains with canvas thread and greases the wound, frail first aid for bestial bloodsport.

For his survey of human bondage, Paulsen extracted from Southern plantation history the bestialization of slaves by bigots who fed bondsmen twice daily in troughs. As a scheme of astute husbandry, the master makes double use of a unified meal at one site for both nourishment and roll-call. To ensure a fair share, slaves quickly gather around the animal bin. In Sarny's words, "Everybody passes the gourd and eats with their hands" to scoop up the vegetables cooked in pork fat and buttermilk, the leftover liquid from churning (*ibid.*, 31). The narrative validates language as an antidote to degradation. Although additional strictures on religion and free speech relegate slaves like Delie to whispered prayers, the wisps of courage and consolation buoy demoralized spirits.

Sexuality and breeding incite worse brutality because procreation means profits to the planters, who raise and sell crops of black children as though they were calves or piglets. For falling asleep while courting on the sly, Pawley endures emasculation, a farmer's method of gelding or slicing off genitals that causes Pawley to bleed to death. Obsessed with altruism to better his people, John endures dismembered middle toes, which Waller lops with a "thunk" of the chisel (*ibid.*, 74). Mammy greases the wounds, salts them, and wraps the feet in rags cleansed in boiling water. The primitive ministrations represent the most that Waller's slaves can do to relieve the agony of torture and inhibit blood loss and infection. For the exhibition of cruelty, Sarny wishes for Waller "a good goddamn hell with demons eating at you, pulling your guts out" (*ibid.*, 76–77).

Emboldening the Soul

The description of a ditch school or brush school captures the crudeness of the first clandestine slave training site, which Sarny calls a "pit school" (*ibid.*, 87). The one-on-one method countered laws such as the North Carolina statute of 1830, which sentenced violators to 39 lashes on the bare back. Three years later, Alabama legislators upped the punishment to 50 lashes for the first offense and 100 for subsequent infractions, a certain death penalty. Lit by pitch torches, John's outdoor classroom welcomes seven pupils, all smiling at the opportunity to learn white magic—scratching letters in dirt with a sharpened stick and reading words on paper. Although warned of the danger, Sarny obeys the urge to animate shapes with sound—"BAG. BAG. BAG." (*ibid.*, 61).

The magic of letters to make words emboldens Sarny during the fall of the Confederacy, a chaotic time that accords rough justice to Waller. Despite her lack of cash or salable goods, literacy assures her a means of reading war accounts in newspapers and locating her children. Among Greerson's bills of sale, she digs for the truth and discerns, "Lives. These were lives," a revelation to a woman who clings to recorded fact to reunite with son Tyler and daughter Delie (Paulsen, *Sarny,* 39). Paulsen uses the predicament of scattered families as an object lesson about the evils of the flesh trade and the lack of education that leaves freedmen unable to access official papers, data, maps, and roads.

See also The Legend of Bass Reeves; literacy; *Nightjohn; Sarny.*

Source

Edmonds, Arlene. "Deltas Open Festival with Discussion about 'Nightjohn,'" *Philadelphia Tribune* (13 November 1998): D1.
Gilson, Nancy. "Survival Saga Takes New Twist," *Columbus* [Ohio] *Dispatch* (18 June 1998): 27.
Holden, Stephen. "Literacy, a Weapon for a Slave," *New York Times* (31 January 1997): 8.
Robertson, Judith P. "Teaching about Worlds of Hurt through Encounters with Literature: Reflections on Pedagogy," *Language Arts* 74:6 (October 1997): 457.

Soldier's Heart

Paulsen's historical fiction *Soldier's Heart* empathizes with a boy volunteer in the American War between the States and, by extension, with all child soldiery, beginning with 13-year-old Samuel Lehi Smith's enlistment in *Woods Runner* and including Apache raider Coyote Runs in *Canyons* during the Indian Wars. For 15-year-old Charles E. "Charley" Goddard, a real infantryman in Company K of the First Minnesota Volunteers, the introduction to army life begins at Fort Snelling after his three-year enlistment on April 29, 1861, when he intends to "go to see what a war was like" (Paulsen, *Soldier's,* 4). Despite scuttlebutt that recruits will replace regular army on the western frontier, the need for Union regiments forces President Abraham Lincoln to call for volunteers four days later on May 3.

The narrative pictures Charley's enthusiasm for battle as evidence of naiveté. His high-spirited anticipation of wartime adventure begins 17 days after the firing on Fort Sumter, South Carolina, but a week before the Confederate States of America formally declares war on the United States. From Fort Snelling, Minnesota, the budding soldier writes to his mother, Catherine McLure Fruit Goddard, and his seven-year-old brother Orren about "rough fare" at mealtime, a lack of uniforms, boring drills, and a salary of $11 per month (*ibid.,* 14). Significantly, Charley gives no thought to the effects of shooting and slaughter on his morale and conscience.

Off to War

On June 22, 1861, five weeks after Union troops occupied Baltimore, Charley moves out by steamer to St. Paul and by train southeast toward Maryland, where pro–Confederate secessionists had rioted on April 19. The train trip provides a misleadingly comfortable journey through Illinois, Indiana, Ohio, and Pennsylvania for homesteaders unused to travel. On the way, he exults in girls waving flags, distributing candy and hankies, and urging him on to Richmond, Virginia, the Confederate capital and bastion of rebel president Jefferson Davis. From Charley's limited experience, the send-off is "a simply grand way to go off to fight a war," strong evidence of his shallow values and inexperience (*ibid.,* 13).

The historical novel creates contrast in the Goddard family's snug homestead that Charley leaves behind and the farms and shacks of the South's "poor white trash," whom the Union army battles (*ibid.,* 18). The narrative directs the thinking of Charley and his comrade Swenson to the overall effects of black poverty, a national disgrace that lasted far beyond the 1860s into present time. Upon learning of shortages of cotton and tobacco and viewing the rag-wrapped feet of a rebel Alabaman, Charley misjudges the enemy by thinking, "This ain't going to be much of a war" (*ibid.*). Paulsen returns to the issue of the fight for freedom in *Sarny,* in which the title figure muses on Abraham Lincoln's freeing of slaves on January 1, 1863. A second glimpse of liberation in *The Legend of Bass Reeves* pictures him galloping toward Indian Territory—a free man at last.

Real Conflict

The author emphasizes the difference in ambition and achievement for officers and grunts. By July 21, 1861, boredom ends for Charley after he receives an introduction to mayhem in Manassas, Virginia, at the Battle of Bull Run. At the war's first major face-off, rebel general Pierre Gustave Toutant Beauregard clashed with Union General Irvin McDowell, winning a major victory and a day of thanksgiving at the Confederate headquarters in Richmond's Court End. Because of McDowell's poor leadership, Lincoln transferred command of Union troops to Major General George Brinton McClellan, a reconnaissance specialist during the Mexican-American War in 1847. In contrast to initial enlistment expectations, Charley abandons illusions of bravado.

Paulsen's abrupt fictional pacing plunges the enlistee into the fray. Charley shudders at the smoke and sounds of bullets piercing the flesh of horses and men and forgets to fire his weapon. The pumping of Lieutenant Olafson's legs after his fatal shooting and the decapitation of Massey by a cannon ball send Charley to the woods to vomit, a normal physiological rejection of an horrific bloodbath. His only solace—cold, raw salt pork on dry bread—repudiates in dietary terms the inaccurate slogans, banner waving, and songs of glory. The text later depicts Charley mechanically cleaning, oiling, and loading his weapon, evidence of the muscle memory imbedded by training exercises at Fort Snelling. The author drew on his own military training for such details as "half cock," "earthworks," and "port arms" (*ibid.*, 34, 38, 36).

Battlefield Lessons

Dotted with sense impressions as revolting as brook water stained with the blood of floating corpses, rebel yells, and soldiers wetting themselves in fear, the cautionary tale pummels the reader with proofs of unremitting foreboding. For Charley, the eating of two apple pies purchased from a sutler fails to obliterate the aura of approaching death. Dysentery, a lethal result of unsanitary privies and polluted drinking water, prevents him from "[digging] toilet holes fast enough" (*ibid.*, 44). The debilitating diarrhea, dehydration, cramps, and weakness send him to a military doctor, a professional who must evaluate capabilities and return the most stable men to the front line for more fighting. The main treatment for acute diarrhea involved dosing with calomel, a compound of mercury, honey, and chalk. The author's ratio of four Union deaths from dysentery to each demise from war trauma explains why Charley avoids admittance to the hospital.

Because of the hopelessness of head, chest, and gut wounds, Civil War triage typically left victims untreated, a policy that medics state in *Sarny.* After a second assault, Charley's assistance with Nelson's suicide to spare him the anguish of dying from a belly shot compounds the terrors of the war's first summer and brings on tears in both enlistees. Paulsen stresses that four months of Washington camp life in a log shed produce more trepidation of rampant infections, cold autumnal rains, and rumors of failing leadership and desertions that keep the 90,000 bluecoats on edge. Charley's part in slaughtering 11 captured horses to feed casualties and in piling corpses for a hospital windbreak five feet high and 30 feet long contributes to his jitters. The author notes the top-down command that keeps the grunts fighting.

Arms for the Civil War soldier include muzzle-loading muskets and bayonets, which Charley thrusts at the fleeing Rebs on August 30, 1862, at the second Battle of Bull Run. Fought over the same part of eastern Virginia as the first battle, the clash cost the Union 1,747 dead, 8,452 casualties, and 4,263 prisoners of war. A march of the First Minnesota Volunteers northwest to Pennsylvania reveals the denuded trees and devastation that war has caused over a two-year span, elements the text shares with Stephen Crane's *The Red Badge of Courage*. At his third battle that winter, Charley faces a cavalry charge with a veteran's comprehension of "nasty work" (*ibid.*, 83). He recoils from shooting blameless horses, but has no qualms about killing their Confederate riders, a shift in attitude that Paulsen blames on too much familiarity with death.

Massacre and Despair

At Gettysburg on July 2, 1863, General George Gordon Meade's Union artillery fired 80 Federal cannon against the Army of Northern Virginia, led by Confederate General Robert E. Lee, an experienced veteran of the Mexican War. Charley observes such courage in the advancing secessionists that he pities the mangled carcasses. The bayonet clipped to his rifle does nothing to shield him from bullet wounds in his left thigh and shoulder. Declining consciousness leaves him thinking "At last he was right, at last he was done, at last he was dead" (*ibid.*, 96). His injuries spare his life, but require his admittance to a Philadelphia hospital.

The final accounting at Gettysburg shocks combatants and the nation. Behind Charley lie 953 of the First Minnesota Volunteers, more than 95 percent of his comrades, a fact that Paulsen revisits in *Brian's Hunt*. Far more devastating than Bull Run, Gettysburg soaked up the blood of 3,155 Union dead and 14,529 wounded, with an estimated 28,000 casualties on the Confederate side. Much worse than physical maiming, according to columnist Kendal Rautzhan, a writer for the Newport News, Virginia, *Daily Press*, is the devastation to Charley's heart, which Rautzhan pictured as "scarred beyond repair" (Rautzhan, 1999, C3). Paulsen's surmise about the irrevocable ruination of the soldier's spirit honors all military personnel—Union and Confederate—left alive to suffer an unending hell.

During the clash of Lee and General Ulysses S. Grant in the Wilderness at Spotsylvania, Virginia, Charley mustered out of the unit on May 5, 1864, and returned to Winona, Minnesota. Henry Mayer, a literary critic for the *New York Times Book Review*, saluted Paulsen for "not only [rendering] a historical epoch with documentary fidelity, but also [creating] a work that poses the hard questions" of war literature (Mayer, 1998, 40). The author deliberately focused on horror, explaining "*Soldier's Heart* doesn't make war some kind of pap that's not true; it's what it's really like" (Arnold, 1998, 3). Mayer demands, "What was it about? Was it worth it? Could I have done it?" (Mayer, 1998, 40).

Like many of the 282,000 Union wounded and 137,000 Confederate casualties of a four-year conflict, the veteran reaches home with unhealed injuries and a severe emotional syndrome—alternately referred to as the thousand yard stare, shell shock, battle fatigue, post-traumatic stress disorder—from events "so horrific and devastating that it simply cannot be tolerated by the human psyche" (Paulsen, *Soldier's*, xiii). Over two years after Lee's surrender to Grant at Appomattox, Virginia, on April 9, 1864, Charley passes blood, leans on a cane to walk, and quails at sounds reminding him of artillery fire. In June 1867, he grasps a captured Confederate pistol, a bleak suggestion that he fantasizes about suicide as a release from suffering. In premature decline from echoing memories, he survived another 18 months, dying of consumption on December 9, 1868, at age 23.

See also maturity; violence; war.

Source

Arnold, Martin. "Finding Stories Boys Will Read," *New York Times* (15 October 1998): 3.
Hannings, Bud. *Every Day of the Civil War: A Chronological Encyclopedia.* Jefferson, NC: McFarland, 2010.
Mayer, Henry. "The Boys of War," *New York Times Book Review* (15 November 1998): 40.
Rautzhan, Kendal. "Reading Aloud Lets Kids Enjoy Complex Books," [Newport News, VA] *Daily Press* (5 January 1999): C3.

storytelling

As Paulsen states in the introduction to *The Beet Fields,* he relies on the past for material, "mining my life for the ore that makes each piece of fiction" (Paulsen, *Beet,* ix). In reflections on his three-year army hitch in "The True Face of War," published in the spring 1999 issue of *Riverbank Review,* he marveled at "stories fill with the vicious humor and the fierce love that come with war—stories where death became funny and life became cruel, where joy was morbid and sadness the engine that ran life" (Paulsen, "True," 25–26). He has testified repeatedly that stories saved him, such as the life accounts of women who come in out of the cold in Poplar, Minnesota, in the story "The Library" and the alcoholic veteran's repetition of war stories in "The Madonna."

In *Shelf Life: Stories by the Book,* the writer rhapsodized on "found joys and aches and torture and great rolling hills and towering storms and things quick and hot and slow and dull ... a crazy dance of words" that fill his body of work (Paulsen, *Shelf,* 9). He reprises oral family history in *The Island,* in which Wil Neuton relives his grandmother's explanation of heating curling irons on the stove to smooth her long hair. In the telling of her first encounters with Clarence, her beau and future husband, the wealth of love in her voice explains why she spent time and energy on curls. The story so captivates her grandson that he sighs, "Oh my grandmother, I thought, oh my grandmother" (Paulsen, *Island,* 88).

As an example in *Woods Runner,* the casual rumors of Olin Smith, Coop, Caleb Clark, Abner McDougal, Matthew, Whitby, and Micah augur the events of the War for Independence. Lacking reliable forms of communication, witnesses verbalize the attitudes and qualms of backwoodsmen, who live too far from rebel centers in Boston, Philadelphia, and New York City to comprehend the rationale for defying a British monarch and the world's greatest military. Similarly, in *Soldier's Heart,* Charley Goddard gains scraps of information about the Civil War that lure him into joining the First Minnesota Volunteers, a decision he rues after learning the rest of the story of war. The models attest to the power of word-of-mouth revelations on patriotism.

For characters, verbalizing emotions and events like war, poverty, and natural phenomena divulges personal traits, as with the optimistic fantasies of a trans-border journey to America for Mexican beggar Manny Bustos in *The Crossing,* a P-51 fighter pilot telling Richard Allen Mesington about World War II in *The Rifle,* Bill Halverson's stereotypical vampire ghost stories in *Canyons,* and Mammy's educating her son on silk-clad octoroons living in New Orleans "high houses" in *The Legend of Bass Reeves* (Paulsen, *Legend,* 39). After Bass's initiation into town life in Paris, Texas, he returns the favor of stories to Mammy. Still unrecorded in general histories, the Trail of Tears transects his route, introducing him to the hunger and sorrow of the Creek and Cherokee after their forced removal from the Great Smoky Mountains to Indian Territory in the Midwest. Ironically, this episode of human degradation escapes Bass's attention.

Like putting dreamscapes into words for Janet Carson in *The Night the White Deer Died,* another dreamer, Orson, the captain of a religious pilgrimage in *Tucket's Home,* intends to learn from the orphan Lottie the perils of the frontier by hearing her adventures. Offering open-hearted hospitality, he urges, "You must come and visit with us for a time and tell us the stories" (Paulsen, *Home,* 53). In a more creative blend of clan history with magical thinking in *Winterkill,* Uncle Harvey shapes his farm narratives to "[make] stories come out with the right ending even if it didn't really happen that way" (Paulsen, *Winterkill,* 46). To the unnamed 13-year-old, a beleaguered delinquent and foster child, droll stories make endearing memories, the intangible gifts that bolster his spirit.

STORIES OF SELF-DISCOVERY

The author incorporates personal stories into disclosures of self, the dance-pantomime insights into a manly fight against a beast that introduce hiker Mark Harrison to a primitive tribe in *The Transall Saga.* Other models strengthen Russel Susskit, the restless Inuit in *Dogsong;* Sue Oldhorn, an Ojibwa granddaughter, in *Sentries;* the braggart cousin in *Harris and Me;* and the freedwoman heroine of *Sarny.* For David Alspeth in *The Voyage of the Frog,* keeping a log enables him to vent rage at storms and wind to an anonymous audience. After writing "Date unknown.... I am hate," he reconsiders the exaggeration and cuts to the heart of his anguish with an admission, "I am alone" (Paulsen, *Voyage,* 95). For literary effect, in describing the composition of *Liar, Liar,* Paulsen declared that a single fictional statement from Kevin Spencer, the main character, seized the author's mind and instilled a plot. The madcap results, Paulsen added, "are like dog teams—they run out ahead of you and you hold on and see where you're going" (Maughan, 2011).

For a master raconteur like the author, narrative achieves a rhythm and timbre like the music of a stream, the source of a story in *The Rifle* that "came together just ... exactly ... right" (Paulsen, *Rifle,* 5). In *The Winter Room.,* the protagonists, brothers Eldon and Wayne, internalize episodes from Uncle David without realizing the importance of storytelling in keeping alive memories of David's dead wife and child. His traditional lore harks back to the carved name of Grandfather Karl, who emigrated from Norway to homestead a farm in Minnesota. The boys know only that tales "became part of us so that [David's] memory became our memory" (Paulsen, *Winter,* 84). According to Jessica Harrison, on staff at the *Deseret News,* the author distinguished the result of allowing stories to take their own shape and pacing as "a river that goes under you or around you. You dip a bucket in, and you don't know what you get" (Harrison, 2010). The metaphor of an ongoing flow as old as time betokens endless material for recital, a reserve awaiting the opportunity for retelling.

The critical shaper of episodes remains the unfettered mind of youth, the fans who have elevated the writer to a literary institution for adventure novels like *The Rock Jockeys;* memoirs of childhood in *Eastern Sun, Winter Moon;* and stirring tales, such as "Stop the Sun" in *Boys' Life* and "The Last Great Race" in *Reader's Digest.* Analyst Bernice Golden isolated the humanistic inquiry that undergirds Paulsen's tales: "Where do I fit into my family? Who are my heroes, and why do I need them" (Golden, 1999, v). Of the role of teller of archetypal sagas, the author asserted the worth of the storykeeper: "That's who we are, who we as humans have always been—we are [creatures] who tell stories to one another" (Dar, 2015). The value of one-to-one transmission sets the tone and direction of *The River,* in which Brian Robeson recounts his 54 days of isolation in south central Canada to scientists who want to learn from his experience. To express the crucial cycle of cause and result in *Sarny,* the memories of the title character, a 94-year-old former slave, impart acts of resistance during evil times during the Civil War and Reconstruction. For the first generation of freedmen, oral tradition aids those who never gain literacy, but who learn just the same by listening.

Recovering the Past

Paulsen affirms a special reverence for reflections on aging and recall, which he reveals by the "many stories of hard journeys told by old people" in *Canyons* and in the winter storytelling around the stove by a World War I veteran of the Battle of Verdun in *The Foxman* (Paulsen, *Canyons,* 30). Opal Moore, a literary critic for the *Washington Post,* explains that "Storytelling was once part of the texture of daily life, of the extended family unit" (Moore, 1993, X-11). In the latter novel, the title figure accounts for combat tales that become roses from manure, of tellers "trying to find some use in all that waste" (Paulsen, *Foxman,* 87). In his own experience in *Woodsong,* the author sits by Storm, his old wheeler husky, and reminisces about "young things and old things, long runs and short runs, puppies and cold and wind, northern lights," a symbol of edification (Paulsen, *Woodsong,* 77). One model of the very old, Gunnar Pederson, the visiting horse lover in *Clabbered Dirt, Sweet Grass,* has no one to inherit his acreage or farming career. The author muses over the implied ritual in old Pederson's story: "Who will make him go on and on so that the things of him, the way of him will not stop, will not end?" (Paulsen, *Clabbered,* xv). The rhetorical question touches the heart of oral chronicle—the true recall of a mortal who will die and leave worthy memories unuttered.

A featured element in *Fishbone's Song,* the story-songs and song-stories of the title character inform his foster son of yin and yang—the nature of love and details of death in the Korean War from cholera and wounds. From the old hermit's cache of experiences, the unnamed boy gleans seeds of wisdom, a source of man-to-child guidance as old as Eli and Samuel's relationship in I Samuel 3, Merlin and Arthur's preparation for kingship in E.B. White's *The Sword in the Stone,* and Luke's Jedi training under Obi-Way Kenobi, the noble mentor in George Lucas's space opera *Star Wars.* Paulsen celebrates the successive tellings as a legacy imbued with the wisdom that philosopher Carl Jung termed the collective unconscious, the shared human lore marked by archetypal motifs. Fishbone's foster son values the sessions "like going up a stairway or a ladder," a form of ascending into manhood (Paulsen, *Fishbone's,* 17).

Women's Stories

From a feminine perspective, Paulsen features gendered "quilt stories" in *The Quilt,* a lasting source of verities hand-stitched in scraps of wedding gowns, curtains, tablecloths, and everyday dresses and aprons. The memoir reprises how he learned childbirth mysteries and marital lore at age six through "the music of the old stories," a metaphor for oral cadence and pacing of talk-story (Paulsen, *Quilt,* 66). During the long labor of Kristina Jorgensen with her first child, female relatives caress the family quilt and recite reasons for the embroidered words on each six-inch square in the checkerboard rectangle. By highlighting the sisterhood of Norwegian-American relatives, the text commends clan lore for bolstering lone women throughout World War II. The author stresses that family unity comprises fellowship as well as loss when a member "passes away," the fate of the boy's great-grandfather Karl and of Pearl, a beloved matriarch (*ibid.,* 66).

Paulsen's salute to women's work envisions oral history as a kind of patchwork of cherished scraps of human events, which he centers in a photo album shared with Wil Neuton's grandmother in *The Island*. From memory, Grandmother Alida Peterson Moen, the family griot, retraces "old Norse tales of gods and goddesses and spirits of another world" (Paulsen, *Quilt,* 62). She honors quilt scraps for preserving beneficial reminiscences: "Sometimes it is good to think of old things, old ways, and do the old stories when there is nothing to do but wait" (*ibid.*, 57). At an epiphany in his understanding, her grandson deduces that the reverence is a form of love: "They loved the cloth, loved the quilt, no, loved each other" (*ibid.*, 59). Imbued with tender story weaving, the episodes capture both the joy of weddings and births and the poignance of matriarchal deaths, the natural rhythm of mortality that binds each generation to the past and buttresses clan virtues and aims. Like beating a relic of a drum in a museum, the tellers enable the story to live again.

See also Sarny; Tucket's Home.

Source

Dar, Mahnaz. "'This Side of Wild': A Conversation with Gary Paulsen," *School Library Journal* (13 October 2015).
Golden, Bernice. *Critical Reading Activities for the Works of Gary Paulsen*. Portland, ME: Walch, 1999.
Harrison, Jessica. "'Hatchet' Author Gary Paulsen to Bring Boyhood Tales to Salt Lake," *Deseret News* (11 April 2010).
Moore, Opal. "Tellers and Their Tales," *Washington Post* (13 June 1993): X-11.
Wood, Susan Nelson. "Bringing Us the Way to Know," *English Journal* 90:3 (January 2001): 67–72.

survival

The tension between survival and danger has intrigued Paulsen from his tumultuous childhood, when he learned to value solitude and native savvy from boyhood capers like those of the cousins in *Harris and Me* and neighborhood friends in *Masters of Disaster*. Whether in the wild or in cities, the situations in *Popcorn Days and Buttermilk Nights, Dogsong,* and *Winterkill,* he equips his characters with the same "vicious determination" he manifested in boyhood (Salvner, 1996). He remarked in an interview with Anne Goodwin Sides, a journalist with the *New York Times*, "I'd run away to live in the woods, trapping and hunting game to survive. The wilderness pulled at me; still does" (Sides, 2006, B7). His reveries of the wild continue to invest his writings with memorable exploits and the outdoor lore that kept him alive. He explained to Randy Lewis, on staff at the *Los Angeles Times*, "We did what didn't hurt, and as it didn't hurt more and more, we spent more and more time in the woods and on the rivers—a natural flow of survival" (Lewis, 1994, 1).

For historical fiction, Paulsen veered from terse woods lore to realistic tellings of Afro-American bondage, which occurs in *The Legend of Bass Reeves* and *Soldier's Heart*. In the writer's vision of slavery in *Nightjohn* and *Sarny,* field hands work agricultural tasks until they die, the fate of Sarny's husband Martin, who collapses in 1861 at age 27—two years shy of the Emancipation Proclamation. Those with dreams of freedom risk lashing, dog mauling, and excision of their thumbs when they flee through the woods and along the streams, but they seldom achieve self-liberation. Because John, the alphabet teacher, accepts the punishment of unjust laws, he earns the fame of a legendary spreader of literacy, a source of power that lives on in Sarny's notebooks and in the imagination of proponents of civil rights.

Like the novels of Karen Cushman, Robin McKinley, Will Hobbs, Avi, Cynthia Rylant, and Ben Mikaelson, Paulsen's stories rely on what critic Eden Ross Lipson, a reviewer for the *New York Times,* identified as typical heroes—"underdogs, youngest children, orphans, or, like Harry Potter, some combination of these," such as hiker Mark Harrison, the lone human among primitive tribes in *The Transall Saga* and the orphaned title heroine of *Molly McGinty Has a Really Good Day* (Lipson, 2000, B7). One outstanding example, the loner Manny Bustos, the 13-year-old mestizo beggar and thief in *The Crossing,* survives stalking by the street thugs and pedophiles of Juárez, Mexico, by "moving, always moving," an exhausting means of eluding danger, especially by night (Paulsen, *Crossing,* 4). Embracing darkness as a fail-safe, he obscures his shiny teeth and squints over the whites of his eyes to conceal himself in a culvert. He triumphs by clinging to a dream of crossing from the mean alleys into a more promising life in the United States.

Living Through Battle

The author applies the wiliness of runaways like Nightjohn and the Gary character in *The Beet Fields* and urchins like Manny to the willingness of soldiers to help a dying comrade in "The Madonna" and the verve of John Byam, a sharpshooter for McNary's Rangers in *The Rifle.* For *Woods Runner,* the protagonist, 13-year-old Samuel Lehi Smith, learns in late childhood to trust his sense impressions. Sound, sight, and smell configure a reading of the wilderness from crackling twigs, wind aromas, the musk and urine of wild animals, and his assessment of the size and direction of smoke. On his way into the dense groves of western Pennsylvania, he arms himself with a flintlock, dry powder, and a hunter's skinning knife, the essentials of protection from large animals and recovering meat from carcasses. While waiting for a sighting of game, he turns to the hunter's task of remaining alert and focused while "[checking] the priming on his rifle" (Paulsen, *Woods,* 3). His survival hinges on preparation for "a world that did not care about man any more than it cared about dirt, or grass, or leaves," a milieu that had often gobbled up trappers, settlers, and Native Americans (*ibid.*, 4).

In existential straits, particularly war and challenge, solitary figures like Sam epitomize isolation and frustration, two sources of anguish in the lives of Wil Neuton in *The Island,* Jake in *Paintings from the Cave,* and John Borne in *Tracker.* For lone sailor David Alspeth in *The Voyage of the Frog,* a battle with a vicious storm seems "just at the limits of the plausible," yet, nine days afloat in the Pacific Ocean elevate the young skipper from boy to confident adult (MacCallum, 1989, E6). Educator Bernice Golden summarized the impetus to the daring voyage in a single question, "Can I make it through and survive?" (Golden, 1999, v). The question states the obvious enemy—drowning in the stormy sea, the risk that David takes to inter his Uncle Owen's ashes in the Pacific Ocean.

Of Paulsen's romantic zest for writing about the challenges and triumphs of companionless, tortured youth like David, he describes storytelling as an atavistic ritual. He envisions the performance of the cave-dwelling dancer swathed in bloody pelts as he whirls about the fire to dramatize the quest. To attain verisimilitude, the author prefers hands-on research—"to get my hands dirty, my bones broken, my face dragged through the snow, my head whacked with the beam of a sailboat to really savor the experience" (Blasingame, 2004, 273). Among the minutiae he adds to Civil War lore in *Soldier's Heart,* he comments on death from dysentery and the infections caused by bullets carrying scraps of filthy clothing into wounds. Such details convince readers of the insidious variety of perils.

Conflict and Youth

After his personal initiation into extreme situations, the author recognizes a fierce truth: "I know many people say that 'rite of passage' is the predominant theme in children's literature, but I think it's survival" (Gilson, 1994, B-8). He plunges his young protagonists into hellish terrors, such as a knife fight in *Tiltawhirl John* and Janet Carson's hallucinatory dreams in *The Night the White deer Died.* On fleeing Blade's armed gang in *Paintings from the Cave,* Jake, the urban survivor, has learned of menace in the dark: "Night people with night eyes are in the alleys, in the halls. They're watching and waiting" (Paulsen, *Paintings,* 38). Scurrying between buildings, Jake avoids Blade and Petey, gangbangers intent on shooting him with their Glocks. Of the constant dread, Jake advises, "You stop moving too long, you're done," advice identical to that of Manny Bustos in Juárez *(ibid.,* 61). Paulsen implies that the wisdom of the street equips Jake—and Manny—with instincts and experience far too mature for their age.

For his most influential hero, Brian Robeson, Paulsen immerses the 13-year-old in unforeseen peril—the trauma of watching a pilot die of heart attack in *Hatchet* and, two years later in *The River,* the coma that results from a lightning bolt striking psychologist Derek Holtzer. Without assistance in landing a plane, Brian survives impact, thirst, mosquito swarms clogging his airways, and serious illness from a snack on gut cherries. The protagonist remarks that movies tend to picture the stereotypical survivor "finding a clear spring with pure sweet water to drink," while reality debunks romanticism and easy-out solutions (Paulsen, *Hatchet,* 42). For that reason, Brian has become a classic survivor whom "people chew over long after they turn out the lights" (Lipson, 2000, B7).

See also violence; war.

Source

Blasingame, James. "Books for Adolescents," *Journal of Adolescent & Adult Literacy,* 48:3 (November 2004): 269–273.
Gilson, Nancy. "A Survivor of Childhood, Gary Paulsen Imbues Books with Intensity," *Columbus* [Ohio] *Dispatch* (8 November 1994): B-8.
Golden, Bernice. *Critical Reading Activities for the Works of Gary Paulsen.* Portland, ME: Walch, 1999.
Lewis, Randy. "He Owes It All to Librarians and Dogs," *Los Angeles Times* (31 July 1994): E6.
Lipson, Eden Ross. "The Dark Underbelly of Writing Well for Children," *New York Times* (8 July 2000): B7.
MacCallum, Elizabeth. "Tales of Freedom and Self-Reliance," [Toronto] *Globe and Mail* (18 November 1989): E6.
Maughan, Shannon. "Spring Audio 2011," *Publishers Weekly* 258.6 (7 February 2011).
Rosenberg, Merri. "Some Must Reading among Suggestions," *New York Times* (21 May 2000): 15.
Salvner, Gary M. "Brian's Winter," *ALAN Review* (Fall 1996).
Sides, Anne Goodwin. "On the Road and Between the Pages, an Author Is Restless for Adventure," *New York Times* (26 August 2006): B7.

trust

Paulsen's body of works leans heavily on the theme of trust, whether faith in self displayed in *The Beet Fields,* backpacker Mark Harrison's reliance on language teacher Leeta in *The Transall Saga,* or a "sweet" flintlock, the salvation of John Byam, a marksman during the American Revolution in *The Rifle* (Paulsen, *Rifle,* 5). The author's abiding love for the outdoors, whether the New Mexican desert, South Dakota agricultural fields, Alaskan wilds, Pacific Ocean, or Minnesota woods, instilled a belief in nature and its fierce truths. From age 12, he found faithful companions in librarians and books, a credence that he continues to share with young adult audiences. The combination of literacy with woodsmanship, tracking, mushing, sailing, horseback riding, and reliance on self saved him and prepared him for an amazing career in writing and speaking. Confidence undergirds the plots of *Winterkill* and *Dancing Carl,* his first successful novels. At decisive points in later stories and memoirs, especially *Caught by the Sea, Dogteam,* and *Woodsong,* he dramatizes how reliance on reading, outback and sea competencies, and dogs shaped his decisions and philosophy.

The formation of links between characters enhances the author's alliance of teen hunter Samuel Lehi Smith with colonial tinker and spy Abner McDougal in *Woods Runner* and of the slave Sarny with John, the daring runaway and literacy instructor in *Nightjohn.* Sam accepts Abner's judgment calls about safety from British cavalry patrols, by which "they would be caught, probably killed" (Paulsen, *Woods,* 108). John, the peripatetic slave tutor on plantations, clings to an ambition to learn: "It eats at you then—to know it and not have it" (Paulsen, *Nightjohn,* 58). He lives for his dream of educating a student to become the historian of and for black Americans. His aspirations come true in *Sarny,* a sequel that revisits the storykeeper at age 94, when John's faith in truth reaches its culmination in Sarny's notebooks. She deifies the trust in literacy as something that "must have come from God in some way" (Paulsen, *Sarny,* 136).

For the sake of humor, Paulsen stresses the reliance of Amos Binder on Duncan "Dunc" Culpepper in *Coach Amos* and *Amos and the Vampire.* In these narratives and in *Amos's Killer Concert Caper, Dunc and Amos Go to the Dogs, Amos Goes Bananas,* and *Dunc and Amos on Thin Ice,* Dunc mesmerizes his pal's flustered mind with repetitions of "trust me," a chant that wears thin in *Super Amos* after a cycle of failure in previous escapades (Paulsen, *Super,* 4). In *Amos Gets Married,* the victim declares, "Every time you say that, something goes wrong" (Paulsen, *Married,* 3). Iffy situations leave Amos in tenuous straits, such as his switched identities with Gustav of Moldavia in *Prince Amos,* a resetting of Mark Twain's *The Prince and the Pauper* and Anthony Hope's doppelgänger novel *The Prisoner of Zenda.* At an ebb of Amos's respect for his friend's advice in *Amos Gets Famous,* the perennial dupe charges, "The last time you said that, I wound up getting turned into a dog and had to fight my way out of a nest of pit bulls, and before that a parrot swore at me" (Paulsen, *Famous,* 6). The exasperation heightens Paulsen's satire of misplaced trust, the dominant cause of trouble between Dunc and Amos and the daredevil boy cousins in *Harris and Me.*

Trust between Strangers

Paulsen retains the motif of faith in self and others in realistic fiction, a controlling theme during Carley's adaptation to country life in *Popcorn Days and Buttermilk Nights* and Terry Anders's ambition to build a Bearcat from a kit in *The Car.* From the perspective of historical fiction, the author applies self-trust to a neophyte Apache raider, Coyote Runs, in *Canyons* and to a Western hero, Deputy U.S. Marshal Bass Reeves. On the run from a slave master, Reeves, the hero of *The Legend of Bass Reeves,* has little hope of trusting whites in Oklahoma Territory. To survive during pursuits of criminals, he relies on instinct and savvy and, according to Nebraskan critic Pat Leach for the *Lincoln Journal Star,* "his remarkable ability to adapt to the landscape and recall his surroundings" (Leach, 2007, 1). The combination elevates Reeves above less adept lawmen of the frontier period.

Paulsen stresses the complexity of trust in a bilingual relationship. An ironic pairing, the orphaned beggar Manny Bustos with a broken warrior, Sergeant Robert S. Locke, in *The Crossing,* depicts two people in need of mutual trust. Covering for 13-year-old Manny at the Santa Fe Bridge by lying to a Mexican police officer, Locke tacitly states his confidence in the orphaned beggar, who needs an adult to stave off hunger, coyotes, gangs, and callous officials. The symbiotic friendship results in a full cafe meal for Manny and a source of tickets, liquor, and snack food at the bullfight for Locke.

The wrenching conclusion at the bridge to El Paso, Texas, which pits Locke against four of Manny's stalkers, exalts the faith of a dying Viet vet. He believes so strongly in the ambitious mestizo street waif that he relinquishes his wallet while breathing his last. In what critic Stephanie Loer, a writer for the *Boston Globe,* called "a strange relationship of trust," Locke escapes the torture of post-traumatic stress disorder by sacrificing himself to save Manny from the mean streets of Juárez (Loer, 1988, 48). An ironic twist on relief from anxiety, the narrative implies that in ending a period of mental and physical anguish for both characters, Locke, before expiring, passes to Manny a future worth living.

Faith in Dogs

Beyond writings on human-to-human assurance, Paulsen deepened his knowledge and understanding of working animals and their dedication to responsibility. He demonstrated the human reliance on beasts, particularly the faithful lead dog Cookie in *Puppies, Dogs, and Blue Northers;* the alert border collies in *The Haymeadow;* the wise counselor Atticus in *Field Trip;* and the collie Radar and ranch guardian Old Molly in *Grizzly.* In "Brian's Hunt," an excerpt for the January 2004 issue of *Boys' Life,* the author restated his faith in watchdogs through the protagonist's comment, "He trusted in the dog's warning ability and dozed enough for his mind and body to rest" (Paulsen, "Brian's," 39). Reliance proves well founded after the dog helps save Brian from a bear attack. In the novel version of the story, the lesson in trust comes at an embittering pass in Katie Robeson's marriage that causes her to divorce her husband. Kevin Thomas, a literary critics for the *Los Angeles Times,* explains: "The urgent matters of food, shelter, and defense against predatory animals allow Brian to gain perspective toward his troubled emotional state. Rage and fear gradually give way to resourcefulness and resilience; Brian finds he has little time for self-pity" (Thomas, 1990, 8).

The author pinpointed additional canine trustworthiness in the paired border collies William and Wallace in *Woods Runner.* For cultural reasons, the grizzled tinker/spy Abner McDougal named the dogs for a Scots knight who led clansmen during the Wars of Scottish Independence from England, beginning in September 1297. Abner outlines the bestial attributes—pricked ears, rigid stance, hair raised on the back—that express a visceral canine distrust of strangers. In a subsequent encounter on the road to New York City, Abner affirms the ESP of dogs, who "kind of feel things, in the air, maybe, or along the ground" (Paulsen, *Woods,* 105). From experience, the Scotsman, like the author, has come to trust canine know-how and depend on his dogs to protect himself and his passengers.

See also integrity.

Source

Leach, Pat. "Authors, Illustrators Offer Up surprises in These Books," *Lincoln* [Neb.] *Journal Star* (2 February 2007): 1.

Loer, Stephanie. "A Satisfying Depression Era Tale," *Boston Globe* (21 February 1988): 48.

Thomas, Kevin. "Grace under Pressure in the Wild," *Los Angeles Times* (21 September 1990): 8.

Tucket's Gold

Without pause after an escape from drunken Comancheros in *Tucket's Ride*, the fourth part of the five-novel Tucket saga speeds on with *Tucket's Gold.* The venture initiates a death-defying installment in the young plainsman's ongoing quest to save two orphaned children and reunite with his pioneer parents and sister Rebecca. Alerting readers to "death, brutal death," the author readies Tucket for a homicidal showdown, a clash more destructive than YA fiction usually features (*ibid.*, 1). While Coop Renner, a book critic for *School Library Journal,* demeaned the narrative as "nonnutritive," *Kirkus Reviews* lauded the story for its trio of adventurers combatting a world of meanness and ill treatment of the young (Renner, 1999, 156).

Flight from the relentless Comancheros introduces the preface to the third sequel with Tucket's exhaustion and the erosion of his moccasins, a testimonial to his arduous journey and the vulnerability of bare feet in the desert, symbols of tender youth. The attempt at making green-hide moccasins proves more difficult than he anticipates. By revving up the odds with thirst in bareheaded travelers on a "sunbeaten, airless plain," a rattlesnake bite treated by Pueblo Indians, and a possible sale of Billy and Lottie into slavery by the stalkers, Paulsen endorses the fact that "the three travelers had become a team" (Paulsen, *Gold,* 1, 35). Lottie sums up the concept of camaraderie to Billy in her simple dialect style: "You go where we go, that's how it works" (*ibid.*, 88).

Adept at varied exigencies, Tucket grabs runaway horses and acquires enough sign language to "hand-talk" with Kashi, his Indian friend (*ibid.*, 85). Already "so dry he croaked," Tucket directs his companions' digging into ground water to increase seepage (*ibid.*, 12). The refugees, Lottie and Billy, have heeded their rescuer as a mentor, who taught them how to make camp, hunt with bow and arrow, and slaughter and cook raw meat over a small fire. The progression from neophyte to experienced plainsman suggests a normal rite of passage by which young men like Tucket take their place among seasoned elders.

Wealth and Health

The trio acquires accidental wealth after Billy dismisses the discovery of "just a skull" and a sword before realizing that an ancient grave of a Spanish conquistador contains armor and real treasure dating to the New World explorations of Coronado and Hernán de Soto in the 1540s (*ibid.*, 42). The text creates irony out of the worthlessness of precious metals in the wasteland, where rare opportunities for commerce rely on barter rather than cash. Still only eight years old, Billy views treasure as a source of rock candy at the next store they pass. A second irony, the problem of weight, demands careful balance of 30 pounds of Spanish silver and gold bars on a worn packhorse. Paulsen adds a touch of humor in Billy's fierce possession of the Spanish sword, a symbol of the boy's entry into the ancestral growth pattern that turned Francis Alphonse Tucket into a man.

The narrative rewards hardihood with Spanish loot, but lauds a month's hospitality by Pueblo villagers as a more valuable find. The trio apply Pawnee fishing methods, which aid them in snagging trout with a braided line of horsehair pulled from the pony's tail. Folk medicine enables the Pueblo to cut into the rattlesnake fang marks on Tucket's shoulder and apply a life-saving poultice before the poison can afflict his heart or brain. In an effort to reduce tension with humor, the author contrasts native expertise with Lottie's reliance on a "spit-and-mud poultice" as traditional first aid for snakebite (*ibid.*, 75). To ensure plenty of curative juice, she forces Billy to drink water and spew it into a gourd until he produces one quart. Amid the comedy and emergency medical care, Tucket undergoes a renewal similar to "[becoming] reborn" (*ibid.*, 72).

Trail Wisdom

Central to the themes of *Tucket's Gold* is the growing know-how that turns the protagonist into a reliable rescuer and guardian on a par with his former mentor, Jason Grimes. Tucket becomes alert to game tracks and reminds himself, "He had to think of three mouths and three stomachs instead of just his own" (*ibid.*, 39). Like a watchful father, he superintends adequate rest for Lottie and Billy and cuts a deer hide into foot shapes for moccasins. Even near the breaking point from a fierce storm, travail, hunger, thirst, and lack of sleep, he ponders "what would happen to Lottie and Billy" if Comancheros capture them for sale as slaves (*ibid.*, 8). The possibilities chill his heart. Of the dangers, Enicia

Fisher, a reviewer for the *Christian Science Monitor,* warns: "This book is not for sensitive types.... Readers will have to be tough-minded" (Fisher, 1999, 20).

Significant to the Tucket series, Paulsen tempers pejorative scenes among the Pawnee and Comanche and negative comments about the Apache and Crow with the courtesies of the Pueblo, a Southwestern people known for settled life and irrigated croplands at their "castle in the clouds" (*ibid.,* 63). For the protagonist, the respite at the adobe village offers a month-long break from the long trek, new gear and clothing, and a buckskin packsaddle. He takes the opportunity to acquaint himself with Kashi and Annas, the cook who bakes cornbread in earthen ovens to serve with rabbit stew. The narrative states that Tucket "had found a new kind of peace here and loved life in the village" (*ibid.,* 85). A recovery of community values prepares the boy for the fifth novel, *Tucket's Home,* and a renewed enthusiasm for family.

Source

Fisher, Enicia. "Harrowing Adventures on the Oregon Trail," *Christian Science Monitor* (14 October 1999): 20.
Renner, Coop. "Tucket's Gold," *School Library Journal* 45:10 (October 1999): 156.

Tucket's Home

At the completion of a five-book quest series, Paulsen moves full circle to an amicable finale and an opportunity to congratulate the novice for all he has learned about compassion and survival. Within a few paragraphs, the narrative summarizes the misadventures of teen frontiersman Francis Alphonse Tucket in the previous four books. Throughout, according to reviewer Victoria Kidd, "Paulsen trusts his readers to handle sometimes graphically violent scenes and accept them" as part of the history of "Westward expansion," particularly the scalping of the Pawnee war leader Braid, slaughtering buffalo, escaping Comanchero enslavers, and the summary judgment and execution of a murderer by the U.S. Cavalry (Kidd, 2000, 236).

Reunions dominate the narratives. The trio—Tucket and two orphans, Lottie and Billy—encounter "a fancy man," William James Bentley the Fourth and his three servants, a carefree party reprised from *Call Me Francis Tucket* (Paulsen, *Home,* 7). Paulsen restores the British tenderfoot to the Oregon Trail to account for the casual decimation of 50,000,000 American bison by meat hunters for wagon trains and railroad crews and by sport shooters on "a grand adventure," which requires servants to load rifles while William fires them (*ibid.,* 9). To Tucket, such a cavalier attitude toward animal life "stinks of death" (*ibid.,* 12). The text illustrates the boy's outback expertise in stripping a dead cow of her hump, tenderloins, and belly fat, a domestic staple for oiling bow strings and waterproofing tents.

The Final Trek

After reuniting with his mentor in *Tucket's Home,* the protagonist and Grimes overwhelm five heavily armed brigands—"scavengers who worked the trail, preying on travelers" (*ibid.,* 13). Grimes characterizes their vitriol toward Bentley and his servants as "crazy—like wolves with crazy-water" (*ibid.,* 32). The concluding episodes involve Tucket in concealing 75 pounds of gold and 60 of silver, lashing wagons into cedar log rafts with bark twine and rope to cross the Columbia River, and covering 500 miles on the way to Oregon before snow-fly. Following tips from Iktah, Tucket learns to catch salmon and to avoid the dangerous current. He aims the pilgrims once more toward a rugged trail and manages the arrival into the "golden valley" (*ibid.,* 52).

As Paulsen illustrates in the epilogue, settling the West came at a price of suffering and loss, beginning with departures from homes and friends, the collapse of a wagon on Orson's foot, and the slaughter of Jason Grimes, "shot and cut to pieces" (*ibid.,* 33). Wagon master Orson, the captain of a religious pilgrimage, has stories to share with Lottie and Tucket of separation from home folks. Tucker volunteers to scout and hunt for the train while Lottie grudgingly accepts cooking as woman's work. In private, Tucket struggles with the death of Grimes, whose corpse he held in the green light of hope for a day and night. Weeping for what he has lost, the boy "used up all his grief when Grimes was killed" and left unburied at the base of a tree (*ibid.,* 75). Of Tucket's advance into sturdy manhood, Paulsen honors the character of a survivor "limited only by himself—and by nature" (*ibid.,* 92).

The Return Home

Once more a member of the family who had lost their boy, Tucket views them from a distance like a painting before he joins the "crying and hugging all at once" (*ibid.,* 82). He stands taller than his ecstatic parents, a suggestion of the physical and emotional growth he completed over two years on his own. He re-acclimates himself to sleeping indoors, eating meals home-cooked by his mother and Rebecca, and undertaking the bucolic work of tilling his father's fields. Perhaps because of Grimes's death, Tucker values hearing his father call him "son." Billy and Lottie find places with a family bereft of children, a common form of adoption on the cross-country passage.

In separate households, the trio remains unified. For Billy, the investment of Spanish loot in Chinese trade introduces the sub-theme of capitalism as the end result of the westward movement. Lottie, who has learned to be silent and observant, accepts marriage to her rescuer as her reward for loyalty. Their union produces a stereotypical ending legitimating matrimony and the nuclear family, a serene, staid lifestyle foreshadowed by Tucket's study of a herd of buffalo cows with yearling calves and two bulls and his memories of a peaceful encounter with Kashi and Annas in a Pueblo village.

The reunion of the Tucket household implies that Francis, now a man with remarkable experience in the outback, has acquired a perspective on pioneering that will enhance his family's settlement in Oregon Territory while satisfying his craving for adventure. In retrospect, the author honors his boy plainsman for "[living] to be an old man and [dying] in 1923"—approximately 89 years old—leaving behind the children he sired with Lottie and the nieces and nephews produced by Billy and his wife (*ibid.,* 87). In a survey of Paulsen's genre elements, reviewer Michael Maschinot, a critic for the *St. Petersburg* [Florida] *Times,* declares the Tucket saga "a standard adventure story with echoes of American classics from *The Deerslayer* to *Shane* to *Dances with Wolves*" (Maschinot, 1994, D-6).

Source

Kidd, Victoria. "Tucket's Home," *School Library Journal* 46:9 (September 2000): 235–236.
Maschinot, Michael. "Journeys of the Spirit Series," *St. Petersburg* [Florida] *Times* (27 February 1994): D-6.
McCarthy, Cheryl Stritzel. "Homecoming Puts the Wraps on Wild West Series," [Cleveland, Ohio] *Plain Dealer* (8 July 2001): I-1.

Tucket's Ride

In Mexican territory in *Tucket's Ride,* the second sequel of the five-part Tucket series progresses from wagon trains coursing the Oregon Trail into historically complex obstacles heightened by racial antipathies. By opening on a scream from an adobe hut, Paulsen plunges his 16-year-old protagonist into a new situation where "he couldn't stay and not help" (Paulsen, *Ride,* 3). The statement identifies a mounting altruism in Francis Alphonse Tucket, an outgrowth of his home training and relationships with settlers and mountain man Jason Grimes. Diana Penner, a book reviewer for the *Indianapolis Star,* noted that "Francis's primary goal is to find his own family, but now he finds that he is building his own" (Penner, 1995, D-6).

Criticism, including that of the *Washington Post Book World,* praised the grit and thrills of another Tucket adventure. On this route away from the Oregon Trail, he and two refugees, Billy and Lottie, evade winter cold by swinging south through dangerous territory toward the Rio Grande on the Mexican border. In an unforeseen draw-down, Tucket kills an Irish trooper named Flannagan, stopping him from what the orphan Lottie describes as "being 'rageous, that soldier, simply 'rageous" (*ibid.*, 118). The escalation jacks up the moral themes to a life for a life, a mature consideration for an armed horseman like Tucket.

Traditional Western Battles

In slow cinematic motion, Paulsen's text unfolds a standard Western shooting scenario that stops the rape of a lone woman under the protective code of the West. Details picture the opening of the rapist's holster and the hip shot from Tucket's rifle to the victim's chest for an instant kill, leaving the villain in the dust. The author introduces the milieu of the Mexican War by alerting Tucket that he has shot an American soldier. The action takes the protagonist within ten miles of Taos, New Mexico, disputed territory northeast of the Rio Grande since the onset of hostilities in 1846. At the office of a drunken commandant, Tucket reacts to an unlikely verdict: "Take him out and hang him" (*ibid.*, 122). Fortunately, the tin cup filled with tequila wipes all thought of punishment from the commander's mind, but leaves in Tucket's imagination "the feeling of the noose around his neck" (*ibid.,* 129).

The narrative introduces a raid by Comancheros, a band of vicious, "universally feared" Mexican slave traders complicit with the Southwestern Comanche in making "raids for plunder and prisoners as far as the northern edge of the Texas frontier" (Paulsen, *Ride,* 57). The loot empowers them to buy supplies with ill-gotten gold. In addition to Gothic descriptions of the ruthless abductors, general lawlessness in the Southwest includes scavengers from Tennessee "running and killing out here for nearly two years" following the Treaty of Guadalupe Hidalgo signed on February 2, 1848 (Paulsen, *Ride,* 132).

Paulsen's Deus ex Machina

By employing a Dickensian coincidence, Paulsen sends the scroungy trader Jason Grimes once more to rescue the apprentice frontiersman, noting sardonically, "Grimes was still Grimes—a rough man in the company of other rough men" (*ibid.,* 178). Tucket expands on Grimes's amorality by picturing him crawling under a snake. The down-and-dirty trading commences, with Grimes using the same swapping of arms, powder, and lead that he had plied on the Pawnee in *Mr. Tucket.* Grimes refuses to barter for the two captive children and presses the Comancheros to drink from his whiskey barrel, a method rebuked by critics for exonerating the white man's exploitation of Native Americans through alcohol and firearms.

Paulsen's narrative exonerates Grimes by picturing his success at selling out his goods for "a small sack of gold coins" (*ibid.,* 177). By freeing the captive children from the drunken enemy's brush hut, Grimes enables Tucket to spirit Billy and Lottie from the village, seize fresh horses, and hustle them north. A standard Western ruse, directing the Indians toward the trail of Grimes and his packhorses in the dark rather than Tucket's party extends the time that the escapees flee undetected. The direction allows Paulsen to connect the narrative thread to motifs of the fourth Tucket novel, *Tucket's Gold.*

See also names.

Source

Hurst, Carol Otis. "Four Literature Webs You'll Be Glad to Get Caught In," *Teaching Pre-K-8* 26:1 (September 1995): 112.
Penner, Diana. "Review: *Call Me Francis Tucket,*" *Indianapolis Star* (4 June 1995): D-6.
Salvner, Gary M. *Presenting Gary Paulsen.* New York: Twayne, 1996, 79–133.

violence

Paulsen's vivid memories of childhood reprise startling scenes of menace, rape, maiming, and death, specifically, Brian's savage brawl with Carl Lammers, a schoolmate in *Brian's Return,* Apache raider Coyote Runs's facing a bullet in the stomach in *Canyons,* Pawnee war chief Braid's intention to provoke a war in *Mr. Tucket,* the senseless burning of a garage in *Popcorn Days and Buttermilk Nights,* and the sudden bold stand of Sergeant Robert S. Locke against Mexican child procurers in *The Crossing.* At the introduction of Wil Neuton to Pinewood, Wisconsin, in *The Island,* he encounters Ray Bunner, the town Godzilla and "real bottom-feeder" (Paulsen, *Island,* 61). From friend Susan, Wil learns that "everybody has to fight Ray" in a ritual intended to establish teen male primacy (*ibid.*). In the story "Rape," the main character learns, as Wil discovers, the lie that circulates among young men that they "should seek danger to prove" manhood (Paulsen, *Madonna,* 43).

In *The Legend of Bass Reeves,* historical fiction about a black lawman in the trans-Mississippi West, the author opens a plantation culture by which blows of the whip turn Flowers into a mute and progresses to Comanche territory and the skinning and burning of a hapless wagoneer. The narrative details a deputy U.S. marshal's daily entanglement in lynchings and gory shootings against his credo of not "killing things without a good reason" (Paulsen, *Legend,* 5). While wrapping a slaughtered naked daughter of the Garnetts in a blanket, "there were marks on her that Bass's eyes found against his will," a reflection of the future lawman's attempt at decorum and respect for the innocent, especially females (*ibid.,* 36).

In addition to cut-throat fiction, brutal episodes permeate Paulsen's memoirs. In *The Quilt,* at age six, the author ponders why Germans and Japanese attack Americans ships and troops and why Uncle Olaf Jorgensen dies in the Pacific in the last months of World War II. When Gary questions Grandmother Anita Halverson about when the war will end, she lashes out, "When men are sick and tired of being men," a gendered charge against males for world mayhem (Paulsen, *Quilt,* 5). Out of earshot, Alida later generalizes to Kristina: "Men. It's how they fix things.... Just like bulls," a remark rife with bestiality and one-sided blame (*ibid.*, 28).

In post–World War II Manila, the setting of *Eastern Sun, Winter Moon*, the author, at age seven, recycles a crashed Mitsubishi Zero into a playground and witnesses a typhoon turn metal roofing into a flying guillotine that lops a man's torso from his legs. In another episode, Gary's houseboy Rom decapitates a 12-foot snake before it can digest a neighbor's monkey. To his maternal grandmother in *Alida's Song,* the Gary character confesses his distaste for army life, but conceals the space left by "the back tooth kicked out by another recruit in a barracks fight during basic training" (Paulsen, *Alida,* 4). The revelation might have disclosed something about his self-control and maturity that Paulsen preferred to keep secret. In *This Side of Wild,* he revealed his dread of huge bombs by which people "could simply be evaporated into nothingness without knowing that it had happened" (Paulsen, *Wild,* 66). The statement expresses his loathing of a military job as instructor on the devastating power of missiles.

YA Literature

Early in his career, the novelist placed young protagonists in peril as a means of examining self-discovery and problem solving, the task faced by Terry Anders amid a trio of criminals in *The Car,* two cousins pulling pranks while performing heavy farm labor in *Harris and Me,* and a troubled delinquent boy in *Winterkill* in the hands of boozy parents and a sadistic foster father, Gib Nymen, a vicious bible thumper. For Francis Alphonse Tucket, the 14-year-old Missouri farm boy in *Mr. Tucket,* imagination heightens fears of Indian attack along the Oregon Trail. When he falls into the clutches of seven Pawnee, he makes the mistake of struggling against grown men, who knock him unconscious. Leashed by an elderly tribeswoman, the captive becomes a target for young Pawnee bullies. At a height of terror, the leader Braid brandishes a blonde scalp and a china doll seized from Francis's nine-year-old sister Rebecca. Paulsen soft-pedals the horror of violent death for a little girl by omitting the identity of the mutilated corpse.

During research for the historical fiction *The Rifle,* the writer acknowledged the senselessness of American havoc, the gun deaths that grew into daily headlines in the late 1990s and continued to rise in the 2000s and 2010s. For episodes of *Winterkill,* the fine line between police endangerment and an officer's outright murder of suspects anticipated ongoing confrontations between the authorities and citizens, some unqualified or forbidden to own and fire weapons. By describing the shootings in the career of child rescuer Nuts Duda, Paulsen alerts young readers to the danger of selecting a flawed role model and of expecting heroism as a daily outcome of struggles for justice.

As viewed by Brian Robeson in *Hatchet,* recovery of a rifle from a downed Cessna 406 resets the adventure from boy-against-nature to boy-with-firepower. He realizes the gun as a game-changing element: "Suddenly, he didn't have to know; did not have to be afraid or understand" (Paulsen, *Hatchet,* 174). The power shift forces him to re-evaluate his place in the wild, as with the earthling Mark Harrison's assessment of threats to the Tsook tribe from the cannibal Rawhaz in *The Transall Saga.* The re-balancing of power with guns in teen lives recurs in *Paintings from the Cave,* in which Jake acknowledges the menace of gang leader Blade. Formerly a knifer of enemies, Blade advances to a Glock Nine that "holds more bullets than God made" (Paulsen, *Paintings,* 4). The jocular reference to the Almighty indicates Paulsen's rejection of religious dogma as a solution to childhood face-offs against armed gangbangers.

Eras of Mayhem

For patriots facing the "Wall of British Steel" in *Woods Runner,* destruction increases from the Redcoat strategy of quelling colonists with "fire and sword" (Paulsen, *Woods,* 52, 151). Muskets extended with a three-foot bayonet enabled a charging line to continue unleashing death after the discharge of their minié balls. More Gothic images attach to victims of Iroquois arrows and tomahawks, which scar the forehead of 13-year-old protagonist Samuel Lehi Smith. For realism, Paulsen explains that scalping allows facial skin to droop, thus obscuring identity of victim Ben Overton, a village friend. The physiological fact contributes to Sam's horror at glimpsing Ben's hacked remains and to the taste and smell of carnage, sense impressions that embed violent scenes.

From early nineteenth-century history, the author extracted the sufferings of black slaves in the plantation South under the control of sadistic owners, a motif of *The Legend of Bass Reeves*. In *Nightjohn*, the lashing of Delie, a mother figure, and tethering her to a buggy precedes the historic mutilation of runaways, depicted by dogs chewing the breasts of the slow-witted Alice and by enslaver Clel Waller's emasculation of Pawley and the lopping of middle toes from John, the title character. At the era's worst retaliation for running away "to be more" in the sequel *Sarny,* freedom lovers "get whipped, get cut, get hung sometimes, get killed sometimes," but the flow of slaves to the north continues over the path of "the drinking gourd" (Paulsen, *Sarny,* 10). Paulsen counters with the death of Waller by a Union soldier's bayonet through the gut, a protracted demise to curtail the enslaver's meanness and overlay his suffering with justice.

During the war to free slaves, Charley Goddard, the protagonist of *Soldier's Heart,* fears missing out on war and cajoles his mother with reasons for joining the First Minnesota Volunteers. Two years later in Pennsylvania, he displays agrarian sensibilities at the sight of horses "torn and dying" at the Battle of Gettysburg, fought on July 1–3, 1863 (Paulsen, *Soldier's Heart,* 80). Already inured to killing enemy Rebs who might shoot him, Charley feels nausea at the thought of slaughtering 11 of the great innocent war steeds for food to nourish hospital patients. The narrative relates a fact about horse deaths, which occur in greater proportion than human deaths because horses make larger targets and expose their vulnerable underbellies to cannon and artillery.

Paulsen creates a brilliant backdrop for a naive town boy in *The Foxman.* The bizarre memories of Hans, the nighttime storyteller, about non-alcoholic champagne and the attacks "a-screaming and a-hollering and a-shooting," seemed like "the only part of their life worth remembering" (Paulsen, *Foxman,* 41, 43). The boy wonders why Hans makes his combat stories outlandish—"the kind of story you're *supposed* to laugh at" (*ibid.*, 42). While he learns to cope in the woods, he finds himself returning weekly to the title figure's shack for grotesque inklings of the Battle of Verdun during World War I. The contrast between war yarns and realistic recall enlightens the listener to the lasting damage that combat does to survivors.

Unlike Hans, the Foxman plucks raw elements from his time in France. In the resolution, his gradual expiration from lung ills caused by wartime gassing ends with the narrator's tears for a fragile veteran isolated in the northern woods to conceal his scarred visage from outsiders. The old recluse relives "the beauty of being human. And beauty lost," the result of the ten-month bombardment at Verdun in 1916, when 305,000 men died out of a total of 976,000 French and German casualties (*ibid.,* 86). Of a war intensified by machine guns, biplanes, howitzer cannon, and mustard gas, he concludes, "Science kills beauty—just like war destroys life" (*ibid.,* 74). As a coda to a diminished life, the boy burns the Foxman's remains in his shack, saving only a single fox hide as a memory of the old veteran's precarious esthetics. The fiery celebration of the Foxman recaptures a Nordic rite, the interment of chieftains in burning boats set adrift on the ocean, a worthy conclusion for an author from a Scandinavian lineage.

See also Canyons; The Rifle; slavery; storytelling; survival; war.

Source

Mayer, Henry. "The Boys of War," *New York Times Book Review* (15 November 1998): 40.

Robertson, Judith P. "Teaching about Worlds of Hurt through Encounters with Literature: Reflections on Pedagogy," *Language Arts* 74:6 (October 1997): 457.

vulnerability

Paulsen balances his more macho writings with episodes of fragility, epitomized by the meager ashes of Uncle Owen that eighth-grader David Alspeth sprinkles on the Pacific Ocean during nine days at sea in *The Voyage of the Frog,* a farm boy's scuffle with a bull in *Harris and Me,* and the unfathomable Christmas Eve death of Richard Allen Mesington from a gunshot wound in *The Rifle.* Disparate examples include diffident juvenile delinquents in *Popcorn Days and Buttermilk Nights* and *Winterkill;* the stillbirth of a husky in *Puppies, Dogs, and Blue Northers;* and women overcome by religious fervor in *The Tent.* To explorer Mark Harrison in *The Transall Saga,* life on a distant planet apart from his own species leaves him pregnable to poisonous plants and insects, killer beasts, and uncivilized tribes, particularly the cannibal aggressor Rawhaz. Among illegal Mexican migrants in *The Beet Fields,* wisdom keeps the laborers out of town, where they feel "like ghosts that [people] see but do not recognize" (Paulsen, *Beets,* 43). So long as the workers hoe beets like slaves and accept a peon's wages, they shield themselves from government authorities and racists.

In reference to his preference for youthful characters, Paulsen remarked, "Young people are always the victims" (Nickelson, 1993). The plight of Manny Bustos, an undersized mestizo beggar with red hair, begins in infancy with abandonment behind the Church of Our Lady of Perpetual Sorrow, a name replete with despair. Dwelling alone leaves him open to bullying by Pacho and swarthy "street wolves" in the alleys of Juárez, Mexico (Paulsen, *Crossing,* 41). More disgusting by their predations, adult kidnappers like Raoul troll for handsome young teens to exploit for sex. Like Alice and Sarny in *Nightjohn* fearing for the lashings faced by grown women and Francis Alphonse Tucket's fear of the capture and enslavement of children by Comancheros in *Tucket's Ride* and *Tucket's Gold,* Manny must scramble to keep out of the grasp of enslavers. With astute imagery, he compares his ability to those of "an alley rat" and concludes, "Not for any was there help" (*ibid.,* 22, 25).

Additional narratives on parentless children such as the plight of orphans Billy and Lottie on the prairie in *Call Me Francis Tucket* and *Tucket's Ride* and Rachael Ellen "Rocky" Turner in *The Monument* elevate Paulsen among contributors to the helping professions. In musings on the American Revolution, Samuel Lehi Smith, the 13-year-old protagonist of *Woods Runner,* speaks the author's concern by recognizing defenselessness in Anne Marie Pennysworth "Annie" Clark, an eight-year-old war orphan. Of his labors burying villagers clubbed and shot by Iroquois and Hessian mercenaries, Sam mutters a parallel concern for Annie: "The innocent ones were the worst part of all," an allusion to Paulsen's distaste for the random violence of war (Paulsen, *Woods,* 91). To compensate for seeing her parents massacred, Annie slips into her remarks a casual "our folks" in reference to Abigail and Olin Smith, whom she appears to adopt as mother and father (*ibid.,* 95). Of her loss, she declares to Sam, "You're the only family I have" (*ibid.*). Her candor precedes acknowledgment of him as a brother, a relationship that satisfies their mutual needs.

Drawing on historical research, the author salts fiction with realistic barbarity, such as the tossing of coins to Mexican children to generate a fight along the Rio Grande in *The Crossing,* cannon fire against American infantry during World War I in *The Foxman,* the study of exploding artillery shells in *Fishbone's Song,* and the death of 27-year-old Martin from overwork in the fields in *Sarny.* Imprisonment and starvation threaten Cody Pierce and Toni McLaughlin, protagonists who scrounge for food with other camp inmates in *The White Fox Chronicles.* Hunger and homelessness reduce the children of post–World War II Okinawa to begging in *Eastern Sun, Winter Moon;* a late-in-the-war killing of soldier Olaf Jorgensen leaves fatherless his infant son and namesake in *The Quilt*. For less virulent, but no less daunting episodes of boyhood trauma, the author depicts harassment by the strong over the weak as a normal part of growing up, a motif complicating the life of Chris Masters in *The Seventh Crystal*, Brian Robeson in *The River*, and the author himself in *My Life in Dog Years*.

Bullying the Weak

The adventure writer opens *Captive!* with a model of group taunting as Jeff Dodsen leads a class in the chant, "Stuff him. Stuff him" (Paulsen, *Captive!*, n.p.). The impetus to Roman Sanchez's vengeance against Woody "the Worm" Winslow, the chant fails to produce retaliation against the undersized prey, but does lead to humiliation after Roman drops Woody like a pup in his desk. Paulsen relieves the one-sided encounters by awarding Woody craftiness and an eidetic memory, the sources of a daring rescue. Sanchez states a valuable theme: "We've all got something to contribute" (*ibid.*). The balancing of talents indicates the author's faith that spindly nerds have skills lacking in big bruisers.

An unusual pairing of teenaged males with a veteran of World War II creates poignant reflection in *Dancing Carl*. The title figure, Carl Wenstrum, who spent the mid–1940s piloting a B-17 bomber, came home broken and expresses his hidden post-traumatic stress disorder with silence and a strangely evocative dance. Townsfolk recognize the symptoms and commiserate that "something happened and he needs help" (Paulsen, *Dancing*, 21). In contrast to "the big, four-engined bomber," Carl in his tattered sheepskin flight jacket seems spent and depleted because "he had done something wrong and couldn't live with the memory" (*ibid.*, 61). His fault, known as survivor's guilt, results from not dying in battles that killed his buddies.

Honor to Carl's wartime record as a pilot and his fascination with Helen Swanson epitomize a community's attempt to rehabilitate a haunted veteran without knowing the details of his pain. Critics ventured from standard war novel descriptors to locate insight and lyricism, the conclusion of a review in *Horn Book*. *Booklist* lauded Carl's story for impacting the perceptions of innocent 12-year-olds with complex post-war trauma, the subject of Paulsen's *Boys' Life* story "Stop the Sun" and the four-part novella *Sentries*. On the negative side, reviewer Jill Webb, in a critique for *School Library Journal*, disparaged the slow narrative pacing and dismissed as anticlimactic the gift of a rose and a performance for Helen, the culmination of *Dancing Carl*.

Exploiting Hispanics

In an article for *Jeunesse*, a questionable premise for *Lawn Boy* caused Slovenian English teacher Lilijana Burcar to rebuke Paulsen for turning the protagonist from straightforward investment schemes to outsourcing to the underclass. By hiring and underpaying migrant laborer Pasqual and 13 other illegal employees, the author ignored substandard living conditions and dehumanized the edgers, trimmers, fertilizers, and lawn caretakers by failing to treat and remunerate them as a real service staff. Burcar scorned the author's excuse that Hispanics are "always looking for work," a handy generalization for abusers of the poor (Paulsen, *Lawn*, 24). To conceal the gross mistreatment of needy workers surviving on a pittance, Paulsen's text keeps them out of sight like "lawn fairies," a ploy that Burcar called "invisibilization" (*ibid.*, 65; Burcar, 2012, 49).

As Bursar asserts, Paulsen's *Lawn Boy* bares a reprehensible underside of colonial racism. By implying that exploiting undocumented workers is a wise business move, the novel treats them like faceless robots and inconspicuous assets. In a lame excuse for complicity in splitting wages with his employer, Pasqual cheerfully concedes, "That's the way it's done" (Paulsen, *Lawn,* 28). Burcar declares that Pasqual's abetment of "an institutionalization of below-subsistence-level wages" betrays the founding premise that the lawn boy is not at fault (Burcar, 2012, 54). She blames Paulsen for desensitizing young adult audiences to the hurt inflicted by white entrepreneurs on Latino laborers, who reflect the myth of "happy plantation darkies" of early 20th-century literature and film (*ibid.*).

See also coming of age; war.

Source

Burcar, Lilijana. "(Global) Capitalism and Immigrant Workers in Gary Paulsen's *Lawn Boy:* Naturalization of Exploitation," *Jeunesse* 4:1 (Summer 2012): 37–60.
Golden, Bernice. *Critical Reading Activities for the Works of Gary Paulsen.* Portland, ME: Walch, 1999.
Nickelson, George. *Gary Paulsen.* New York: Trumpet Club, 1993.
Webb, Jill. "Dancing Carl," *School Library Journal* 58 (2012).

war

Paulsen examines the effects of combat atrocities on young recruits, the most defenseless of warriors, whom politics heedlessly "fed into the madness" (Paulsen, *Soldier's,* xv). The archetypal struggle in *The Transall Saga* indicates that tribal warfare was a given in primitive societies like the ones Mark Harrison encounters on a distant planet. For "The Madonna," the author opens the story with excruciating sounds of incoming shells, a barrage he wards off with alcohol. In *Pilgrimage on a Steel Ride,* he charged that "all healthy men in the United States have a hidden eight-year military obligation … and hundreds of thousands of them were slaughtered in ways that are unspeakable" (Paulsen, *Pilgrimage,* 162). Of his son Jim's brush with enlistment, Paulsen detailed a personal terror: "I hadn't felt fear for a while, and there was an intense bolt of fear and I could see him being hit. I could see the bullet entering him. I could see the exit wound.… I couldn't breathe" (Miller, 1988, 6). Ironically, the fervor with which children play-act at bitter fighting becomes a delight for the cousins in *Harris and Me,* in which they take the parts of GI Joe vs. a "commie Jap" (Paulsen, *Harris,* 150).

The writer surprised literary critics by publishing *Nightjohn* and *Sarny,* a two-part fictional study of slavery and the Civil War. The sudden gut-stabbing of Clel Waller with a Northern soldier's bayonet in *Sarny* signals the liberation of his plantation workers by Union bluecoats. In the upheaval, slaves run for town past their liberators, "riders … wearing blue, brass buttons, glinting in the sun," a hopeful sign to blacks, but certain destruction to soldiers in gray and "nothing but ruin" to Southern socioeconomics (Paulsen, *Sarny,* 29, 33). Sarny realizes the significance of uniforms by the fact that the blue-clad men are "fighting and dying and for you," causing "terrible, terrible damage," a one-person overview of the rebellion that applied to all Civil War battlefields (*ibid.,* 46, 47).

In addition to his two works on emancipation of slaves, the author incorporates in much of his oeuvre allusions to the most destructive world conflicts, including "the damned war" that killed a neighbor boy that Wil Neuton's grandmother missed in *The Island* (Paulsen, *Island,* 90). For Hans in *The Foxman,* the worst of the German onslaught in World War I began with cannon fire that wiped out whole units of Americans. Remembering the ten-month offensive at Verdun, France, in 1916, the Foxman relives "steel against flesh, science against beauty" (Paulsen, *Foxman,* 86). Battle proves no less horrific on volunteer militiamen, officers, and noncombatants, who gain nothing from international hostilities, imprisonment, and indiscriminate killing. For the Foxman, the wholesale butchery ends his sociability. To live in peace, he hides his grotesquely scarred face in the north woods and retreats behind a mask and into books, which make no judgments about his appearance or his flashbacks to Verdun. In contrast to the hermit, the neighbor of Richard Allen Mesington in *The Rifle* prefers describing World War II and flying a P-51 "to satisfy the need to tell these parts of his life to somebody" (Paulsen, *Rifle,* 78).

Ruined Lives

Integral to the author's musings on casualties, commentary on battle fatigue generalizes to broken soldiers from all conflicts. In *The Crossing,* Sergeant Robert S. Locke represents the Viet veteran who "had seen and been and done" and who had watched men die "when there was nothing I could do for them" (Paulsen, *Crossing,* 51, 108). After a career of campaigns in Vietnam, Honduras, and El Salvador, he marvels at a lieutenant's perverse joy in warfare, "the smell of it, the rattle of it, the fire and maneuver," a seemingly normal person's enthusiasm for rampant killing (*ibid.,* 30). In an interview for *Children's Book Review*, Paulsen posited his own abomination of combat by asserting, "The essence of war is insanity. Destruction, death, women widowed, children orphaned, lands plundered, property destroyed, lives decimated—it's all bad" (Lynch, 2009).

To recreate the panic of front-line fighting, in "Stop the Sun," a short story for January 1986 issue of *Boys' Life,* Paulsen plays out an attack of post-traumatic stress disorder in Terry Erickson's father. To the boy's horror, his father crawls along the floor at a shopping mall, "crying, looking terrified, his breath coming in short, hot pants like some kind of hurt animal," an apt description of a physiological flashback (Paulsen, "Stop," 36). Better than histories of the Vietnam War, the episode informs Terry of a soldier's replay of the day when he "couldn't stop the morning" (*ibid.*). The surreal response portrays a human mind pressed beyond rationality. Of the change wrought by time, Paulsen described mid–20th-century veterans as "old now and as misunderstood as dinosaurs" (Paulsen, *Pilgrimage,* 163).

The author's memories of wartime devastation in *Eastern Sun, Winter Moon* consist of a child's view of the homeless, starving islanders on Okinawa and shell-shocked Filipinos in Manila. The remnants of city life incorporate potholes, rusty metal, and "shacks and huts and lean-tos" (Paulsen, *Eastern*, 123). Sergeant Ryland, the Paulsens' jeep driver, explains to Eunice Paulsen: "Bombs, shells, mines—They blew hell out of the city" (*ibid.*, 121). The destruction overpowers seven-year-old Gary when he encounters rats chewing flesh from human corpses jettisoned into a cave. The startling scenarios rack his psyche for the remainder of his life. In "The True Face of War," an article for the spring 1999 issue of *Riverbank Review,* he reviles "the horror of war, the madness of war, the total destruction that is war, ever since" (Paulsen, 1999, 25). He returns to the reason for war tales in *The Foxman,* where the hermit declares, "The men telling those stories are only trying to remember some of the parts of the war that might be worth remembering—trying to find some use in all that waste" (Paulsen, *Foxman,* 87).

War in American History

With *Woods Runner,* written under the influence of James Fenimore Cooper's *The Last of the Mohicans*, the author examines the truism that conflict never ends, even from the good wars. The British and French, vying for control of the New World, conducted a series of engagements, beginning with the French and Indian War from 1754 to 1763. Military debts and festering animosities over the Stamp Act in 1775 extended antagonism into the American Revolution, when the French allied with North American patriots and contributed cash, armaments, ships, and men to defeat colonialism. A collapse of the French economy precipitated the French Revolution, which began with rioting and the storming of the Bastille on July 14, 1789. In retrospect of interlinked strife, the author sighed, "Perhaps it has never ended" (Paulsen, *Woods,* 161). The comment suggests his regret for past martyrs and for his father's involvement in World War II and the loss of Paulsen's army buddies in Vietnam.

The author focuses tales of protagonist Samuel Lehi Smith's late boyhood on the misery inflicted by the War for Independence, a slog-fest of New World persistence and courage extending from 1775 to 1783. The text admits colonial missteps and the heinousness of Iroquois and Hessian mercenaries, whom the farmer/spy Micah demeans as "mad dogs" (Paulsen, *Woods,* 118). According to an interview with Christy Corp-Minamiji, the author aims "to dispute the mythic, clean, even antiseptic qualities in many histories, because war is never ever clean" (Corp-Minamiji, 2010). For British motivation, he returns to the issue in *The Rifle* and blames the English fear of competition from American "produce and products" (Paulsen, *Rifle,* 32). In the blunt retrospect of Sam's mentor, tinker/spy Abner McDougal, "Some get, some don't, some live, some … don't," a reference to 4,400 war deaths and an estimated 60,000 post-battle losses from filth, malnutrition, and infection (Paulsen, *Woods,* 139).

Of his anti-war theme, Paulsen extols the bottom level of the Continental Army: "It was eight years of slaughter. And the guys who took it were these grunts" (Harrison, 2010). Episodes in *Woods Runner* partition the daily work, as with the job of burying nine victims of Iroquois arrows and tomahawks—six adults, two little boys, and a girl—which falls to 13-year-old Sam, even though he suffers from a serious clout to the forehead from a war club. Small details—his vomiting and "twitches and jerks and whimpers" in sleep—communicate permanent harm to the boy's spirit (Paulsen, *Woods,* 31). The author reprises the theme of teen sacrifice with *Sentries.* In four brief chapters entitled "Battle Hymns," he reveals the dead-end destinies of soldiers bereft of satisfying lives because of appalling episodes of gunfire producing slaughter or permanent disability.

Civil War

For the biography of a Civil War survivor in *Soldier's Heart,* Paulsen fictionalizes the eyewitness accounts of 15-year-old Charley Goddard, one of 47 of the 1,000 First Minnesota Volunteers to survive the Battle of Gettysburg over July 1–3, 1863. At a telling moment in the recruit's coming to knowledge about ideals and survival, he views the gore caused by artillery fire: "Next to him Massey's head suddenly left his body and disappeared, taken by a cannon round that then went through an officer's horse, end to end, before plowing into the ground" (Paulsen, *Soldier's*, 21). In the evaluation of Martin Arnold, a book reviewer for the *New York Times,* Private Goddard's breakthrough to wartime reality yields "truth and the self-esteem that comes with coping with tough truths" (Arnold, 1998, 3).

Charley Goddard's biography reveals what reviewer Kari Wergeland termed "the gruesome toll war exacts on the soul," an existential distress that leaves the infantryman feeling doomed and alone (Wergeland, 1999, F-4). He experiences a perverse "aha" that he is capable of bloodthirsty vengeance against the Rebs. Familiarity with bloated cadavers and the maiming of horses by large-caliber bullets prompt him to vent his wish "to kill them…. All of them. Stick and jab and shoot them and murder them and kill them all" (Paulsen, *Soldier's*, 51). He challenges God to account for the unspeakable battlefield outrages that afflict his mind. The author resumes the thread of pity for mounts in *Sarny,* in which the protagonist comments, "Never saw anything so hard on horses as war" (Paulsen, *Sarny,* 55).

Paulsen indicates that the killing fields are the wrong place to seek identity in the years preceding adulthood. Hopeless from battle fatigue, Charley, a blighted veteran at age 21, feels "old from too much life, old from seeing too much, old from knowing too much" (Paulsen, *Soldier's,* 98). The author rounds out the story with Charley's riverbank picnic and a hint of suicide in his thoughts. In *Journal of Adolescent & Adult Literacy,* Becky Ramsey, an English education student, noted the coercion of child soldiery: "Most 'men' fighting were frightened young boys who did not want to fight and be killed" (*ibid.*). Ramsey's fellow pupil, Susan Charbauski, made a gendered observation about the boy-meets-war motif of *Soldier's Heart*: "To go off to war and mutilate a hundred people does not make one a 'man,'" the stereotypical verdict of battlefield literature and movies (Davenport, 1999, 204).

A second-hand reprise of the horrors of the Battle of Verdun in *The Foxman* peruses individual responses to combat narratives and compares dread of mustard gas and fire. The limited interaction of the title figure, a disfigured infantryman residing apart from civilization, causes his teenage friend to ponder the loss of a valuable woodsman to disillusion and death. The theme recurs in the author's revelation of post-traumatic stress disorder in the alcoholic Korean War veteran in *Fishbone's Song* and Carl Wenstrom, the title figure of *Dancing Carl,* a pilot during a World War II conflagration that killed nine airmen in a B-17 bomber. A single inkling informs Marsh, the narrator, of the basic illogic of even the best-intentioned war: "I thought how awful it was that you could mean well and do so much damage to someone" (Paulsen, *Dancing,* 80).

See also healing and death; *The Rifle; Soldier's Heart; Tucket's Ride;* violence; *Woods Runner.*

Source

Arnold, Martin. "Finding Stories Boys Will Read," *New York Times* (15 October 1998): 3.
Corp-Minamiji, Christy. "Conversation with a Master: An Interview with Acclaimed Author Gary Paulsen," http://blogcritics.org/conversation-with-a-master-an-interview/, 2010.
Davenport, Stephen. "Soldier's Heart," *Journal of Adolescent & Adult Literacy* 43:2 (October 1999): 204–206.
Harrison, Jessica. "'Hatchet' Author Gary Paulsen to Bring Boyhood Tales to Salt Lake," *Deseret News* (11 April 2010).
Lynch, Amanda. "Gary Paulsen," *Children's Book Review* (26 January 2009).
Miller, Kay. "Suddenly Fame and Fortune," [Minneapolis] *Star Tribune* (10 July 1988): 6.
Wergeland, Kari. "'Hatchet' Author Tells Civil War Tale," *Hartford Courant* (2 March 1999): F4.

wisdom

Paulsen avoids moralizing in his works, which illustrate with action how "not to be driven down by bad things" such as loss, war, torture, arson, theft, rape, and butchery, as with the crimes of Carley, a confused delinquent in *Popcorn Days and Buttermilk Nights,* robbery by a deputy sheriff in *The Beet Fields,* and the martyrdom of Sergeant Robert S. Locke in a knife fight at the Santa Fe Bridge linking Juárez, Mexico, to El Paso, Texas, in *The Crossing* (Fitzpatrick, 2011, D1). The author replaces preaching with pragmatism, some proposed by his judicious lead dog Cookie, the star of *Puppies, Dogs, and Blue Northers,* and by the border collie Atticus in *Road Trip* and *Field Trip.* In *Clabbered Dirt, Sweet Grass,* Paulsen recalls seeing an elderly man, Gunnar Pederson, and musing: "Some are old, done, ended at forty and look it and some are never done" (Paulsen, *Clabbered,* ix). The observation alludes to the author's intention to stay active and to continue learning and writing about survivalism and dogs all his life.

Of realism, in the introduction to *Captive!,* the fiction specialist describes true adventure as "danger and daring and sometimes even a struggle for life or death," the situation faced by backpacker Mark Harrison in a surreal jungle in *The Transall Saga* and by sharpshooter John Byam during the American Revolution in *The Rifle* (Paulsen, *Captive!*, n.p.). In *The Cookcamp*, five-year-old Gary learns from his grandmother, Anita Halverson, that "All men must know how to sew in case they must live alone" (Paulsen, *Cookcamp,* 39). The remark suits the surroundings—an androcentric milieu of road builders who put stress on work clothes and boots from driving trucks and operating the great "road cat," which can tear flesh and require on-site stitches to save a limb or a life (*ibid.,* 78). The natural outflow of advice reflects Paulsen's penchant for organic theme development, a style that dominates his output.

Training the Young

For character study, Paulsen favors subtlety, particularly revelations of negative influences in youngsters' lives from violence, alcoholism, and drudgery, the daily existence of migrant workers in *Tiltawhirl John* and *The Beet Fields.* In *Winterkill,* police officer Nuts Duda's insistence that personal values are "the only rules that count" reflects a cop's diagnosis of the juvenile delinquent syndrome (Paulsen, *Winterkill,* 116). As the Civil War engulfs the title figure in *Sarny*, Lucy, her road companion, considers treating the wounded but concludes, "Easy say, hard do," a summation of medical skills lacking to freedwomen attempting to save their rescuers (Paulsen, *Sarny,* 73). In the training of Sarny in kitchen duties, the valet Bartlett advises "Just keep on keeping on," an allusion to the unending cycle of human work and the empirical nature of learning from hands-on experience (*ibid.,* 113).

The author fills his canon with examples of counsel by tight-lipped elders, notably, the Apache warrior Magpie in *Canyons,* who warns Coyote Runs not to turn stolen horses toward the village lest followers attack women and children of the tribe. At a tense moment in *Mr. Tucket,* the Pawnee leader Braid knocks the protagonist head over heels and states the difference between courage and bravado: "Bravery in youth is a good thing.... It is not good to be stupid" (Paulsen, *Mr.,* 14). Of the slaughter and composting of farm animals in *The Winter Room,* Uncle David reflects humor on the fact that "we're all fertilizer in the end," a witty riposte to the fear of death (Paulsen, *Winter*, 8).

For 13-year-old Samuel Lehi Smith, a Pennsylvania frontiersman in *Woods Runner,* Uncle Ishmael warns of lethal consequences to tramping the wild: "Nothing dies of old age in the forest ... something eats you" (Paulsen, *Woods,* 5). At a tenuous advance in the action of the American Revolution, Sam discovers the pernicious essence of international war, a vast contrast to an outdoorsman used to solitude. Matthew, the patriot boat captain, mutters, "What isn't seen isn't noted," a terse reminder to Sam to assume an inconspicuous air among the Redcoats in New York City. Both Uncle Ishmael and Matthew speak from experience that can save the boy pain, capture, and possible execution.

Mentoring

The author returns repeatedly to the apprentice youth and his relationship with older males, particularly Russel Susskit and the sage elder Oogruk, an aged shaman in *Dogsong;* the Gary character and Uncle Knute in *Harris and Me;* and Arnold the entrepreneur in *Lawn Boy Returns,* who enjoys "a great feeling a person gets from good, old-fashioned hard work" (Paulsen, *Returns,* 16). Like the lad paired with a learned graybeard in Lois Lowry's *The Giver,* protagonist Russel Susskit learns from Oogruk the concept of the internal song, a mystic melody as individual as a fingerprint. To ready himself for a long run over a snowy waste behind a husky team, Russel senses his sled's vibration through his mukluks, stays alert for pack ice, and gives way to dream-trance of the Arctic dwellers' hunt for a mammoth millennia in the past. From pure absorption in the chase, Russel follows his mentor's advice and guides his team as far from civilization as the mythic home of the wind's mother. In a critique for *CU Commons*, reviewer Randy Bush concluded that dreaming saves Russel's sanity: "The Eskimo transcends the immediate because that's what it takes to survive" (Bush, 1994, 14).

In an existential probe of challenge in *The Island*, Paulsen offers the terse advice on "gut-love" from Aunt Pam in Ensenada to 15-year-old Wil Neuton (Paulsen, *Island*, 43). She compared "sex things" to wealth and religion: "People who really had it didn't talk about it" (*ibid.*). The author stresses that young adults avoid slick idealism and easy solutions to locate a unique truth like that of Oogruk. The protagonist chooses trial and error enlightenment over glib advice from sententious elders. As Mark Vogel and Anna Creadick observed in *English Journal*, Wil realizes that he "must carve out his precepts even as he listens to advice from all sides" (Vogel and Creadick, 1993, 37). By reconciling parental and media responses to his need for solitude, Wil, a model of self-discovery on a par with Brennan Cole in *Canyons*, suits his inner need to exist Thoreau style in isolation and to satisfy his thirst to know more about his place in nature.

See also mentors.

Source

Bush, Randy. "Vibrations in Eskimo Dog Sled Runners: Paulsen's *Dogsong*, Art and the Transcendent," *CU Commons* 2 (Spring 1994): 14–18.

Fitzpatrick, Andy. "Author Gary Paulsen to Speak in Battle Creek," *Battle Creek Enquirer* (6 February 2011): D1.

Lipson, Eden Ross. "The Dark Underbelly of Writing Well for Children," *New York Times* (8 July 2000): B7.

Vogel, Mark, and Anna Creadick. "Family Values and the New Adolescent Novel," *English Journal* 82:5 (September 1993): 37.

Woods Runner

To inform young readers of boy soldiery and civilian spying during the American War for Independence, Paulsen creates a fictional eyewitness, 13-year-old Samuel Lehi Smith, protagonist of *Woods Runner*. *Kirkus Reviews* translated "woods runner" into the historical French "coureur du bois," a wilderness expert from his early teens who excels at hunting bear and deer to feed settlers of western Pennsylvania. Echoing the limited scope of Howard Fast's *April Morning* and James Lincoln Collier and Christopher Collier's *My Brother Sam Is Dead,* the plot focuses on the usurpation of a farming community by an alliance of Iroquois with British Redcoats and Hessian mercenaries, all of whom indiscriminately slaughter colonists.

Rumors over the initial conflict rouse from Olin Smith, an idealistic, peace-loving western Pennsylvanian, too curt a dismissal of "just some trouble in Boston," a naive anticipation that distance will spare him from clashes to come (Paulsen, *Woods,* 15). To Olin, a war against Britain, the world's greatest military might, seems unthinkable, "too huge to even contemplate" (*ibid.,* 16). Tinker/spy Abner McDougal places the question of loyalty within the zeitgeist by reminding Sam that, "A while ago, we were all loyal Englishmen," a commitment eradicated by the Stamp Act of 1765 and the odious tax on tea, passed by Parliament on May 10, 1773 (*ibid.,* 112). The statement reminds the reader of the urgent choice that colonists made in 1775 between past support of monarchy and anticipation of independence from George III, a new concept in the world order. Later, however, Paulsen sullied the glory of the American Revolution in *Fishbone's Song* for freeing "all except women and black people and native Americans" (Paulsen, *Fishbone's*, 67).

From Protest to Battle

Surveying the fighting up close through the experience of a farm boy, the author strips history of the myths of Boston's Sons of Liberty and stalwart Massachusetts Minute Men found in Esther Forbes's *Johnny Tremain* and Seymour Reit's *Guns for General Washington*. By concentrating on details like bayonet attacks and imprisonment on floating hulks and in a sugar mill, Paulsen's narrative develops a graphic glimpse of eight miserable years of combat and incarceration, often resulting in starvation or death from firing squad, hanging, or contagion, the indiscriminate killer that fells sharpshooter John Byam in *The Rifle*. News of the battles of Lexington and Concord from April 19, 1775, omit the rush of patriots to a continental army grown to 3,960 enlistees. Total casualties cost the colonists 94 to the British loss of 300. At the Battle of Bunker Hill on June 17, 1775, the patriots counted 450 casualties among their 2,400 men, while the Redcoats' 3,000 troops sank to 2,946 from minimal battle deaths. The teetering back and forth of victory and defeat until England's surrender on September 3, 1783, kept colonists like Olin Smith and Abner McDougal in suspense about the future of North America.

For Sam, the true cost of separation from the British crown lies in the arson that destroys his homestead, the nine bodies he buries, and a search for his parents among 5,000 starving prisoners of war in New York City. Marjorie Kehe, in a review for *Christian Science Monitor*, remarked on the blend of "harsh scenarios with moments of unexpected camaraderie," a common juxtaposition in war literature such as Stephen Crane's *The Red Badge of Courage* and Erich Maria Remarque's *All Quiet on the Western Front* (Kehe, 2010). According to Beth Martin, a book writer for the *Wausau* [Wisconsin] *Daily Herald*, the key to Sam's survival lies in his ability to submerge sorrow for his home and fears for the homeless child Anne Marie Pennysworth "Annie" Clark while plotting a logical means of freeing Abigail and Olin Smith.

Noncombatants

While tending Annie, an eight-year-old orphaned by Hessian marauders, Sam ruminates on a vital concern for Tories and patriots—the problem of trust. Abner McDougal, an itinerant tinker and purveyor of information to patriots via carrier pigeon, decides to trick British troopers with a forged pass. He cautiously sets the plan in operation after observing his two border collies and their response to the intruders. The authenticity of the printed merchant's pass escapes the Redcoats' perusal, a subterfuge that enables Abner to ferry Sam closer to his parents. Paulsen indicates that seemingly inconsequential merchants like the tinker/spy could move freely along the roads and collect and pass on information useful to refugees and other enemies of the British, including Micah the farmer and Matthew the riverboat captain.

Critics differ over Paulsen's decision to round out the fictional quest narrative with fact by inserting snatches of essays about prison ships, Hessian barbarism, and spy rings. *Publishers Weekly* approved the alliance of fiction with nonfiction in an exciting book that "candidly and credibly exposes the underbelly of that war," including death from dysentery and Iroquois scalping ("Woods," 2009, 61). Ian Chipman, a reviewer for *Booklist*, admired Paulsen for "steering his narrative through an unsentimentalized and deglorified depiction of the American Revolution" (Chipman, 2010, 72). For its literary quality, characterization, and historical authenticity, *Booklist* named *Woods Runner* among the Year 2010's Best Fiction for Young Adults.

See also war.

Source

Chipman, Ian. "Woods Runner," *Booklist* 106:9–10 (1 January 2010): 72.
Kehe, Marjorie. "Two Good Books for Boys," *Christian Science Monitor* (22 May 2010).
Soltan, Rita S. "Woods Runner," *Horn Book* (Fall 2010): 380.
"Woods Runner," *Kirkus Reviews* 78:1 (1 January 2010): 47.
"Woods Runner," *Publishers Weekly* (21 December 2009): 61.

writing

Perhaps the nation's most obsessive YA writer, "Prolific Paulsen" has maintained a killing pace over a half century of work, interlacing moods and atmospheres with the nuances of a symphony. In the epilogue to *Six Kids and a Stuffed Cat,* he muses on the tiny sense impressions that spawn topics. He ponders the strangeness of "a wisp of a millionth of a volt of electric energy through brain cells," the source of his scenario featuring a cluster of school children immured in a bathroom during a tornado drill (Paulsen, *Six,* 75). In his head, Paulsen uses those wisps by "[spending] months—years, sometimes—chewing away at different story ideas" before committing them to a final manuscript (Thomson, 2003, 76). Of self-doubts, he acknowledges in *Pilgrimage on a Steel Ride* the role of fear "of failing again, and again, and again, that needs to be there, that is the engine that drives the writing" (Paulsen, *Pilgrimage,* 17).

Paulsen's affinity for androcentric philosophy and adventure in such comedies as *Harris and Me* and *Masters of Disaster* earned him the titles "the Hemingway of Children's literature" from Matt Berman of the New Orleans *Times-Picayune* and "the quintessential writer of guy lit" from Bob Biastre and Doug Poswencyk of the Bridgewater, New Jersey, *Courier News* (Berman, 1999, D-6; Biastre and Poswencyk, 2005, 11). Children's author Jon Scieszka toasted Paulsen's output of testosterone-soaked literature: "He gets that guy mentality. He understands that, for a good book, you need weaponry and vehicles. Or you need to be out in the middle of nowhere and just have your hatchet to survive" (Jacobs, 2008). Educators added that the maleness resonating through such classics as the Tucket series, *Hatchet, The Beet Fields, The Crossing,* and *Soldier's Heart* draws fathers and sons together for read-alouds.

Jubilant over his first acceptance letter, in *Shelf Life: Stories by the Book,* Paulsen acclaims his initial published work a composite of labor, hopes, thoughts, songs, and breath. The acknowledgment resonates in his mind and soul much like adventures on his Harley-Davidson, the focus of *Pilgrimage on a Steel Ride,* or on the sloop *Felicity,* which he cherishes in *Caught by the Sea.* With what Amazon reviewer Maria Dolan calls "exaggerated manliness" and Carol Peace Robins, a book critic for the *New York Times Book Review,* labels "a macho, introspective, kaleidoscope remembrance," he summarized the transcendent biking as "out of myself, out ahead of myself, into myself, into the core of what I was, what I needed to live" (Robins, 1997, 21; Paulsen, *Pilgrimage,* 36). To his profit, he concluded, "And I knew, my core knew that I would never be the same again" (*ibid.*).

Dog sledding elicited a similar out-of-body experience. While completing *Dogsong,* Paulsen bedded down in an Alaskan dog lot and wrote by headlamp with a pencil because pens froze up in temperatures below -80. For ten years, he stayed at the task for 18 hours a day, a compulsion he described as dipping his bucket into the perpetual flow of a river. He juggled multiple works at a time and zipped through revisions on plots he had mapped out in his thoughts, eschewing modifiers and commas while metering "the pulses of words" (Paulsen, *Winterdance*, 253). For *Dogteam,* he incorporates onomatopoeia in "the high-soft-shusshh-whine of the runners and the soft jingle of their collars" (Paulsen, *Dogteam*, n.p.) Critic James Blasingame remarked, "He has a way of putting the reader right there with him so that the sights and sounds come through clearly and loudly" (Blasingame, 2004, 268). The episodes prove so realistic that readers and reviewers frequently make the error of assuming that every scene that Paulsen describes is a personal adventure.

Paulsen's Ambition

Out of faith to fans, the author has vowed to write until death. He rivets his audience with economy, fidelity, and juice, in part by strip-mining his past and segueing from one episode to another, as with the three meetings between street urchin Manny Bustos and Sergeant Robert S. Locke in *The Crossing,* the primal war of the Tsooks with the Rawhaz cannibals on a distant planet in *The Transall Saga,* and face-offs between outlaws and a black deputy U.S. marshal in *The Legend of Bass Reeves*. Terse dialogue encapsulates the folk wisdom found in Samuel Lehi Smith's assessment of Old Bobby, a crazed survivor of Iroquois slaughter in *Woods Runner,* and tinker/spy Abner McDougal's personal philosophy that "we all do what we can do" (Paulsen, *Woods,* 143). Of Paulsen's choice of details, he declares, "You use what you are," a succinct bit of advice on a par with Old Bobby's sorrow song and Abner's practical heroism (Buchholz, 1995, 29).

In a remark about absorption in print, Paulsen informed critic James Blasingame, "Good writing should immerse the readers in the story to the point where they look up hours later and are surprised to find themselves in a chair in the living room or under the sheets with a flashlight" (Blasingame, 2004, 270). For *Six Kids and a Stuffed Cat,* he shifted into stage mode in what *Publishers Weekly* termed "rapid-fire dialogue" and "a theatrical quality," both lures to the creative mind ("Six Kids and a Stuffed Cat," 2016). For *The Amazing Life of Birds,* he turned "The Twenty-Day Puberty Journal of Duane Homer Leech" into what Shannon Maughan, an analyst for *Publishers Weekly,* called a "journal-cum-bird-watching manual" on teen maturation (Maughan, 2005, 147).

Paulsen's Style

Much of the author's clarity derives from a solid moral base. As described by Maureen Conlan, "There's an aquifer that feeds Paulsen's stories, made up of intensity, compassion, hatred of oppression—and a belief in stating the bald truth" (Conlan, 1995 B1). Each text invigorates words—making them serve multiple duties via repetition, kenning, alliteration, and puns, an effective source of humor in *The Schernoff Discoveries* and the 30-book Amos Binder and Dunc Culpepper comedy series. In the purview of Susan Perren, a critic for the Toronto *Globe and Mail,* Paulsen balances "potentially sentimental material" with specifics, such as the influence of cowboy movies and comic book heroes on impressionable kids in *Super Amos* and *Eastern Sun, Winter Moon* (Perren, 1998, D15). The result is a "'just the facts' sort of writer," a master of authenticity devoid of excessive modifiers and fussy or self-aggrandizing philosophy (*ibid.*).

In the Paulsen canon, action rules, as with reflections on the collaboration of Mexican farmers and workers in *The Tortilla Factory,* Grandma's promotion of the prizefighting career of Joey Pow in *Lawn Boy Returns,* and memories of Jean-claude Killy's championship skiing in the 1960s in *Thunder Valley*. For *Dunc's Halloween,* the stringing of action verbs—

"fighting each other and digging holes looking for something to fight and rip to pieces and kill and eat and chew up and spit out and maim and dismember"—adds a witty dash to the escapades involving Duncan Culpepper and his pal, Amos Binder (Paulsen, *Dunc's*, n.p.). Anne Goodwin Sides, a journalist for the *New York Times* dismissed the author's application of fantasy and feats as "writing to conquer his own dark, painful experiences" (*ibid.*).

Central to Paulsen's purpose lies his reverence for literacy, the key to understanding history and the evolution of human character. In an interview, he declared the give and take of composition his main purpose: "The dance with words and the way the hair on the back of my neck raises when it works right is what I live for" ("Q&A"). A recurrent visual trope, hyperbole replicates the teen choice for overstatement as a means of establishing significance, as with "rats as big as ponies" in *Paintings from the Cave*, freckles "so large he seemed to move inside them" in *Harris and Me*, and "a belt buckle the size of Montana" in *Cowpokes and Desperadoes* (Paulsen, *Paintings*, 7; *Harris*, 7; *Cowpokes*, 4). In *The Amazing Life of Birds*, protagonist Duane Homer Leech exaggerates the faults of his older sister Karen as "demon spawn born in the fires of Hades," a touch of satanic overreaching (Paulsen, *Amazing*, 4). An adult version of exaggeration in *The Haymeadow* cites the senior John Barron's assertion that Tink, an elderly ranch hand, is "meaner than nine Hells" (Paulsen, *Haymeadow*, 5). In more lyrical mode in *Shelf Life: Stories by the Book*, Paulsen rejoices in "hay so sweet you could eat the grass," the conclusion to a *tour de force* rhapsody (Paulsen, *Shelf*, 6).

Testosterone Writing

With judicious placement, the author interprets the lingual style of poorly educated and unrefined male speakers in brusque, disjointed sentences, as with Carl's comment in *The Cookcamp* "We're late. You got a crescent wrench?" (Paulsen, *Cookcamp*, 17). For younger characters, Paulsen makes two- and three-word clusters zing with boyhood fervor, for example, "You'll … never … guess!," a lead-in to conversation between Amos and Dunc in *The Wild Culpepper Cruise* (Paulsen, *Cruise*, n.p.). Repetition furthers Dunc's assessment of Amos in *Cowpokes and Desperadoes*, in which Dunc disparages his friend's hopeless expectation of phone calls from his beloved. Dunc muses to himself, "It couldn't have been Melissa. It was never Melissa. Had never been Melissa. Would never be Melissa," an ongoing gag about Amos's self-delusion throughout the series (Paulsen, *Cowpokes*, n.p.).

The writer envisions young readers overcome by a curiosity about sensory details picturing grisly wounds, suffering, and loss in war stories and about ancient lifestyles, the source of raw, oily scents permeating Oogruk's quarters in *Dogsong*, cold monster eyes in *The Creature of Black Water Lake*, and dry riverbeds and burial chambers in *Canyons*. Paulsen's work offers hope and perspective on reality, even raw accounts of torment, disease, old age, and feuds. For humor, he overlays specifics with contrast. In *The Boy Who Owned the School*, the author introduces protagonist Jacob Freisten leaning on a Dumpster, a visualization of the boy's self-image and lack of confidence. The text records the boy's memories of birthday cakes from Discount Doug's bakery featuring "dancing drunk little elephants made of gushy pink frosting that looked like blown styroform," a retreat into the absurd to augment changes in self-identity in Jacob's teens (Paulsen, *Boy*, 10).

For immediacy and validity, Paulsen probes the unknown, such as child labor in Mexico for *The Tortilla Factory;* a teen prostitute in Houston, Texas, for *Sisters/Hermanas;* and antique technology from the colonial era to the 1860s for "The Case of the Dirty Bird," *Culpepper's Cannon*, and *The Rifle*. His recreation of the harrowing battles of Bull Run and Gettysburg in *Soldier's Heart,* according to reviewer Kari Wergeland, appeared in "crystalline, simple prose [built] to a grim crescendo" (Wergeland, 1999, F4). To understand the Civil War armaments, the author bayoneted pig carcasses suspended from trees and shot them with flintlock rifles and cannon. For a study of child labor in London from 1780 to 1850, he read about the 100,000 urban children forced into early graves while working in mills. In ignominy, the ones caught stealing met their end on a gibbet. The non-stop juggernaut of research and composition reminds the author of his younger days: "I write the way I used to run the Iditarod.... I can't not work.... I'll explode or something" (Metella, 1993, D6).

See also humor; kenning.

Source

Berman, Matt. "Getting Real," [New Orleans] *Times-Picayune* (31 January 1999): D-6.
Biastre, Bob, and Doug Poswencyk. "Books Guys Will Sit Still For," [Bridgewater, NJ] *Courier-News* (14 June 2005): 11.
Blasingame, James. "Books for Adolescents," *Journal of Adolescent & Adult Literacy* 48:3 (November 2004): 269–273.
_____. "Outrageous Tales about Extreme Sports," *Journal of Adolescent & Adult Literacy* 48:3 (November 2004): 267–268.
Buchholz, Rachel. "The Write Stuff," *Boys' Life* (December 1995): 29–30, 53.
Conlan, Maureen. "A Writer with Stories to Fill Two Lifetimes," *Cincinnati Post* (15 April 1995): B1.
Jacobs, Mary. "Guys Read Guy Books," *Scouting Magazine* (September 2008).
Maughan, Shannon. "The Amazing Life of Birds," *Publishers Weekly* 252:28 (18 July 2005): 139–150.
Metella, Helen. "I Write the Way I Used to Run," *Edmonton Journal* (31 October 1993): D6.
Perren, Susan. "Umbrellas, Dogs, Puppy, Fairy Tales," [Toronto] *Globe and Mail* (28 March 1998): D15.
"Q&A with Gary Paulsen," https://www.crackingthecover.com/2859-2/.
Robins, Carol Peace. "Pilgrimage on a Steel Ride," *New York Times Book Review* (30 November 1997): 21.
Sides, Anne Goodwin. "On the Road and Between the Pages, an Author Is Restless for Adventure," *New York Times* (26 August 2006): B7.
"Six Kids and a Stuffed Cat," *Publishers Weekly* 263:8 (22 February 2016).
Thomson, Sarah L. *Gary Paulsen.* New York: Rosen, 2003.
Wergeland, Kari. "'Hatchet' Author Tells Civil War Tale," *Hartford Courant* (2 March 1999): F4.

Glossary

The following abbreviations refer to titles by Gary Paulsen:

AA *Amos and the Alien*
AV *Amos and the Vampire*
AGB *Amos Goes Bananas*
AGF *Amos Gets Famous*
AGM *Amos Gets Married*
AL *The Amazing Life of Birds*
AS *Alida's Song*
BF *The Beet Fields*
BH *Brian's Hunt*
BR *Brian's Return*
BW *Brian's Winter*
BWO *The Boy Who Owned the School*
C *Canyons*
Car *The Car*
CBS *Caught by the sea*
CC *The Cookcamp*
CCa *Culpepper's Cannon*
CD *Cowpokes and Desperadoes*
CDB "The Case of the Dirty Bird"
CDS *Clabbered Dirt, Sweet Grass*
CM *Call Me Francis Tucket*
CR *The Crossing*
Cr *Crush*
CS *A Christmas Sonata*
CuR *Curse of the Ruins*
DAGD *Dunc and Amos Go to the Dogs*
DAH *Dunc and Amos Hit the Big Top*
DAMS *Dunc and Amos Meet the Slasher*
DART *Dunc and Amos and the Red Tattoos*
DATI *Dunc and Amos on Thin Ice*
DBW *Dunc Breaks the Record*
DF *Dunc and the Flaming Ghost*
DGS *Dunc and the Greased Sticks of Doom*
DC *Dancing Carl*
DD *Dunc's Dump*
DGT *Dunc Gets Tweaked*
DH *Dunc's Halloween*
DHC *Dunc and the Haunted Castle*
DMR *Danger on Midnight River*
DS *Dogsong*
DT *Dogteam*
EF *Escape from Fire Mountain*
ES *Eastern Sun, Winter Moon*
FB *Flat Broke*
FS *Fishbone's Song*
FT *Family Ties*
FTr *Field Trip*
FW *Father Water, Mother Woods*
FX *The Foxman*
G *Guts*
GC *The Glass Cafe*
H *Hatchet*
HAP *How Angel Peterson Got His Name*
Hay *The Haymeadow*
HES *Hook 'Em, Snotty!*
HM *Harris and Me*
I *The Island*
LB *Lawn Boy Returns*
LBR *The Legend of Bass Reeves*
LL *Liar, Liar*
LRHC *The Legend of Red Horse Cavern*
M *The Monument*
MD *Masters of Disaster*
MG *Molly McGinty Has a Really Good Day*
MS *Madonna Stories*
MT *Mr. Tucket*
Mud *Mudshark*
ND *Notes from the Dog*
NJ *Nightjohn*
NW *The Night the White Deer Died*
PC *Paintings from the Cave*
PDBM *Popcorn Days and Buttermilk Nights*
PDBN *Puppies, Dogs, and Blue Northers*
PSR *Pilgrimage on a Steel Ride*
Q *The Quilt*
Rif *The Rifle*
Riv *The River*
RJ *The Rock Jockeys*
RR *Rodomontade's Revenge*
RT *Road Trip*
S *Sarny*
SC "Skate-Chuting"
SD *The Schernoff Discoveries*
SCr *The Seventh Crystal*
SE *Sentries*
SH *Sisters/Hermanas*
SHe *Soldier's Heart*
SK *Six Kids and a Stuffed Cat*
Sky *Skydive!*
SL *Shelf Life*
SS "Stop the Sun"

T *Tracker*
TG *Tucket's Gold*
TH *Tucket's Home*
THa *The Time Hackers*
TJ *Tiltawhirl John*
TP The Treasure of El Patrón
TR Tucket's Ride
TS The Transall Saga
TSW This Side of Wild
TT *Tucket's Travels*
V *Vote*
VF The Voyage of the Frog
WD Winterdance
WF The White Fox Chronicles
WK Winterkill
WRo The Winter Room
WRu Woods Runner
WS Woodsong
Z *Zero to Sixty*

---

adobe (*CD*, 4; *CuR*, 2; *LBR*, 5; *NW*, 44; *PSR*, 43; *SE*, 8; *TR*, 1; *TS*, 172) a building material formed of natural elements—mud, clay, animal dung and hair—and shaped between staves into walls and stockades. *See also* pueblo.
adze (*WRu*, 116) a bladed axe that slices planks from tree trunks.
aggie (*CDS*, 10; *HM*, 84) a playing marble made of agate, which is suitable for shooting.
alloy (*I*, 21) a blend of two or more metals.
aortic (*SK*, 83; *TSW*, 15) concerning the major blood vessel from the heart.
arpeggio (*MG*, 17) the separate notes making up a chord, usually played from low note to high.
arroyo (*C*, 138; *TG*, 29; *WF*, 83) a ditch or gully sliced in dry soil by running water.
aspen (*H*, 39; *Hay*, 153; *LBR*, 108; *MT*, 110; *TR*, 28) a tree common to cold regions in high plains or mountain ridges.
auger (*FW*, 91; *HM*, 142; *M*, 32; *TH*, 67; *TSW*, 20; *WK*, 49) the boring tip of a drill for making holes in wood or the ground.
bairn (*WRu*, 98) the Scottish term for "child."
barking (*BF*, 135) talking loud to draw customers.
barrio (*CR*, 29; *CuR*, 16) ghetto or slum.
beauty mark (*BH*, 7) a patch made from felt or velvet that women glued to the face to accentuate lips and cheeks.
Blackhawk (*WF*, 15) a twin-blade helicopter incorporated in war readiness in 1979 and used in subsequent Middle Eastern engagements, particularly for transporting medical teams.
blackstrap (*LBR*, 2; *WRu*, 45) molasses, a by-product of sugar cane processing in Jamaica, Haiti, and Martinique used to make a strong, heavily aged dark rum.
blockade (*CCa*, 5) a bottleneck of harbors by which the Union navy halted supply lines to the South during the Civil War.
bluebellies (*C*, 4; *SHe*, 60) an Indian term denoting U.S. cavalry dressed in blue uniforms.
bluff (*C*, *38*; *CBS*, 95: *CM*, 4; DS, 102; *H*, 102; *Hay*, 10; *LBR*, 87; *SD*, 37; *TR*, 5; *TS*, 111; *WF*, 182) a steep riverbank or promontory eroded by moving water.
break country (*LBR*, 132) badlands, dry terrain heavily eroded by wind and water.
breechclout (*DS*, 14; *LBR*, 22; *NW*, 4; *TS*, 104) a loincloth or modesty shield covering male genitals.
broadhead (*BH*, 5; *BR*, 31; *FW*, 167; *G*, 93; *HAP*, 39) an arrow tipped with a wide barbed head shaped from two or three blades.
B-17 (*AS*, 4; *DC*, 61; *PSR*, 105–106; *RJ*, 3; *SD*, 64; *SE*, 61) a workhorse four-engine bomber favored in World War II.
Bull Durham (*BF*, 21; *CDS*, 25; *G*, 37; *HM*, 20) a brand of loose tobacco for pouring into a rolling paper to make a cigarette.
bullwheel (*TJ*, 62) the source of power and direction driving a farm implement or mechanism.
butte (*TG*, 67) A flat-topped hill that arises sharply and vertically from flatter ground.
caliber (*C*, 120; *FW*, 24; *G*, 67; *Hay*, 17; *LBR*, 24; *MT*, 6; *Rif*, 9; *RJ*, 4; *SE*, 62; *SHe*, 4; *TG*, 6; *TSW*, 23; WRu, 10) the diameter of the opening in a gun barrel.
cantina (*C*, 137; *MS*, 9; *NW*, 36; *SE*, 8) a wine bar or saloon.
carbine (*Rif, 58*; *SHe*, 78) a lightweight rifle with a short barrel favored by cavalrymen.
cerveza (*SE*, 8) Spanish for "beer."
chain shot (*SHe*, 93) artillery ammunition created from two half-balls attached by metal links to make a destructive swipe across a massed enemy.
chinga! (*BF*, 40) a Spanish exclamation of pain; Oh!
chokecherry (*AS*, 41; *BH*, 2; *CDS*, 39; *FX*, 12; *HAP*, 17; *Q*, 6; *Riv*, 18, 42) a plant in the rose family that yields clusters of bitter red to purplish-black fruit.
chub (*FS*, 6; *TSW*, 132) a stubby freshwater whitefish resembling a carp.
chute (*Riv*, 116) a rocky waterfall or rapids.
cinch (*C*, 67; *EF*, 6; *HES*, 6; *LBR*, 83; *TG*, 61–62; *TSW*, 93) a belt, band, or cord fastening a saddle or blanket around a horse.
clinkers (*AS*, 7–8) the unburned residue and ash left over from a coal fire.
Comanchero (*TG*, 3; *TH*, 157; *TR*, 57) a Mexican trader with the Comanches of north central New Mexico.
compost (*DH*, 5; *LR*, *2*) decaying plant matter used as a cover and weed suppressor for flower and vegetables beds.

conchos (*TSW*, 12) round or oval metal ornaments attached to Southwestern clothing and gear.
Conestoga wagon (*MT*, 2) a workhorse covered wagon moving people and cargo in North America from 1717.
conquistador (*CDB*, 28; *TG*, 103; *TH*, 3) a Spanish explorer and exploiter of New World wealth.
crackers (*NJ*, 57; *SHe*, 16) poor, rural Southern whites.
croup (*CM*, 58; *FS*, 38; *HM*, 8; *LBR*, 95) bronchitis.
culls (*MT*, 89) cast-offs.
D&D (*I*, 36) Dungeons and Dragons, a fantasy game of role playing issued in 1974.
demerit (*Cr*, n.p.; *DAGD*, cover; *DART*, cover; *DATI*, cover; *MG*, 25) a mark of bad conduct or fault; a penalty.
deviated septum (*SK*, 83) the misalignment of the divider between human nostrils.
diorama (*BR*, 33; *HM*, 139) a realistic scene in a three-dimensional miniature or shadowbox.
doppelgänger (*MD*, 12) a double, spectral twin, or counterpart.
Doppler effect (*HM*, 146) a change in sound pitch as an object speeds by the hearer.
doubletree (*FX*, 17; *Hay*, 132; *WRo*, 40) a crossbar that holds parallel bars at each end for harnessing a team of horses. *See also* singletree.
dragoons (*WRu*, 98) infantrymen who fight on horseback.
dunderfunk (*Q*, 76) a military baked dish consisting of sea biscuits and molasses.
edamame (*V*, 7) a fresh soybean.
eddy (*H*, 164; *Rif*, 94; *TH*, 73; *VF*, 140) a whirlpool or swirl of air or water.
Edsel (*DC*, 5) a failed Ford sedan issued between 1958 and 1960 and named for Edsel Ford, a scion of the company founder, Henry Ford.
electron (*SD*, 4; *THa*, 5) a negatively charged particle orbiting the center of an atom.
epoxy (*BR*, 51; *FT*, 92) a polymer glue formed of two resins.
fandango (*BF*, 47) taunting, passionate mating duet performed among Iberian peasants.
fault line (*I*, 2) a fracture in a rock.
feint (*CR*, 112; *LB*, 5; *MT*, 65) trick or deceive; pretend to strike.
fetal (*C*, 105; *I*, 119; *LBR*, 9; *MD*, 45; *SK*, 38) in a pre-birth, developmental state.
F-15s (*DART*, n.p.) twin-engine tactical fighters that dominated Air Force maneuvers in the 1970s and 1980s.
filigree (*Rif*, 6) lacy metalwork.
flintlock (*FW*, 124; *Rif*, 15; *WRu*, 3) a long gun equipped with a flint in the hammer that generates a spark to light the charge of gunpowder.
forestay (*VF*, 12) a guy rope or stabilizer connecting the foremast to the deck of a sailing vessel.
founder (*TR*, 134; *WRu*, 63) eat too much and vomit.
frijoles (*BF*, 11; *CR*, 2; *SE*, 8; *SH*, 15) Spanish for "beans."
froe (*WRu*, 116) an L-shaped cutting tool that applies torque to the splitting of wood along the grain.
frotch (*NJ*, 76) slang for "fetch."
galleon (*TP*, n.p.) a square-rigged 15th-century Spanish sailing vessel introduced as a warship and later used as a transport ship.
gangline (*PDBN*, 51; *WD*, 10; *WS*, 2, 6) the central cord that attaches to a dog sled and secures each dog's tugline or tether.
gedunk (*BF*, 129) snack, junk food.
geek (*AA*, 4; *AGM*, 6; *BF*, 116; *BWO*, 38; *DAH*, 5; *DAMS*, 5; *DATI*, 2; *DGS*, 2; *DMR*, 4; *GC*, 19; *MG*, 4; *MUD*, 59; *ND*, 3; *SCR*, 6; *SD*, 14; *TH*, 63; *TJ*, 69; *Z*, 31) an eccentric or freak.
Gitchee Goomee (*DART*, n.p.) Henry Wadsworth Longfellow's poetic name for Lake Superior in *The Song of Hiawatha,* the American epic.
Glock Nine (*PC*, 4) the 9mm. handgun of choice for 21st-century gangbangers.
grapeshot (*SHe*, 93; *WRu*, 26) a pouch of small metal balls that mimic the effect of a shotgun blast when fired from larger artillery.
guano (*AV*, n.p.; *BF*, 16; *DBR*, 8; *LRHC*, n.p.; *MD*, 70) dung, manure.
gyroscope (*PSR*, 166) a free-spinning disc in a gimbal or frame; a wheel that can rotate in multiple directions.
Habla español? (*TR*, 6) "Do you speak Spanish?"
haggis (*DHC*, n.p.; *FT*, 84) a Scottish delicacy made from a sheep's stomach stuffed with organ meats.
halyard (*CBS*, 25; *SL*, 130; *VF*, 12) any rope that raises or lowers a sail or flag.
hames (*HM*, 47) a pair of curved iron connectors on a horse collar for attaching traces on harness. *See also* trace.
Hare Krishna (*DGT*, n.p.) a member of a Hindu religious sect who practices celibacy and vegetarianism and chants to the god Krishna.
Hawken (*MT*, 6, 44) the standard muzzle-loading rifle of plains traders, explorers, fur trappers, and buffalo hunters from the 1820s to 1882. It bore the surname of gunsmiths Jacob and Samuel Hawken of St. Louis, Missouri.
highbinder (*LBR*, 44) rogue.
Hoka-ha (*MT*, 13) the Lakota phrase "Hokahey" means "Let's go."
horse pistols (*C*, 59) a pair of large pistols

holstered in connected pockets and draped over a saddle pommel for firing with one hand.

Huks (*ES,* 124, 177) Filipino farmers who formed a Communist guerrilla movement in the late 1940s.

hummock (*BW,* 45; *DS,* 45; *H,* 37; *MT,* 91; *TSW,* 5; *WD,* 130) a low hill or berm.

Ice Age (*AA,* 2; *DS,* 193; *I,* 2; *MD,* 83; *WS,* 7) the Pleistocene Age from 1,588,000 to 11,700 B.C., when glaciers sculpted the earth's surface.

Igorots (*ES,* 215) natives of the Philippine highlands.

jackpine (*DC,* 44; *I,* 2; *T,* 70) short, scrubby pine that can survive on poor soil.

jib (*CBS,* 54; *SL,* 129; *VF,* 12) a triangular sail on the foremast that absorbs the brunt of the wind.

jig (*FW,* 147; *G,* 80) a clamp or stabilizer that holds arrows while the author glues on feathers.

journeyman (*Rif,* 6) artisan or skilled crafter.

Juneberry (*CDS,* 47) serviceberry, a bush fruit native to Minnesota that received its name from blooms that appeared before Easter service.

kachina (*NW,* 48, 59) a Pueblo Indian doll that carries messages to the gods.

Kafka (*Car,* 84) an early 20th-century Czech writer of absurdist stories and novels.

Kevlar (*BH,* 22; *BR,* 5; Riv, 132) fabric made of polyamide strands that have strength and resistance to permeation by bullets.

kimchi (*FT,* 84) a Korean condiment made from fermented cabbage.

kiva (*TG,* 82) an underground worship center among Pueblo Indians.

koi (*ND,* 17) goldfish.

knot (*CBS,* 22; *G,* 7; *VF,* 17) one nautical mile of speed or 1.151 mph of land speed.

krokono (*AS,* n.p.; *WK,* 49) a board game in which participants shoot wood rings toward high-scoring areas.

lath (*HM,* 119) a thin wood strip placed under shingles.

Lazarus (*HM,* 82) a New Testament figure at Bethany whom Jesus raises from the dead in John 11: 1–44.

lefsa (*CS,* n.p.; *ES,* 237; *Q,* 6) Norwegian flatbread made from potatoes, flour, butter, and milk or cream.

linsey (*S,* 45) a coarse twill formed by weaving wool yarn over linen warp threads.

longhorn (*Hay,* 39; *LBR,* 3; *S,* 176; *TSW,* 11) a breed of cattle indigenous to the Texas desert that sports a curving span of horns up to nearly seven feet long.

lucifer (*C,* 4; *FS,* 95; *LBR,* 53) a mid–19th-century name for friction matches.

lunker (*FW,* 62; *Q,* 71) an oversized person or animal, particularly fish.

lutefisk (*CS,* 65; *Q,* 65) a Scandinavian fish delicacy made from dried whitefish tenderized in lye.

magneto (*WRo,* 35) a forerunner of the automatic push-button starter; a magneto electric power source that generated current for igniting gas in a cylinder.

mandibles (*I,* 93; *RR,* 2) jaws.

matador (*CR,* 82) bullfighter.

medicine (*BR,* 93; *C,* 3) a Native American term denoting anything possessing supernatural power.

mesa (*C,* 145; *MT,* 74) a flat-topped hill.

mesquite (C, 25; CuR, n.p.; *G,* 147; *LBR,* 3; *S,* 176; *TG,* 83; *TR,* 185; *TSW,* xiii, 60) a low-growing, bean-producing shrub common to shallow desert soil.

mestizo (*CR,* 24) half-breed Hispanic.

midway (*BF,* 105; *HAP,* 86) section of a carnival containing sideshows.

Missouri (*ES,* 107) a fast U.S. battleship commissioned in June 1944 and chosen as the site of the Japanese surrender on August 29, 1945.

momentum (*AGF,* n.p.; *BR,* 90; *BWO,* 24; *CDS,* n.p.; *Cr,* 97; *DAMS,* n.p.; *DD,* n.p.; *FB,* 35; *FT,* 12; *HM,* 69; *MD,* 20; *RR,* n.p.; *RT,* 43; *WD,* 6; *WF,* 243; *WS,* 66) impetus or forward motion.

Morgan horse (*CM,* 4) a powerful equine breed suitable for stagecoaches, cavalry mounts, and harness racing.

Mountie (*BH,* 87; *HAP,* 25; *WS,* 11) member of the Royal Canadian Mounted Police.

nematode (*AGF,* 5; *I,* 74) a microscopic roundworm that feeds on bacteria and fungi.

neuron (*HM,* 12; *PSR,* 91) nerve cells that transmit electrical impulses.

nicad battery (*Riv,* 28) a dry-cell rechargeable power source tipped with a nickel anode and a cadmium cathode.

nock (*BR,* 31) a groove or notch on an arrow for fitting onto a bowstring, which can be toughened with a smear of glue.

Norski (*Q,* 53, 59) the Norwegian language, which Paulsen's grandmother and female relatives speak to conceal from the boy the rigors of childbirth.

obfuscate (*V,* 65) conceal by confusing or clouding the issue.

occupation (*ES,* n.p.; *HM,* 37; *LL,* 95; T, 13; *WRo,* 29) the seizure, conquest, or control of a people or territory by a foreign army.

parabolic (*HM,* 60; *MD,* 22) of symmetrical curves giving mirrored images of each other.

paradox (*G,* 75; *TH,* 9; *WD,* 120; *WS,* 2) a self-contradictory statement; an inconsistency or ambiguity.

patch (*LBR*, 24; *MT*, 42; *Rif*, 10; *TG*, 13) a small piece of fabric placed in a rifle muzzle beneath the ball to capturing expanding gases.
pathology (*C*, 114; *WS*, 62) a study of cause of disease or death by laboratory analysis of skeletal remains and bodily fluids.
patrón (*BF*, 16; *TP*, cover) Spanish for boss, land owner.
petroglyph (*TSW*, xv) a carved or scratched image in the surface of smooth rock.
philtrum (*SK*, 2) a channel between the nose and upper lip.
phosphoresce (*VF*, 26) luminesce, glow, or emit a murky, opaque light, such as the sheen of fireflies, plankton, and angler fish.
picket (*C*, 141; *Hay*, 146; *SHe*, 65; *TH*, 58; *TSW*, 19; *WD*, 140) a sentry or squad of men standing guard; also a line, chain, or fence.
pictograph (*MS*, 59; *TH*, 90) symbolic images etched into rock by preliterate people.
piñon (*HES*, 6; *PSR*, 43; *TH*, 4; *TR*, 7) a pine species indigenous to the U.S. southwest.
plug (*Hay*, 11) an old, worn-out horse; a hack or nag.
popple (*WRo*, 10; *WS*, 31) poplar.
portage (*BR*, 36) hauling a boat or canoe from one body of water to another or over shallows or around falls and cataracts.
positive reinforcement (*BWO*, 1) a psychological term for encouragement.
possibles (CM, 16, 49; MT, 83; *TG*, 9; *TR*, 80; *WRu*, 42, 6) supplies, ammunition, or personal necessities.
poultice (*TG*, 69; *TS*, 160; *WRu*, 78) a pad or dressing dampened with a healing solution.
prime (*BH*, 48; *CBS*, *27; FX*, 38; *S*, 73; *SE*, 167; *TSW*, 103; *WD*, 141; *WR*, 30) top grade; superior quality.
pueblo (*NW*, 94; *SE*, 40; *TR*, 40) a multifamily adobe residence built in the spare style of Pueblo Indians. *See also* adobe.
pulse fencer (*HM*, 130) an electrically charged barrier that keeps stock from crossing a boundary.
punk-ball slug (*G*, 96) lead orb used in a scattergun, a primitive shotgun.
quarters (*LBR*, 14; *NJ*, 17; S, 14) housing for slaves; cabins or shacks.
Qué? (*BF*, 34) Spanish for "What?"
quill (*C*, 162; *G*, 80–81, *H*, 76; *NW*, 75; *PDBN*, 13; *SL*, 129) the hollow shaft of a feather, which the writer sanded flat to fit to a boxwood shaft.
rat-tail file (*G*, 81) a thin tubular file that Paulsen used to shape grooves in arrow shafts.
revenuer (*FS*, 77) a U.S. treasury agent who arrests and fines makers of moonshine for avoiding taxes on liquor.
rifling (*AL*, 48; *Rif*, 4; *SHe*, 4; *TG*, 18; *WRu*, 33) grooves cut inside a rifle barrel that cause the bullet to spin.
Roman nose (*LBR*, 9) a convex face on a horse.
route step (*WRu*, 113) a loose form of military march that allows soldiers to walk normally and chat.
rudder (*CBS*, 13; *H*, 3; *Riv*, 24; *VF*, 107) the vertical hinged vane on the tail of a Cessna, which alters the flight path horizontally, or on the stern of a ship for steering.
Sadie Hawkins (*AA*, 2) a folk holiday taken from Al Capp's comic strip "Li'l Abner" during which women ask men to dance.
sage hen (*LBR*, 17) grouse.
scan (*I*, 92) follow a metrical verse pattern.
schottische (*AS*, 80; *DC*, 88) a popular hopping folk dance that spread from Bohemia to Norway and Ireland.
sear (*T*, 62) the part of a trigger that holds the hammer, striker, or bolt.
sextant (*CBS*, 63) a navigational guide divided into a 60-degree arc for measuring the altitudes of stars, moon, and sun to estimate longitude and latitude.
sheepshead (*DC*, 14; *FW*, 10) a blunt-nosed freshwater fish.
shill (*BF*, 133; *TJ*, 69; *Z*, 48) an accomplice in acts of fraud.
shoepac (*DS*, 7; *WD*, 103) a waterproof boot.
shrapnel (*CR*, 14; *SE*, 65) a shred of hot metal detonated from a shell, bomb, or bullet.
silage (*CC*, 107; *CDS*, 66; *HM*, 149; *T*, 38; *WRo*, 1) winter feed for ruminants that involves the fermentation of compressed grains and green crops in a silo.
singletree (*Hay*, 131; *PDBN*, 15; *WRo*, 65) a cross bar that balances the pull of a pair of horses hitched to a wagon. *See Also* doubletree.
slit lantern (*WRu*, 142) a tall cylinder split on one side to focus light from a candle or flame.
slit trench (*WRu*, 160) latrine.
smudge (*BF*, 114; *BR*, 33; *FW*, 106; *WRu*, 20; *WS*, 59) a smoky fire lighted to repel insects or protect tender plants of fruit trees from frost.
snoose (*CC*, 19; *FX*, 5; *Hay*, 20; *I*, 25; *TJ*, 13; *WRo*, 19–20) powdered tobacco called *snustobakk*, a Danish-Swedish form of snuff developed in the early 1700s.
snowhook (*DS*, 38; G, 123; *PDBN*, 49; *WD*, 10; *WS*, 5) a wire loop or snelled apparatus on a pole that acts as an emergency brake for a dogsled by digging into ice or banked snow.
soil money (*BF*, 71) a federal program of the late 1950s that paid farmers to leave cropland land unplanted for 10 years to keep prices high and reduce surpluses.

span (*LBR,* 42) a line of two or more dray animals by pairs.
spillway (*FW,* 9; *HAP,* vii; *PSR,* 106) a chute that controls the release of water from a dam or levee.
spinnaker (*VF,* 12) a lightweight triangular headsail marking the effects of wind.
strawberry roan (*HES,* 2) a horse colored chestnut and white.
striker (*CM,* 45; *TG,* 97; *TH,* 145; *TT,* 45; *WRu,* 66) high carbon firesteel struck against flint or quartz to ignite tinder.
Stroganoff (*Car,* 62; *I,* n.p.; *FTr,* 3; *TSW,* 56) sliced beef sautéed in sour cream and served over noodles or rice.
struts (*BF,* 24; *BR,* 62; *BW,* 133; *Sky,* n.p.) wood supports for girders or metal braces under airplane wings.
swale (*C,* 58) a depression in the landscape, especially marshy ground.
switchback (*WD,* 176) a sudden trail reversal, often referred to as a hairpin turn.
swivel gun (*WRu,* 96) a small rotating cannon.
syndrome (*SHe* xii; SS, 27) multiple abnormal behaviors; a pattern of symptoms of a psychological disorder.
tack (*CBS,* 94; SC, 57; *VF,* 139; *WRu,* 136) a sailing term for changing direction by advancing into the wind.
tang (*CDS,* 79.; *Rif,* 11) a projection on the end of a tool or firearm that fits snugly into a handle or stock.
the Territory (*LBR,* 49) Indian Territory (Oklahoma) the land where Andrew Jackson had the Cherokee and Creek settled after the Trail of Tears.
Texican (*LBR,* 44) a resident of Mexican Texas or the Republic of Texas.
Thirtieth Foot (*WRu,* 157) a regiment of a volunteer Philadelphia militia dating to the 1760s.
thrum (*BW,* 9; *DS,* 174; *FS,* 39; *H,* 11; *I,* 98; *T,* 29; *VF,* 85; *WS,* 2) vibrate.
timberline (*BH,* 7; *Hay,* 7; *WS,* 183) the altitude beyond which trees cannot survive.
tow (*LBR,* 4; *S,* 26; *SHe,* xvii) cord or coarse cloth woven from hemp or flax.
trace (*Hay,* 132; *HM,* 46; *S,* 15; *T,* 22; *WRo,* 40) a side strap, lead, or chain connecting the harness of a dray animal to a farm implement or vehicle.
trajectory (*DGT,* 5; *HM,* 60; *Rif,* 4; *TSW,* 4) the arc or path followed by a bullet or missile.
triceratops (*DF,* n.p.; *HM,* 61) a bulky dinosaur armed with three horns around the eyes.
trysail (*VF,* 12) a stabilizing sail on the mainmast that holds a vessel into the wind.
tundra (*DS,* 5; *H,* 6; *PDBN,* 79; *WD,* 220; *WS,* 122) treeless land of the far north covered in moss and sedge.
ulu (*DS,* 8, 10) a semicircular cutting blade sometimes called a mezzaluna (half moon).
vaquero (*C,* 59; *LBR,* 52; *SH,* 87) Spanish for "cowboy."
velvet (*BH,* 56; *BR,* 2; *G,* 54; *I,* 45) a soft, fuzzy covering of deer, elk, moose, and caribou antlers that oxygenates the bone during growth.
vision quest (*DS,* 186; *FT,* 80; *WS,* 5) an intense personal venture into self among plains Indians, who fast and cleanse their spirits in anticipation of a supernatural awareness of creation.
whist (*CC,* 53; *Q,* 75) a card game for four people played like bridge.
widowmaker (*CBS,* 7; *TJ,* 17) a rodeo term for a horse that kills its riders.
yellow rose (*LBR,* 45) a legendary nickname for Emily D. West, an abductee by General Santa Anna in mid–April 1836, who occupied him in his tent at the Battle of San Jacinto.
yucca (*C,* 162; *Z,* 43) a perennial desert shrub that provided natives with fruit and seeds rich in calcium for making jelly and candy, stalks to quench thirst, petals for eating, a stout heart for roasting, tips for arrowheads, seeds for dye, pain relief for aching joints, soap from the roots, tinder for fire starting, and fiber for huaraches, rope, and baskets.

Appendix A
Timeline of Historical References

11,700 B.C. During the Pleistocene or Ice Age, glaciers sculpted the earth's surface. (*The Island*)

18,000 B.C. Humans migrated into the American West. (*Mr. Tucket*)

15,000 B.C. Hunters in Dordogne, France, painted large animal shapes on a cave wall. (*Six Kids and a Stuffed Cat*)

1320 B.C. King Tutankhamun began a nine-year rule of Egypt's New Kingdom until his death, when Horemheb replaced him. (*Time Benders; Six Kids and a Stuffed Cat*).

1250 B.C. Hebrew followers of Moses received God's law as the Ten Commandments. (*The Legend of Bass Reeves*)

700s B.C. The prophet Isaiah foresaw the birth of a religious leader in Bethlehem. (*The Tent*)

100 B.C. Julius Caesar was born in Rome to a patrician family. (*The Time Hackers*)

8 A.D. During a Roman census in Palestine, a virgin teenager gave birth in Bethlehem and migrated to Egypt. (*The Tent*)

ca. 41 Pontius Pilate, a Roman governor, condemned Jesus to death. (*The Tent*) Jesus the evangelist suffered mockery and pain from a crown of thorns on his head before his crucifixion. (*Dogsong*)

453 Attila the Hun formed an empire of tribes that terrorized central and eastern Europe. (*Dunc and Amos and the Red Tattoos*)

September 1297 Sir William Wallace, a Scots libertarian, led an anti–English force to victory at the Battle of Stirling Bridge on the River Forth. (*Woods Runner*)

1492 Christopher Columbus set out from Spain to the west and discovered the Western Hemisphere. (*Mr. Tucket*)

May 19, 1536 Henry VIII sent to the block his second wife, Anne Boleyn, the mother of Elizabeth I. (*The Time Hackers*)

1540s Spanish explorers began roaming the American West in search of gold. (*Mr. Tucket; Tucket's Gold*)

August 18, 1576 English privateer Martin Frobisher became the first white man to see Canadian Eskimos. (*Dogsong*)

1610 Spaniards established Santa Fe, New Mexico. (*Mr. Tucket*) late August 1619 Virginia colonists imported black slaves to Jamestown to produce tobacco. (*Nightjohn; Sarny*)

1716 Privateer Edward Teach began a career of piracy under the name Blackbeard. (*Dunc and the Flaming Ghost*)

December 13, 1717 The Conestoga wagon received its first mention as transport for German Mennonites across southern Pennsylvania. (*Mr. Tucket*)

1718 The Spanish founded San Antonio, Texas. (*Mr. Tucket*)

August 10, 1728 Russian-Danish explorer Vitus Bering sighted Inuit on Saint Lawrence Island, Alaska. (*Dogsong*)

1740 South Carolina lawmakers banned education for slaves. (*Nightjohn*)

June 10, 1752 During a lightning storm, Benjamin Franklin experimented with electricity by attaching a key to a kite. (*The Schernoff Discoveries*)

1759 Georgia prohibited writing for slaves, but allowed them to read as part of Christian education. (*Nightjohn*)

1768 Previous to the American Revolution, Philadelphia gunsmith Cornish McManus learned rifling from expert John Waynewright. (*The Rifle*)

1769 Spanish settlers founded San Diego, California. (*Mr. Tucket*)

April 19, 1775 Months after the first military engagements of the American Revolution at Lexington and Concord, Massachusetts, the news filtered west to Pennsylvania pioneers. (*Woods Runner; The Foxman; The Rifle*)

June 17, 1775 The Battle of Bunker Hill introduced to the war a dismaying destruction and terror instilled by British muskets equipped with bayonets. (*Woods Runner; The Rifle*)

late June 1775 General Daniel Morgan organized 69 sharpshooters armed with rifles for use against the Redcoats. (*Woods Runner*)

1776 Mexican settlers founded San Francisco, California. (*Mr. Tucket*)

1776 To boost trade with the Pacific Coast, the Spanish opened the Santa Fe Trail from New Mexico to Monterey, California. (*Mr. Tucket*)

February 1776 George Washington took his first major command in New York. (*The Rifle*)

July 4, 1776 The Declaration of Independence, primarily the writing of Thomas Jefferson, expressed patriot anger because George III contracted with German states for the service of 30,067 Hessian mercenaries in the American colonies. (*Woods Runner; The Rifle*)

August 15, 1776 The first Hessian auxiliaries landed in Staten Island, New York, and earned a reputation for savagery and pillaging. (*Woods Runner*)

August 29, 1776 At the Battle of Brooklyn Heights, Redcoats outflanked General George Washington's Continental Army. (*Woods Runner*)

September 15, 1776 The British took control of New York City after the Battle of Long Island, forcing patriots to flee south to Philadelphia. (*Woods Runner*)

December 26, 1776 After moving the Continental Army across the Delaware River on Christmas night, General George Washington surprised Hessian troops in Trenton, New Jersey, to ensure the safety of Philadelphia, the heart of the revolution. (*Woods Runner*)

1777 Henry Hamilton, the governor of Fort Detroit, paid the Iroquois to turn in scalps and prisoners of war for pay. (*Woods Runner*)

September 19, 1777 French investments in the patriots enabled the Continental Army to triumph over the British at Saratoga, New York. (*Woods Runner*)

September 23, 1777 British forces invaded Philadelphia and held it until June 18, 1778. (*Woods Runner*)

February 6, 1778 The French allied with the colonists against Britain. (*Woods Runner*)

1781 Spaniards in California established Los Angeles. (*Mr. Tucket*)

1791–1794 Pennsylvania farmers rebelled against tax on distilled spirits during the Whiskey Rebellion and faced an army led by President George Washington. (*Fishbone's Song*)

1804 Lewis and Clark set out from St. Louis, Missouri, to survey the Pacific coast. (*Mr. Tucket*)

1811 Fur trappers blazed the Oregon Trail. (*Mr. Tucket; The Rifle*). As settlers crossed the Mississippi Valley, their approach launched the Indian Wars. (*The Legend of Bass Reeves*)

1819 To protect lands southwest of the Great Lakes from Chippewa and British \attack, the U.S. Department of War built Fort Saint Anthony, later called Fort Snelling, Minnesota. (*Soldier's Heart*).

1823 Stephen F. Austin formed colonial vigilantes into the first Texas Rangers. (*The Legend of Bass Reeves*)

1825 For a century, one-third of all Norwegians emigrated to North America, producing 800,000 Norwegian-Americans by 1925. (*The Winter Room*)

August 1826 Kit Carson began his career as a mountain man by traveling with Jim Bridger to New Mexico. ("The Madonna," *The Legend of Bass Reeves*)

winter 1831 The spread of disease along the Oregon Trail reduced the Pawnee from smallpox and killed pioneers from cholera, typhus, malaria, and typhoid fever. (*Tucket's Home*)

March 6, 1836 In San Antonio, Texas, the Alamo fell to Mexican general Santa Anna's forces, who killed former U.S. Representative Davy Crockett. (*The Legend of Bass Reeves*)

April 21, 1836 During the Texas Revolution, the Texians won a quick victory over General Santa Anna, who dallied in his tent with Emily D. West, an abductee popularized as the Yellow Rose of Texas. (*The Legend of Bass Reeves*)

May 1838 On the Trail of Tears, Andrew Jackson's troops forced the Cherokee, Creek, and

Choctaw to march toward Oklahoma. (*The Legend of Bass Reeves*)

December 19, 1843 Charles Dickens published *A Christmas Carol.* (*Dunc's Doll*)

1846 The Mexican War ended Hispanic dominance of the American Southwest. (*Mr. Tucket; Tucket's Ride; The Legend of Bass Reeves*)

1846 Jeremiah Johnson traveled west from New Jersey in search of gold. (*The Legend of Bass Reeves*)

1853 To stave off problems with the Sioux, the U.S. army built Fort Ridgely in south central Minnesota. (*Soldier's Heart*)

1855 American epic poet Henry Wadsworth Longfellow, author of *The Song of Hiawatha*, referred to Lake Superior as Gitche Gumee. (*Dunc and Amos and the Red Tattoos*)

March 22,1858 Monticello, Kansas, elected Wild Bill Hickok as constable. (*The Legend of Bass Reeves*)

April 3, 1860 The Pony Express covered a mail route from Missouri to Sacramento, California. (*The Legend of Bass Reeves*)

April 12, 1861 Newspapers reported the onset of the American Civil War and stirred rumors of emancipation. (*Sarny; The Legend of Bass Reeves; Pilgrimage on a Steel Ride*)

April 19, 1861 President Abraham Lincoln blockaded Southern ports, thus halting the exportation of cotton and sugar. (*Sarny*)

April 29, 1861 During the recruiting of Union soldiers, 15-year-old Charles E. Goddard lied his way into the First Minnesota Volunteers. (*Soldier's Heart*)

July 21, 1861 Legislators and their families picnicked on a hill while they watched the First Battle of Bull Run in Manassas, Virginia. (*Soldier's Heart*)

August 20, 1861 President Abraham Lincoln summoned General George B. McClellan to reorganize the Union military into the Army of the Potomac. (*Soldier's Heart*)

March 9, 1862 The ironclad Monitor and Merrimack clashed off Hampton Roads, Virginia, producing no clear victory for either navy. (*Culpepper's Cannon*)

March 11, 1862 President Lincoln lost confidence in McClellan and reduced his command from general-in-chief to leader of only the Army of the Potomac. (*Soldier's Heart*)

April 7, 1862 General Ulysses S. Grant gained a reputation for victory after defeating rebels under Beauregard at Shiloh, Tennessee. (*Soldier's Heart*)

August 28, 1862 At the second Battle of Bull Run, General Thomas J. "Stonewall" Jackson mounted the war's largest mass assault against Union General John Pope, causing him some 14,500 casualties. (*Soldier's Heart*)

September 17, 1862 At Sharpsburg, Maryland, generals George B. McClellan and Joseph Hooker prevented a Confederate invasion. (*Sarny*)

January 1,1863 Abraham Lincoln's Emancipation Proclamation freed slaves. (*Sarny; The Legend of Bass Reeves*)

July 2, 1863 During the Battle of Gettysburg, the First Minnesota Volunteers led a counterattack and lost 82 percent of their number. Corporal Charley Goddard sustained wounds to the left thigh and shoulder that forced his hospitalization in Philadelphia. (*Soldier's Heart; Sarny; Brian's Hunt*)

November 19, 1863 At the dedication of a national graveyard, President Abraham Lincoln delivered the Gettysburg Address. (*The Voyage of the Frog*)

May 5, 1864 Charley Goddard mustered out of Company K as a wounded veteran. (*Soldier's Heart*)

April 9, 1865 The Civil War ended with General Robert E. Lee's signing of a surrender to Union General Ulysses S. Grant. (*Sarny*)

Of the 370,000 Union soldiers from New York State, a total of 33,621 died of wounds or disease. (*Soldier's Heart*)

late 1865 The American West drew pioneers and settlers for a period of 30 years. (*Mr. Tucket*)

1866 Confederate veterans started the Ku Klux Klan in Pulaski, Tennessee. (*Sarny*)

July 28, 1866 The Tenth Cavalry, a unit of freedmen, fought during the Indian Wars. (*Pilgrimage on a Steel Ride*)

December 9, 1868 Five and a half years after the Battle of Gettysburg, Charley Goddard died of consumption at age 23 in Winona, Minnesota. (*Soldier's Heart*)

March 4, 1869 Ulysses S. Grant began the first of two terms as U.S. president. (*Pilgrimage on a Steel Ride*)

May 10, 1869 The Transcontinental Railroad opened travel from the east coast to the Pacific coast. (*Mr. Tucket; Tucket's Home*)

November 17, 1869 Wyatt Earp accepted appointment as constable of Lamar, Missouri. (*The Legend of Bass Reeves*)

December 23, 1869 Author Ned Buntline began issuing a series of dimes novels about Western outlaws and heroes in the *New York Weekly. Legend of Bass Reeves*)

December 1872 Buffalo Bill Cody debuted in a Chicago Wild West show. (*The Legend of Bass Reeves*)

1875 Isaac Parker accepted appointment as federal judge over Indian Territory and named Bass Reeves a U.S. Marshal. (*The Legend of Bass Reeves*)

1907 Bass Reeves became the first black deputy U.S. marshal and served in Arkansas and Oklahoma. (*The Legend of Bass Reeves*)

September 16, 1875 Billy the Kid committed his first crime in Silver City, New Mexico, by stealing food. (*The Legend of Bass Reeves*)

1876 Alexander Graham Bell invented the telephone. (*Brian's Hunt*)

June 25, 1876 General George Armstrong Custer led the Seventh Cavalry into a fatal ambush at the Little Big Horn against a coalition of Cheyenne, Arapaho, and Sioux, who were better armed than U.S. soldier. (*Pilgrimage on a Steel Ride; The Rifle*)

October 22, 1879 Thomas Edison perfected the carbon filament lightbulb. (*The Schernoff Discoveries*)

early 1880s Apache raiders stole mounts and cattle from ranchers in El Paso, Texas. (*Canyons*)

June 24, 1889 Butch Cassidy became a wanted felon for robbing a bank in Telluride, Colorado. (*The Legend of Bass Reeves*)

October 11, 1899 The Boer War brought British troops in conflict with Dutch farmers in South Africa. (*The Monument*)

1901 Irish explorer Ernest Shackleton led the first of three expeditions to the Arctic. (*Sentries*)

December 17, 1903 The Wright brothers completed their first powered flight at Kitty Hawk, North Carolina. (*Brian's Hunt; Molly McGinty Has a Really Great Day*)

November 16, 1907 When Oklahoma becomes a state, the U.S. marshal service turns local policing over to town constables. (*The Legend of Bass Reeves*)

February 17, 1909 Apache leader Geronimo died in U.S. custody at Fort Sill, Oklahoma. (*Fishbone's Song*)

November 20, 1910 Mexico's provisional president, Francisco Madero, encouraged the raids of Pancho Villa against wealthy hacienda owners. (*The Crossing*)

July 28, 1914 The assassination of Austrian archduke Franz Ferdinand in Sarajevo, Bosnia, incited World War I. (*The Foxman*)

late May 1915 Baron Manfred von Richthofen became the most feared German fighter pilot of World War II. (*The Treasure of El Patron*)

February 21, 1916 Over ten months, the Battle of Verdun killed 305,000 soldiers. (*The Foxman*)

January 16,1920 A U.S. Prohibition law banned alcoholic beverages. (*Father Water, Mother Woods*)

January 1925 Gunnar Kaassen, a musher in Anchorage, Alaska, and lead dog Balto began a relay through -40 degrees to carry diphtheria serum to Nome, arriving on February 2. (*Winterdance; Dogsong*)

September 4, 1929 The collapse of the stock market launched the Great Depression. (*The Haymeadow*)

August 8, 1934 Boeing developed for the U.S. Army Air Corps the four-engine B-17 omber, a symbol of the nation's air power. (*Dancing Carl*)

1935 Nuremberg race laws banned mating between darker peoples with Aryans, the master race. (*The White Fox Chronicles*)

July 26, 1941 President Franklin D. Roosevelt named General Douglas MacArthur the command of U.S. forces in the Far East. (*Masters of Disaster*)

December 7, 1941 Japan's surprise assault on Hickam Field in Hawaii brought U.S. forces into World War II, a two-front conflict. (*Tracker; Pilgrimage on a Steel Ride; This Side of Wild; How Angel Peterson Got His Name; Eastern Sun, Winter Moon; A Christmas Sonata; Sentries;* "The Case of the Dirty Bird"; *The Legend of Bass Reeves; The Beet Fields*)

February 1942 Adolf Hitler appointed Albert Speer to head German production of weaponry. (*Pilgrimage on a Steel Ride; Amos and the Chameleon Caper;* "The Killing Chute")

August 23, 1942 Nazi Germany fought the Soviet Union for more than five months to claim Stalingrad. (*Pilgrimage on a Steel Ride*)

July 9, 1943 General George Patton's Seventh Army led an invasion of Sicily to free the island from the forces of Benito Mussolini. (*A Christmas Sonata*)

September 2, 1945 The U.S. and its allies occupied Japan after its surrender in Tokyo Bay aboard the U.S.S. *Missouri*. (*Eastern Sun, Winter Moon; Tracker; Harris and Me*)

1945 Occupation forces settled in the Philippines. (*Eastern Sun, Winter Moon;* "The Liberty Ship")

June 25, 1950 A clash between north and South Korea on the Ongjin peninsula began the Korean War (*Fishbone's Song; The Foxman; Sentries; Winterkill; Pilgrimage on a Steel Ride*)

November 1, 1955 A clash between North and South Vietnam incited the Vietnam War. (*Sentries; Canyons; Pilgrimage on a Steel Ride;* "Stop the Sun")

January 20, 1961 John F. Kennedy took the oath of office of U.S. President. (*Pilgrimage on a Steel Ride*)

January 21, 1961 President Kennedy named Robert McNamara the Secretary of Defense. (*Pilgrimage on a Steel Ride*)

October 16, 1962 A Russian transport of ballistic weapons to Cuba launched the Cuban missile crisis. (*Pilgrimage on a Steel Ride*)

January 1968 King Norodom Sihanouk protested U.S. air strikes in Cambodia. ("The Killing Chute")

March 16, 1968 A massacre at My Lai, South Vietnam, brought criminal charges against the American army. (*Winterdance;* "The Killing Chute")

Spring 1973 Alaskans held the first Iditarod race. (*Woodsong*)

January 20, 1981 Ronald Reagan began the first of two terms as U.S. president. (*Pilgrimage on a Steel Ride*)

November 13, 1982 The Vietnam Wall honored 58,307 soldiers killed or missing in Vietnam. (George Nickelson interview)

September 10, 1989 Paulsen's beloved lead dog Cookie died. (*Puppies, Dogs, and Blue Northers*)

January 1, 1994 The North American Free Trade Agreement began luring American factories to Mexico. (*The Tent*)

Appendix B

Writing, Art and Research Topics

1. What are Paulsen's strongest comments about racism? war? heroes? forest animals? child abuse? poverty? hunger? boyhood daring? achievement? contentment? Choose the most memorable remarks for poster art.

2. Summarize the wisdom of grandmothers in *The Quilt, Molly McGinty Has a Really Good Day, The Island,* or *Alida's Song* and one of these works: Richard Peck's *A Long Way from Chicago*, Maya Angelou's *I Know Why the Caged Bird Sings,* Rudolfo Anaya's *Bless Me, Ultima,* or Ray Bradbury's "The Electric Grandmother." Which grandma expresses love more openly? Which uses food as a display of affection? What methods do the grandmothers choose to protect grandchildren from harm?

3. Characterize the motivation and purpose of nature in the works of Paulsen and those of Theodore Taylor, Mark Twain, Marjorie Kinnan Rawlings, Avi, Willa Cather, Jack London, Natalie Babbitt, Ursula Le Guin, Scott O'Dell, or Will Hobbs. Which authors admire the attitude of Native Americans toward creation and conservation? Which authors predict losses to Mother Earth?

4. Summarize the effects of a raid, torture, intimidation, bullying, or militarism in *Soldier's Heart, Nightjohn, The Island,* or *Danger on Midnight River* and one of these works: Robert Cormier's *I Am the Cheese,* Elizabeth George Speare's *The Sign of the Beaver,* Walter Dean Myers's *Monster,* Robin McKinley's *Beauty,* Orson Scott Card's *Ender's Game,* Esther Forbes's *Johnny Tremain,* James Lincoln Collier and Christopher Collier's *My Brother Sam Is Dead,* Paula Fox's *Slave Dancer,* Walter Dean Myers *Fallen Angels,* or Stephen Crane's *The Red Badge of Courage.*

5. Summarize the significance of one of these details to Paulsen's works: counseling, flintlock, medicine arrow, Comancheros, Iditarod, Gettysburg, mestizo, B-17, PTSD, husky, dream-trance, World War II, Pawnee, Redcoats, Huks, Apache legends, slave sale records, or Norwegian-Americans.

6. Propose the choice of Paulsen's *The Glass Café, The Beet Fields,* or *Dogsong* as a community read or a celebration of young adult literature. Suggest an annotated character web, taped readings, improvised dialogue, or dramatic timeline to express periods of stress or change. Provide a list of alternate texts by Gish Jen, Gary Soto, Yoko Kawashima Watkins, Gayle Ross, Joseph Bruchac, Conrad Richter, Jeanne Wakatsuki Houston, or Carmen Deedy.

7. Compare the turmoil of political and socio-economic change in *Sentries* and *Eastern Sun, Winter Moon.* Include adaptations to employment, food, parenting, music, fear, betrayal, love, and transportation.

8. Analyze dangers to marginalized people in *The Night the White Deer Died* and *The Monument,* particularly alcoholics like former Navajo chief Billy Honcho and handicapped women like Rachael "Rocky" Turner. Contrast other works about needy characters, for example, Clyde Cothern in Ben Mikaelsen's *Petey,* Rob Peck in Robert Newton Peck's *A Day No Pigs Would Die,* Brat in Karen Cushman's *The Midwife's Apprentice,* the unnamed boy in William H. Armstrong's *Sounder,* or Frankie in Carson McCullers's *The Member of the Wedding.*

9. Account for varied types of confrontations in Paulsen's writing, particularly the arrival of reporters in a boat in *The Island,* Brian Robeson's fistfight with Carl in *Brian's Return,* a classroom raid in *Captive!,* Braid's scalping by Jason Grimes in *Mr. Tucket,* Atticus's new brother Conor in *Road Trip,* a Civil War skirmish in *Sarny,* the arrival of John to the plantation in *Nightjohn,* and alien encounters in *The Transall Saga.*

10. Contrast types of resistance in several of Paulsen's works. Include the following models:

- against an escaped gerbil in *Mudshark*
- against war memories in "Stop the Sun"
- against juvenile delinquency in *Winterkill*
- against a storm in *The Voyage of the Frog*
- against divorce in *Hatchet*
- against bullies in *The Island*
- against racists in *Sarny*
- against Redcoats in *The Rifle*
- against cancer in *Notes from the Dog.*

11. Compare the gifts of heritage in Gary Paulsen's *Alida's Song, Sentries, The Island,* or *The Winter Room* with kinship in Gish Jen's "Fish Cheeks" or Sylvia Lopez-Medina's *Cantora,* freedom in Avi's *True Confessions of Charlotte Doyle,* or learning in Lois Lowry's *The Giver* or Paulsen's *Winterdance.*

12. List types of curiosity about self and nature in *The Island, The Amazing Life of Birds, The Voyage of the Frog,* or *Woodsong.* Which protagonist achieves the greatest satisfaction from learning? from experience? from compromise? from solitude?

13. Summarize Paulsen's views on the disempowerment of nonwhite peoples in *Canyons, Dogsong, The Night the White Deer Died, The Beet Fields, The Legend of Red Horse Cavern, The Crossing,* or *Tucket's Gold.*

14. Determine the source of pride in Paulsen's *The Tortilla Factory, Worksong, Escape from Fire Mountain, Danger on Midnight River, Six Kids and a Stuffed Cat,* or *Hook 'Em, Snotty!* How do hard labor, practice and teamwork produce satisfaction?

15. Account for humor in difficult situations in Paulsen's *The Schernoff Discoveries, Lawn Boy, Brian's Winter,* or *Molly McGinty Has a Really Good Day* with scenarios in Marjane Satrapi's *Persepolis,* Mark Twain's *The Adventures of Huckleberry Finn,* or Laura Ingalls Wilder's *Little Town on the Prairie.*

16. Compare standard rules for behavior in Paulsen's *Sisters/Hermanas* or *The Glass Café* with similar expectations in Jessamyn West's *The Friendly Persuasion,* William Gibson's *The Miracle Worker,* Louisa May Alcott's *Little Women,* Robert Edwin Lee and Jerome Lawrence's *The Night Thoreau Spent in Jail,* John Steinbeck's *The Red Pony,* or Harper Lee's *To Kill a Mockingbird.*

17. Discuss the tone and atmosphere of supernatural intervention in character action, particularly in *The Time Hackers, The Treasure of El Patrón,* or "Wolfdreams." How does Paulsen present foreknowledge in the Foxman and Oogruk, instinct in Harris Larson and Cookie, and age-old wisdom in Grandfather Borne, Johanna, Sgt. Robert S. Locke, Nuts Duda, Laura Harris, Fishbone, Anita Halverson, Matthew the boatman, Al the stripper, Jason Grimes, or Delie?

18. Summarize the traits of a broken soldier, such as the survivors in *The Crossing,* "Stop the Sun," *Dancing Carl, Fishbone's Song, Woods Runner, The Foxman, The Rock Jockeys, Soldier's Heart, Winterkill,* or *Eastern Sun, Winter Moon.*

19. Account for positive images of solitude in the lives of Jo-Jo the Dog-faced Girl, Wil Neuton, Brian Robeson, John Barron, Terry Anders, Nightjohn, David Alspeth, Daniel Martin,

Rachael "Rocky" Turner, Dancing Carl, Jason Grimes, or the Foxman. How does Paulsen's personal life validate close relations of lone humans with animals in the woods or sea?

20. Select contrasting scenes and describe their pictorial qualities, for example:

- making a raft in *The River*
- seeing reindeer in *A Christmas Sonata*
- locating a foundling in *Fishbone's Song*
- eating at a diner in *Pilgrimage on a Steel Ride*
- burying a stillborn dog in *Puppies, Dogs, and Blue Northers*
- writing on a laptop in *Caught by the Sea*
- seeing wolf packs in *Dogteam*
- applying first aid in *Masters of Disaster*
- arresting an outlaw in *The Legend of Bass Reeves*
- spying on a spy in *The Island*
- looking for clues in *Mudshark*.

21. Discuss the sources of affection or antipathy between one of these character pairs:

- Dunc Culpepper and Amos Binder
- Harris Larson and his summer guest
- Ben and Mr. Duffy
- Henry Mosley and Reed Hamner
- Finn and Johanna
- Russel Susskit and Oogruk
- Sarny and Laura Harris or Bartlett
- Wil and Jim Neuton
- Mrs. Barrancs and Tracy
- Bass Reeves and Mammy
- Kevin Spencer and Tina.

22. Contrast flaws and strengths in two of these secondary characters:

Rom	Abner McDougal	Mick Strum	Helen Swanson
Uncle David	Oogruk	Rebecca Tucket	railroad porter
Clay Borne	Lottie	Annie Clark	Bledsoe boys
Aunt Emily	Ice Shackleton	David Smallhorn	Richard Allen Mesington
Olin Smith	Waylon or Suze	Irene Flynn	Corpsman Harding
Little Bear	Magpie	Matthew	Troy or Brandon

Which characters recognize their own weaknesses? talents? inescapable memories? needs for food, music, and camaraderie?

23. Write an extended definition of *conflict* using as an example Amos Binder and Melissa Henson, Jacob Freisten and his sister, Terry Anders and teen criminals, Jake and Skinny Tony, Manny Bustos and Pacho, Gary's mother and Sergeant Ryland, Charley Goddard and Coops, William James Bentley the Fourth and Francis Alphonse Tucket, or Brian Robeson and the skunk Betty.

24. List types of comfort in these scenes: Paulsen riding a Harley-Davidson to Alaska, six kids retreating from a tornado, Mick Strum designing a monument, Pueblo applying a poultice to snakebite, Scandinavian women touching wedding dress fabric on a quilt, Brian sharing food with David Smallhorn, Gary clutching a stuffed toy named Dog, violin music and a waltz after Alida's dinner, Derek Holtzer's arrival at the pier, Helen Swanson receiving a rose from Carl on the ice, Paulsen drinking hot tea during the Iditarod, Henry Mosley directing boys in daredevil stunts, Samuel Lehi Smith burying nine victims of Iroquois raiders, and Grandma giving her grandson a lawn mower.

25. Compare shifts in everyday stresses in *Winterkill* after Officer Nuts Duda rescues a delinquent from a child abuser, in *Mr. Tucket* after Jason Grimes trades with Braid and the Pawnee, and in *Hatchet* after Brian Robeson recovers food and emergency supplies from the sunken Cessna 406. Emphasize the compromises that allow individuals to cope with unlovable people like the bible-thumping foster father, grumpy Pawnee squaws, and realtor Katie Robeson, Brian's divorced mother.

26. Improvise a dialogue among Paulsen's comic characters, including Amos Binder, Harris Larson, Kevin Spencer, Atticus, Duncan "Dunc" Culpepper, Henry Mosley, Jacob Freisten, and Molly McGinty. As a model, explain through character speeches a variety of attitudes toward school, friends, and home.

27. Compose letters to characters in need of support and advice, especially Wil Neuton, Rocky Turner, Brian Robeson, Sue Oldhorn,

Daniel Martin, Francis Alphonse Tucket, David Garcia, Annie Clark, Sgt. Robert S. Locke, Carley, Roman Sanchez, and Olin Smith.

28. Cite occasions for storytelling in Paulsen's works, such as these:

- discussing a photo album in *The Island*
- educating children about Scandinavian immigration to America in *The Winter Room*
- helping a sick cousin cope with a lethal disease in *A Christmas Sonata*
- preserving an Apache hero story in *The Legend of Red Horse Cavern*
- thinking about the Korean War in *Fishbone's Song*
- alerting delinquents to the consequences of crime in *Winterkill*.

29. Discuss the repeated motif of conservation in Paulsen's works such as *Guts, Dogsong, Tucket's Ride, Caught by the Sea, Escape from Fire Mountain,* and *Father Water, Mother Woods*. Explain how he applies to human stories the settings and themes of wise use of fish, game, water, and hardwood.

30. Account for the significance of secondary characters, such as Rebecca in *Tucket's Home,* the pilot in *Hatchet,* Mr. Henderson as Santa Claus in *A Christmas Sonata,* John in *Tiltawhirl John,* Uncle David in *The Winter Room,* Grandfather Hawkes in *The Flight of the Hawk,* Arnold the stockbroker in *Lawn Boy,* Radar in *Grizzly,* Anne Kelleher in *The Island,* and Sergeant Ryland, Corpsman Harding, or Maria in *Eastern Sun, Winter Moon*.

31. Contrast the sources of drama in these situations: Finn befriending Johanna, Janet Carson tracking a doe, Olin and Abigail Smith escaping British sentries outside a sugar mill in New York City, Peter Shackleton writing fresh rock music, Coyote Runs becoming an Apache raider, Paulsen sailing the Pacific Ocean in a sloop, Katie and Sam searching for Dr. Crockett, Sven and Altag eating at a cookcamp on a new road from Minnesota to Canada, and Charley Goddard surviving the Battle of Gettysburg. Which provide visual effects for film or stage? Which suit oral storytelling, radio, petroglyph, puppetry, or pantomime?

32. Characterize the importance of setting to these scenes: skydiving, baking apple pie, hoeing beets, joining a carnival crew, building a kit car, locating the crash of a B-17, supervising a skating rink, thwarting a drug smuggling operation in Seattle, recovering treasure from a sunken galleon, escaping from a mysterious computer game, rescuing dogs from the pound, burying an Apache skull, performing triage on injured plane crash survivors, introducing Rex to Cookie, avoiding a moose, preaching to a gullible congregation, rubbing salt into a lash wound, living alone on an island, buying 'shine, or burying a stillborn baby.

33. Compose an annotated global map featuring these landmarks in Paulsen's life: Cleveland, Thief River Falls, Madison, Anchorage, Organ Mountains, Juárez, Seattle, Hawaii, Cincinnati, Verdun, Catalina, El Paso, Rainy Pass, Columbia River, Southern plantation, Manila, Jicarilla Mountains, Alamogordo, New York City, Vietnam, Missouri, Madison, Pacific Ocean, Milwaukee, Korea, Nome, Chicago, Tres Pinos, Yukon River, the Oregon Trail, Minneapolis, Okinawa, New Orleans, Eden Prairie, New Mexico, and the Minnesota woods.

34. Explain the significance of three of the following terms to Paulsen's works:

medicine arrow	tugline	fool birds	Cessna 406
Harley	flintlock	border collie	Pueblo
U.S. Marshal	mask	carny	piracy
lefsa	rose	raw seal meat	turtle eggs
chicken pox	snoose	Hessians	blacksmith

35. Locate examples of journeys as symbols of ambition, escape, and healing, particularly Paulsen's retreat to the seashore after leaving the army, Charley Goddard traveling to Fort Snell to enlist in the Minnesota Volunteers, Wil Neuton avoiding the media, Devon and Taylor retreating to the RJ Glavine Middle School bathroom for a tornado drill, David Alspeth sprinkling Uncle Owen's ashes in the sea, Paulsen completing a second Iditarod, Carley hitching plow horses, Grandma Alida visiting a pregnant farm wife, Mr. Henderson dressing like Santa Claus, Paulsen driving a truckload of huskies to Alaska, and Russel Susskit sledding to the home of the wind's mother.

36. Debate the wisdom of two of the following choices: Brian Robeson's return to Canada, Bass Reeves's pursuit of outlaws, dipping cattle with Harris and the Larsons, Molly's keeping a notebook of events, Gary's trapping wild animals for profit, Corpsman Harding treating wounds from shark bite, boys spending a night in a Dumpster, displaying a model B-17 to a veteran, Paulsen sailing to Hawaii, Tucket rescuing orphans from a wagon train, John Barron protecting sheep from a bear attack, Peter Shackleton writing music for a rock band, Al working as an exotic dancer, mushers delivering diphtheria vaccine to Inuit children, boys examining explosives left from the Civil War, a Vietnam veteran crouching in a mall from war memories, Grandma Alida writing letters to a disappointing daughter, and burning the Foxman's body in a cabin.

37. Discuss the role of history in two of Paulsen's works. Include the Cuban Missile Crisis, Emancipation Proclamation, Vietnam War, the Battle of Verdun, formation of the Ku Klux Klan, Custer's defeat at the Little Big Horn, Edison's lightbulb, the Korean War, the settlement of the frontier, and the legendary lives of Wyatt Earp, Billy the Kid, Kit Carson, Buffalo Bill, Jeremiah Johnson, Jim Bridger, and Ernest Shackleton.

38. Discuss the effectiveness of the following rhetorical devices:

- *Gothicism* "Night people with night eyes" (*Paintings from the Cave*)
- *black English* "what they doing to us" (*Nightjohn*)
- *aphorism* "If you have good friends, you can consider yourself truly wealthy" (*Lawn Boy Returns*)
- *neologism* "moneywood" (*Clabbered Dirt, Sweet Grass*)
- *verse* "All around me is beauty" (*This Side of Wild*)
- *euphemism* "um, the whole odor thing you've got going here" (*Masters of Disaster*)
- *parallelism* "a deep, grunting, ripping sound that turned into a piercing shriek and ended in panting murmurs" (*The Quilt*)
- *synesthesia* "the smell that had a copper taste" (*The Crossing*)
- *humor* "a roommate with a terminal hygiene problem" (*Brian's Winter*)
- *understatement* "just some trouble in Boston" (*Woods Runner*)
- *run-on* "cold and ugly and raw and cruel and vicious" (*Paintings from the Cave*)
- *sobriquet* "Uncle Casey" (*The Cookcamp*)
- *hyperbole* "will kill you for your shoes" (*Tucket's Home*)
- *allusion* "football coach—Nazi beast" (*The Schernoff Discoveries*)
- *cacophony* "to jerk your guts out and just about wreck you" (*The Foxman*)
- *command* "Die you commie jap pigs" (*Harris and Me*)
- *caesura* "Grown.... You ... know things" (*Woods Runner*)
- *simile* "like sharks smelling blood" (*The Boy Who Owned the School*)
- *dialect* "Can't have nothing much fresh" (*The Haymeadow*)
- *slang* "I wanted to be a jock" (*The Island*)
- *metaphor* "a soulless midlevel corporate drone" (*Field Trip*)
- *impressionism* "Fight wait. Death wait" (*The Crossing*)
- *alliteration* "shone like silver" (*The Rifle*)
- *periodic sentence* "not one thing on God's earth wanted to die" (*Brian's Winter*)
- *cadence* "I—am—the—killer—of—the—terrible—Howling—Thing" (*The Transall Saga*)
- *repetition* "Disappear me.... Disappear me, now" (*The Boy Who Owned the School*)
- *allegory* "true scars—the scars that covered other parts of his body and all of his mind and thoughts" (*The Crossing*)

39. Survey the rewards and recriminations of advanced age in two of Paulsen's characters. Consider the actions of Grandfather Hawkes, Tink, Delie, the Foxman, Sue Oldhorn's Ojibway grandfather, Uncle Owen, Grandfather Clay, Irene Flynn, Fishbone, Billy Honcho, Braid, Eldon and Wayne's Uncle David, Anita Halverson, John Barron's father, Wil Neuton's grandmother, and Grandma in *Lawn Boy Returns*.

40. Summarize two of the following dilemmas as themes in Paulsen's works: alcoholism, exhibitionist males, intimidation by the military, harassment of migrant workers, forced bondage, bullying a slow learner, disagreements between siblings, biracial children, cancer treatment, limited educational opportunity, neglectful parents, drug smuggling, and illegitimate birth.

41. Contrast two love relationships from Paulsen's writings, for example, Paulsen/Cookie, Francis Alphonse Tucket/Lottie, Alida/"Little Thimble," Bonnie/Nuts Duda, Helen Swanson/Carl Wenstrum, Amos Binder/Melissa Hansen, Cornish/Clara, and Gary's mother/Uncle Casey, Corpsman Harding, or Sergeant Ryland.

42. Describe how Paulsen presents social issues in fiction, such as labor exploitation, spousal abuse, prostitution, child abandonment, patriarchy, police corruption, banditry, post-traumatic stress disorder, gang violence, alienation, amputation, religious fanaticism, at-risk learners, and the extermination of Indian culture.

43. Arrange a literature seminar to introduce students to adventure lore in one of Paulsen's mysteries or quest novels, particularly *Curse of the Ruins, How Angel Peterson Got His Name, The Creature of Black Water Lake, Captive!, Rodomonte's Revenge,* or *Cowpokes and Desperadoes*. Conclude discussion of action writing with proposals for cover art, computer games, or illustrations.

44. Propose alternate titles for these books: *Project: A Perfect World, The Night the White Deer Died, Popcorn Days and Buttermilk Nights, Prince Amos, Family Ties, The River, The Gorgon Slayer, Field Trip, Winterkill,* and *Hook 'Em, Snotty!*

Bibliography

Primary Sources

Novels by Gary Paulsen

Alida's Song. New York: Random House, 1999.
The Amazing Life of Birds. New York: Random House, 2006.
Amos and the Alien. New York: Random House, 1994.
Amos and the Chameleon Caper. New York: Bantam, 1996.
Amos and the Vampire. New York: Bantam, 1996.
Amos Gets Famous. New York: Bantam, 1993.
Amos Goes Bananas. New York: Bantam, 1995.
Amos's Killer Concert Caper. New York: Bantam, 1994.
The Beet Fields. New York: Random House, 2000.
The Boy Who Owned the School. New York: Bantam, 1990.
Brian's Hunt. New York: Random House, 20203.
Brian's Return. New York: Random House, 1999.
Brian's Winter. New York: Random House, 1996.
Call Me Francis Tucket. New York: Random House, 1995.
Canoe Days. New York: Random House, 1999.
Canyons. New York: Bantam, 1990.
Captive! New York: Random House, 1995.
The Car. Orlando, FL: Harcourt, 1994.
Caught by the Sea. Orlando, FL: Harcourt, 2003.
The CB Caper. Milwaukee, WI: Raintree, 1977.
A Christmas Sonata. New York: Random House, 1992.
Clabbered Dirt, Sweet Grass. New York: Harcourt, 1992.
Coach Amos. New York: Bantam, 1994.
The Cookcamp. New York: Random House, 1992.
Cowpokes and Desperadoes. New York: Random House, 1994.
The Creature of Black Water Lake. New York: Bantam, 1997.
Crush: The Theory, Practice and Destructive Properties of Love. New York: Random House, 2012.
Culpepper's Cannon. New York: Bantam, 1992.
Curse of the Ruins. New York: Bantam, 1998.
Dancing Carl. New York: Simon & Schuster, 1983.
Danger on Midnight River. New York: Bantam, 1995.
Dogsong. New York: Simon & Schuster, 1985.
Dogteam. New York: Random House, 1993.
Dunc and Amos and the Red Tattoos. New York: Bantam, 1993.
Dunc and Amos Go to the Dogs. New York: Bantam, 1996.
Dunc and Amos Hit the Big Top. New York: Bantam, 1993.
Dunc and Amos Meet the Slasher. New York: Bantam, 1994.
Dunc and the Flaming Ghost. New York: Bantam, 1992.
Dunc and the Haunted Castle. New York: Random House, 1993.
Dunc and the Scam Artists. New York: Bantam, 1993.
Dunc Gets Tweaked. New York: Bantam, 1992.
Dunc's Doll. New York: Bantam, 1992.
Dunc's Dump. New York: Bantam, 2011.
Dunc's Halloween. New York: Random House, 1992.
Eastern Sun, Winter Moon: An Autobiographical Odyssey. Orlando, FL: Harcourt, 1993.
Escape from Fire Mountain. New York: Random House, 1995.
Family Ties. New York: Random House, 2014.
Father Water, Mother Woods: Essays on Fishing and Hunting in the North Woods. New York: Random House, 1994.
Field Trip. New York: Random House, 2015.
Fishbone's Song. New York: Simon & Schuster, 2016.

Flat Broke: The Theory, Practice and Destructive Properties of Greed. New York: Random House, 2012.
Flight of the Hawk. New York: Bantam, 1998.
The Foxman. New York: Scholastic, 1990.
Full of Hot Air: Launching, Floating High, and Landing. New York: Delacorte, 1993.
The Glass Café. New York: Random House, 2004.
The Gorgon Slayer. New York: Random House, 1995.
The Grass Eaters. Milwaukee, WI: Raintree, 1976.
Grizzly. New York: Bantam, 1998.
Guts. New York: Random House, 2001.
Harris and Me. Orlando, FL: Harcourt, 1993.
Hatchet. New York: Simon & Schuster, 1987.
The Haymeadow. New York: Random House, 1992.
Hook 'Em, Snotty! New York: Bantam, 1995.
How Angel Peterson Got His Name. New York: Random House, 2003.
Ice Race. New York: Macmillan, 1997.
The Island. New York: Scholastic, 1988.
Lawn Boy. New York: Random House, 2007.
Lawn Boy Returns. New York: Random House, 2010.
The Legend of Bass Reeves. New York: Random House, 2008.
The Madonna Stories. Orlando, FL: Harcourt, 1989.
Masters of Disaster. New York: Random House, 2010.
Mr. Tucket. New York: Random House, 1994.The
Molly McGinty Has a Really Good Day. New York: Random House, 2004.
The Monument. New York: Random House, 1991.
Mudshark. New York: Random House, 2009.
My Life in Dog Years. New York: Random House, 1998.
The Night the White Deer Died. New York: Random House, 1978.
Nightjohn. New York: Bantam, 1993.
Notes from the Dog. New York: Random House, 2009.
Paintings from the Cave. New York: Random House, 2011.
Pilgrimage on a Steel Ride: A Memoir about Men and Motorcycles. Orlando, FL: Harcourt, 1997.
Popcorn Days and Buttermilk Nights. New York: Penguin, 1983.
Prince Amos. New York: Bantam, 1994.
Project: A Perfect World. New York: Random House, 1996.
Puppies, Dogs, and Blue Northers. Orlando, FL: Houghton Mifflin, 2007.
The Quilt. New York: Random House, 2004.
The Rifle. Orlando, FL: Harcourt, 1995.
The River. New York: Random House, 1991.
Road Trip. New York: Random House, 2013.
The Rock Jockeys. New York: Random House, 1995.
Rodomonte's Revenge. New York: Bantam, 1994.
Sarny. New York: Random House, 1997.
The Schernoff Discoveries. New York: Random House, 1997.
Sentries. New York Simon & Schuster, 1986.
Shelf Life: Stories by the Book. New York: Simon & Schuster, 2003.
Sisters/Hermanas. Orlando, FL: Houghton Mifflin, 1993.
Six Kids and a Stuffed Cat. New York: Simon & Schuster, 2016.
Skydive! New York: Random House, 1996.
Soldier's Heart. New York: Random House, 1998.
Super Amos. New York: Bantam, 2011.
The Tent. Orlando, FL: Harcourt, 1995.
This Side of Wild: Mutts, Mares, and Laughing Dinosaurs. New York: Simon & Schuster, 2016.
Thunder Valley. New York: Random House, 1998.
Tiltawhirl John. New York: Penguin, 1977.
Time Benders. New York: Random House, 1997.
The Time Hackers. New York: Random House, 2005.
The Tortilla Factory. San Diego, CA: Harcourt Brace, 1998.
Tracker. New York: Simon & Schuster, 1984.
The Transall Saga. New York: Random House, 1998.
The Treasure of El Patrón. New York: Random House, 1996.
Tucket's Gold. New York: Random House, 2001.
Tucket's Home. New York: Random House, 2000.
Tucket's Ride. New York: Random House, 1997.
Tucket's Travels. New York: Random House, 2009.
Vote: The Theory, Practice, and Destructive Properties of Politics. New York: Random House, 2013.
The Voyage of the Frog. New York: Scholastic, 1989.
The White Fox Chronicles. New York: Random House, 2000.
The Wild Culpepper Cruise. New York: Random House, 1993.
The Winter Room. New York: Bantam, 1989.
Winterdance: The Fine Madness of Running the Iditarod. Orlando, FL: Harcourt, 1994.
Winterkill. Nashville, TN: Thomas Nelson, 1976.
Woodsong. New York: Simon & Schuster, 1990.
Woods Runner. New York: Random House, 2010.
Worksong. Orlando, FL: Houghton Mifflin, 1997.
Zero to Sixty: The Motorcycle Journey of a Lifetime. Orlando, FL: Houghton Mifflin, 1999.

Stories and Essays by Gary Paulsen

"Boy vs. Bear." *Scholastic Scope* 10:5 (February 1999).
"Breaking the Record." *Boys' Life* 93:5 (May 2003): 28–33.

"Brian's Hunt." *Boys' Life* 94:1 (January 2004): 36–42.
"Brian's Hunt." *Scholastic Scope* 52:15 (22 March 2004): 12–13.
"Brian's Return." *Boys' Life* 89:3 (March 1999): 32–35, 52.
"Brian's Winter." *Boys' Life* 86:2 (February 1996): 42–45, 60.
"Brian's Winter." *Catholic Library World* 66:4 (1996): 53.
"The Case of the Dirty Bird." *Boys' Life* 82:7 (July 1992): 30–34; 82:8 (August 1992): 28–32.
"The Deer." *U.S. Catholic* (1982).
"Fabulous First-Line." *Scholastic Scope* 62:2 (October 2013): 24.
"The Gift of Words." *Writing* 30:3 (November/December 2007): 22.
"Guts." *Boys' Life* 91:12 (December 2001): 22–27.
"A Heart for the Run." *Reader's Digest* (April 1997): 82–88.
"Henry Mosley's Last Stand." *Boys' Life* 91:7 (July 2001): 24–27.
"Ike, a Good Friend" in *In Praise of Labs*. St. Paul, MN: MBI, 2007, 120–129.
"It Could Happen." *Read* 54:1 (27 August 2004): 8–14.
"The Last Great Race." *Reader's Digest* 144:863 (March 1994): 181–208.
"Lost at Sea." *Boys' Life* 78:11 (November 1988): 32–36, 58; 78:12 (December 1988): 36–40, 74.
"My Favorite Fan" in *A Printz of a Man*. Chicago: American Library Association, 1997.
"The Night the Headless, Blood-Drinking, Flesh-Eating Corpses of Cleveland (Almost) Took Over the World." *Boys' Life* 94:7 (July 2004): 34–39.
"1997 Margaret A. Edwards Award Acceptance Speech." *Journal of Youth Services in Libraries* 11:1 (Fall 1997): 24.
"People Call Me Crazy." *Scholastic Scope* (May 2014): 14–18.
"The 'Perfect' Book Tour." *Children's Books* 250:11 (17 March 2003).
"Skate-Chuting." *Boys' Life* 59:12 (December 1969): 57.
"Speed Demon." *Scholastic Scope* 54:10 (23 January 2006): 18–19.
"Stop the Sun." *Boys' Life* 76:1 (January 1986): 34–38.
"This Side of Wild." *Boys' Life* (October 2015).
"The True Face of War." *Riverbank Review* (Spring 1999): 25–26.
"The Way Stories Dance." *Voices from the Middle* 8:1 (September 2000): 60–65.
"Winterdance" in *Alaska: Tales of Adventure from the Last Frontier*, ed. Spike Walker. New York: Macmillan, 2002.
"Wolfdreams." *Boys' Life* (February 2017): 22.

Secondary Sources

Reviews

"Alida's Song." *Publishers Weekly* (31 May 1999): 94–95.
Atherton, Tony. "Literacy Fable Wrapped in Slavery Melodrama." *Calgary Herald* (16 June 1996): E5.
Belden, Elizabeth A., and Judith M. Beckman. "Torn Up and Transplanted." *English Journal* 80:2 (February 1991): 84–85.
Blasingame, James. "The Time Hackers." *Journal of Adolescent & Adult Literacy* 49:6 (March 2006): 543–544.
Bush, Randy. "Vibrations in Eskimo Dog Sled Runners: Paulsen's *Dogsong*, Art and the Transcendent." *CU Commons* 2 (Spring 1994): 14–18.
Bynum, Mollie. "Puppies, Dogs, and Blue Northers." *School Library Journal* 42:7 (November 1996): 130.
Campbell, Patty. "A Spyglass on YA 2000." *Horn Book* 77:1 (January/February 2001): 131–136.
Chipman, Ian. "Woods Runner." *Booklist* 106:9–10 (1 January 2010): 72.
Coats, Karen. "Fishbone's Song." *Bulletin of the Center for Children's Books* 70:2 (October 2016): 89.
"The Cookcamp." *Publishers Weekly* 81 (1990).
Cvengros, Stephen. "Review: *Call Me Francis Tucket*." *Chicago Tribune* (4 July 1995): 2.
"Dancing Carl." *Booklist* 79 (1 June 1983).
Davis, Gina. "A 2nd Book to Return to Carroll High Schools." *Baltimore Sun* (12 January 2006): B-2.
"Dear Gary Paulsen." [Saint John, N.B.] *Telegraph-Journal* (21 May 2008): D11.
Donelson, Ken. "Soldier's Heart." *English Journal* 89:2 (November 1999): 147–148.
Durichen, Pauline. "Review: *Canyons*." *Kitchener-Waterloo Record* (16 February 1991): H6.
Edmonds, Arlene. "Deltas Open Festival with Discussion about 'Nightjohn.'" *Philadelphia Tribune* (13 November 1998): D1.
Ernst, Shirley B. "Brian's Winter." *Language Arts* 74:7 (November 1997): 566.
Erickson, Barbara. "Read-Alouds Reluctant Readers Relish." *Journal of Adolescent and Adult Literacy* 40:3 (November 1996): 212–217.
Estes, Sally. "Sisters/Hermanas." *Booklist* 90 (1 January 1994): 816.
Fenly, Leigh. "Just for Kids." *San Diego Union-Tribune* (1 March 2001): 5.
Fisher, Enicia. "Harrowing Adventures on the Oregon Trail." *Christian Science Monitor* (14 October 1999): 20.
Flaherty, Dolores, and Roger Flaherty. "When Gary Paulsen Went Utterly Mad and Ran the Iditarod." *Chicago Sun-Times* (26 February 1995): 19.
Flint-Ferguson, Janis. "Review: The Legend of Bass Reeves." *Kliatt* 4 (July 20006): 12.

Garvie, Maureen. *"Bookstand."* Kingston, Ontario, *Whig-Standard* (30 January 1988): 1.
Gilson, Nancy. "Survival Saga Takes New Twist." *Columbus* [Ohio] *Dispatch* (18 June 1998): 27.
"The Glass Café." *Brilliance Audio* (2016).
"The Glass Café." *Journal of Adolescent and Adult Literacy* 49:3 (November 2005): 227–234.
"The Glass Café." *Kirkus Reviews* (1 June 2003): 809.
Harding, Susan M. "The Cookcamp." *School Library Journal* 37 (1991).
Harrison, Jordan. "A Shift in Time." *Toronto Star* (7 April 2005): P12.
Holubitsky, Kathy. "Brian's Hunt Unearths Some Dubious 'Facts.'" *Edmonton Journal* (4 April 2004): D11.
Hurst, Carol Otis. "Four Literature Webs You'll Be Glad to Get Caught In." *Teaching Pre-K-8* 26:1 (September 1995): 112.
Kehe, Marjorie. "Two Good Books for Boys." *Christian Science Monitor* (22 May 2010).
Kelley, Annie J. "Gary Paulsen: A Book Can Change a Life." *Battle Creek* [Michigan] *Enquirer* (11 February 2011).
Kenney, Edwin J., Jr. "The Island." *New York Times* (22 May 1988): A30.
Kidd, Victoria. "Tucket's Home." *School Library Journal* 46:9 (September 2000): 235–236.
Larking, Kate. "Haunting Tale of Deceit." *Calgary Herald* (11 September 2004): ESO5.
"Lawn Boy." *Booklist* (15 April 2007): 44.
"Lawn Boy." *Kirkus Reviews* 75:10 (2007): 507.
"The Legend of Bass Reeves." *Kirkus Reviews* 74 (1 July 2006).
"The Legend of Bass Reeves." *Publishers Weekly* 253:30 (30 July 2006): 76.
Ley, Terry C. "The Monument." *English Journal* 83:3 (March 1994): 90.
Loer, Stephanie. "A Satisfying Depression Era Tale." *Boston Globe* (21 February 1988): 48.
MacCallum, Elizabeth. "Tales of Freedom and Self-Reliance." [Toronto] *Globe and Mail* (18 November 1989): E6.
Maschinot, Michael. "Journeys of the Spirit Series." *St. Petersburg* [Florida] *Times* (27 February 1994): D-6.
Maughan, Shannon. "The Amazing Life of Birds." *Publishers Weekly* 252:28 (18 July 2005): 139–150.
Mayer, Henry. "The Boys of War." *New York Times Book Review* (15 November 1998): 40.
McCarthy, Cheryl Stritzel. "Homecoming Puts the Wraps on Wild West Series." [Cleveland, Ohio] *Plain Dealer* (8 July 2001): I-1.
McCracken, Lin. "Awards Honor Women Writers, American Indian Themes." *Colorado Springs Gazette-Telegraph* (13 October 1991): F-4.
McGrath, Charles. "Lawn Boy." *New York Times* (12 August 2007).
"Mr. Tucket." *Journal of Reading* 38:1 (September 1994): 70–71.
O'Mahony, Michael. "The River." *Los Angeles Times* (30 June 1991): 13.
Patrick, Jean. "Paging through Paulsen." *Kids Today* (28 January 1996): 4.
Penner, Diana. "Review: *Call Me Francis Tucket.*" *Indianapolis Star* (4 June 1995): D-6.
Perren, Susan. "Umbrellas, Dogs, Puppy, Fairy Tales." [Toronto] *Globe and Mail* (28 March 1998): D15.
Peters, John. "The Legend of Bass Reeves." *Booklist* 102 (1 June 2006): 75.
"Pilgrimage on a Steel Ride." *Kirkus Reviews* 65:12 (3 November 1997).
Potyandi, Barry. "Warm Embrace of Pastoral Life Is Long Lost." *Calgary Herald* (24 June 1995): B14.
Price, Rodney. "Harley Journey a Rough Ride." *Rocky Mountain News* (30 November 1997): E3.
"Puppies, Dogs, and Blue Northers." *Kirkus Reviews* (1996).
Quealy-Gainer, Kate. "Family Ties." *Bulletin of the Center for Children's Books* 68:1 (September 2014): 53–54.
"The Quilt." *Kirkus Reviews* (1 April 2004).
Rae, Arlene Perly. "Poignant Story Grapples with Abuse at School." *Toronto Star* (3 February 1996): L-16.
Ralston, Jennifer. "The Rifle." *School Library Journal* 49:10 (1 October 2003): 98.
Renner, Coop. "Tucket's Gold." *School Library Journal* 45:10 (October 1999): 156.
Richmond, Dick. "'Friends' Separated by a Century." *St. Louis Post-Dispatch* (19 September 1991): G-3.
"The Rifle." *Kirkus Reviews* (1 September 1995): 17.
Robins, Carol Peace. "Pilgrimage on a Steel Ride." *New York Times Book Review* (30 November 1997): 21.
Rosenfeld, Judith B. "Canyons." *Baltimore Sun* (8 November 1990): G-8.
Salvadore, Maria B. "The Amazing Life of Birds." *School Library Journal* 52:10 (October 2006): 166.
Salvner, Gary M. "Brian's Winter." *ALAN Review* 23 (Fall 1996).
"Sarny." *Ottawa Citizen* (15 March 1998): E5.
Scotten, Neil. "A Feel-Good Story in a Simple World." *Edmonton Journal* (4 October 1992): B4.
"Sentries." *Kirkus Reviews* 54 (1 April 1986).
"Six Kids and a Stuffed Cat." *Publishers Weekly* 263:8 (22 February 2016).
Soltan, Rita S. "Woods Runner." *Horn Book* 86 (Fall 2010): 380.
Thompson, Laura. "It's a Dog's Life." [London] *Sunday Times* (5 March 1995): 11.

Turvey, Shannon Lee. "The Trouble with Sequels." *Vancouver Sun* (23 May 1998): I-10.
"The Voyage of the Frog." *Kirkus Reviews* (15 February 1988).
"Washed by the Wave." *Ottawa Citizen* (1 February 1998): E6.
Webb, Jill. "Dancing Carl." *School Library Journal* 58 (2012).
Wecker, David. "Story Has Whiff of Authenticity." *Cincinnati Post* (5 March 1998): B1.
Weller, Frances Ward. "One Boy's Solitary Fight for Survival." *Los Angeles Times* (12 December 1987): 6.
"Woods Runner." *Kirkus Reviews* 78:1 (1 January 2010): 47.
"Woods Runner." *Publishers Weekly* (21 December 2009): 61.

Commentary

Abilock, Debbie. "The Politics of Reading." *Knowledge Quest* 30:3 (2002): 7.
Alexander, Victoria N. "Children's Novel about Stripping Causes Controversy." *Digital Journal* (21 December 2012).
Arnold, Martin. "Finding Stories Boys Will Read." *New York Times* (15 October 1998): 3.
Austin, Jane. "The Best Doggone Pooches, Vampire Bunnies and Extreme Survival Tips Are Contained in the Fall's Best Books." [Fort Worth] *Star-Telegram* (14 September 1999): E-8.
Barron, Ronald. "Gary Paulsen: 'I Write Because It's All I Can Do.'" *ALAN Review* 20:3 (Spring 1993): 27–30.
Beers, Kylene. "The Power of Publication." *Voices from the Middle* 8:1 (September 2000): 4–7.
Bentley, Rosalind. "'Nightjohn' Offers Lesson to Remember." [Minneapolis] *Star Tribune* (6 June 1997): E-15.
Berman, Matt. "Getting Real." [New Orleans] *Times-Picayune* (31 January 1999): D-6.
Biastre, Bob, and Doug Poswencyk. "Books Guys Will Sit Still For." [Bridgewater, NJ] *Courier-News* (14 June 2005): 11.
Blasingame, James. "Books for Adolescents." *Journal of Adolescent & Adult Literacy* 48:3 (November 2004): 269–273.
_____. "Outrageous Tales about Extreme Sports." *Journal of Adolescent & Adult Literacy* 48:3 (November 2004): 267–268.
Bookman, Julie. "Paulsen's Tale Gets to 'Heart' of the Civil War." *Atlanta Journal-Constitution* (9 January 1999): E5.
Bradburn, Frances. "Middle Books." *Wilson Library Bulletin* (January 1993): 88.
Brewbaker, James M. "Because a Book Can't Have Smells, Sound, Light." *English Journal* 81:2 (February 1992): 87.
Broz, Bill. "Memoir: Reading Life." *ALAN Review* 36:3 (Summer 2009): 59–64.
Buchholz, Rachel. "The Write Stuff." *Boys' Life* 85:12 (December 1995): 28–29, 53.
Burcar, Lilijana. "(Global) Capitalism and Immigrant Workers in Gary Paulsen's *Lawn Boy:* Naturalization of Exploitation." *Jeunesse* 4:1 (Summer 2012): 37–60.
Burton, Art T. "Lawman Legend Bass Reeves: The Invincible Man Hunter." *Wild West* 19:5 (February 2007): 50–57.
Bush, Elizabeth. "The Legend of Bass Reeves." *Bulletin of the Center for Children's Books* 60:2 (October 2006): 89.
Caillouet, Ruth. "The Adolescent War: Finding Our Way on the Battlefield." *ALAN Review* 14 (Fall 2005): 68–73.
Carroll, Pamela S., and Steven B. Chandler. "Sports-related Young Adult Literature." *Strategies* 14:5 (2001): 35–37.
Cary, Alice. "Gary Paulsen on the Go: Sleds, Motorcycles, and Sailboats." *Children's Literature Review* 82 (2003).
Cindrich, Sharon Miller. "Gary Paulsen's Love Affair with Writing." *Writer* (June 2004): 22.
Conlan, Maureen. "A Writer with Stories to Fill Two Lifetimes." *Cincinnati Post* (5 April 1995): B-5.
Creager, Ellen. "Two Tough Reads for Preteens." [Bergen, NJ] *Record* (22 April 1993): C-9.
_____. "View from the Outside the Wilderness Resonates for Children's Author." *Detroit Free Press* (13 April 1999): 4.
Cummins, Amy. "Border Crossings: Undocumented Migration between Mexico and the United States in Contemporary Young Adult Literature." *Children's Literature in Education* 44:1 (March 2013): 57–73.
Davenport, Stephen. "Soldier's Heart." *Journal of Adolescent & Adult Literacy* 43:2 (October 1999): 204–206.
Davis, James S. "Memoir: Reading Life." *ALAN Review* 36:3 (Summer 2009): 7.
Engel, Sue. "'Bad Feeling' Offers Some Slapstick Fun." *Wausau* [Wisconsin] *Daily Herald* (3 September 2015): 5.
Faust, Susan. "Young Soldiers Face War's Horror." *San Francisco Chronicle* (25 October 1998): 8.
Fitzpatrick, Andy. "Author Gary Paulsen to Speak in Battle Creek." *Battle Creek Enquirer* (6 February 2011): D1.
Galehouse, Maggie. "A New Challenge for Author." *Houston Chronicle* (16 April 2010): E1.
Gallo, Don. "The Promise and Seduction of Sequels." *English Journal* 94:4 (March 2005): 124–128.
"Gary Paulsen." *Beacham's Guide to Literature for Young Adults.* Vol. 11. Farmington Hills, MI: Gale, 2001.

"Gary Paulsen." *Major Authors and Illustrators for Children and Young Adults*. Farmington Hills, MI: Gale, 2002.

"Gary Paulsen Awarded 2007 Chicago Tribune Prize for Young Adult Fiction." *PR Newswire* (11 September 2007).

Gerber, Lisa. "The Art of Intimacy." *Philosophy in the Contemporary World* 8:2 (Fall/Winter 2001): 79–83.

Giles, Rebecca M., and Karyn W. Tunks. "Read the Past Now! Responding to Historical Fiction through Writing." *The Councilor* 75:1 (2014): 15–22.

Giles, Valerie. "Quotable Quotations." *Prince George Citizen* (27 June 2005): 13.

Gilson, Nancy. "A Survivor of Childhood, Gary Paulsen Imbues Books with Intensity." *Columbus* [Ohio] *Dispatch* (8 November 1994): B-8.

Grant, Adam. "Dog Life." *Scholastic Scope* (26 January 1996): 17–18.

Gregory, Kristiana. "Commodore Perry in the Land of the Shogun." *Los Angeles Times* (11 May 1986): 7.

Holden, Stephen. "Literacy, a Weapon for a Slave." *New York Times* (31 January 1997): 8.

Jacobs, Mary. "Guys Read Guy Books." *Scouting Magazine* (September 2008).

Jacobson, Ann. "Paulsen Revisits Bush in Finale of 'Hatchet' Series." *South Bend* [Ind.] *Tribune* (14 March 1999): F6.

James, Caryn. "To the Cabin of Slaves, a Gutsy Girl Brings Light." *New York Times* (1 June 1996): 13.

Jensen, Joyce. "From Fences to Fast Getaways, the All-Time All-American Greats." *New York Ties* (6 November 1999): 11.

Johnson, Nancy, et al. "Language of Music." *Reading Teacher* 53:7 (April 2000): 602–604.

Jones, Patrick, Dawn Cartwright Fiorelli, and Melany H. Bowen. "Overcoming the Obstacle Course: Teenage Boys and Reading." *Teacher Librarian* 30:3 (2003): 9.

Kent, Susan I. "Saints or Sinners?." *Social Education* 63:1 (January/February 1999): 8–12.

Lacy, Meagan. "Portraits of Children of Alcoholics." *CUNY Academic Works* 46:4 (December 2015): 343–358.

Leach, Pat. "Authors, Illustrators Offer Up surprises in These Books." *Lincoln* [Neb.] *Journal Star* (2 February 2007): 1.

Lehr, Susan. "Beauty, Brains, and Brawn: The Construction of Gender in Children's Literature." *ERIC* (2001).

Lesesne, Teri S., Rosemary Chance, and Lois Buckman. "Books for Adolescents: Journeys: Traveling Toward the Unknown." *Journal of Adolescent & Adult Literacy* 39:4 (December 1995–January 1996): 332–336.

Levy, Paul. "One for the Books." [Minneapolis] *Star Tribune* (30 October 2002): E1.

Lewis, Randy. "He Owes It All to Librarians and Dogs." *Los Angeles Times* (31 July 1994): 1.

Lipson, Eden Ross. "A Children's Author Joins the Immortals." *New York Times* (20 June 1986): A31.

_____. "The Dark Underbelly of Writing Well for Children." *New York Times* (8 July 2000): B7.

Louie, Belinda Y, and Douglas H. Louis. "Empowerment through Young-Adult Literature." *English Journal* 81:4 (April 1992): 53.

MacCallum, Elizabeth. "Rude, Outrageous: An Ideal Book for Kids." [Toronto] *Globe and Mail* (5 February 1994): C17.

_____. "What We Need to Know about Natives." [Toronto] *Globe and Mail* (17 November 1990): C20.

Mallon, Linda. "Someone Their Age Is Telling the Story." *USA Today* (20 October 1998): D9.

Mao, Xin-geng. "The Protagonist's Coming-of-Age Is the Reproduction of the Author's Own Life." *Journal of Yunmeng* 2 (2009): 25.

Martin, Claire. "'Soldier's Heart' Melds Civil War Fact with Fiction." *Denver Post* (5 November 1998: H2.

Maughan, Shannon. "Spring Audio 2011." *Publishers Weekly* 258:6 (7 February 2011).

McCaleb, Joseph L. "Story Medicine." *English Journal* 93:1 (September 2003): 66–72.

Metella, Helen. "I Write the Way I Used to Run." *Edmonton Journal* (31 October 1993): D6.

Miller, Howard M. "Victims, Heroes, and Just Plain Folks." *Reading Teacher* 51:7 (April 1998): 602–604.

Moss, Meredith. "'Hatchet' Author to Appear." *Dayton Daily News* (14 March 1999): E3.

_____. "Novelist's Life Is In, Out of the Woods." *Dayton Daily News* (5 February 2004): E1.

Napoli, Donna Jo. "Promoting Conceptual Mathematical Thinking through Books." *Journal of Education* 189:1/2 (2008–2009): 209–211.

Nappi, Rebecca. "Books That Mentor." *McClatchy-Tribune Business News* (19 April 2009).

Nilsen, Allen Pace, and James Blasingame, Jr. "Getting Up Close and Personal with Living Authors." *English Journal* 98:3 (January 2009): 15–21.

Parmer, Janet. "Author on Tour Chronicling Life of 'Brian,'" [Santa Rosa, CA] *Press Democrat* (6 February 2004): 3.

Pemberton, Mary. "Writing, Mushing Are Man's Twin Passions." *Whitehorse Star* (1 April 2005): 10.

"The Perfect Book Tour." *Publishers Weekly* (17 March 2003): 34.

Phillips, Anne K. "James Fenimore Cooper's Literary Descendants: American History for 21st

Century Adolescent Readers." *James Fenimore Cooper Society Journal* (Fall 2015): 7–10.

Phillips, Barbara D. "TV, the Flickering Teacher." *Wall Street Journal* (3 June 1996): A12.

Rautzhan, Kendal. "Reading Aloud Lets Kids Enjoy Complex Books." [Newport News, VA] *Daily Press* (5 January 1999): C3.

_____. "Teach Children the Value of Their Freedom." [Newport News, VA] *Daily Press* (24 July 2001): D3.

Robertson, Judith P. "Teaching about Worlds of Hurt through Encounters with Literature: Reflections on Pedagogy." *Language Arts* 74:6 (October 1997): 457.

Rodesiler, Luke, et al. "Teacher to Teacher: What Literature Related to the Environment and Nature Do You Enjoy Teaching?." *English Journal* 100:3 (2011): 27–29.

Rosenberg, Merri. "Some Must Reading among Suggestions." *New York Times* (21 May 2000): 15.

Royte, Elizabeth. "Grumpy Old Man and the Sea: Adventures with Gary Paulsen." https://www.outsideonline.com/1919481/grumpy-old-man-and-sea-adventures-gary-paulsen, 2013.

Schmitz, James A. "Gary Paulsen: A Writer of His Time." *ALAN Review* 22:1 (Fall 1994): 15–18.

Stetson, Nancy. "Been There, Done That: Gary Paulsen Spreads the Words on Survival." *Chicago Tribune* (12 March 1996): 7.

Stix, Andi, and Marshall George. "Using Multi-Level Young Adult Literature in the Middle School American Studies." *Social Studies Journal* (Jan-Feb 2000): 25–31.

Thomas, Kevin. "Grace under Pressure in the Wild." *Los Angeles Times* (21 September 1990): 8.

Vander Staay, Steven. "Young-Adult Literature: A Writer Strikes the Genre." *English Journal* 81:4 (April 1992): 48.

Vogel, Mark, and Anna Creadick. "Family Values and the New Adolescent Novel." *English Journal* 82:5 (September 1993): 37.

Wenger, Laurie. "Books for Building Circle of Courage: Independence." *Reclaiming Children and Youth* 8:1 (Spring 1999): 56–57.

Wergeland, Kari. "'Hatchet' Author Tells Civil War Tale." *Hartford Courant* (2 March 1999): F-4.

Winton, Tim. "Boy's Life His Own World War." *Los Angeles Times* (21 March 1993): 1.

Wood, Susan Nelson. "Bringing Us the Way to Know." *English Journal* 90:3 (January 2001): 67–72.

Interviews

Bartky, Cheryl. "An Interview with Gary Paulsen." *Writer's Digest* 74:7 (July 1994): 42–44.

Beckman, Rachel, James Chryssos, and Candice Hahm. "Talking with Gary Paulsen." [Long Island, NY] *Newsday* (27 April 2004): 1.

Bieselin, Robert. "Novelist Gary Paulsen Talks about His Drive to Continue to Write for Kids." *McClatchy-Tribune News Service* (8 April 2010).

Carey, Joanna. "A Born Survivor Joanna Carey Meets the Engaging Best-selling American Author Gary Paulsen." *The* [Manchester] *Guardian* (28 May 1996).

Conlan, Maureen. "A Writer with Stories to Fill Two Lifetimes." *Cincinnati Post* (15 April 1995): B1.

Corp-Minamiji, Christy. "Conversation with a Master: An Interview with Acclaimed Author Gary Paulsen."

Dar, Mahnaz. "'This Side of Wild': A Conversation with Gary Paulsen." *School Library Journal* (13 October 2015).

Fraser, Stephen. "Adventure Stories: Exciting Tales of Challenge and Survival." *Christian Science Monitor* (6 November 1987): B-5.

Gale, David. "Gary Paulsen." *School Library Journal* 43:6 (June 1997): 24.

"Gary Paulsen In-Depth Written Interview." https://www.teachingbooks.net/interview.cgi?id=91&a=1, 2010.

"Gary Paulsen Interview." https://www.youtube.com/watch?v=Q7ADtOjxmRs.

Goodson, Lori Atkins. "Singlehanding: An Interview with Gary Paulsen." *ALAN Review* 31:2 (Winter 2004): 53–59.

Handy, A.E. "Gary Paulsen." *Book Report* 91:10 (May/June 1991): 28–31.

Harrison, Jessica. "'Hatchet' Author Gary Paulsen to Bring Boyhood Tales to Salt Lake." *Deseret News* (11 April 2010).

"Iditarod Race Across Alaska." eacher.scholastic.com/activities/iditarod/top_mushers/index.asp?article=gary_paulsen.

"In Defense of Getting Outdoors." *Hutchinson* [Kansas] *News* (20 April 2010).

Lewis, Randy. "He Owes It All to Librarians and Dogs." *Los Angeles Times* (31 July 1994): E6.

Lodge, Sally. "Q&A with Gary Paulsen and Jim Paulsen." http://www.publishers weekly.com/pw/by-topic/authors/interviews/article/55019-q-a-with-gary-paulsen-and-jim-paulsen.html, 2012.

Lounds, Sue. "St. Johns Students Earn Honors in Writing Contest." *Lansing State Journal* (2 June 2013).

Lynch, Amanda. "Gary Paulsen." *Children's Book Review* (26 January 2009).

Miller, Kay. "Suddenly Fame and Fortune." [Minneapolis] *Star Tribune* (10 July 1988): 6.

Moore, Opal. "Tellers and Their Tales." *Washington Post* (13 June 1993): X-11.

Morris, Anne. "'An Inch Ahead of the Fireball,'" *Austin American Statesman* (7 March 1999): K6.
Nickelson, George. *Gary Paulsen.* New York: Trumpet Club, 1993.
North, Arielle. "The Newbery and Caldecott Awards." *St. Louis Post-Dispatch* (17 January 1988).
"Q&A with Gary Paulsen." https://www.crackingthecover.com/2859-2/.
Scott, Caroline. "Gary Paulsen." [London] *Sunday Times* (21 July 1996): 12.
Shadle, Laura Smith. "Author Uses Own Life Experiences in Teen Novels." [Spokane, WA] *Spokesman Review* (2 February 2004): B1.
Sides, Anne Goodwin. "On the Road and Between the Pages, an Author Is Restless for Adventure." *New York Times* (26 August 2006): B7.
Stan, Susan. "Conversations: Gary Paulsen." *Children's Literature Review.* Vol. 82, Farmington Hills, MI: Gale, 2003.
Stevens, Susan. "Adventure Author Gives Audience Wild Ride." [Arlington Heights, Illinois] *Daily Herald*] (14 March 2002): 1.
Thomas, Jane Resh. "Slavery Tale Piles on Description." [Cleveland, Ohio] *Plain Dealer* (4 April 1993): H-11.
_____. "'Superkid' Aura Mars Paulsen's Latest." [Minneapolis] *Star Tribune* (16 June 1996): F-17.
Weisman, Kay. "Talking with Gary Paulsen." *Book Links* 13:1 (September 2003); 26–28.
Woodman, Tenley. "Acclaimed Author Takes on Awkwardness of Adolescence." *Boston Herald* (19 June 2006): 26.
Zvirin, Stephanie. "Gary Paulsen." *Booklist* 95:9–10 (1 January 1999): 864.

Books

Blasingame, James. *Gary Paulsen.* Westport, CT: Greenwood, 2007.
Davis-Secord, Jonathan. *Joinings: Compound Words in Old English Literature.* Toronto: University of Toronto Press, 2016.
Fine, Edith Hope. *Gary Paulsen: Author and Wilderness Adventurer.* Berkeley Heights, NJ: Enslow, 2000.
Galda, Lee, Lauren A. Liang, and Bernice E. Cullinan. *Literature and the Child.* Boston: Cengage, 2017.
Golden, Bernice. *Critical Reading Activities for the Works of Gary Paulsen.* Portland, ME: Walch, 1999.
Hahn, Mary Lee. *Reconsidering Read-Aloud.* Portland, ME: Stenhouse, 2002.
Hannings, Bud. *Every Day of the Civil War: A Chronological Encyclopedia.* Jefferson, NC: McFarland, 2010.
Kaywell, Joan F., ed. *Using Literature to Help Troubled Teenagers Cope with Abuse Issues.* Westport, CT: Greenwood, 2001.
Lowery, Ruth McKoy. *Immigrants in Children's Literature.* New York: Peter Lang, 2000.
Macken, JoAnn Early. *Gary Paulsen: Voice of Adventure and Survival.* New York: Enslow, 2008.
Powell, Jim, and Nancy Lafferty. "Tracking Adolescent Responses to Cancer" in *Using Literature to Help Troubled Teenagers Cope with Health Issues.* Westport, CT: Greenwood, 2000.
Salvner, Gary M. *Presenting Gary Paulsen.* New York: Twayne, 1996.
Snodgrass, Mary Ellen. *Encyclopedia of World Folk Dance.* Lanham, MD: Rowman & Littlefield, 2016.
Thomson, Sarah L. *Gary Paulsen.* New York: Rosen, 2003.
Trelease, Jim. *Read All About It.* New York: Penguin, 1993.
Ward, Barbara, Terrell A. Young, and Deanna Day. "Crossing Boundaries: Genre-Blurring in Books for Young Adults" in *Teaching Young Adult Literature Today.* Lanham, MD: Rowman & Littlefield, 2012.

Index

accomplishment 14, 18, 24, 31–33, 98
adaptation 1, 33, 34–36, 39, 49, 66, 67, 72–73, 85, 121, 139, 172
adoption 43, 104, 121, 127, 143, 148
Alida's Song 42, 44, 64, 65, 67, 74, 87, 110–111, 114, 145, 172, 173, 174
The Amazing Life of Birds 22, 23, 63, 79, 112, 157, 159, 173
alcoholism 6, 7–8, 12, 14, 15, 36–38, 39, 78, 96, 100, 102, 104, 106, 120, 133, 139, 144, 146, 150, 153, 154, 170, 173, 176
ambition 16, 19, 32, 34, 37–39, 55, 80, 103, 105, 106, 111, 117, 131, 139, 158, 175
American Revolution 4, 20, 25, 31, 34, 35, 43, 54, 60, 74, 77–78, 84, 90, 92, 94, 100, 115, 122, 123–124, 138, 148, 151–152, 154, 155–157, 168
Amos and the Alien 112
Amos and the Chameleon Caper 105
Amos and the Vampire 139
Amos Gets Famous 139
Amos Goes Bananas 113
Amos's Killer Concert Caper 139
Apache 3, 4, 39, 50, 52, 55, 76, 83, 84, 90, 100–101, 106, 113, 130, 139, 142, 145, 154, 170, 172, 175
"Aunt Caroline" 12, 88

Beautyway 91
The Beet Fields 3, 6, 8, 22, 23, 36, 40–41, 53, 59, 61, 63, 65, 70, 74, 76, 83, 88, 97, 100, 101, 102, 106, 107, 109, 110, 114, 115, 116, 119, 133, 137, 138, 148, 153, 154, 157, 169, 172, 173, 175
belonging 4, 41, 42–44, 45, 48, 71, 81, 118
"Bickerbits" 87, 120
Black Hills 3, 104, 108
books 7, 9, 15, 19, 62, 76–77, 80, 95, 96, 138, 156; *see also* censorship; libraries; reading
The Boy Who Owned the School 2, 8, 17, 54, 61, 66, 80, 84, 89, 159, 176
"Breaking the Record" 25
Brian Robeson series 4, 16, 72, 115
Brian's Hunt 33, 34, 45–47, 55, 56, 57, 59, 62, 72, 73, 114, 115, 121, 132, 169, 170
"Brian's Hunt" 140
Brian's Return 32, 47–48, 60, 72, 105, 115, 145, 173
Brian's Winter 1, 48–50, 72, 103, 173, 175, 176
bullying 24, 56, 61, 83–84, 108, 146, 148, 149, 172, 173, 176

Call Me Francis Tucket 3, 4, 19, 34, 50–51, 63, 68, 74, 107, 108, 142, 148
cannibals 3, 96, 112, 117, 146, 148, 149
Canoe Days 1, 21–22
Canyons 1, 3, 6, 51–53, 55, 63, 73, 75, 84, 97, 100–101, 106, 110, 114, 115, 120, 130, 133, 135, 139, 145, 154, 155, 159, 170, 171, 173
Captive! 1, 61, 84, 113, 114, 149, 154, 173, 177
The Car 3, 8, 68, 120, 139, 146
"The Case of the Dirty Bird" 38, 63, 77, 79, 159, 170
Caught by the Sea 86, 116, 138, 157, 174, 175
The CB Caper 97
censorship 2, 22, 70
Cherokee 93, 133–134, 166, 168–169
Chickasaw 93
childbirth 61–62, 63, 99, 100, 101, 114, 126, 135, 136, 163, 164, 172, 176; midwifery 61, 68, 114
Choctaw 93, 168–169
Christmas 67, 120, 124, 148, 168, 170
A Christmas Sonata 2, 6, 18, 37, 67, 85, 100, 109, 121, 174, 175
Civil War 3, 4, 21, 39, 54, 60–61, 75, 76, 77, 78, 79–80, 84, 94, 95, 98, 102, 110, 118, 127, 129–130- 133, 135, 137, 150, 152, 154, 160, 162–169, 173, 176
Clabbered Dirt, Sweet Grass 1, 18, 57, 88, 114, 135, 153, 176
Coach Amos 79, 139
Comanche 59, 78, 92, 93, 142, 144, 145
Comancheros 1, 3, 34, 37, 44, 100–101, 128, 138, 140–141, 142, 143, 148, 162, 172
coming of age 3, 5, 14, 39, 40, 44, 52, 53–55, 60, 86–88, 92, 99, 102, 108–109, 121, 135, 141, 158
computer games 3, 175, 177
conservation 3, 172, 175
"The Cook Camp" 6, 7, 74
The Cookcamp 3, 6, 17, 33, 36, 42, 43, 45, 61, 63, 64, 65, 68, 74, 87, 88, 96, 105, 106, 107, 110, 114, 154, 159, 175, 176
Cookie 13, 14, 17, 24, 57, 58, 69, 75, 79, 82, 83, 112, 120, 140, 153, 171, 173, 175, 177
Cowpokes and Desperadoes 33–34, 59, 89, 159
The Creature of Black Water Lake 89–90, 159, 177
Cree 46, 49, 62, 69, 93, 114, 168–169
Creek 74, 93, 133–134, 166, 168–169

The Crossing 1, 4, 7, 11, 12, 15, 21, 31–32, 34, 37, 38, 39, 44, 55, 58–59, 60, 63, 68, 75, 76, 78, 85, 90, 95–96, 98, 100, 102, 106, 111, 112, 117, 133, 137, 139, 145, 148, 151, 153, 157, 158, 170, 173, 176
Crow 4, 78, 142
Crush: The Theory, Practice and Destructive Properties of Love 1, 25, 63, 120, 121
Culpepper's Cannon 77, 96, 113, 159, 169
Curse of the Ruins 1, 65, 113, 114, 177

Dancing Carl 4, 14, 21, 34, 36, 60, 65, 78, 80, 105, 110, 114, 138, 149, 153, 170, 173
Danger on Midnight River 1, 35, 72, 73, 83–84, 100, 106, 172, 173
death *see* healing and death
"The Deer" 14
delinquency 3, 12, 42–43, 44, 53, 83–84, 103–104, 106, 115, 116, 134, 146, 148, 153, 154, 173, 174, 175
disease 51, 75, 83, 85, 100, 115, 125, 129, 131, 137, 152, 156, 159, 165, 169, 175; cancer 3, 14, 25, 32, 37, 55, 64, 75, 103, 112, 116, 173, 176; chicken pox 7, 75, 175; cholera 51, 74, 135, 168; consumption 133; dysentery 25, 74, 92, 104, 122, 131, 137, 156; Ebola 90, 97–98; malaria 168; pneumonia 7; seasickness 75; smallpox 168; typhoid fever 168i; typhus 168
divorce 4, 8–9, 39, 73, 84, 121, 140, 173, 174
dog team 3, 13, 14, 15, 17, 19, 21, 23, 34, 56, 57, 58, 63, 76, 79, 81–83, 89, 91, 99, 101, 106, 114, 116, 117, 134, 138, 140, 155, 157–158, 163, 165, 170, 176
dogs 1, 2, 4, 9, 14, 26, 46, 55–59, 61, 62, 64, 68, 78, 81–82, 83, 88, 89, 91, 96–97, 98, 109, 112, 116, 117, 120, 123, 128–129, 136, 138, 139, 140, 147, 153, 170, 174, 175; *see also* Cookie
Dogsong 3, 15, 37, 45, 54, 56, 57, 59, 61, 63, 67, 81, 88, 89, 90, 99, 101, 106, 110, 112, 114, 134, 136, 154, 157, 159, 172, 173, 175
Dogteam 1, 18, 57, 83, 86, 88, 89, 110, 115, 138, 158, 174
dreams 13, 24, 32, 35, 39, 42, 50, 52, 53, 59, 62, 63, 64, 65, 69, 87, 89, 91, 104, 134, 136, 137–138, 139, 155, 172, 173
Dunc and Amos and the Red Tattoos 167, 169
Dunc and Amos Go to the Dogs 59, 139
Dunc and the Scam Artists 98
Dunc Gets Tweaked 112
Dunc's Doll 98, 121
Dunc's Halloween 80, 158–159

Eastern Sun, Winter Moon: An Autobiographical Odyssey 3, 6, 36, 37, 38–39, 43, 61, 64, 68, 75, 100, 110, 117, 120, 134, 148–149, 151, 158, 172, 173, 175
Emancipation Proclamation 1, 89, 118, 136, 169, 176
Escape from Fire Mountain 62, 173, 175
evangelism 1, 76, 112, 123, 167
exhibitionism 80, 176
exploitation 3, 25, 37, 78–79, 111, 144, 149, 163, 177; *see also* slavery

"The Face of the Tiger" 6, 7, 100
Family Ties 25, 42, 63, 110, 177
farm work 3, 5, 8, 10, 14, 16, 18, 33, 40–41, 42–43, 44, 68, 70, 71, 75, 83, 87, 96, 100, 102, 105, 106, 107, 110–111, 114, 136, 129, 134, 135, 146, 148, 154, 158, 162, 165, 166
Father Water, Mother Woods: Essays on Fishing and Hunting in the North Woods 3, 8, 9, 19, 35, 58, 69, 116, 175
fear 1, 26, 49, 51, 55, 59–62, 68, 87, 89, 95, 102, 103, 106, 112, 131, 140, 144, 146, 147, 148, 150, 152, 154, 156, 157, 170, 172
female persona 1, 18–19, 32, 34, 41, 43, 61–62-66, 68, 95–96, 98, 101–102, 108, 110, 111, 126, 130, 135–136, 151, 154, 156, 165
Field Trip 26, 40, 59, 80, 120, 140, 153, 176, 177
Fishbone's Song 4, 26, 36, 37, 78, 89, 105, 106, 109, 113, 117, 135, 148, 153, 156, 173, 174, 175, 176
Flat Broke 25, 112–113
Flight of the Hawk 63, 89–90, 98, *175*
food 6, 7, 8, 9, 15, 20, 32, 34, 37, 41, 43, 44, 46, 48, 50, 51, 53, 54, 55, 56, 57, 58, 62, 63, 64, 66–70, 71, 72, 73, 82–83, 86, 101, 117, 123, 125, 127, 129, 130, 131, 139, 140, 142, 143, 147, 148, 163, 170, 172, 174; rationing 67, 68
The Foxman 4, 7, 8, 12, 16, 32, 37, 42, 45, 53, 55, 60, 68, 73, 75, 76, 78, 88, 90, 103–104, 106, 109, 114, 115, 116, 135, 147, 148, 150, 151, 153, 173, 174, 176
frontier 4, 12, 20, 31, 34, 44, 50, 54, 64–65, 78, 84, 90, 91, 92, 93, 95, 96, 99, 104, 105, 107, 109, 110, 113, 115, 117, 123, 130, 134, 139, 142, 144, 154, 176; Oregon Trail 4, 12, 20, 74, 78, 84, 96, 99, 107, 108, 113, 142, 143–144, 146, 168, 175
Full of Hot Air: Launching, Floating High, and Landing 18

gangs 20, 34, 55, 56, 62, 80, 85, 93, 99, 100, 102, 112, 137, 138, 139, 146, 148, 156, 163, 177
The Glass Café 3, 6, 22, 63, 84, 120–121, 172, 173
The Gorgon Slayer 177
The Grass Eaters 3
Grizzly 3, 45–46, 63,116, 140, 175
"The Grotto" 91
guns 1, 8, 20, 42, 53, 62, 89, 92, 112, 115, 120, 132, 146, 162, 163, 165; artillery 11, 39, 77, 79–80, 147, 152, 156, 166; bayonets 43, 74, 77, 100, 104, 127, 132, 146, 147, 150, 156, 160, 168; cannon 61, 77, 100, 131, 132, 147, 148, 150, 152, 159, 160, 166; rifles 4, 9, 63, 65, 90, 92, 98, 105, 107, 108, 120, 122–124, 132, 137, 138, 148, 160, 168
Guts 1, 22, 37, 39, 62, 69, 91, 103, 115

Harris and Me 2, 8, 19, 33, 35, 36, 37, 38, 44, 45, 53, 62, 66, 70–71, 74, 79, 81, 83, 96, 98, 100, 102, 104, 105, 106, 111, 112, 114, 115, 120, 134, 136, 139, 146, 148, 150, 154, 157, 159, 173, 174, 176
Hatchet 3, 15, 17, 21, 22, 26, 32, 33, 35, 45, 47, 55, 63, 69, 72–74, 84, 97, 100, 101, 103, 109, 114, 121, 125, 126, 128, 146, 157, 173, 174, 175
The Haymeadow 3, 18, 54, 55, 56, 63, 68, 75, 88, 91, 92, 102, 113, 140, 159, 176
healing and death 6, 7, 11, 16, 20, 22, 24, 37, 38, 41, 45, 46, 48, 55, 56, 57, 60–61, 62, 65, 74–76, 77, 78, 87, 89, 91, 92, 94, 98, 100, 101, 102, 104, 117, 118, 121, 124, 127, 129, 132, 133, 135, 137, 140, 141, 142, 143, 145, 146, 147, 148, 150, 151, 152, 153, 154, 156, 167, 169, 170, 171, 175, 176; broken bones 77, 80, 117, 137; faith healing 1, 11, 19, 74, 76, 112, 119, 121, 148; herbalism 74, 77, 129, 141, 165, 174; mystic medicine 49, 52; snakebite 44,

74, 97, 141, 174; triage 7, 75, 131, 175; *see also* alcoholism; disease; loss; mortality; post-traumatic stress disorder; *The Rifle*
"Henry Mosley's Last Stand" 25
Hessians 3, 60, 77, 84, 100, 104, 148, 152, 155, 175
history 3, 4, 9, 13, 17, 19, 20, 21, 23, 24, 35, 42, 44, 45, 47, 50, 51, 52, 54, 60, 65, 69, 74, 75, 76–79, 82, 83, 84, 85–86, 89–90, 92, 94, 95, 96, 100, 102, 104, 105, 107, 108, 111, 113, 118, 119, 122, 123, 127, 128–130, 132, 133, 134, 135, 136, 139, 142, 143, 145, 146, 147, 148, 151, 152, 155, 156, 157, 159, 167–171, 176
Hook 'Em, Snotty! 63, 173, 177
How Angel Peterson Got His Name 1, 7, 9, 38, 98, 114, 170, 177
humor 1, 12, 18, 22, 23, 25, 26, 49, 51, 55, 58, 59, 61, 66, 70, 71, 79–81, 82, 83, 89, 96, 98, 107, 109, 112, 113, 120, 133, 134, 139, 141, 154, 158, 159, 173, 174, 176
hunger 2, 7, 8, 41, 51, 56, 60, 62, 64, 69, 70, 77, 80, 85, 125, 126, 133–134, 139, 141, 148, 151, 172
hunting 7, 9, 13, 15, 20, 39, 44, 45–47, 48, 50, 56, 60, 62, 67, 80, 90, 94, 95, 99, 101, 103, 107, 113, 116, 117, 125, 136, 137, 139, 141, 142, 155, 163, 167

Ice Race 81–82
Iditarod 14, 15, 17, 19, 23, 56–58, 76, 81–83, 85, 107, 117, 120, 160, 171, 172, 174, 175
immigrants 3–4, 10, 16, 32, 36, 40, 42, 61, 66, 70, 76, 78–79, 85, 89–90, 96, 100, 102, 106, 107, 108, 134, 148, 149, 154, 167, 168, 175, 176
Indian Wars 51, 76, 78, 84, 92–93, 130, 151, 168, 169
integrity 3, 14, 19, 25, 33, 78, 83–85, 92, 94, 110, 118, 120
Inuit 3, 15, 34, 37, 47, 49, 54, 56, 63, 82, 83, 90–91, 99, 101, 107, 114, 134, 167, 176
Iroquois 25, 60, 74, 77, 84, 100, 104, 110, 115, 146, 148, 152, 155, 156, 158, 168, 174
The Island 1, 16, 32, 33, 35, 40, 42, 45, 53, 56, 61, 64, 65, 70, 74, 79, 80, 84, 86–88, 94, 100, 101, 102, 103, 107, 109, 111, 113, 114, 115, 116, 120, 133, f136, 137, 145, 150, 155, 172, 173, 174, 175, 176

kenning 1, 88–89, 158
"The Killing Chute" 65, 75
Kiowa 78
Korean War 9, 36, 81, 89, 135, 153, 171, 175, 176

labor 3, 5, 8, 9, 10, 14, 22, 24, 25, 36, 40–41, 44, 50, 68, 71, 76, 78–79, 92, 96, 105, 110–111, 112, 114–115, 127, 129, 135–136, 146, 148, 149–150, 157, 158, 160, 173, 177; *see also* farm work
"The Last Great Race" 21, 134
Lawn Boy 4, 24, 25, 40, 78–79, 105, 112, 115, 120, 121, 149, 173, 175
Lawn Boy Returns 24, 25, 64, 105, 114, 154, 158, 176
legend 1, 89–92, 96, 112, 166, 172, 176
The Legend of Bass Reeves 4, 24, 31, 33, 36, 54, 59, 63, 64, 66, 67, 72, 74, 76, 78, 83, 84, 90, 92–94, 95, 98, 100–101, 109, 114, 115, 127, 128, 131, 147, 158, 170, 174
The Legend of Red Horse Cavern 91, 114, 133, 136, 139, 145, 173, 175
Liar, Liar 25, 31, 85, 134
"The Liberty Ship" 75, 170
libraries 2, 3, 9, 14, 21, 22, 33, 53–54, 65, 66, 69, 72, 79, 94, 113, 138
"The Library" 12, 65, 133
literacy 1, 3, 18, 75, 91–92, 94–97, 118–119, 126–127, 129–130, 135, 136, 138, 139, 159, 165; *see also* libraries; reading
logic 1, 16, 31, 35, 48, 49, 50, 55, 60, 65, 71, 72, 73, 80, 87, 95, 97–100, 104, 123–124, 153, 156
loss 23, 34, 38, 41, 42, 45, 46, 48, 49, 55, 56, 57, 60–061, 71, 74, 75, 77, 78, 88, 91, 97, 99, 100–102, 104, 106, 116–117, 120, 127, 129, 135, 143, 147, 148, 152, 153, 156, 159, 172; *see also* healing and death
"Lost at Sea" 16, 72

"The Madonna" 7, 62, 74, 100, 133, 137, 150
The Madonna Stories 4, 16
Masters of Disaster 25, 55, 64, 65–66, 80, 105, 113, 120, 136, 157, 174
maturity 1, 14, 33, 34, 46, 47, 53, 54, 55, 66, 73, 75–76, 80, 81, 86, 88, 99, 102–104, 107, 108, 111, 121, 124, 138, 143, 144, 146, 157, 158
memory 3, 4, 8, 17, 25, 26, 32, 33, 36, 38, 44, 53, 56, 60, 61, 64, 69, 70, 73, 75, 83, 86, 88, 90–91, 93, 101, 104, 109, 110, 111, 112, 120, 121, 124, 125, 133, 134–136, 138, 143, 145, 147, 149, 150, 151, 157, 158, 159, 172, 173, 174, 176; *see also* post-traumatic stress disorder
mentors 1, 4, 31, 32, 34, 54, 55, 57, 60, 75, 84, 99, 100, 102, 104–107, 108–109, 112, 113, 117, 119, 120, 135, 141, 142, 152, 154–155,
military 7, 22, 31–32, 37–38, 39, 40, 41, 42, 43, 45, 47, 52, 54, 60–61, 65, 74, 75, 76, 77, 78, 81, 96, 100, 101, 102, 110, 111, 113, 121, 124, 125, 127, 130–133, 146, 150–153, 155, 163, 165, 166, 168, 169, 172, 176; boy/child soldiery 84, 96, 102, 130, 153; *see also* post-traumatic stress disorder; war
Mr. Tucket 12, 19–20, 34, 37, 44, 50, 53, 78, 79, 84, 105, 107, 108–109, 112, 114, 117, 144, 145, 146, 154, 167–169, 173, 174
Moen, Alida Peterson 5, 6, 10, 17, 23, 42, 44, 61, 64, 65, 67, 74, 87, 96, 101, 110–111, 114, 136, 145, 172, 173, 174, 176, 177
Molly McGinty Has a Really Good Day 1, 23, 42, 45, 53, 54, 63, 64, 80, 96, 100, 113, 136–137, 172, 173, 174
The Monument 2, 17, 37, 40, 44–45, 65, 75, 106, 148, 173
mortality 3, 6, 36, 48, 55, 58, 60, 62, 74–76, 112, 135, 136; *see also* disease; healing and death; loss
motorcycles 20, 80
Mudshark 25, 78, 98, 113, 173, 174
music 2, 37, 40, 83, 87, 88, 89, 90, 101, 107, 109–111, 131, 134, 135, 154–155, 157, 158, 172, 174, 175, 176; birdsong 109, 115; folk dance 41, 52, 109, 111, 165; folk songs 10, 90–91, 101, 106, 110, 111; instrumental 41, 52, 90, 109–110, 111; story-song 89, 109, 135
My Life in Dog Years 21, 36, 56, 89, 96, 120, 149

names 1, 10, 39, 41, 51, 71, 80, 89, 93, 95, 112–115, 148; ethnic 44, 111, 113, 114, 144; namesake 148–149; nickname 94, 115, 166, 168; patronyms 111, 112, 113, 126, 163
nature 3, 4, 5, 7, 8–10, 12–14, 18,

22–22, 26, 32, 44, 46, 47, 48, 51, 52, 53, 54, 56, 57–58, 62, 69, 71, 72, 73, 81–82, 85, 86–88, 94, 98, 101, 102, 104, 107, 108, 112, 114, 115–117, 121, 125, 126, 136, 137, 138, 141, 146, 154, 155, 174, 176
Navajo 64, 91, 105, 109–110, 173
"The Night the Headless, Blood-Drinking, Flesh-Eating Corpses of Cleveland (Almost) Took Over the World" 25
The Night the White Deer Died 13, 37, 53, 59, 64, 91, 101, 102, 105, 109–110, 114, 134, 137–138, 173, 177
Nightjohn 3, 19, 20, 33, 34, 44, 55, 58, 60, 64, 68, 78, 85, 89, 91, 95, 97, 98, 100, 102, 105, 112, 115, 118–119, 121, 126–130, 136, 137, 139, 147, 148, 150, 172, 173, 176; *see also* Civil War; *Sarny*; slavery
nonviolence 88
Notes from the Dog 4, 8, 25, 55, 63, 64, 67, 69, 75, 79, 84, 89, 105, 109, 111, 112, 114, 173

Oglala Lakota 91, 163
Ojibwa 110, 114, 134, 176
orphans 3, 15, 19, 23, 32, 34, 35, 38, 39, 40, 44–45, 46, 54, 60, 63, 64, 68, 80, 90, 95, 98, 100, 102, 111, 112, 118, 128, 134, 136–137, 139, 140, 142, 144, 148, 151, 156, 176

Paintings from the Cave 1, 3, 8, 9, 18, 26, 35, 37, 42, 43, 44, 54, 56, 62, 70, 112, 137, 146, 159, 176
parenting 1, 3, 7–8, 10, 14, 17, 22, 31, 35, 36, 37, 39, 43–44, 45, 54, 60, 63, 66, 67, 68, 70, 71, 72, 74, 77, 79–80, 83–84, 87, 96, 100, 101, 104, 109, 115, 119–122, 128, 143, 146, 148, 155, 156, 172, 176; father 3, 6, 8–9, 10, 13, 26, 33, 34, 35, 36, 37, 40, 42, 43, 52, 53, 54, 55, 59, 60, 65, 67, 69, 73, 74–75, 76, 78, 80, 86, 88, 94, 98, 99, 101, 106, 108, 110, 112, 119–120, 121, 143, 148–149, 151–152, 157, 176; foster parent 26, 35, 44, 60, 65, 70, 100, 105, 106, 117, 120, 121, 127, 134, 135, 141, 146, 148, 174; grandfather 14, 32, 75, 91, 92, 98, 101, 103, 105, 107, 110, 112, 114, 116, 117, 134, 135, 173, 175, 176; grandmother 5, 10, 17, 23, 42, 43, 44, 53, 61, 63, 64, 68, 84, 87, 101, 105, 107, 109, 114, 133, 135–136, 145, 147, 150, 154, 164, 172, 176; mother 3, 5, 6, 8–10, 18, 22, 33, 34, 35, 36, 37, 41, 42, 43, 44, 47, 50, 52, 54, 61, 63, 64, 65, 67, 73, 75, 76, 77, 80, 84, 85, 87, 96, 98, 100, 101, 102, 103, 105, 107, 117, 119, 120, 121, 125, 126, 130, 143, 148, 174, 177; *see also* adoption; alcoholism; childbirth; divorce; orphans
Paulsen, Eunice Hazel Moen 5, 6, 7–8, 36, 37, 64, 75, 85, 151
Paulsen, Gary 3, 5–27, 31, 36, 37, 38, 40, 41, 42, 43, 44, 45, 53, 55–56, 61, 64, 68, 70, 71, 72, 74, 75, 80, 83–84, 85, 96, 97, 100, 102, 105–107, 110–111, 115, 116, 137, 145–146, 151, 154, 174, 176
Paulsen, James Wright 12–13, 16, 26, 59, 85, 96, 110, 112, 150
Paulsen, Oscar 5, 6, 78, 10, 36, 78, 152
Paulsen, Ruth Ellen Wright 1, 12, 16, 18, 65, 85
Paulsen genealogy 29
Pawnee 4, 63, 79, 107, 108–109, 113, 142, 144, 146, 174
pedophilia 6, 34, 43, 61, 64, 85, 102, 112, 137, 148
"People Call Me Crazy" 55, 59
Philippines 7, 37, 43–44, 56, 61, 151, 164, 170–171
Pilgrimage on a Steel Ride: A Memoir about Men and Motorcycles 11, 20, 31, 62, 66–67, 81, 107, 116, 150, 157, 174
police 8, 10, 12, 13, 47, 62, 85, 104, 106, 112, 121, 139, 146, 154, 177
Ponca 53, 78, 114
Popcorn Days and Buttermilk Nights 5, 14, 34, 42–43, 53, 60, 63, 66, 76. 83–84, 88, 100, 103–104, 106, 107, 114, 115, 116, 118, 119, 136, 139, 145, 148, 153, 177
post-traumatic stress disorder 4, 38, 61, 76, 77, 78, 99, 110, 132, 140, 147, 149, 151, 153, 177
Prince Amos 139
prisoners of war 7, 31, 61, 63, 74, 77, 99, 100, 104–105, 121, 132, 144, 148, 154, 156, 168
Project: A Perfect World 1, 20, 116, 119–120, 177
Pueblo 4, 44, 74, 109, 114, 141, 142, 143, 162, 164, 165, 174, 175
Puppies, Dogs, and Blue Northers 1, 24, 37, 54, 75–76, 79, 83, 96–97, 112, 115, 140, 148, 153, 171, 174; *see also* Cookie
The Quilt 1, 3, 5, 17, 23, 42, 59, 61, 64, 65, 68, 76, 84, 87, 89, 95–96, 101–102, 113, 114, 135–136, 145, 148–149, 172, 174

"Rape" 88, 103, 144, 145
reading 4, 6, 7, 9, 12, 22, 49, 50, 76–77, 78, 80, 95–96, 97, 108, 113, 115, 118, 119, 125, 126, 129–130, 138 *See also* libraries.
refugees 3, 7, 43, 51, 62, 74, 113, 141, 144, 156
The Rifle 4, 20, 31, 35, 40, 42, 53, 58, 59, 63, 65, 67, 74, 77, 78, 83 90, 92, 94, 98, 100, 103, 105, 112, 115, 120, 122–124, 133, 134, 137, 138, 146, 148, 151, 152, 154, 156, 159, 168, 170, 173
The River 2, 3, 17, 32, 45, 72, 79, 84, 110, 121, 124–126, 134–135, 138, 149, 174, 177
Road Trip 1, 26, 40, 59, 110, 112, 153, 173
The Rock Jockeys 4, 76, 77, 78, 96, 112, 134, 173
Rodomonte's Revenge 81, 90, 113, 177

sailing 3, 10, 11, 13, 17, 21, 22, 23, 25, 32, 34, 43, 68, 83, 99, 137, 138, 163, 164, 166, 175, 176
Sarny 1, 20, 33, 34–35, 36, 43, 44, 55, 60, 64–65, 68, 75, 78, 85–86, 88, 89, 91, 95, 97, 98, 100, 102, 103, 105, 109, 115, 118–119, 121, 126–128-130, 131, 134–135, 136, 139, 147, 148, 150, 152–153, 154, 169, 173, 174
Sarny's genealogy 127
The Schernoff Discoveries 8, 10, 21, 33, 63–64, 69, 80, 113, 158, 173
school 9, 10, 13, 14, 15, 23, 26–27, 32, 33, 35, 40, 42, 44, 54, 60, 65, 72, 73, 77, 80, 84, 85, 89, 91, 95–96, 98, 106, 118–119, 125, 127, 129, 157, 173
Sentries 4, 10, 15, 37, 40, 55, 76, 102–103, 105, 110, 111, 112, 114, 134, 149, 152, 170, 171, 172, 173
The Seventh Crystal 90, 112, 149
Shelf Life: Stories by the Book 9, 39, 44, 64, 89, 96, 133, 157, 159
Sioux 78, 108–109, 114
Sisters/Hermanas 18–19, 85, 102, 121, 159, 173
Six Kids and a Stuffed Cat 1, 26, 33, 79, 85, 89, 157, 158, 167, 173
"Skate-Chuting" 7
slavery 19, 20, 24, 33, 34–35, 36, 44, 55, 57, 60, 65, 68, 75, 76, 78, 84, 85–86, 89, 91, 93–95, 97, 98, 100–101, 103, 105, 112,

115, 118–119, 121, 126–127, 128–130, 131, 135, 136, 139, 141, 142, 144, 147, 148, 150, 165, 167, 168, 169, 172
Smith genealogy 43
"The Soldier" 11, 37, 111, 112
Soldier's Heart 3, 4, 21, 39, 45, 54, 60, 77, 85, 96, 100, 102, 112, 114, 121, 128, 130–133, 136, 137, 147, 152, 153, 157, 159–160, 169, 172, 173
The Special War 12, 60, 76, 78
"Speed Demon" 98
"Stop the Sun" 4, 60, 78, 99, 134, 149, 151, 173
storytelling 1, 4, 8, 16, 31, 38, 39, 49, 50, 51, 65, 88, 89, 90, 102, 105, 111, 118, 119, 133–136, 137, 143, 147, 175; story-song 89, 109, 135; talk-story 16, 89, 135
survival 2, 3, 4, 6, 7, 9, 13, 15, 16, 21, 26, 31, 32, 34, 35, 36, 38, 39, 46–49, 50, 51, 55, 60, 63–65, 69, 70, 73, 74, 78, 84, 97, 98, 100, 101, 103, 104, 107, 108, 116, 117, 118, 125, 133, 136–138, 139, 142, 143, 147, 149, 152, 153, 155, 156, 157, 158, 173, 175

The Tent 1, 11, 19, 74, 76, 112, 119, 121, 148
This Side of Wild: Mutts, Mares, and Laughing Dinosaurs 1, 3, 7, 17, 23, 36, 62, 64, 91, 109, 146111, 114, 115
Thunder Valley 54, 98, 158
Tiltawhirl John 1, 3, 10, 12, 35, 36, 40, 50, 58, 70, 110, 114, 137–138, 154, 175
Time Benders 23, 33, 80, 89, 114
The Time Hackers 23, 81, 173
The Tortilla Factory 1, 20, 158, 159, 173
Tracker 1, 14, 32, 44, 55, 63, 75, 88, 101, 103, 105, 107, 109, 112, 116, 117, 120, 137
The Transall Saga 4, 9, 21, 31, 34, 61, 63, 66, 69, 72, 74, 76, 81, 85, 87, 90, 94, 97, 100, 102, 110, 112, 117, 128, 134, 136–137, 136, 146, 148, 150, 154, 158, 173
The Treasure of El Patrón 77, 112–113, 173
"The True Face of War" 7, 10, 11, 21, 133, 151
trust 21, 44, 52, 58, 73, 75, 84, 96, 104, 137, 138–140, 142, 156
Tucket's Gold 1, 3, 20, 44, 63, 99–100-101, 105, 107, 108, 114, 128, 140–142, 145, 148, 173
Tucket's Home 1, 20, 34, 37, 60, 63, 66, 74, 96, 103, 107, 108, 113, 114, 121, 134, 142–143, 175
Tucket's Ride 1, 20, 37, 44, 80, 107, 108, 113, 140, 143–145, 148, 175
Tucket's Travels 20, 69

Vietnam War 4, 11, 12, 13, 15, 37–38, 39, 52, 60, 74, 76, 78, 85, 102, 139, 151, 152, 171, 175, 176
violence 1, 9, 20, 32, 36, 52, 53, 65, 76, 78, 92, 100, 104, 108–109, 115, 116–117, 127–128, 142, 145–147, 148, 154
Vote: The Theory, Practice, and Destructive Properties of Politics 120
The Voyage of the Frog 16, 32, 34, 37, 44, 50, 58, 59, 100, 106, 134, 137, 148, 173
vulnerability 1, 3, 71, 74, 103, 110, 118, 141, 147, 148–150

war 3, 4, 5, 7, 9, 10, 11, 12, 13, 14, 16, 18, 21, 22, 25, 31, 32, 33, 34, 35, 36, 37, 38, 39, 41, 42, 43, 45, 51, 52, 53, 54, 56, 60, 61, 62, 63, 64, 65, 67, 68, 71, 73, 74, 75, 76, 77, 78, 79–80, 81, 84, 85, 89, 90, 92, 98, 99, 100, 102, 103, 104, 105, 106, 108, 110, 112, 115, 117, 118, 120, 121, 127, 128, 129–130-133, 135, 137, 139, 140, 142, 144, 145, 147, 148, 149, 150–153, 154, 155, 156, 158, 159, 160, 172, 173, 175, 176
Whiskey Rebellion 78, 168
The White Fox Chronicles 3, 11, 22, 23, 59, 66, 97, 112, 148
The Wild Culpepper Cruise 113, 159
wilderness 3, 4, 5, 7, 8, 12, 22–22, 32, 44, 46, 47, 48, 53, 54, 56, 57–58, 69, 72, 73, 81–82, 85, 94, 98, 102, 104, 107, 108, 112, 114, 115–117, 121, 125, 126, 136, 137, 138, 141, 146, 154, 155; wild animals 9, 10, 13, 14, 18, 26, 46, 47, 48, 52, 55, 58, 62, 67, 71, 75, 82, 91, 101, 103, 108, 115–116, 117, 137, 140, 174, 176
The Winter Room 4, 14, 16, 17, 21, 31, 64, 74, 76, 89, 96, 106, 114, 134, 154, 173, 175
Winterdance: The Fine Madness of Running the Iditarod 3, 19, 36, 58, 59, 79, 81, 82, 83, 85, 88, 89, 117, 120, 173
Winterkill 4, 8, 12, 13, 14, 45, 65, 83–84, 88, 99, 104, 106,114, 115, 119, 134, 136, 138, 146,148, 154, 173, 174, 175, 177
wisdom 1, 4, 26, 31, 47, 54, 64, 67, 75, 84, 85, 90–91, 93, 99, 101–102, 105, 106, 107, 108, 111, 112, 117, 120, 124, 125, 135, 138, 140, 141–142, 148, 149, 153–155, 158, 172, 173, 175, 176
"Wolfdreams" 2, 3, 57, 89, 96, 116, 173
Woods Runner 1, 4, 25, 26, 31, 35, 37, 43, 44, 54, 60, 63, 67, 73, 74, 77, 80–81, 84, 90, 91, 95, 96, 99100, 104–105, 106, 110, 113, 115, 117, 121, 130, 133, 137, 139, 140, 146, 148, 151, 152, 154, 155–157, 158, 168, 173
Woodsong 1, 3, 9, 17, 21, 44, 56, 57, 62, 86, 88, 91, 107, 109, 112, 115, 117, 135, 138, 173
Worksong 1, 22, 173
World War I 4, 11, 73, 75, 76, 105, 135, 147, 148, 150
World War II 3, 4, 5, 14, 18, 33, 34, 37, 41, 42, 43, 64, 65, 67, 71, 76, 78, 110, 120, 133, 135, 145, 148, 149, 151, 152, 153, 172
writing 1, 3, 5, 7, 9–27, 33–34, 35, 36, 38, 39, 40, 42, 43, 44, 47, 48, 56, 57, 59, 63, 64, 65, 66–67, 71, 72, 74, 75, 76–79, 82–85, 87, 90, 93, 94–97, 98, 110, 111, 115, 116, 119, 121, 126–127, 128–129, 130, 133, 134, 136, 137, 138, 140, 146, 148, 149, 150, 151, 153, 157–160, 168, 173, 174, 175, 176, 177

Zero to Sixty: The Motorcycle Journey of a Lifetime 20, 36, 37, 80